She's Gone

A Novel

Joye Emmens

Copyright © 2015 Joye Emmens
All rights reserved.

ISBN: 0990687600
ISBN 13: 9780990687603
Library of Congress Control Number: 2014915362
Heart Rock Press, Ventura, CA

To Ché, Nick and David
My love and my thanks

All good things are wild, and free.
Henry David Thoreau

1

Oil and Water

The chop of a helicopter drew Jolie through the French doors and onto the deck of her parents' Spanish style home. From there she could see the harbor, the red tiled roofs of Santa Barbara, and the iridescent catastrophe. It was February 1, 1969 and the fifth day that crude oil had been spewing uncontrollably from an offshore drilling platform.

Rage spread though her. Overnight, the brownish-black slick radiating from the Union Oil platform had increased in size. It thinned and meandered south along the coastline, melting together in a glistening sheen. Jolie squinted in the morning sun. A second slick had formed. It looked to be five miles long and three miles wide. Its rainbow hue snaked toward the Channel Islands that hovered on the horizon, blue and inviting, twenty miles offshore. A sickening sensation welled within her. Why did they have to drill in the ocean?

Twelve oil platforms rose from the water, twenty stories high, the island cliffs their backdrop. At night they sparkled like crystal ships floating in the dark ocean. She scanned the horizon. Her dad was out there now, advising on how to cap the well, a boiling cauldron, an ecological crime. He worked for one of the oil companies, fortunately not Union Oil. It was bad enough that he was an executive in the oil industry, but now with the blowout she felt guilt by association. All of

1

the control efforts had failed, and the flow of oil from the new well was unstoppable. Two helicopters circled the massive slick. A single oil well was responsible for all of the devastation; the other eleven platforms loomed ominously.

Jolie went back inside. She'd see Will soon, at the protest. She warmed in anticipation, nervous and happy at the same time. She hadn't seen him for a week.

She carefully picked out her clothes and dressed in a hand-embroidered peasant blouse and a short green skirt. She slipped on knee-high suede moccasins, brushed her long blonde hair, and slung her beaded purse over her shoulder.

"Mom," she called, "I'm walking to Zoe's."

"Call me if you need a ride home." Her mom's voice came from the far reaches of the house.

Jolie walked down the driveway to the street, where she passed more Spanish-style homes with sweeping gardens. Deep red bougainvillea, white honeysuckle, and pink-throated jasmine spilled over walls, archways, and trellises. She breathed deep, inhaling the intoxicating fragrances. She paused to pick a sprig of honeysuckle and tucked it behind her ear.

At the main road, a safe distance from her neighborhood, she stopped, turned toward the first oncoming car, and stuck out her thumb. An older turquoise Chevy sedan pulled over. She scanned the driver's face, a guy in his early twenties with shaggy brown hair framing soft brown eyes. He looked normal, nice even. She hopped in the car, tugging her skirt down as they drove off down the hill.

"Where're you going?" he said.

"The harbor."

"It's a mess down there. I read in the morning paper the slick now covers one hundred fifty square miles. It's boiling up around the platform."

"There's a protest today. We're going to stop them from drilling."

He looked at her and then back to the road. "You're protesting? How old are you?"

"Almost fifteen."

He glanced sideways at her.

As they neared the harbor, traffic stalled. A stream of pedestrians crossed the street, ignoring the traffic lights, headed to the protest.

"I'll get out here," she said.

"Sure, kiddo."

She hopped out of the car. A few steps later she glanced back, smiled at the driver, and flashed him a peace sign.

A dense petroleum aroma hung in the air. Handmade signs with the slogan GOO—Get Oil Out were set up in front of a speaker's platform. She eased her way through the crowd. There he was. Will stood tall in the sea of bodies. His tan, handsome face was set off by straight, dark hair pulled back neatly in a ponytail. He wore the hand-woven headband she'd made for him. She waved.

He smiled wide and strode through the swelling mass of protestors toward her. "You made it."

She smiled up at him. "This crowd is huge." They hugged, his faded jeans and T-shirt were warm from the sun. A soul-stirring current spread through her. Only he had this effect on her. He wasn't anything like the boys at school.

Will was twenty-four, a political science graduate from U.C. Berkeley. She'd first seen him when she stumbled into a Vietnam War protest in Pershing Park. Will had stood on the stage of the amphitheater speaking to a large crowd. Jolie was mesmerized by his words. He argued to stop the immoral Vietnam War, put an end to racial discrimination and fight to create a classless and equal society. The crowd had erupted with chants of support. His words were simple yet eloquent and they struck a chord with her. She began attending all of the rallies hanging close to the stage, drawn to his words and presence.

After the rallies Jolie stayed on and joined Will and a small group discussing the need for change. Mature for her age, everyone assumed she was older. When Will asked her age months later she had told him the truth. She wouldn't lie, not to him. But it was too late. They had fallen for each other. He treated her as an equal. He liked her innocence and her desire to make the world a better place. He said her age didn't matter.

The crowd around them began to chant: "Get Oil Out! Get Oil Out!"

He brushed her lips with his. She glanced around, but there was no need to be anxious. Her parents or any of their acquaintances would never be at a protest.

A man in a yellow shirt and checkered sport coat stepped onto the platform. He seemed out of place amid the crowd dressed in blue jeans and sandals. When the chanting died down, the speaker introduced himself as their former senator and the leader of the newly formed GOO organization.

"We are calling for an immediate halt to oil drilling in the Channel and the permanent removal of all oil platforms and drilling rigs. The chemical dispersants aren't working and their bales of hay can't save us. Only *we* can Get Oil Out!"

The crowd resumed the chant: "Get Oil Out! Get Oil Out!" A defiant current surged through the protesters. Swallowed up in the moment Jolie joined the slow chant. They would stop oil drilling in the Channel.

At dinner that night, Jolie sat with her father and two older brothers as her mother served. "What's happening with the oil spill?" James, one of her brothers, asked.

"The Feds have taken over control of the drilling operation," her dad said. "They're putting in log booms to contain the slick, and straw is being delivered to the beaches to absorb the oil and start the cleanup."

"How can they start the cleanup when oil is still gushing out of control?" Jolie asked.

"They're working twenty-four hours a day," he said.

Her mother sat down at the other end of the table.

"I was down at the harbor today, and there was a group called GOO—Get Oil out—protesting. They're demanding that oil drilling in the Channel be stopped," Jolie said.

In unison, her brothers turned to look at her, their eyes cautioning.

Her dad shot her a stern look. "I don't want you involved with that group."

"I thought you were at Zoe's house," her mom said.

"It's a disaster out there." Jolie's hand waved toward the oil rigs sparkling in the night. She looked at her brothers. Weren't they going to say anything? They were just as upset as she was. Two days earlier, oil had first come ashore on black waves at their favorite surf break.

"I don't want you hanging out with those beatniks and hippies," her dad said.

"Well, I don't want you working for big oil." A stab of pain ran up her shin, a warning kick from one of her brothers.

Her dad's blue eyes bored into her. "Oil puts a roof over your head."

"Why do you have to drill in the ocean? It's a crime against nature," Jolie exclaimed.

Her brother Jon's eyes widened at her open defiance.

Her dad's cocktail glass hit the table with a sharp crack. "Go to your room. Anymore back talk and you'll end up at Saint Mary's so fast, you won't know what hit you."

She rose and moved past her mother. Their eyes met. Jolie knew the look. She'd gone too far again. But hadn't they taught her to stand up for what she believed in? He'd been threatening her for some time now with Saint Mary's, the strict Catholic girls' school. She was already on thin ice at school, and her father didn't know the half of it. The latest incident was getting caught selling a baggie of oregano as pot to another student. The principal was not amused. She smiled inwardly. She and her mom hadn't told her dad and they didn't plan to. Her mom tried to protect her from his strict ideals, but he was adamant about the threat he'd made. One more incident, and she would be enrolled in Saint Mary's—and they weren't even Catholic.

In her room Jolie put on a Buffalo Springfield album and turned up the volume to "Something's Happening Here." How could her dad be so uncaring? He was the one who had taught them to appreciate the beauty of nature. On their first trip to the Channel Islands, she'd been in paradise. The wild and rugged coastline was a haven to birds and foxes. On the boat she'd seen her first whale and dozens of dolphins. Her dad had taught her to snorkel, and for hours she floated blissfully, undulating in the swell, in the underwater world of colorful fish and sea grass. Now it was all threatened by an unstoppable blowout.

⟳

A week later, Jolie was in the kitchen making a carrot cake from scratch, her dad's favorite. It would be easy to get back on his good side. Her mom worked beside her, cooking dinner while the kitchen radio serenaded them with top fifty hits. On the deck, her dad sat reading the paper. She glanced out the kitchen window at him and the panoramic view of the ocean. There was no ignoring the oil slick that flowed like a glistening black river, constantly changing its course with the current and tides.

The phone rang and she shot into the dining room to answer it. It was usually for her. "Can you talk?" It was Will's deep voice. She had told him not to call in the evenings. It was too risky.

She glanced at the French doors open to the deck and then to her mom in the kitchen, intent on her recipe. "Briefly."

"I know you'd want to hear this. President Nixon has temporarily suspended drilling in the Channel."

"Really?" She smiled into the phone. Their efforts had paid off. "We have a victory."

"It's only temporary. I don't trust that warmonger."

"I've got to go."

"I love to hear your voice."

"Same here."

She hung up the phone. She had to be more careful. The smell of the cake wafted in from the kitchen.

"Who was that?" her mom asked.

"A friend. Oil drilling has been stopped in the Channel. But it's only temporary."

"You're not still on the anti-oil thing, are you?"

"Mom, everybody is talking about it."

"Don't get involved. It's too close to home."

"But it's a big deal. Look out there." Jolie turned her gaze out the window at the slick. "It's a world gone wrong."

"Your dad is serious about Saint Mary's. I can't talk him out of it. Don't pit me against him."

A wave of resistance rose within her. Not Saint Mary's again. They couldn't force her to go, could they? She'd seen what happened to girls that went there. First they were stripped of their identities, made to wear uniforms. Pleated skirts, cardigan sweaters, knee-high socks, and ridiculous Oxfords or Mary Jane's. Their one and only choice was between the two shoe styles. In the end they came out like lambs, without an individual thought in their heads, brainwashed with Catholic doctrine and devotion, the hypocritical religion hardwired in their brains. All that Catholic dogma would destroy her soul. She would never go. She'd stand up for her beliefs no matter what the consequences.

✎

The oil blowout was finally controlled eleven days after it began. The *Santa Barbara News-Press* reported that two million gallons of oil had flowed into the Channel. Small fissures still seeped oil and the slick randomly drifted up and down the coast two months later.

On a Friday afternoon in April, President Nixon was scheduled to view the environmental disaster and cleanup effort. Under an overcast sky, a crowd of three thousand people gathered in a roped off area at the harbor, waiting for his arrival. Over one hundred news crews were set up to report on the event.

Jolie and Will stood with the GOO supporters, holding signs and chanting "Get Oil Out." She had skipped her last two classes to get there on time, to be a part of it. She was invisible in the mob, but her voice would be heard.

Jolie scanned the crowd. Aside from the boisterous GOO protesters, everyone stood politely in military attention, waiting for their savior, the president. Didn't they know the truth about him? He was a warmonger who was destroying their country. He couldn't be trusted. The Vietnam War was supposed to be ending but more and more troops had been deployed and the casualties grew each month.

"Here he comes," someone shouted.

Nixon and his wife landed in a helicopter after flying over miles of oily ocean and tar-drenched beaches. Surrounded by reporters, the mayor and presidential party walked the beach. Jolie strained to see Nixon. Even now after seeing the disaster she doubted he would do anything permanent. Although the oil leases were on federal land owned by the people, big corporations would win. They would change that. She began to chant louder.

At the shoreline, Nixon chatted with the cleanup crew while they raked oil-soaked straw into piles. He paid no attention to the roped-off crowd of onlookers or the chanting GOO group. As he stood talking, a small black wave came ashore and soaked his shoes. A wild cheer went up from the GOO supporters. Nixon nonchalantly looked down at his oily shoes, walked toward the helicopter, and the presidential party was airborne, whirling away toward the Union Oil platform.

That night, Jolie and her family sat in the living room for their nightly ritual—watching the news of the Vietnam War.

The news announcer could hardly look at the camera when he announced that 386 US troops had been killed in Vietnam that week.

"If I get drafted, I won't go," Jon, her oldest brother muttered.

"You'll do what your country asks you to do," her dad said.

The coverage of the president's visit to view the oil spill came on next. Jolie could see the protesters off to the side. They'd gotten some good footage. Her bare toes gripped the beige shag carpet. What if her dad found out she'd been there? She wanted to change the TV channel, but he watched with rapt attention.

The president droned on that the incident had touched the conscience of the American people. He vowed his administration would do a better job on environmental problems, and he promised to consider a permanent ban on offshore drilling. Jolie's dad swore under his breath. She sat up straighter. Yes, that's what they wanted, a permanent ban. The crowd of GOO protesters filled the TV screen.

Her dad's knuckles whitened around his drink as he took a sip. "Damn them. It's un-American. Oil powers our country."

The camera continued to pan the crowd. There, standing with Will, was Jolie, holding a Get Oil Out sign, chanting with the GOO crowd. She was the opposite of invisible. She sat still, riveted to the TV.

"Is that you, Jolie?" her brother James asked. "It is. You're on TV!"

She held her breath and glanced at her dad. The anger in his eyes pierced the air between them. She looked back at the screen. He rose, turned off the TV, and stared down at her. Her brothers slipped out of the living room. They'd be hovering nearby, within earshot. Her mom sat silent on the couch.

"I will not allow my daughter to protest the oil industry." His tone waivered as he fought to stay calm. "It's a personal affront. Why can't you conform?"

Why couldn't she conform? It wasn't in her nature for one thing and voicing her opinion wasn't a crime. She didn't respond.

"Answer me." Frustration broke through in his voice.

"I'm sorry but I feel strongly about the oil spill."

"I don't like it any more than the rest of the town, but I asked you not to get involved with that group. You're too young for this."

"No, I'm not." Her eyes locked with his before she lowered her gaze. He knew she was mentally mature. It was built into her character. She couldn't help it. He'd read the comments from her teachers on report cards that repeatedly stated she was precocious and advanced for her age. They said it wasn't a bad thing, only an observation.

Her mom's voice interrupted her thoughts. "Who is that man you were with?"

Jolie hesitated. She couldn't tell them about Will. They would never understand.

"He looks like a long haired...a long haired..." Her mom hesitated, at a loss for words.

"A long-haired radical. They're all radicals," her dad said.

9

"Not hardly Dad. The group is led by an ex-senator."

"I'm enrolling you in Saint Mary's on Monday. You need to learn discipline."

Her brows furrowed. How could he say that? She was disciplined in everything she did. "Discipline? I've already skipped a grade and I still get straight A's. How's that for discipline?" Her eyes darted wildly to her mother, who sat silent, looking apologetic. Please Mom, stand up to him for once!

Her mom met her gaze. "She isn't going to change schools in April. Besides, there's an application process to get in."

"Fine, I want you to get the ball rolling Monday and enroll her in the fall."

This could not be happening. Her heart pounded. She would not go to Saint Mary's.

Summer came and the shroud of Saint Mary's hovered over her. She had to work on her dad to change his mind, but he would come around. She'd enlist her mom to help. In the meantime, she did everything she could to be helpful at home, doing more than her share of the chores and cooking her dad's favorite desserts, the exemplary daughter. Away from home, she and Will became inseparable.

One day in July, Will picked her up a few blocks from her house in his friend's Volkswagen Bug.

"Today you're going to learn to drive," he said.

Jolie laughed. "Okay, I'm game."

Will drove to a grassy meadow by the beach and taught her how to shift. After numerous jerks and stalls, she mastered the clutch, laughing with each lurch. After the driving session they sat on the grass on a blanket. Will tuned his guitar and played Jimi Hendrix's *Little Wing*. He sang softly, his long fingers flying over the frets. Jolie lay back captivated by his voice and the clear notes of the guitar.

After a few more songs he lay back and stroked Jolie's cheek. "I've got it bad."

She turned on her side. "What do you mean?"

He cupped her chin in his hand. "I can't get enough of you." He gently pushed her onto her back and kissed her neck and face. Small kisses that became more hungry and warm and moist. When his lips met hers, he pulled back and traced them with his finger. "Jolie, my sweet Little Wing. Soon you'll be riding with the wind."

His eyes were soft with longing and then his mouth was on hers, salty, musky, and warm. She closed her eyes and melted into him and let herself go in the warm crush of love. Nothing had ever felt this good.

Will rolled onto his back and she rested her head on his shoulder.

"We can leave here and start a new life. There's a whole world out there," Will said.

She rose up onto her elbows. "Leave? Where would we go?"

"I have friends all over we can stay with."

She glanced at him. "But what would we do?"

He remained on his back looking up at the sky. "We'll fight to create a society where misery and poverty are eliminated, a classless society. We'll abolish capitalism, and socialism will reign."

"I want that too, an equal society."

"That's why I love you. You're not like the other women I know. They're all so cynical. But you're not jaded."

She laughed and wrapped her arms around him. He was her warrior, but he was also tender. They shared an interest in changing the world. He was smart and captivating. She was drawn to him by his passion for wanting to help the oppressed and his desire to end the evils of capitalism. The world was changing. Anything was possible.

"I'm speaking at an anti-war rally in San Francisco this weekend. Come with me."

"You know I can't and it's my birthday. My family is camping at the beach."

"We're expecting over 100,000 people. I'm going to introduce the anti-war crowd to the socialist revolution."

She closed her eyes and envisioned him onstage with the crowd. If only she could be there. He wanted a revolution and she wanted her

11

freedom. Freedom from her parents' rules. Freedom to let her spirit soar.

Then Saint Mary's Girls School flashed before her, and her harmonious mood crashed.

⌒♡

"What do you want for your birthday?" her mom asked at dinner that night.

Jolie looked around at her family. This was her chance. They were all together and they'd support her. She looked at her dad at the head of the table. "All I want is to not go to Saint Mary's." Their eyes met. "That's all I want."

He shook his head. "You're already enrolled. You need to learn respect for authority and become a proper young lady."

And after she became a proper young lady? Then what? Become a proper wife to someone? "What do you mean, proper?"

He picked up his knife and fork. "Respectful. Know your place in society. Conform to the rules."

"Dad, I am not someone you can mold. I have my own thoughts and ideas and my own path to follow."

"Well, for the next few years that path is Saint Mary's."

She looked at her brothers to plead for support. They were both focused on passing the basket of French bread.

2

Run

⁓

Jolie woke to the sound of plates clattering far off down the hall in the kitchen. Today was the day. Adrenaline pulsed through her. She lay in bed and looked around her room, wanting to remember everything. The ceiling sparkled with shiny flecks. Her papier-mâché Jimi Hendrix head sculpture that sat on the dresser. The psychedelic Janis Joplin concert poster that was taped to the pink wall above her record player.

She took her time getting ready. She stepped into the blue plaid skirt, the hemline exactly three inches above the bend in her knee. She buttoned the white blouse over a white bra. All undergarments were required to be white. She pulled on navy-blue knee socks and slipped into the clunky white-and-black Oxfords.

Jolie paused in the doorway to the dining room. Her brothers were eating breakfast while her mom stood talking with them, her purse and car keys in hand. Her dad was already at work. The conversation halted. Her brothers gaped at her.

"Whoa," James exclaimed. "I never thought I'd see the day."

"At least you won't have to think about what to wear," Jon said.

Her mother shot them a look and smiled at Jolie. "I'm going to be late for my Women's League meeting." She looked into Jolie's eyes and gave her a hug. "It's going to be fine sweetheart. You'll see. Don't miss your bus. I want to hear all about it tonight." And she was gone, out the door.

Her brothers left shortly after. Jon off to college in his VW Bug and James to high school in her father's old, green Ford pickup. The house was still.

Jolie walked back into her bedroom and changed into a skirt, tie-dyed T-shirt, and her butter soft knee high moccasins. She opened her closet and picked up her pack. From her top desk drawer she plucked out an envelope and walked back through the house.

On the kitchen counter was a note from her mom. The note pad was printed with *Have a Nice Day* next to a yellow smiley face.

Jolie,
Saint Mary's is not as bad as you think. You'll meet new friends. Focus and I know you'll graduate early.
Love, Mom XOXOXO

She tore off the note, folded it, and put it in her wallet. Her stomach was in knots. Breakfast was out of the question. Out on the deck, she gazed over the red tile roofs and canopy of green trees. Boats in the harbor looked miniature, bobbing in the blue water. After seven months, the oil slick had dissipated into small seeps. It was a beautiful morning, and she drank it in.

A muscle car groaned up the street and turned up the driveway. They were on time. She walked back through the kitchen, picked up her pack, and placed the envelope on the counter next to the note-pad. She paused, lifted the letter and brushed it to her lips. "I love you, Mom and Dad," she whispered. "Please understand, I have to do this."

She set it back down and walked out of the house, not daring to glance back. A newer blue Camaro idled in the driveway. Will sat in the passenger seat. A young woman stood by the open driver's door. She was dressed in pale yellow poplin shorts, a matching top, and a wide, white plastic belt.

"I'm Pattie. I guess I'm your ride."

"Nice to meet you, Pattie. I'm Jolie."

14

Jolie pulled the seat forward and slipped into the backseat. Pattie got in, and the car purred down the driveway. Will looked back at her and smiled his wide disarming smile.

"Emancipation day!" he said.

"Isn't she a little young for you?" Pattie asked, scowling at Will. "Where exactly are we going?"

"700 miles north of here. It's on your way. It's just a short detour outside of Dunsmuir. You can drop us off at the ranch and be on your way."

"What's at the ranch?" Pattie said.

"Friends."

All Jolie knew about the ranch was that it was located somewhere in the mountains of Siskiyou County, in Northern California.

Pattie studied her in the rear view mirror. "How old are you, Jolie?"

Jolie glanced at Will. Hadn't this all been prearranged? He had told her Pattie was going back to college in Portland and would give them a ride. She looked into the rearview mirror. Jolie could hardly speak. Her heart was in her throat. "Eighteen."

So this was how it was going to be. She was already lying about her age. She put her head back and closed her eyes. The engine's steady hum and vibration cradled her as Pattie drove north on the 101 freeway. Will periodically reached back and squeezed her hand. They stopped only for gas and food. More than once, Jolie caught Pattie's concerned gaze in the rearview mirror. If Pattie suspected she wasn't eighteen, would everyone else?

Pattie and Will talked up front. "I want to become a journalist," Pattie said.

"You don't need a degree for that. Write for an underground news press," Will said.

"No, I want to have the skills and credentials to work for a big news agency. I want to work overseas, on assignment."

"Trust me, you're wasting four years of your life. Plus, they don't send women overseas. That's a man's job," Will said.

Jolie cocked her head toward Will. What did he just say? A man's job? That didn't sound like the Will she knew. Wasn't he all about equality?

Pattie shot him a glance. "We'll see about that."

Jolie gazed out the window. The knot tightened in her stomach. She was with Will, and they'd be together now. They'd been drawn to each other from the moment they'd met. He had persuaded her they could make it together, out there, wherever that was and she had put her trust in him.

Pattie drove north into the fading light. Will changed the radio station every time they lost the signal. Jolie inhaled deeply and closed her eyes. This was really happening. She sank back into the seat.

By now her parents would have read her good-bye letter and would be mad. Mad she hadn't followed through with the first day at Saint Mary's. Mad she wouldn't conform and obey. But their mold for her couldn't contain her free spirit.

Hours later they neared Lake Shasta. "I can't drive anymore," Pattie said.

"Let's find a rest stop and crash for the night. We'll start fresh in the morning," Will said.

Pattie cruised into a rest stop. Jolie curled into a ball in the cramped back set. Her world would never be the same. What were her parents doing right then? Had they called the police? She lay awake a long time before falling into a fitful sleep.

In the early morning darkness, a rumble woke them as truckers idled their diesel engines. At dawn they piled out of the car and stretched. They drove on and stopped at a roadside café in Dunsmuir and ordered the Logger's Special: pancakes, eggs, and hash browns. Will made notes in his well worn leather notebook.

Pattie fidgeted with her spoon and coffee cup, glancing repeatedly at Jolie. "Let's hit the road. I want to be in Portland tonight, and we have no idea where this so-called ranch is."

Will turned to a page in his notebook. Cryptic directions were scrawled on the bottom of a song he was writing.

"X marks the spot." Will pointed to a small *x* drawn at the end of a squiggly line.

From Dunsmuir they drove toward Sawyers Bar through Fort Jones and Etna. The pavement ended abruptly, and a cloud of dust enveloped the car. They had gone too far. Pattie did a U-turn and slowed when they came upon a store, a phone booth, a ranger station, a few houses, and a small post office.

"This is the middle of nowhere," Pattie said. "I thought you said it was a short detour?"

Jolie peered out the back window. "Do people really live here?" Where was the ranch? She'd imagined a horse ranch off the side of the highway with a white fence that ran for miles and horses galloping wild and free.

Will looked at the map and guided them on. They turned off the main dirt road onto a rutted one lane track. "The ranch is eight miles ahead."

"This is so primitive. I'm not sure my car will make it," Pattie said.

"I'll drive," Will said.

After switching drivers, Will drove, up and up, mile after mile, until they reached a crest. "Look at this." Will stopped the car. When the dust settled, they got out and looked over the valley. Folds upon folds of blue green mountains were stacked against each other as far as they could see. Small cloud wisps wrapped the far off peaks. An emerald green river snaked through the lush fir and pine forest far below.

The tightness in Jolie's stomach relaxed. Two brown and gold mosaic-patterned hawks rode air currents, floating effortlessly in large meandering circles over the forest valley. They were free, and she was free. Free from her parents. Free from Saint Mary's.

"Are you sure about the directions?" Pattie turned the ring on her finger over and over. "I mean, there is nothing out there."

Will nodded. "I trust my friends."

They drove on, bumping down the twisted mountain, granite cliffs on one side and the green winding river far below on the other. A rusted brown station wagon lay overturned partway down the mountain. Jolie closed her eyes to calm her stomach. The drop-off was dizzying. If the wheel got too close to the loose edge it would be all over. Will inched down the rutted road, navigating hairpin turns for three more miles. At the bottom, the forest opened up and the road ended in a meadow.

Will parked in the grass. "We have arrived."

Jolie took a deep breath and exhaled, relieved to be off the harrowing road. An old homestead with a hulking brown farmhouse sat on one side of the meadow. Opposite the farmhouse was a teetering barn. Both were in need of repair.

Will got out of the car. Pattie and Jolie paused and then eased out and stationed themselves by the Camaro, the car almost unrecognizable under layers of dust. Will strode toward the farmhouse.

Jolie glanced around furtively. A dozen or more goats nibbled tall meadow grass on the knoll and bleated incessantly. This was nothing like the ranches she'd been to. Where were the horses and riding corrals?

The screen door creaked open. Out stepped a young woman with waist-length brown hair wearing a long skirt and halter top. A bearded man with a blond ponytail, jeans, and no shirt appeared behind her. A bowie knife poked out of a sheath strapped to his belt. They stood rigid on the porch.

Jolie clasped her hands together. Who were these people? Why was the man wearing a bowie knife?

Will stopped twenty yards from them and addressed the man. "Peace, brother. We're here to visit Allen and Haley."

"They're away," he said.

Jolie stood straighter. They weren't there? Now what would they do?

Will paused. "I'm Will. They invited us to visit."

"They're in San Francisco," the man said, studying Will. "How do you know them?"

Jolie clasped her hands tighter; a sinking feeling ran from her head to her stomach. The man looked her way. His gaze was too intense to hold, and she dipped her head.

"Allen and I were roommates at Berkeley."

Jolie hadn't thought about his life in Berkeley. There was a lot she didn't know about him. The man stood silent on the porch.

"And after college we shared a house. Haley, too."

The man studied them and then conferred with the woman in a low voice. Jolie wiped the sweat off her brow with her hand. It was unbearably hot in the sun.

The couple descended the porch steps and walked over to Will. "I'm Mark and this is Jasmine." He held out his hand to shake Will's. "Friends of Allen's are friends of ours."

Jolie smiled and murmured, "Hi." She followed Mark's gaze to Pattie. The girl looked wildly out of place in her matching yellow outfit standing rigid with her arms crossed.

"If I'm going to make it to Portland tonight, I'd better head out now," Pattie said.

"We're getting ready for lunch. Don't you want to stay and join us?" Jasmine asked.

"No thanks, I need to be off."

"Don't you want to see the ranch?" Mark asked.

"No, no thanks." Pattie looked at Will. "Do you want to get your packs from the car?" Jolie gave Pattie a hug. The steep winding road they had traversed loomed behind them. Pattie could not be looking forward to the drive out by herself.

"Thanks for the ride and everything," Jolie said.

Pattie hugged her back. "Are you sure about this? This ranch? And Will?"

Jolie nodded. Was she sure about this? She hid her fear and put on a smile, but she did wonder. The ranch wasn't what she had expected. She watched Will get their things out of Pattie's car. Everything would work out. He had told her that. She just wasn't used to it yet. This was her new life, a new adventure.

Will stacked his guitar, their packs, and bedroll in the grass and hugged Pattie. "Thanks for the ride."

Jolie stood rooted in place, her eyes riveted on the trail of dust as Pattie's car disappeared from view on the spiral assent up the crude road. Jasmine's voice startled her, and she turned back to them.

"Let's put your packs in the house. We're getting ready to join the others for lunch, down the way, in the summer kitchen."

Jolie followed Jasmine's gaze. The others? Who were the others?

3

Free People

೭ᴖᴏ

They stepped over a black lab on the porch, too hot to move. The dog's tail thumped against the wood planks. Inside the farmhouse the heat was unbearable. They set their things in a corner. Books lay stacked on the floor in the large open living room. Neatly folded clothes lay in piles. Jolie was surprised to see a piano, three guitars, hand drums, and a mandolin in the far corner.

On the kitchen counter next to the wood-fired oven, eight loaves of whole wheat bread rested on cooling racks. Jasmine put four loaves into a cloth flour sack.

"Can I use your bathroom?" Jolie asked in a quiet voice.

"It's outside. We'll go past it on the way," Jasmine said.

Jolie glanced around the old farmhouse. A house this big didn't have a bathroom? Will and Jolie followed them out of the house.

Jasmine pointed to a crude outhouse. "We'll meet you by the orchard."

Near the outhouse door was a bucket of water, a bar of soap, and a hand towel. Jolie held her breath and hurried in to pee. At least there was soap and water.

Jolie walked through the meadow past a large garden to an old orchard. Gnarled apples dripped from the trees. "Try one," Mark said, picking some off the tree.

Jolie and Will each picked an apple and took a bite. "They're sweet," Jolie said. Juice ran down her chin. "And tart."

Smiling, Will wiped the juice off her face with his long fingers. She felt his calluses from the hours he spent playing the guitar.

They moved along a path to a crude log bridge. Mark and Jasmine continued over it. Jolie walked behind Will and kept her eyes on her footing and not at the stream twenty feet below. The path led them through another meadow and up a rise. A grove of fir and madrone trees stood off in the distance. As they drew nearer she noticed a group of twenty or more people under the trees on a large wooden platform. It was covered with a dome type roof. Jolie hung back. She hadn't expected all these people. Some sat on benches at a long wooden table. A wood cook stove anchored a corner and an array of cooking implements lay next to overflowing five-gallon compost buckets.

Jolie reached for Will's arm. This was the summer kitchen? It was more like primitive camping.

Mark introduced her and Will to the group. There were too many names to remember: River, Sky, Acorn, Crazy Bob, Grace, Jade, and various other tree and flower names. The women mostly wore long skirts and halter tops. Two of the women's bellies bulged in pregnancy. The men, many of them long-haired and bearded, were dressed in jeans. Some were shirtless. The odor of sweat sent a shiver through Jolie. Most of the men sported bowie knives strapped to their belts. A few wore animal skin vests despite the heat. Two young children clamored for food.

Jasmine and two other women worked together to lay out the lunch of sliced bread, soft white cheese, sliced apples and blackberries. The group assembled around the large table. The woman on Jolie's right reached over and took her hand. Jolie flinched at her unexpected touch.

"I'm Grace," she said.

Everyone joined hands. Will reached for her other hand and squeezed it.

Mark began to speak and rambled on, giving thanks for the food. He ended by welcoming Will and Jolie. There were murmurs all around, then hands unclasped and the food was passed around on plates.

"What's your trip here?" Will asked.

"We've formed a new culture. We're a band of Free People," Mark said. "We bought the one-hundred-acre ranch last year and started the commune. We're a family of freedom, acceptance, and love."

"There are thirty-five of us living in harmony with nature," Jasmine added.

"It's like the wild west," Mark said. "We're trying to become self-sufficient."

"But we're city people, learning as we go. I'd never built a shelter or cut firewood before I came here. But we're surviving," said a man in a leather vest with no shirt.

Jolie took in the scene around her. She had been dropped into another world. Thirty-five people living way out here? She hadn't known what to expect but it certainly wasn't this. Will caught her eye and smiled. She attempted a smile. All that mattered was she was with him.

"We've torn down the walls of society and have created a utopia, a radical wilderness utopia," a man with startling blue eyes said.

Jolie's brow furrowed. She thought she knew what utopia meant but this was not it by any means.

"I came here to get away from the United States of America," said Crazy Bob, a burly man with an eagle tattooed on his bicep.

Jolie studied him. Well, he'd attained his wish. This was the most isolated end of the road place in the wilderness you could get. There was no electricity, running water, or proper bathrooms and they were forty long miles from anywhere. But they were free and no one was telling them what to do out here. She doubted anyone could even find the ranch.

The group continued to talk after lunch. "Can we stay until Allen and Haley get back?" Will asked, looking at Mark.

The table went silent. Jolie stiffened. What if they said no? Where would they go? Will didn't have another plan that she knew of and Pattie was long gone. Mark, Crazy Bob, and River got up from the table and walked a short distance away. They stood under a madrone tree, talking. The conversation resumed at the table. Will stroked her hand to relax her grip. The three men returned and sat down.

"You can stay in one of the old miners' shacks," Mark said. "A couple left last month. Make yourselves at home with whatever's there."

Jolie exhaled, her shoulders relaxed a bit. The conversation turned to the projects that needed to be done: chopping wood, barn repair, garden irrigation. No one could agree on what to work on as a group that day. Slowly they disbanded and wandered off to do whatever they each wanted. Some went to repair their houses. Some headed to the swimming hole and others to the main house. A few women stayed in the summer kitchen to clean up and start working on dinner.

Jasmine offered to show Jolie and Will around. They walked along a well-worn path past five geodesic domes nestled in a circle around a meadow. The domes were patched together with tin, plywood, tar paper and whatever building material was available. Plexiglas skylights adorned the roofs. The whole place was surreal.

"Most live in their own shelters and some live in the main house, especially in the winter," Jasmine explained. "We are trying to perfect the domes. They're one of the most efficient dwellings to live in. Mark and I built this one."

Jasmine walked onto a wooden deck and opened the door. Will and Jolie followed and peered in the door. The large open room was framed by a series of triangles from floor to ceiling. It looked like a giant honeycomb. Sun poured in through the skylight onto a bed laden with a patchwork quilt. A wood stove and small kitchen area were off to one side. Everything was clean and neat. Jolie felt the calmness of the place, a retreat from the chaos of the noisy summer kitchen.

They walked back across the creek to a string of collapsing wood-framed miners' shacks.

"You can stay here," Jasmine said. She opened the door to one cabin and led them in. It was blazing hot inside. A gray-and-white striped canvas mattress rested on a metal bed frame. A chipped ceramic wash basin and a few cups had been left on a wooden table. In the corner was a tin wood stove. The stovepipe exited skyward out of the roof and daylight streamed in from cracks.

"It's perfect," Will said.

Jolie stood rigid in the center of the small room looking at mouse droppings on the rough plank floor. It was far from perfect. A couple had actually lived there? It needed a cleaning, that was for sure.

Will and Jolie walked back to the main house with Jasmine. "This is our only link to civilization right now." Jasmine nodded toward an old Dodge Power Wagon parked by the main house. "And of course people like you who stop by now and then."

The oversized truck with the rusty bed did not inspire confidence. Four other vehicles rested inoperable amid rusting car parts and tires.

In the main house Jolie and Will retrieved their packs, bedroll, and Will's guitar. Jasmine gave them a broom, a bucket, and some rags for cleaning.

Jolie swept and cleaned the dusty cabin, trying to make it somewhat habitable. Will sat outside on a log bench, talking to one of the bearded men. She unfolded the bedroll on the mattress and lay back on the bed in the stifling heat.

Pattie's words echoed in her mind. Was she sure about this? Less than thirty hours earlier she had been at home and now she was at the end of a dirt road in the middle of the wilderness, in a miner's shack with thirty-five mountain men and women and one vehicle that worked. She breathed deep, exhaled slowly, and closed her eyes. There was no going back. It was all about survival now.

Jolie and Will joined the group for dinner at the summer kitchen. Kerosene lanterns hung from the dome roof and bathed the group in a golden glow. Someone strummed a guitar.

"What's happening out there in the evil world?" Mark asked Will.

"The socialist movement is gaining a foothold around the country," Will said.

"Nothing will come of that," Mark responded. "It's been tried so many times."

"No, the Revolutionary Socialist Movement is gaining ground especially on college campuses," Will said.

"Ha, that's because the rich kids feel guilty. It's a revolt of privilege," Mark argued.

Someone played a harmonica and the blues tune floated overhead.

"It's a different movement now," Will replied. "We're building a political platform to overthrow the capitalists."

"What's the platform?" one of the men asked.

"We're fighting to end poverty and racism. To create a better world with an equal and classless society."

"Good luck with that," Mark said.

"How we do that?" someone asked.

Will talked about his vision of a socialist society where everyone is equal and the industries, services and natural resources are collectively owned by the people. "It means that for the first time the government of the people, for the people and by the people will become a reality."

"Right on," someone said.

"Take our natural resources," Will explained. "The people own the oil under the land the government leases but the oil companies take the profit. In a socialist society the people own the oil and the profit."

The group listened, their enthusiasm growing as ideas spilled forth. Mark listened silently, his eyes on Will.

Jolie sat close to Will, warily observing the group. He was in his element. He was the handsomest, with his high cheekbones, straight black hair, and captivating smile. She smiled inwardly. She was with him now. All evening she didn't say a word and no one noticed. Occasionally Mark's intense gaze met hers and she quickly looked away.

In their cabin that night, Will held her. "You're free." He caressed her face and then her breasts.

She didn't feel free. All of these new people. What if they saw through the lie about her age?

"My sweet Little Wing. We're together now."

She melted under his strong warm touch and moved her hands gently over his taut body. She closed her eyes and lost herself in their lovemaking.

Later she lay wrapped in his arms listening to the sound of the night forest. Crickets chirped. An owl hooted. "They'll never find us here," Will whispered.

A far off howl pierced the night.

4

Moonchild

Jolie woke to the sound of muffled bells and bleating goats. She held her breath. Where was she? Sunlight spilled through the cracks in the roof, sending streaks of light onto the rough plank floor. The coarse wood walls were patched with black tar paper. The past forty-eight hours slowly rained down on her. She was at the ranch.

Will was still asleep, his arm wrapped around her. She closed her eyes. She was here with Will. That was all that mattered, they were together now.

Will stirred. "I thought I was dreaming, but we're really here." He smiled at her and she rolled into him. "Hungry?"

She nodded and swung her feet over the side of the bed. "Ouch." A sliver of wood pierced her foot.

They dressed and walked to the stream to wash up. She splashed water on her face and sucked in her breath from the icy blast. Fully awake and invigorated, they followed the path to the summer kitchen. Mark sat drinking coffee talking with a small group at the long table. Jasmine and Grace flipped whole wheat pancakes. They were dressed alike in halter tops and long skirts, their long hair woven in braids.

"We're going to chop firewood before it gets too hot," Crazy Bob said, looking at Will. "Want to join us?"

Will hesitated. Jolie couldn't picture him chopping wood. Mark looked at Will expectantly. Crazy Bob stood waiting for his response. "Sure."

"Jolie, you can come with us and milk the goats," Grace said.

Milk the goats? She glanced at Will and then back to Grace. "You'll have to show me how."

After eating, the group broke up and went about their tasks. Jolie went with Grace and three other women to the goat barn. The animals' peculiar smell engulfed her and scorched her throat as they entered the barn. A herd of bleating goats swarmed them, nudging their thighs with long curved horns. Jolie stood rigid in the middle of the dancing herd while the bells around their necks jingled softly.

"First we have to lure them into their milking stalls and secure their heads or they'll butt," Grace said.

Using oats to coax them into place, they sat on log rounds and set about milking. Jolie, slow in the beginning, got into the rhythm. She listened to the women talk and tried not to breathe too deep. The pungent goat smell overwhelmed her. It took the five of them the better part of the morning to finish.

The women carried the heavy buckets up to the main house and used cheese cloth to strain the odd-smelling milk into bottles. Grace set them behind the house in a stream-fed metal box. Part of the icy stream had been diverted and the constant flow kept the metal box cold.

"I'll teach you how to make cheese and yogurt tonight after the evening milking," Grace said.

"You milk them twice a day?" Jolie asked.

Grace smiled at her. "Yes, and we can't miss a milking or they'll dry up and then where would we be?"

Jolie massaged her sore fingers. That was a lot of work every day. She had a lot to learn. The goat smell still permeated her nostrils. Did the milk taste like it smelled?

That afternoon, Mark and Jasmine invited Will and Jolie to hike with them to the swimming hole. In the ninety degree heat, insects buzzed and heat waves rippled off the knoll. They moved trancelike to the end of the meadow and picked up the trail to the creek. Stately firs and giant red-barked sugar pines soared above them. Two-foot long cones hung from the branches. Jolie padded along the forest floor on the soft layer of pine needles in the fairylike setting. She breathed deep, the scent of pine and cedar infused the air. She hadn't thought to pack a bathing suit. Were they going to swim in their underwear or naked?

The path led them out of the forest alongside a creek, bordered with large smooth boulders. Farther down they came to a deep emerald pool. Jasmine and Mark stripped naked. Mark's tan muscular body arched in a dive and disappeared into the water. Circular ripples patterned the water. Jasmine dove in after him, her shapely curves and long hair swallowed beneath the surface. Will followed, his tall, lean frame perfect, like a Michelangelo statue. She hesitated, then quickly disrobed and slipped in, too inhibited around Mark and Jasmine to make a show of a dive.

The pool was cold and exhilarating. One by one they climbed onto the smooth rocks. Jolie slipped on Will's T-shirt, pulling it down around her thighs.

Will traced the formation of several red blisters on his hands from chopping wood. Jasmine took his hand. "You need some salve on these. I'll make some for you later."

"Get some sun on your body, Jolie," Mark said.

"Leave her be. She's shy," Jasmine said.

They spent the afternoon diving in and out of the cool water and lazing on the sun-kissed rocks. Jolie quickly covered up when she got out of the water and averted her eyes from Mark. Will and Mark talked on about the war machine and imperialistic policies. When Jasmine swam to the far end of the swimming hole Jolie swam after her. At the outlet of the pool, Jasmine picked up a plastic bottle that was nestled by a log and held it out to her: Dr. Bronner's Magic Soap.

"Have you ever read this crazy label?"

Jolie shook her head.

Jasmine read: "*Absolute cleanliness is Goodliness! Teach the Moral ABC that unites all mankind free...*This cat goes on and on and on."

Jolie took the bottle and started to read out loud the principles of *we're all one or none*. They laughed and soaped up, their bodies tingled in an explosion of peppermint. The goat smell faded.

Mark and Will dove in and swam over. Mark's gaze rested on Jolie's breasts. "What's going on here, my bathing beauties?" Mark said.

Jolie wished her breasts were smaller. Men always seemed to stare at her. But they did help her pass for eighteen. She sank lower into the water and turned away. She was not his bathing beauty.

In their cabin that night Jolie rubbed salve on Will's hands. Jasmine had given it to him at dinner. She'd made it from guava leaves, herbs and natural oils. The smell was pungent but not unpleasant. Jolie breathed deep to get the goat smell out of her nostrils from the late afternoon milking. After they had finished the milking, Grace taught her how to make yogurt.

Tired to the bone, she rubbed the balm on his blisters. She had worked twice as long as he had that day. After she and Grace finished the yogurt they joined everyone in the summer kitchen where dinner was already underway. She was proud of the work she had done and was warmed by Will's smile when she sat down at the end of the table.

Will closed his eyes as she massaged the balm on his hands. "I'm not cut out for that kind of labor."

"What do you mean?"

"I'm a leader not a worker."

"But in a socialist society everyone is equal. Everyone shares in the work."

Will shook his head. "There are still roles in socialism."

"But the ranch already has a leader," Jolie said. "Grace told me that Mark helped start the commune and he owns the only working vehicle which gives him power over the trips out of the ranch."

Will lay back on the bed. "He's on a power trip alright."

Two weeks after they arrived at the ranch, Mark held a meeting in the summer kitchen after lunch. "We need to share the workload," Mark reminded the group. "We all committed to a minimum of three hours of work a day. Three hours for the family."

"The women do far more work than three hours a day," Grace said.

"Let's keep track of how much we work and then we can even out the chores," Jade said. "And tell me something, why can't the men milk goats too?"

Jolie suppressed a smile. That was brave. She had wondered the same thing.

Sky looked up from the piece of wood he was whittling. "Whoa, what happened to Free People?"

Duties at the ranch were clearly split into traditional male and female roles. The women hauled water for the summer kitchen from the spring by the main house, tended the garden, milked the goats morning and night, made goat cheese, yogurt, grinded wheat for bread, baked bread, dried fruit, cooked, cleaned, and tended the children.

The men felled trees and chopped wood. Despite the efforts, the winter firewood stockpile seemed to shrink. Some worked on the broken down vehicles, the lifeline to the ranch, although there never seemed to be any progress.

Jolie slid onto the bench next to Will. It was no wonder Mark was laying down the law. She knew Will wasn't pulling his weight which compelled her to work harder. The ranch chores didn't fit his personality, a personality she was just getting to know.

"We are free people," Mark stressed. "The ranch is devoted to open-mindedness, free thinking, and the ability to do what one wants. But we also need to keep the work organized to survive."

"We need to elect a leader," Will proposed.

"A leader could hold everyone accountable," River said, as he stroked his beard.

"No," Mark said. "That breeds politics. We're here to get away from traditional governance."

As the conversation continued, Jolie's mind wandered. It was hard to concentrate in the afternoon heat. This wasn't the life she'd envisioned. All she wanted was to be with Will, but now she was with Will and thirty-five other people in the wilderness. She was constantly self-conscious about her age. How could they get out of there?

Since they had arrived the Power Wagon had not moved once. She wondered if it really ran. She needed to talk to Will about leaving. They had only been there two weeks but it seemed like an eternity. Time moved differently there. She thought they were going to make the world a better place. That's what he had promised her. But now he seemed content to fill the pages of his notebook with a socialist manifesto and was in no hurry to leave.

That afternoon Jasmine and Jolie stayed to clean up after lunch. Will wandered off with a group of men to sit in the shade and most likely talk politics, their work being done for the day. Across the meadow they caught a glimpse of Mark and Jade holding hands. The pair walked down the path out of sight. Jolie glanced at Jasmine. Her face was blank.

Jasmine caught her gaze. "We're all free here." But she couldn't disguise the pain in her voice.

"Let's get Will and go swimming," Jolie suggested.

"No, you go on. I need to make an herbal tea for our soon-to-be mothers."

Jolie hesitated. "I'll stay with you. I'd like to learn about natural medicine."

Jasmine appraised Jolie for a few moments. "Well, if you are interested, I could use an apprentice. The family is growing."

Jasmine took out a weathered leather notebook from the outdoor cupboard. She flipped through and opened it to a page with soaring script and sketches of plants. From another cupboard, she pulled out three glass jars full of dried leaves and flowers, labeled in the same flowing script.

Jolie stoked the wood stove and boiled water for the tea and then sat down to watch Jasmine work. Jasmine pulled out an antique scale. Her large brown eyes were intent on the task, and her long, delicate fingers and tan arms flowed as she weighed and mixed herbs and ground them together with a mortar and pestle. Wisps of silken hair escaped from her braid and fell over her paisley halter top. Jolie wondered if she would ever be as beautiful and confident as Jasmine.

Jolie placed the teapot next to the pestle and Jasmine carefully measured a portion of the herbs into the pot. "This will keep their swelling down in this heat," Jasmine explained. "Here, divide the rest into these." She gave Jolie two small glass jars. "And don't be so quiet. You can ask me anything."

"How did you learn all of this?"

"I studied naturopathic and herbal medicine in San Francisco. Some things I've learned through trial and error." Jasmine smiled at her. "I haven't killed anyone yet."

Jolie glanced up from her task and smiled back. When the jars were filled she leafed through the notebook. It contained handwritten instructions on how to prepare and administer herbal cures for any number of ailments. Notes and drawings filled the margins.

After the tea steeped, they walked through the meadow to the circle of geodesic domes. The two pregnant women sat in the shade talking.

"Jolie is my new apprentice," Jasmine said, setting down the teapot.

The women smiled at her. "Ah, another sister of medicine," one said.

Timidly, Jolie handed them each a small jar of the dried tea mixture. "Use one teaspoon per cup in the morning," she said. She had affixed a label of the ingredients and the amount to use on the jars.

"Where are you from?" one of the women asked.

She stiffened. Will had instructed her to be vague. "Near Los Angeles."

"Oh, you're not far from home. I'm from Vermont."

Jasmine disappeared inside the dome and brought out two cups and poured the women tea. They sat in the shade under towering pines. Jolie listened as they talked. The fragrance of warm pine needles drifted down around them. Jasmine placed Jolie's hand on one woman's bulging stomach. Jolie jumped when a sudden lurch pressed her hand. The baby?

The woman laughed. "She wants to say hi."

"You already know it's a girl?" Jolie said.

"That's what Jasmine claims."

Jolie looked at Jasmine quizzically.

Jasmine tucked a wisp of hair behind her ear. "I'll share my secrets with you if you're interested."

Over the next few days Jasmine showed her the herb beds planted at the far end of the vegetable garden. She taught her how to make various remedies for bruises, sprains, colds, earaches, insect bites, and stings. Jolie accompanied her when anyone needed a treatment. One day, instead of milking goats, Jolie went with Jasmine and collected roots and plants from the forest to replenish the supplies. Jasmine explained the timing of the harvests to maximize the potency. They worked side by side under the tall trees.

"Do you know the three things that cannot stay hidden for long?" Jasmine asked after a while.

Jolie stopped digging the Oregon grape root and shook her head.

"The sun, the moon, and the truth."

Her jaw clenched. Did Jasmine think she was hiding the truth?

"Do you know where to find the truth?"

Jolie shook her head and scanned Jasmine's face. Did she suspect something?

"The truth is within you. You can find it through meditation and Buddha's teachings."

Jolie exhaled slowly.

"I can teach you to meditate if you want," Jasmine said.

"Okay, I'd like to learn."

"After we finish here we'll meditate. It will help you relax. You're a bundle of nerves."

Was it that obvious? They walked back to the main house and laid the leaves and roots on drying racks. Jolie inhaled the scent of the woody mixture.

Jasmine got a blanket and a stick of sandalwood incense. Jolie followed her to a shady spot on the edge of the stream. They sat cross-legged facing the water. Jasmine lit the incense and placed it in the ground. "You'll need a mantra."

"A mantra?"

"It's a powerful instrument of the mind. When you silently repeat it you'll disconnect your thoughts and with practice you'll eventually get to the source of your mind."

"You can get to the source of your mind?" Jolie asked.

"Yes, to your pure consciousness, your true being. The source of the universe."

"Wow," Jolie whispered.

"I'll share my mantra with you. It's *om*. When you chant, it sounds like this: ah-oh-mmm."

Jolie smiled. "Om?"

Jasmine nodded. "Silently chant your mantra to quiet your thoughts. If your mind wanders, release it and come back to your breath. Breathe naturally. Inhale and expand your belly. Exhale and relax. When you exhale, your navel wants to touch the front of your spine. It's the way babies breathe." Jasmine demonstrated the breathing technique. "Meditation is a source of inner peace. You can draw strength and courage from it. It will give you the confidence you need in life. Close your eyes and focus on your breath."

Jolie closed her eyes and followed her breath, silently chanting om. The scent of a sandalwood forest filled her. As she exhaled, her thoughts flew to her family. What were they doing right now? How could she let them know she was okay? Her troubled emotions swirled in her mind. When could they leave the ranch? She focused on breathing. When she opened her eyes sometime later Jasmine was still next to her, eyes closed with a serene smile. A wave of homesickness swept over her. She wanted to find Will. He always reassured her that she had done the right thing in leaving home.

⁓‍◯

She found Will in the summer kitchen, the gathering place for afternoon or evening discussions. Will spent his free time there writing in his notebook. He was always at the heart of the debates. Jolie listened to the conversation from the sideline, observing. She tried to catch Will's eye so they could talk but he was in a deep discussion on the politics of the Vietnam War.

Crazy Bob had served in Vietnam, and two of the men were draft dodgers. After burning their draft cards in anti-war protests in New York and San Francisco, they found themselves at the ranch. The isolation proved to be a perfect safe haven.

Crazy Bob rolled another Bugler cigarette and passed the tin around. "We shouldn't be supporting the South Vietnamese regime, let alone sending U.S. soldiers to fight. They brutalize their own people."

"Think about all of the useless deaths in the fight against communism," Will added.

"No, it's more about the messed up U.S. imperialist policies," Mark disagreed.

"No, this war is against the communist aggressor," Will argued.

Jolie frowned, uncomfortable with their constant friction. Did it really matter, when people were dying? Her brothers could get drafted. Her older brother could be sent there at anytime.

"They lied to us," Crazy Bob said. "Nixon said he he'd put an honorable end to our involvement but we have more troops there now than ever, over a half a million. Our government has no idea what is going on there. They have absolutely no idea."

Jolie studied Crazy Bob. His American flag bandana was tied askew around his forehead. Did he get his nickname in Vietnam? "What was it like there?" Jolie asked.

"She talks," Sky said.

Heat rose to her face. It was true. While she listened to the discussions she didn't speak much. Usually no one could get a word in with Will and Mark dominating the debates.

Crazy Bob ignored Sky and met her eyes. "I don't like to talk about it. It's still too raw."

She could see a flint of pain in his sad dropping eyes.

The group slowly disbanded. Jolie and Will walked back to their cabin.

"What's our plan?" Jolie said.

"What do you mean?"

They paused at the cabin door. It was too hot to go inside, and so they sat in front of the ramshackle cabin on a fallen log. "You know, our plan for us and our life?"

Will looked around and spread his hands. "We're here. At the ranch."

She looked around. "This isn't the life I expected."

"You're learning things aren't you? And you're with me." He put his arm around her.

She was with him. That had been what she wanted, but she wanted him all to herself. She'd envisioned their own small house somewhere. Will would get a job, and she'd plant a garden.

"Everyone else thinks this is utopia," Will said.

She looked into his eyes. Utopia? Was he serious? This primitive ranch at the end of a road where the women did most of the work was not her utopia. She couldn't stay quiet any longer. "Maybe for you it's utopia."

His arm dropped from her shoulder and she sensed his mood change. He stood and picked up his notebook. "I'll be back later."

Her chest tightened. Had she hurt him? As he walked away, tears stung her eyes. Was this it? Was this going to be their life? She took in the forest around her and the ever-lengthening shadows. Feeling small and alone, she sank into a deeper, even quieter self.

⤬

Jasmine and Jolie met in the main house the next morning to make blackberry muffins. Jasmine showed her around the pantry. Jolie had never seen such large quantities of food; boxes of dried milk, sixty pounds of honey, one hundred pound sacks of rice, dried beans, and wheat, all stored in big tins to keep out the mice. Jasmine stoked the wood stove with one hand and wiped sweat from her brow with the other.

"It must be a hundred degrees in here," Jolie said. "Don't you like the summer kitchen better?"

"Yes, but there's gravity fed water here from the stream. Plus there aren't as many insects. It's a trade-off."

Grace strode down the stairs. "Life's a trade-off."

"You're up early. Another one bites the dust?" Jasmine asked.

Grace was single and flirted with all of the men. Her relationships lasted about two weeks before she got bored.

"I told him he had to bathe before I'd sleep with him again, and he laughed at me. I think I'll try the single life for a while," Grace said.

"We'll see how long that lasts," Jasmine said.

Jolie laughed.

"No, really. I'm going to wait for the right man to arrive. Someone as smart and handsome as Will."

Jolie's smile faded and jealousy rose through her. Her mood eclipsed across her face. She wasn't sharing him.

"Don't worry," Grace said. "I'm not going after your man."

Jolie relaxed. Of course she wouldn't. They were friends, weren't they?

A moon dance was planned on the knoll for the late September full moon. Preparations lasted two days. The men slaughtered a goat and roasted it. The woman prepared special dishes. It started with a banquet at the summer kitchen. Lanterns and candles glowed in the night. Joints were passed around and the air was pungent with smoke. Homemade elderberry wine flowed into glasses.

Mark toasted. "To Free People. We're all here because we embrace freedom. Freedom to live how we wish. Freedom to express our love for each other openly." As he spoke of love, his gaze was intent on Jolie.

Jolie inched closer to Will and watched the group. The mood was vibrant. Laughter and light-hearted conversation filled the air. They feasted on roasted goat, brown rice, and fresh vegetables. After they finished the last bite of Indian pudding, they streamed to the knoll in a small procession, following the drummers and guitar players.

A circle formed, and a fire was lit in the rock ringed pit. Will and other musicians sat on the ground and began to play. Jolie stood alone and watched from the shadows as the dancing started. The gypsy sound of the tambourine wove together with the guitars. Jasmine and Grace whirled by with the others. The two toddlers twirled in and out of the dancers. The music was hypnotic.

She was aware of a tall presence next to her. She glanced over. It was Mark. She looked back to the dancers. His hand found the small of her back. She didn't dare pull away. She could handle him. He led her to the middle of the dance circle and held her around the waist. He pulled her toward him. They moved together slowly in the shadows. His hands were strong and warm. He began to caress her hips and her waist. His hands moved up her back.

"I've been watching you these past weeks," Mark said, pulling her closer. He was hard against her. "So innocent. Tonight you look like a moon goddess."

He cupped her chin in his hand and tilted her head so her eyes met his. Her throat closed, and she couldn't speak. His other hand was on the small of her back, pressing her toward him. She held her breath.

"I'm going to name you Moonchild."

He pulled her closer, leaned down, and kissed her on the mouth. Her body stiffened. His beard was soft, and he smelled of wood smoke and elderberry wine. She arched away, but he pulled her to him, their bodies pressed tight. He was Jasmine's man. She wanted to get away.

"She's my woman, Mark," Will spoke from behind her.

Mark released her from his kiss but not his hold. "No, she's her own woman here."

Jolie disentangled herself and moved toward Will. His fit body stood tall like a warrior.

"I've been named Moonchild." She exhaled the words, relieved by her rescue.

"You'll always be Little Wing to me. Come dance with me." Will pulled her toward him and into the vibrating dancers.

While she didn't like Mark and his unwanted advances she did like the name. She felt like a Moonchild.

Will kissed her and then leaned into her ear. "Just remember, you're mine, all mine."

5

The Moonstone

The Circle of the Universe was started one day after lunch. Mark, Jasmine and Jade organized everyone into a circle.

"The circle is the symbol of perfection," Jasmine said. "We come together as equals. No one stands higher or apart from the others."

"There is no beginning and no end," Mark said.

"Our unity is more powerful when we clasp hands," Jade said. "Alone we're a single star, together we're a galaxy."

Jolie stifled a laugh. They were serious. Will squeezed her hand. If she looked at him she would lose it.

And so the weekly circle was born. It was used to discuss what had been accomplished that week and by whom. Crazy Bob started a list of what needed to be done and wrote down who volunteered to do it. "Who wants to cut firewood this week?"

There were no takers.

"We need to get another vehicle running," Crazy Bob said.

"How about it, Will?" Mark said.

Will shook his head. "I don't know anything about repairing cars."

Jolie fought back a smile. Will had a degree in political science not engine mechanics.

"Put him on firewood then," Mark said to Crazy Bob, "with Sky and River. We need to build up the winter stockpile."

Everyone's weaknesses were exposed. Jolie volunteered for a number of chores, intent on pulling the weight for the both of them.

One afternoon, Will found her in their shack at the wobbly wooden table. She had created her own herbalist notebook with a chart. She leaned over the notebook, meticulously recording every herb and root and its corresponding culinary, medicinal or cosmetic use. Will came up behind her and wrapped her in his arms.

"You smell so good," he said.

"Lemon balm. I made a skin cleanser. I'm going to make some for all the women."

"You work too hard," he said.

At least he had noticed. "All of the women do. But this doesn't feel like work and I'm learning."

"You're learning more here than you ever would at school."

"Maybe." She was careful not to complain or contradict him and set him off in a bad mood as she had when she questioned the ranch and their plans. He had been cold to her for two days. She had never felt lonelier.

Every day after chores Jolie retreated to the stream or meadow to practice meditation. Meditating became a retreat from the commune, away from the groups and endless debates. At the start of each meditation her chattering thoughts were anything than peaceful. Her mind strayed to her parents. What were they doing? Would they find her? What would the ranch family do if they found out she was underage? Would Mark or another man make a move on her? How long were they going to stay there? She tried to bring her attention back to the rise and fall of her breath and silently chanted om. Eventually the torrent of worries slowed to a trickle. Meditating calmed her troubled mind and brought her some peace and strength.

Jolie woke one morning in mid October with violent stomach cramps. She hurried to the outhouses near the main house. It started with diarrhea, and then she began to vomit. She couldn't leave the outhouse. Did someone not boil the water long enough or not at all? Jasmine constantly reminded them about the risk of waterborne illness from the stream and her dad had taught her not to drink out of streams. But not everyone was diligent. Or maybe it was from undercooked food. Or was she pregnant?

Two hours later Will walked down to the main house looking for her. She lay in the grass near the outhouse, weak, grasping her stomach.

"What's the matter Little Wing?" He bent down beside her and brushed the hair from her forehead.

"My stomach."

She got up and went to the outhouse again. She emerged a while later and sank into the grass in a small heap, racked with severe cramps. Will scooped her in his arms and moved her away from the outhouse and the ever present smell.

He stood over her, his eyes wild with concern. "I'm going to find Jasmine. She'll make you a tea."

She didn't have the energy to respond. Her head ached, her body ached, her stomach heaved in violent cramps. Another wave came. Will took off in a run toward the summer kitchen.

He returned panting and wrapped her in a blanket. He sat with her on the grass, and held her limp body.

Jasmine arrived with tea. "Drink this. It's made with raspberry leaves, mint, golden seal, and Oregon grape root. It'll fix you right up."

Jolie sipped the tea. Will held her and urged her to drink more. Nothing stayed down and her cramps grew in severity. Late afternoon, when she had nothing left but dry heaves, Will and Jasmine moved her from the meadow to an upstairs bedroom in the main house. Will tried to cheer her and played the guitar.

"Please stop." The jangle of noise hurt her head. She closed her eyes and drifted in and out of sleep.

Jasmine came back later. "The herbal tea doesn't seem to be working," Will said. "Is she pregnant?"

"Not with these symptoms. Some newcomers get this, and it usually lasts about three days." Jasmine laid a cold wash cloth on her forehead.

She was burning up, and it was cool on her skin. "Thanks, Mom." Her eyes remained closed against the searing light.

"It's me, Jasmine."

Her eyes fluttered open. Jasmine? She had been back in her room at home. Her mom had brought the cold wash cloth. "Oh, Jasmine," she whispered through dry lips. She wanted her mom.

She lay in the main house for days, dehydrated despite Will and Jasmine's efforts to get her to drink. She couldn't hold anything down and was not getting better.

One afternoon she awoke to whispers. Jasmine and Will smiled down at her. "I think you have a waterborne disease because it's lasted so long," Jasmine said. "It's probably cryptosporidiosis, a protozoan parasite, working its way through your body."

"Doesn't that need treatment?" Will asked.

"Hydration and the tea I've been making should help," Jasmine said.

Fatigued and listless, she felt like dying. She closed her eyes and floated off to sleep, beautiful sleep.

When she awoke, Will was sitting in the chair by the bed writing in his leather notebook. "Are you writing a song?" she whispered.

"No, just notes for the socialist revolution." He set his notebook down. "How are you?" He moved to the bed, sat down and propped her up. "I'm so worried about you." He held a cup of broth to her lips. She took a drink and lay her head back on his arm. He stroked her head and cheek.

"I'll be fine." He leaned in to hear, her voice but a scarce whisper. "Go find your buddies. You don't have to stay here all of the time." She knew he thrived on the political debates and ranch camaraderie. Her eyes closed from the effort. He lay her back down.

"You have to get better, Little Wing."

He kissed her on the forehead and then she felt a breeze wash over her face. Her eyes opened and she saw that he was fanning her with his notebook. She smiled faintly and closed her eyes. He was a good man. Sometime later she heard the door close.

Jasmine and Grace stopped by as often as possible but they had chores. It was harvest time and the ranch women were in high gear canning vegetables in both kitchens. The upstairs bedroom was unbearably hot but she was too weak to move.

The days and nights merged together. She had lost track of time. One day it seemed to be late afternoon. Murmurs and quiet laughter drifted up through the window. What was Will doing? She turned to look out the rusty screen. All she could see were evergreen trees. Was he talking with the other women? Was he off with another woman? He was the handsomest man at the ranch, and he captivated everyone. No, but he loved her and would be faithful. She wouldn't waste energy on jealousy. Who could blame him for not staying in this hot room in the middle of the day with her? She longed to sit on the porch and watch the comings and goings of the ranch, but she was too weak to move. Everything had a dreamlike feeling. Sleep overtook her again.

One evening, during the second week of her illness, she woke to find Will, Mark, Jasmine, Grace, and Crazy Bob standing around her bed gazing down at her.

"How are you, Little Wing?"

Was she dreaming? Will's voice and his touch felt real on her cheek. "I'm a little weak."

"Everyone's concerned about you," Grace said.

"After dinner tonight we had a family meeting," Mark said. "We think someone should take you to the hospital in Shasta."

Jolie looked at Will. What did he think? What about the authorities? They were certainly looking for them. Her parents had seen them together on the news, protesting, and her friend Zoe would have told them about Will. By now they would have pieced together that she was with him.

"Do you want to go to the hospital?" Jasmine asked, stroking her arm.

Jolie probed Jasmine's eyes. She trusted Jasmine's knowledge of natural medicine. She'd seen her cure others. She tried to clear the fog in her mind. It would be a disruption for someone to drive her out in the Power Wagon and stay with her at the hospital. Since they'd arrived at the ranch, no one had driven out. There also could be a problem, a missing person photo of her and a wanted photo of Will. Neither of them had any idea what awaited them out there but she couldn't voice those concerns to the ranch family. They were living there on a false pretense. She continued to probe Jasmine's eyes while her mind swirled. "What do you think?"

Will took Jolie's hand. "No, it's up to you, Little Wing."

She never wanted to burden anyone. "Give me a couple days," Jolie whispered.

Jasmine nodded. Jolie closed her eyes and heard them leave the room. Hushed voices murmured outside her door.

"We can't lose anyone here. Everyone keep a close eye on her," Mark said. "I'll drive her out myself if I have to."

"She has a strong spirit. She'll pull through," Jasmine said.

Jolie felt like dying and was too weak to care. What if she died, there at the end of the road, at the ranch? Would anyone contact her parents? If no one did they would never know what had happened to her. Guilt washed over her. "Please forgive me," she whispered in the dark.

Will came back with broth and helped her sit up to drink. He stayed with her and furiously scribbled in his notebook as she floated in and out of sleep.

Later that night, the door creaked open. Mark and Jasmine slipped in with tea. They sat on either side of her bed. Jolie was awake but listless. Will helped her drink and held the cup between sips.

Mark handed Jolie a small leather pouch. "This is for you."

"What is it?" She struggled to open the pouch. Inside was a green, milky stone, the size of a nickel. She held it in her palm. It shone in the kerosene lamp light.

"It's beautiful," she whispered.

"It's a moonstone for our Moonchild. It's associated with moon goddesses," Mark said.

"Its energy can ease illness and balance upsets," Jasmine said. "It protects travelers from danger."

"Use it to draw in your desires. Moonstones can be used to extend the power of the moon into daylight hours," Mark said.

Jolie smiled at them for the first time in two weeks. She wrapped her hand around the smooth green stone.

"Thank you." Her eyes closed as she clutched the talisman and drifted off to sleep.

6

Winter in Two Moons

∼☉

Three days later, Will held Jolie's arm as she wobbled downstairs. Will went to tell everyone the good news. Grace made her mint tea, and they sat at the kitchen table and ate goat milk yogurt with honey and blackberries. Grace filled her in with the ranch gossip.

Later, Jolie sat on the porch outside the main house soaking up the weak October sun. She read Jasmine's book, *The Wisdom of Buddha*. The moonstone, in its small leather pouch, hung around her neck on a thin leather lace beneath her blouse.

That evening some of the group sat around the fire pit after dinner. It was getting colder as the days passed. Will and Jolie shared a log bench as Will strummed his guitar.

"My vision is to create a higher culture, a true Shangri-La," Mark said.

Jolie could see Mark's s face in the firelight. A Shangri-la? What would that look like?

"But that won't change society or our capitalist government," Will said, impatience rising in his voice.

"This is our society and politics are not part of it," Mark replied. "We don't want to be part of the outside world."

Jolie shifted. She couldn't wait to leave the ranch and join the outside world.

Jade sat down next to Jolie. "Our Moonchild is back. Everyone was worried about you."

Jolie smiled and touched the moonstone in the leather pouch. "Thanks, I'm better now."

"Does anyone know when Allen and Haley are coming back?" Will asked.

"They'd be crazy to come back now," River said. "Winter is in two moons."

Two moons? Two months? The conversation livened. The group that had survived the previous winter, their first, began to share stories. River, Sky, Crazy Bob, Mark, and others told stories of being cold, extremely cold. They'd run out of basic supplies, delivered a baby, and watched record snowfall pile up four feet deep. They shared the tale of Mark and Crazy Bob's heroic trek out by foot to get supplies.

"A four-wheel drive is useless here in the snow. The road is too steep." Mark said.

The group started to plan for the coming winter. Jolie tried to imagine four feet of snow where they sat. How would someone get to the hospital in the winter? Staying in the miners' shack was out of the question. There was no insulation, and the roof had holes. Did the main house have room for everybody? She tried to imagine Will stuck at the ranch all winter. It would be claustrophobic with so many egos.

"We need to make a food run to San Francisco now that we know what to expect," Jasmine said. "Maybe two runs."

The discussion turned serious. No one wanted to endure the bitter cold and meager food conditions of the previous winter. Now there was a baby, two toddlers, and two pregnant women that would give birth that winter. Mark and a few others started planning the trip to San Francisco to load up on supplies.

Jolie glanced at Jasmine sitting between the two pregnant women. Why wasn't she going on the trip? Wasn't she screaming to get out of there for a trip to civilization to buy books and eat some decent food? And it dawned on her. The pregnant women needed her. Jolie looked around at the faces in the firelight, the ranch family. They really did care for each other. But aside from her friendship with Jasmine, she had never felt comfortable there. She inched closer to Will. Their visit had turned into a lengthy stay, and now winter was almost upon them. She felt trapped. A shiver went up her back.

⌒෧

The next day after Will put in his three hours cutting firewood, he found Jolie alone in the kitchen of the big house. She was filling glass jars with dried plants and roots.

"We're leaving the ranch," he said.

She smiled.

He held up his leather-bound notebook. "I've spent my time here writing a revolutionary socialist manifesto and I'm ready to publish and implement it."

Her smile broadened. They would make the world a better place.

"I don't want to be stuck here until spring," he said. "There's work to do."

"Where will we go?"

"I've been talking to some of the men. There's a commune in Eugene, Oregon. They may be open to new members."

Her chest tightened in panic. "Another commune?" Her voice sounded small. Was this his plan for them? Communes? Couldn't they make it on their own? She dreaded getting acquainted with a whole new set of people. "Why another commune?"

"We don't have much money, and the bus tickets will pretty much wipe out what we do have."

This was the first she had learned that they didn't have much money. A few days after they arrived at the ranch she generously placed the money she had brought into the cookie jar, as was expected of newcomers. Will had ignored all the subtle references to contributions so she had felt obligated. Now she regretted giving all of it. Why hadn't he planned better? She had trusted him to take care of her. He promised they would always have everything they needed. He must have access to money once they got back into civilization.

"How will we get out of here?"

"When Mark makes the winter supply run we'll get a ride with him to the nearest town and take a Greyhound bus to Eugene."

She had no choice but to trust his plan. The commune would be temporary. Will would get a job and take care of her as she'd envisioned. But what if the new commune didn't want new members, then what?

❦

The following week, Will and Jolie sat in the Power Wagon's truck bed with Crazy Bob and River. They waved goodbye to a small group that had gathered in the early morning light for the send-off.

Jasmine handed Jolie her well-worn copy of *The Wisdom of Buddha*. Jolie slipped the book into her pack. She leaned over the truck bed and hugged her goodbye.

Jasmine whispered in Jolie's ear. "Follow your heart. All you need to become your own is within you."

Mark was at the wheel. Next to him in the cab was a young couple and their baby boy. The boy had been born the winter before. They were returning to San Francisco. The previous winter had been too harrowing to repeat.

The Dodge rumbled up the dirt road on the long assent to civilization. In the back of the open truck bed, they looked like bandits, their bandanas over their noses and mouths to keep out the dust as they jostled and bumped up the rutted, twisting road. Terrified of the steep drop-off below, Jolie didn't dare look over the side of the truck. On the hairpin turns she closed her eyes.

The Power Wagon lumbered onto the I-5 freeway. Despite the unknown, Jolie liked rolling down the road in the bed of the truck. It was invigorating. They were back in civilization. Two hours later Mark pulled into a small town and stopped near the bus station. Will and Jolie stood, stiff and dusty. They climbed out of the truck with their packs, bedroll, and Will's guitar.

"Good-bye, Moonchild," Mark called from the cab of the truck.

"Good-bye."

51

Will shook Mark's hand. "Thanks for everything."

"Good luck this winter," Jolie called, waving to them as they drove off.

From the back of the truck, Crazy Bob and River flashed peace signs. Jolie hoped the truck would make it to San Francisco and back. Everyone was counting on them.

The bus station was a throwback in time, small with a few chairs, a ticket counter, and bathrooms. To her relief there were no missing persons or wanted photos posted. After Will bought the tickets, they washed the dust off their faces in the bus station bathrooms and stood outside. A truck stop restaurant beckoned from across the street.

"I'm starving," she said. "Let's get a cheeseburger and a chocolate malt."

"No, we have to save our money," Will said. "You wait here, and I'll buy food at the store."

Jolie sat outside the bus station on a wooden bench next to their worldly possessions. She tightened the three leather cords she had braided into a belt to keep her bellbottoms up. Her mouth watered with hunger as she sat fixated on the flashing red sign across the street: CHEESEBURGERS—MILKSHAKES.

Will returned with a grocery bag of food and handed her a Snickers bar. Almost as good as a chocolate malt. She partially unwrapped it, took a small bite. Savoring the chewy chocolate, she watched a woman in the phone booth smiling and laughing.

"I want to call my parents to let them know I'm okay," she said. She owed them that. She didn't want them to worry about her.

"Not now, I'm sure their phone is tapped just waiting for your call. Another time, Little Wing." He took her hand in his.

Her heart sank. It was probably best. They would be mad at her.

7

The Big Yellow House

Will handed the bus driver their tickets. The driver's eyes traveled first over Jolie and then to Will and back to their tickets. She held her breath. Why was he taking so long? Had the police sent their descriptions to all the Greyhound bus drivers? Was it obvious she was underage? The passengers on the bus stared at them. Before they left Santa Barbara Will had obtained a fake drivers license with an assumed last name. At least he had a new identity. Finally, the driver jerked his head toward the aisle, motioning them on. They probably just looked scruffy from the ranch.

Jolie found two empty seats halfway to the back and sat down in the window seat. Will slid in next to her. She leaned her head back on the headrest and exhaled.

The bus rolled down the main street. Out the window was civilization, rural, but civilization nonetheless. They'd been at the ranch two months. She was thankful they weren't staying the winter, all cooped up in the main house. But what would the next commune be like? She didn't want to live in a commune. She wanted freedom. She looked at the small houses they passed. That's what she wanted, their own small house.

"What do you know about the commune in Eugene?" Jolie asked.

"Not much, but we'll find out soon enough."

Apprehension gripped her. She took her moonstone from the pouch and held it in her palm. What had Jasmine and Mark said? It protects travelers from danger? Use it to draw in your desires. She tucked the green gemstone back inside the pouch and clenched the soft suede in her hand. She thought about Jasmine's parting comment. "Follow your heart. All you need to become your own is within you." What did that mean? She pulled out *The Wisdom of Buddha* and began to read.

Late that afternoon, they arrived in Eugene. From the bus station, they walked to the main road. Will stuck out his thumb. A few cars later a brown station wagon pulled over and idled. Will opened the passenger door and spoke with the driver, a long-haired man. He handed him the address.

"Yep, I know the commune, the Big Yellow House." He looked at Jolie. "Hop in, it's on my way."

"Thanks man," Will said.

Will slid their gear into the back seat with Jolie and got in the front.

"Are you going to live there?" the driver asked, accelerating down the road.

"I don't know yet," Will said.

"I know some of the people there. My old lady won't have anything to do with them. She thinks it's a sex cult." The driver grinned at Jolie in the rear view mirror.

Jolie stiffened. A sex cult? That's probably what everyone thinks about communes. But, Jasmine would have told her, warned her at least.

They drove through the suburbs set among green rolling hills. Across from a large wooded park, the driver pulled into a gravel driveway, honked the horn twice, and stopped in front of a three-story wooden house painted a brilliant banana yellow. The window trim on each floor was painted a different shade of psychedelic yellow that radiated a glow of cheerfulness.

A small group of people sat on a large covered porch, soaking up the late afternoon warmth. One of them waved to the driver. Will and Jolie got out of the car with their belongings and walked toward the porch. The driver drove off with a single honk of the horn.

Will looked up at the group. "We've just come from the ranch, the commune in Northern California. The family sends their greetings."

The group on the porch eyed them silently. The men were dressed in jeans and plaid shirts, and the women in bell bottoms or long paisley print skirts. They looked normal enough, not like a sex cult, whatever that would look like. They looked far more normal than the ranch family with their bowie knives and animal fur vests. A tall man in his mid-twenties with short dark hair and a mustache stood up. "I'm Bill. Come on up and join us."

They were offered a seat on an overstuffed couch covered with a faded orange madras bedspread. Bill introduced everyone, Maddy, Michael, Deidre, Kerry and Peter. "We've heard of the ranch. It sounds like nirvana, that far out in the wilderness. How many people are there now?"

All eyes were on Will as he answered their questions. She was surprised he spoke so highly of the ranch since he'd been so critical of Mark's aversion to the outside world.

"How is it governed?" Bill asked.

Will laughed. "It's governed by the Circle of the Universe."

Jolie tried not to smile but it did sound crazy.

Bill stared at him intently. "What does that mean?"

Will explained the family circle. Jolie sat back and did not say a word. Everyone seemed mesmerized by Will and tales of the ranch. She looked out over the gravel driveway to the main road. Across the street, tall trees swayed in the breeze. An occasional car passed on the road a hundred yards away. It dawned on her how trapped they had really been at the ranch, at the end of the road, with no vehicle. They had no control over when they could leave. She thought of how ill she had been and how far emergency medical help had seemed.

This was better. She liked seeing the passing cars. Her attention turned back to the group. Bill asked the most questions and appeared to be the leader. She caught Bill studying her as he stroked his mustache. She quickly looked away and leaned toward Will wishing he would quit looking at her.

"What's the scene here?" Will said.

"My wife, Maddy, and I own the house," Bill said. "It was a lodging house for millworkers. Now, a hundred years later, it's in the middle of suburbia."

"Most of us went to college together. Half of us are psychology majors," Maddy said. "We wanted to start a utopian commune. The neighbors are curious but they leave us alone."

Jolie listened to Maddy, a petite young woman with jet black hair and sparkling brown eyes. They had all gone to college.

"It's an experiment," Michael said.

An experiment? What kind of experiment? Jolie's shoulders straightened. Will took her hand.

"Do you want to join us?" Bill said, eyeing Jolie and then Will. "We could use some new blood. We only ask that you follow the rules."

Jolie uncrossed her legs and tried to stop her foot from jiggling incessantly. New blood? Rules?

"What are the rules?" Will asked.

Bill recited the five rules: "All possessions are shared including vehicles. If you work outside the commune you contribute money to the commune. Everyone contributes to food purchases if you have money. Everyone cooks a group dinner on a rotational basis. Household chores are shared."

She glanced at Will, and their eyes met. There was no mention of sex or cult initiations.

Will nodded. "Yeah, we'd like to join you."

"There's a vacant bedroom on the third floor. The previous couple just moved to Morocco."

Morocco? People just move to Morocco? Maybe she and Will would go somewhere exotic someday. She'd always wanted to travel to far off lands and not just read about it in books.

"Deidre can take you up to see it and get you settled. After the ranch, I'm sure a hot shower will feel good," Bill said. "Dinner is around seven."

Kerrie and Peter got up to start dinner and the group disbanded. Will and Jolie picked up their belongings and followed Deidre into the house. They walked through a room with numerous couches and

56

chairs that looked like a gathering place. Deidre called it the parlor. Out of the corner of her eye, Jolie noticed a built-in bookcase jammed with books. They followed Deidre up the stairs.

"You'll be the third couple on this floor," Deidre said. She had a soft voice and her long brown hair fell loosely around her shoulders. "Michael and I have a room here, and Dawn and Anthony have the other bedroom."

Deidre showed them the large shared bathroom. "Try out the lavender soap I made," she said.

Jolie picked up a bar of soap and inhaled as she looked at the shower and large claw foot bath tub. Luxury, pure luxury. Deidre gathered a set of well-worn sheets and towels from a linen closet and lead them to a room down the hall. She placed them on the bed.

"Welcome to the Big Yellow House. Make yourselves at home," she said. "You'll meet the rest at dinner."

The large room was sparsely furnished with a bed, curtains with large blue flowers, a small writing desk, and two chairs. Jolie went to one of the large windows and peered out. She could see the park across the street and people on the paths and in the gazebo. A house, a room, a bed, a hot shower, a real bathroom, and maybe some real food. Yes, welcome to the Big Yellow House. It would be fine—temporarily.

After making the bed, Jolie went down the hall to take a shower. The hot water and lavender soap melted into her pores. She scrubbed off the ranch layer by layer. The wood smoke and goat smell that always lingered flowed down the drain. She washed her hair three times and combed it out in front the mirror, another luxury. Her cornflower blue eyes stared back at her. She had her father's eyes. Her brothers took after her mom.

She floated back to their room. "Your turn." She smiled wide at Will. "I'll never take hot running water for granted again." He kissed her and headed down the hall to the bathroom.

Jolie unpacked their clothes. All of the clothes she'd bought with her best friend Zoe in vintage clothing shops she had never unpacked at the ranch. They were so out of place in the wilderness. She dressed in a silk blouse and black velvet pants. Will returned from the shower, his long hair sleek and shiny. He, too, was thinner. His face more chiseled and darkly tanned. Will put his arms around her. "You smell like a flower." He stroked her hair. "And you feel like silk." Her blonde strands glowed from months in the sun.

They descended the stairs to the parlor to meet the rest of the group. "Wow," Bill said, looking at Jolie. "You clean up good."

Heat rose to her face, and she caught the glance Maddy shot Bill. He stroked his mustache and smiled. Jolie was painfully aware that everyone's eyes were on her.

Kerrie and Peter announced dinner, and the group filed into the dining room. There were eight couples and a single woman with a five-year-old son living at the Big Yellow House. The long wooden table was laden with multiple casserole dishes of vegetarian lasagna, bowls of green salad, and loaves of homemade bread. The group sat on benches and chairs, no two alike, and passed the food around. Deidre toasted the cooks and their effort.

Over dinner Bill told Will and Jolie more about their new society. "We're a large family that shares everything with each other. I'm sick of mainstream society that allows poverty amid the enormous wealth in America."

"We're all equal here. Our possessions do not define us," Peter said.

The dinner conversation turned to the two-day encounter session the group was planning.

"We've been together for a year now, and we need to hash out our differences and conflicts," Bill said. "We need to share our innermost feelings."

"A professional psychologist, one of Bill's college classmates, has his own counseling practice. He's leading the two-day session," Michael said.

"He's fascinated with our experiment, so he is donating his time," Bill added.

An encounter session? Did she and Will have to go? She didn't know these people. She didn't know what an encounter session was, and she certainly wasn't going to share her innermost feelings with them.

As if on cue, Bill looked at Will and then Jolie. "This will be a good experience. You'll learn more about us, and we'll learn more about you and your relationship."

Kerrie and Peter brought in two large baking pans of hot apple crisp. Deidre brought in bowls, and Michael followed with a gallon of vanilla ice cream. The aroma of cinnamon and baked apples filled the room. Peter and Kerrie stood at one end of the table and dished out bowls of the dessert and passed them down the table. Jolie savored the pure pleasure of the cold ice cream on hot apples and the crunchy brown sugar oatmeal crust. Aside from the upcoming encounter session, life here seemed good.

After dinner some of the group went into the parlor. Jolie and Will joined them. They were a lively bunch, and the conversation ranged from the upcoming apple harvest to Marxism. Jolie browsed the book shelves near the stairs. She pulled out *Silent Spring* by Rachael Carson and read the back cover. "A woman scientist exposes human carelessness, greed and irresponsibility by the reckless use of pesticides and their devastating effect on animals and humans."

She scanned the first chapter, A Fable for Tomorrow, and glanced back at the group. Will and others talked about the history of class struggle between the working class and the bourgeois. She slipped upstairs to their room with the book. Laying on the bed, she reveled in the comfort of a real house with electricity, no holes in the roof, and a smooth hardwood floor. She opened the book and read. The tragedy of man's destruction of nature drew her in. She thought of the oil spill and how it had blackened miles of beautiful shoreline and killed countless birds and sea creatures. She thought of home. Once they were settled she would get a message to her parents.

Will came up much later. "I signed us up for cooking and chores," he said.

"You did?"

"Well, actually, I don't think they would have let me go without an assignment."

"What's an encounter session?" Jolie asked.

"It's an intense analysis of your flaws. They break you down to build you up."

She clutched the moonstone pouch around her neck. "I don't like the sound of it."

"It'll be fine. There'll just be a lot of crying."

"Crying?"

He nodded.

She took a deep breath and let it out slowly. What if she cracked under pressure and the truth about them came out?

8

The Gestalt of Self

❧

That week Jolie and Will settled into the routine at the Big Yellow House. All of the action was either in the dining room, the parlor, or the front porch. The Beatles *The White Album*, the favorite of the month, played constantly on an old phonograph.

"Will you teach me to make soap?" Jolie asked Deidre.

"Sure, but not until next month when all of the fruit and nut harvests are done," Deidre said. "That's a good rainy day project and trust me, we get a lot of rain."

Most of the members volunteered at the Food Cooperative four hours a week, which gave them a discount. They also bartered skills for food and services. Some picked apples and fruit throughout the season.

They talked endlessly about Carl Rogers, a respected psychologist, and his theory of individuals based on nineteen propositions, the gestalt of self. One evening after dinner they moved the discussion to the parlor.

"We need to change our perceptual field of reality to live in a communal society," Bill said.

Jolie frowned; what was he saying? Michael saw her expression and explained. "The perceptual field is the self that has been formed through our interaction with our traditional environments from birth."

"So the concept of self must change in a communal family," Anthony said.

"Why do we have to change?" Dawn said. "I like myself."

Jolie liked herself too, except for what she had done to her parents.

"With the old self, there are barriers to the new society, and tension is created," Michael said.

"When we share more organic experiences, we replace the traditional value system and accept the new one. If any experience is inconsistent with the structure of the self, it's perceived as a threat, and we can't live in harmony," Bill said.

Share organic experiences? Replace the traditional value system? Were they talking about sex? She would only have sex on her terms, not because she was living in the commune. She believed in true love and commitment. Will was all she wanted. She looked around the room at the other women. They were smart and more experienced than she was. Would Will be tempted in this free society? A jealous pang shot through her. Why did they have to live there? She would not surrender to a different sense of order and meaning. She would stay true to herself.

The dreaded Saturday morning arrived. They gathered for the encounter session in the parlor, sitting in a circle of chairs. Bill introduced the group to Tom, the psychologist who was to lead the two-day session. He had short brown hair and neatly trimmed sideburns. He stood in the middle of the circle, exuding confidence.

"Don't be nervous," Tom said, turning around to everyone in the circle. "Don't be shy." He looked straight at Jolie.

How did he know she was scared stiff? She gulped. He was on to her.

"We will engage in intense interaction with each other to improve our own self-awareness and interpersonal relations," Tom said. "You must be completely open and honest and react immediately with your true feelings. Get in touch with your range of emotions and share them with the others."

He paused and looked around the room into the eyes of every person. "You will help others work through their issues in a supportive way. This will strengthen your ties and future communications. We'll go around the room and each of you will have the chance to talk about your concerns, issues, or problems affecting you. Who wants to start?"

Everyone looked around the room expectantly. They were in for a long two days. Jolie sat back, willing herself invisible, terrified of being called upon. She didn't have any problems, at least not yet. She sat, petrified, on the stiff wooden chair.

Bill spoke up. Jolie exhaled. "It's been a year since we formed the Big Yellow House, and we still have so many inhibitions with each other. Some of us are so uptight about things."

No one spoke.

"What kind of things?" Tom said.

Bill's wife, Maddy, closed her eyes.

"Love. We're not sharing the love," Bill said.

The group looked around the room at each other.

"I feel the love," Kerrie said.

"You haven't shared my bed and my love," Bill said. Maddy started to quietly cry.

"I am married to your brother," Kerrie said. "I love you as a brother."

"We can share love without sex," Peter said, coming to her rescue. "I love Maddy, but I don't need to sleep with her to let her know."

Oh boy, the session was in full gear. She glanced at Will, and their eyes met. Why did he look so amused? She was intimidated around this group. He reached for her hand. What if they asked her about her views on sex? Deidre got up and put her arms around Maddy.

Tom seemed to enjoy this exchange. He sat back in his chair and did not intervene.

"Your idea of love doesn't work for everyone," Maddy said, empowered by Deidre's support.

"Sleeping with others has always been a private decision, and optional," Michael said. "It is not a rule of the commune."

Silence ensued. Jolie realized her foot was jiggling madly. She uncrossed her legs and planted her feet firmly on the floor.

"We all agreed to govern without a leader Bill, but you seem to be always in charge and passing judgment," Anthony said.

"I was expressing my disappointment, that's all," Bill said. He smoothed his mustache.

Jolie vowed to steer clear of Bill. She studied the grain of the hardwood floor. Was it cedar?

"Let's explore the leadership comment further," Tom said. "Do you feel you are governed by a democracy or an autocracy?"

There were no takers to the question.

"Michael, since you voiced this concern, can you give us specific examples?" Tom said.

The morning and afternoon wore on, straining the group's emotions.

Will spoke up numerous times regarding the governance. "Why not elect leaders annually? Even a socialist society has someone in charge."

"Decisions have to be made by a consensus or the men will rule," Deidre said. "Men will never elect a woman leader."

Jolie turned to her. That was brave, and it was true. Was there any society where women were equal to men?

When it was time to break for the day, Tom gave them one instruction. "There is to be no lovemaking tonight. This is an emotional experience, and I want you to feel it fully."

The group groaned.

Tom joined them for dinner. It was quiet but not uncomfortable. "This is an interesting social experiment," Tom said. "I'd like to follow your progress."

"Are you going to write a research paper on us?" Bill said.

Tom tilted his head and smiled. "I'll have to come up with a premise."

Jolie's mind danced over a number of sarcastic ideas but her mother's voice filled her head. *"If you can't say something nice, don't say anything at all."*

Exhausted from the day's events, most everyone turned in early. Jolie and Will went up to their room, leaving Maddy and Bill sitting glumly in the parlor.

"I'm not sharing you with anyone," Will said. "If anyone so much as touches you, they'll be sorry."

"I don't want anyone else. Can we even hug tonight?"

"We can do whatever we want." He pushed her hair away from her face and kissed her, drawing her into his arms. Their clothes fell away, and they made love quietly.

The next morning, the group reconvened. There was not a lot of eye contact. Did everyone break the no-lovemaking rule?

Tom explained they would start with a trust exercise. He split them into pairs, but not with their partners, and gave them blindfolds.

"Take turns blindfolding each other and walk around the neighborhood or house and touch and taste things. It's a way to gain trust," Tom said.

Jolie was paired up with Anthony. Will was with Deidre. Anthony didn't make her uncomfortable like Bill did. She and Will shared the third floor with Anthony and his girlfriend, Dawn.

Anthony put the blindfold around Jolie's eyes and tied it tight. "No peeking."

They walked up the driveway. Jolie held on to his arm lightly. Gravel crunched with each step. He paused by the street. Cars passed on the road, and truck engines hummed.

"Do you trust me?" Anthony said.

"I have to," she said.

They walked across the street into the park.

"This is hard," Jolie said. "I feel helpless."

"Here, give me your hand, I have something for you," he said.

She heard someone scream nearby and then laugh. "Is it slimy?"

"You tell me." He placed something in her open palm.

"A flower?"

"What color?" he asked.

"Pink."

"No. It's white and innocent just like you. Don't let the world change you. Here, let me put it in your hair."

His hands were warm as he brushed her face, tucking the flower behind her ear under the blindfold. After a while they switched, and Anthony wore the blindfold.

"Where are you taking me?" he said. He was grinning and looked sweet with his longish black curls flattened by the blindfold.

Arms linked, she led him up the front steps of the house and into the kitchen. She fed him bites of food. He guessed wrong half the time. She dipped a salty peanut in honey and dropped it on his tongue. It was sensual, feeding him blindfolded. A flush of guilt washed over her.

She untied the blindfold. Walking back to the parlor, they passed the window to the backyard. Deidre sat behind Will massaging his shoulders. Instantly, a jealous pang shot through her.

"She gives the best massages," Anthony said. "That's her specialty."

The encounter session reconvened in a more relaxed mood. The group discussion resumed, and Tom pulled out more issues from individuals. The discussion was dominated by a few. Jolie relaxed a bit when it was clear they would never get around to everybody. Finally, the two-day session was ending. Tom wanted to check in with them in six months. Bill seemed reserved but was smiling at Maddy.

At the end of the day, in a circle holding hands, they ceremoniously reconfirmed their commitment to live as a family without power trips.

How long would that last, a week, two weeks? Someone always had to dominate, and Bill did own the house. She had to find a way to move out and get their own place.

9

Down on Peacock Farm

The next week, Will announced to Jolie he was taking her to visit Ken Kesey, the famous author who lived nearby. This was their first outing alone and her first chance away from the commune to talk to Will about their plans, their future. She wanted to move out of the Big Yellow House.

Will borrowed Michael's car, an older, powder blue station wagon of questionable reliability. They drove the eleven miles toward Pleasant Hill. The countryside was dotted with orchards and Christmas tree farms, each field a different shade of green. The sky was baby blue with high, wispy clouds, and the smell of autumn filled the air. Will talked to her about how Kesey had led a group, called the Merry Pranksters, across the country in his psychedelic bus named Further.

"They caused havoc all over the country," Will explained.

When he paused, Jolie jumped in. "I want to move out of the Big Yellow House. I don't want to live in a commune."

Will glanced at her and then back to the road. "And how do you plan to do that?"

She looked at him. This wasn't a game. "Don't you have a bank account?"

He shook his head.

"But you told me we'd always have everything we needed."

67

"We do. We have a house, food and look, we even have a car to use."

She stared at him, incredulous and then closed her eyes and sat back with the crushing weight of reality. She had assumed he had access to funds once they left the isolated ranch. But he had nothing? This was not the life she'd imagined. This wasn't freedom. She felt trapped.

She opened her eyes as Will turned onto the driveway to Kesey's farm. He parked near a fire-engine-red barn that had been converted into a house. An old school bus, painted in an explosion of psychedelic colors, was parked in the cow pasture. Peacocks roamed everywhere, their neon iridescence blended into the colorful scene.

"Come on. Don't be so glum. You're about to meet a great man."

Their situation didn't seem to faze him. Maybe she should lighten up and look for the positive.

The front door opened, and a woman stood in the doorway.

"We're here to see Ken. I met him a few years ago."

"I'm Faye, Ken's wife," she said. "Ken's out in the greenhouse."

She escorted them to the glass structure next to another barn. Ken was standing on a scaffold halfway to the roof, tinkering with a repair. He had a stocky frame and wore a tie-dyed T-shirt and denim overalls. There was a long table in the middle of the room with chairs scattered around. Ken climbed down.

"I'm Will. I met you a few years ago in Berkeley." Will said.

"Berkeley." Ken's eyes squinted as he tried to remember. "I don't recall much about that time."

Will laughed. "Well, the world remembers you."

Ken reached to shake Will's hand and two coins fell out into his palm.

"How did you do that?" Jolie laughed.

"Magic. It extends beyond the visible."

Ken proceeded to tell them about the cross-country trip to never-never land in the 1939 bus named Further with Neil Cassady at the wheel. Faye had heard the story too many times and went back to the house. Will lit a joint and passed it to Ken. When it came around to

Jolie, she shook her head. She wanted to have a clear head and absorb everything Ken was saying over the din of the squawking peacocks.

Will held up his leather notebook. "I've written something I want to share with you."

"Oh?" Ken's eyes sparkled.

"It's a socialist manifesto."

Ken held up his hand. "Sorry, I don't do politics. I stick with the arts."

"Fair enough," Will said.

In the fading light, Will and Jolie got up and said their good-byes.

"Keep love in your hearts," Ken said.

Will drove down the driveway and onto the road back to Eugene.

"That bus trip sounded amazing. What do you think of his idea of life as performance art?" Jolie asked.

"Shit."

"What?" She shot a glance at him. In that instant, she caught the flashing lights of the cop car behind them. Her heart pounded. She sat paralyzed. Would this be it?

Will pulled over onto the gravel shoulder. The cop got out and walked to the driver's side of the station wagon. Will rolled down the window and the cop barked. "Cut the engine."

Jolie, startled by his harsh command, pressed her body against the seat.

"Driver's license and car registration," the cop said.

Will handed him his license and rummaged through the contents of the glove compartment. He found the registration after what seemed like an eternity and handed it to the cop. Jolie, motionless, looked straight ahead, not wanting to attract the cop's attention.

"This isn't your car?"

"No, it's a friend's," Will said.

The cop bent down and peered in at Jolie. "What's your name?"

Panicked, she willed herself to think, think, think. What would her name be? Why hadn't she come up with a name before this?

"Jolie Cassady," she said. They had been talking about Neal Cassady with Kesey.

"How old are you?" The cop's eyes pierced hers.

"Eighteen."

"What's your birth date?"

She had this part down. She told him the date she had memorized. The cop squinted at Will, back to Jolie, and returned his stare to Will.

"Your right taillight is out. I'll give you a warning this time but get it fixed." The cop handed Will his license and the car registration. He walked back to his car, turned off the blue and red flashing lights, and drove off in a screeching U-turn.

"Close one, Jolie Cassady."

She held her face in her hands as tears streamed down her cheeks.

10

Be Here Now

⤳

Bill got the group a two-day job harvesting filberts at a nearby orchard. Saturday morning, a bell clanged at six from the dining room. Will moaned, rolled over, and went back to sleep. Jolie slipped out of bed and into a pair of denim overalls she'd found in the communal clothes bin. In the kitchen, she put on the kettle and placed a large scoop of dried red rose hips into the chipped floral teapot.

Deidre came in, hair tousled, rubbing her eyes, "You look like a farmer."

"Tell me something. Are filberts the same as hazelnuts?" Jolie said.

"In Oregon they're filberts and most everywhere else they're hazelnuts."

"Hmm." Sometimes the simplest things didn't make sense.

They cut slices of homemade bread and packed sandwiches for the group along with crisp, tart apples and homemade cookies Jolie had baked the night before. Cooking for twenty was a lot easier with electricity and running water. The old boarding house kitchen was perfect for a commune. Two stoves and refrigerators were located across from a cavernous pantry full of bulk food and baskets of nuts and apples. A large work table stood in the center of the room, and a wide swinging door lead to the dining room.

Maddy joined them and made a huge pot of oatmeal. Commune members started to assemble in the dining room. Not seeing Will, Jolie slipped up to their room to rouse him. After breakfast, the work party got into three cars and drove out to the orchard. They wound their way along the Willamette River; its wide banks and shimmering green water melted into darker green fields dotted with yellowing oak trees. Dairy cows and an occasional horse grazed in pastures. In the morning fog, the blue outline of the Coastal Range faded into the horizon.

The three car caravan turned onto a long driveway marked by a large sign: WALT'S ORCHARD—WILLAMETTE VALLEY FAMOUS FILBERTS. They rattled down the dirt road to the barn. A man came out and watched the procession arrive. He must be Walt. He looked like a farmer, red plaid shirt, denim overalls, and black rubber boots. His tan face was creased with lines.

"Well, well. Look at all these workers," the man said to Bill. They stood around him in a group. "I'm Walt. So here's what we're going to do. Pair up, every pair takes one rake and one pole. Start on a row and shake the tree with the pole. I want every one of those nuts off the trees. Rake the nuts into a pile at the center of the row. I'll come along after and collect them with the filbert sweeper. Now make sure you get them all. I'll be checking on you," he said.

They all laughed.

Bill moved toward Jolie. "Let's pair up." Jolie looked at Deidre, panic in her eyes.

"We've already paired," Deidre said.

Relief flooded her. Jolie smiled at her friend. She did not want to pair up with Bill for anything.

They grabbed the tools and started the harvest at the far end of the orchard.

"Thanks for saving me from Bill."

Deidre rolled her eyes. "Just ignore him. He'll get the message. But he's really okay. He taught me to be here now."

"Be here now?"

"The here and now are all that exist because the past and future are simply that...the past and future. He taught me to be true to the moment and experience peace and joy."

Jolie raked more nuts. Feel the now. She stopped raking and looked at Deidre. "What if you don't like the now?"

"Then change it, I guess." She turned to Jolie. "What's wrong with the now?"

Jolie shrugged and returned to raking. Everything. Everything was wrong with the now.

"Well, the future is more important than the past. You can change the future."

They worked side by side, shaking the trees and raking nuts. By noon, they had progressed halfway up the row. Walt rang a bell, signaling lunch time. Jolie looked for Will. He and Michael were only a quarter of the way up their row. They stood and talked more than they worked. Will was out to change the world one recruit at a time.

They finished on Sunday as the sun set. At the end of the day everyone helped Will and Michael finish their row. They'd beaten the rain. Walt paid Bill in bushels of nuts and cash.

That night, they roasted hazelnuts in the oven until the skins cracked. They removed the hulls and ate the warm, rich, sweet-flavored nuts. They talked about other jobs they could do. Jolie went into the kitchen to make tea. She stood by the gleaming counter in the soft light, waiting for the water to boil. The door swung open, and Bill sidled up next to her. She moved away.

"Why are you afraid of me?" he said, stroking his mustache.

"I'm not." She moved to get a mug from the cupboard.

"I've got to have you."

A wave of disgust rose in her. "You have Maddy."

"But I want you. I can teach you things."

With a shaking hand, she poured water over an orange pekoe tea bag. Unable to speak, she shook her head and moved toward the door.

"You'll come around. Just you wait and see."

She quietly slipped past Will and the others in the parlor and went upstairs to their room. Later, Will came in. "What are you reading?" He picked up her book and shook his head. "*The Transcendental Movement?* That's mumbo jumbo." He reached for a frayed book on the dresser. "Read this and then we can discuss it."

She took the well-worn copy of *The Communist Manifesto* and set it down.

"I want to get our own house. We need to get jobs and move."

"Move? We just got here," Will said.

"We have to get out of here. I don't want to live like this."

"What's the matter with this?" He motioned with his hand around the room. "Don't act like a spoiled child."

Spoiled child? She was anything but a spoiled child. Should she tell him about Bill? No, first they needed a plan to leave. In the meantime they needed a place to stay, and telling Will would only cause trouble.

11

Mill Race Cafe

೧ಾ

Jolie's social security card arrived from the Social Security Administration office in San Francisco a few weeks after she had mailed her application. She changed her birth date and her last name on the application. It had been that easy. She held out the card. Her new name, Jolie Cassady, leapt off. She could get a real job now. She wanted to get their own place, a small house on a tree-lined street with a flower garden and a dog. She wanted her independence.

She read the Help Wanted advertisements. Topless server? No way. There was an ad for a waitress. She could wait tables couldn't she?

Will drove her to the Mill Race Café, the local coffee shop, and waited in Michael's car. She walked in and squinted. The fluorescent lights were bright in contrast to the gray outside. Red booths glowed against yellow Formica countertops. A cook in a white hat and apron slapped two steaming plates of pancakes and eggs on a stainless steel counter and rang a bell. A middle-aged waitress walked toward the counter and stabbed her pencil through her beehive hairdo. She took the plates and served them to a couple in a booth.

Jolie approached the cash register and waited. She scanned the menu. They served an all-American breakfast and lunch. The waitress walked over, wiping her glasses on her apron and then sliding them back on. She looked like a cat, the eyeglass corners pointing skyward.

Did designers actually believe that style of glasses looked good on anyone?

Jolie asked about the job, and the waitress took out an application from underneath the counter and handed it to her with a pen. She pointed to a stool at the counter, and Jolie sat down and filled it out. She paused occasionally and looked around. There was laughter from the waitress and customers. The decor was hideous, but it was warm and bright. Jolie walked back to the cash register and waited. The waitress came back and reviewed the application.

"Wait here, honey," she said. She took the application and walked back through the kitchen. Jolie watched as she and the cook talked. The cook scanned the paper and glanced out at her. A moment later he stood in front of Jolie, the application in his hand and the waitress at his side. He looked her up and down.

"You don't look eighteen," he said.

She inhaled quickly.

"But all you kids look so young to me. Can you start tomorrow?"

"Yes."

"Your shift is from six in the morning until two, Monday through Friday. We pay minimum wage, and you keep your tips. Georgina here will get you a uniform." He turned and walked back to the kitchen.

"I'll be right back, honey." Georgina disappeared through the swinging door to the kitchen. When she returned, she handed Jolie a uniform and a starched white half-apron with two pockets. "Hallelujah, I have some help. The other girl didn't show up the other day. Not even a courtesy call."

"I promise I'll call if I can't make it in," Jolie said.

"I know you will, honey. We'll see you tomorrow."

Just like that, she had her first full-time job. She announced it at dinner that night. The dinner turned into a meeting of sorts that Bill led, as usual. Will could use Michael's car to drive Jolie to work in the mornings, but she'd have to take the bus home. After some debate, it was agreed that Jolie would turn her paycheck over to the commune but she could keep her tips. That seemed fair.

She was nervous about her new job, but hopeful. She would save her tips, and she and Will would get their own house. He'd get a job too. But he said he needed to remain underground for a while as he feared there was a warrant for his arrest for leaving with Jolie, a minor. He spent his time perfecting his socialist revolution manifesto that he planned to publish under his assumed name.

Later that night Jolie lay on the bed, reading Emerson. She'd methodically been reading through the library in the parlor. She put the book down and pondered his essay on the over-soul. The universe was connected to nature and united all mankind with each other, a common heart. A common heart with the universe. Did she still have a common heart with her family?

Will came in. "You look so sad."

"I miss home."

"We have a new life now," he said, taking her hand.

"I just want to let them know I'm okay."

"We can't risk it right now."

She didn't speak. She closed her eyes. She would find a way. She would get them a message somehow. She needed to give them peace of mind.

Jolie woke at five the next morning. She showered and dressed in her uniform. The pale blue dress hung on her like a sack. The hem fell below her knees. There was no way she would go out in public like that.

Outside the door Will whispered, "Time to go, or you'll be late."

She looked at her reflection, humiliated. Why hadn't she tried it on yesterday? She'd been so nervous about the new job she hadn't even thought of that. She would alter it that night. Maddy had a sewing machine. She walked out of the bathroom. Will stood waiting to drive her, looking sleepy.

She expected some kind of comment about her uniform but none came. There was a slight arch to his eyebrows, but he stayed silent.

Georgina trained Jolie, and her first task every day was to make cake donuts. When they were partly cooled, she dipped them in the frostings, maple, chocolate, and vanilla. The vanilla frosted doughnuts got a dusting of chocolate sprinkles. At the end of the day Georgina sent her home with any leftover donuts. They disappeared instantly at the Big Yellow House.

It was a busy café, and Jolie was on the go her entire shift. Georgina was happy to return to her hostess role. Within a week Jolie had learned the ropes. The owners, it turned out, were the cook and Georgina. They liked her enthusiasm and made light of her mistakes. As the weeks went on she got to know the regulars. The customers liked her good-natured smile and easy conversation, and to her amazement her tips increased with every shift. Every week she painstakingly put her coins from tips into coin wrappers and put them in her drawer. Her dream was to rent a house of their own. That kept her going.

At the restaurant she was always on edge. She scanned the face of each and every customer coming through the door, always expecting her dad to walk in. It was a haunting feeling. Every time the local police came through the door for donuts and coffee, her heart leapt and a rush of panic spread through her.

Will had become a regular at C.J.'s, a downtown coffee house and the political hub of Eugene. The owner, C.J., and Will had become fast friends. Will hung out on the faded, threadbare couches everyday while Jolie was at work. Radical newspapers were stacked by the door; anti-war protest schedules were tacked to the bulletin board. On weekends, musicians jammed on the small stage.

Jolie joined Will on her days off. The coffee house was a cozy refuge from the constant rain. The air was thick with the aroma of fresh ground coffee and herbal tea. She sat in an overstuffed chair and listened with interest to Will's spirited discussion on political change. A small group always encircled him.

One rainy afternoon at the coffee house, Will and C.J. hatched the local chapter of the Revolutionary Youth Movement, the RYM.

Jolie listened to the plan. "What exactly is it?"

"It's a faction of the Students for a Democratic Society, the SDS, but more radical," C.J. said.

"We're going to recruit and build a fighting force of working class youth, a revolutionary movement. A movement to represent the working class of America. A movement to bring down capitalism," Will said.

"Well, I'm a working class waitress. I'll be your first recruit," she said.

And so the recruitment began. Will became the heart and soul of the local RYM. Will used C.J.'s and other local hangouts to recruit members. He hung out at the university student union during the day. The cafeteria near the bookstore, known as the Fishbowl, was the center for student socializing. Jolie joined him one Saturday as he sat in a booth holding court. Male and female students called out to him or joined him in political discussions. She was amazed at how many people knew him.

"How many have you recruited here?" Jolie said.

"Over a hundred. Recruitment is ripe with these students. Our timing is perfect. We're building a strong collective, both on and off campus."

Three male students slid into the large booth with them.

"How's it going?" asked one.

"Good, it's going good," Will said.

Jolie instantly felt the tension. Their eyes were trained on Will. One tapped his fingers on the table. Another ran his hand through his hair repeatedly.

"Instead of two movements, don't you think we'd all be stronger with just one?" the second student said.

"We need more than students. We need all youth," Will said. "Students alone can't bring down capitalism. The RYM represents the entire working class of America."

They didn't argue. He was right. They needed more than students to bring about change.

Jolie picked up the student newspaper and scanned the houses for rent. She'd been looking at the rental advertisements in the paper at work. At the Big Yellow House she could never fully relax or let her guard down. All the drama, spoken and unspoken, and Bill, still made her uncomfortable. She liked going to work to get away from the house. She turned the page to the Help Wanted section. When she looked up the students were gone.

"There are some jobs in the paper," she said.

"I have a job. This is my job."

"I mean a paying job."

"Don't be bourgeois. We don't need any more money. You have a job. We have a roof over our heads. The movement needs me."

She put down the paper and studied him.

He leaned in close to her. "Everything changed for me when we left together. I made a huge sacrifice to be with you. There is a warrant out for my arrest because you are under age. I can't be visible. I can't give speeches. I have to stay underground for a while. But I can publish my manifesto under my assumed name and I can recruit and that is what I plan to do." He sat back.

She gulped, speechless. She had assumed he would work and make some money. They hadn't specifically talked about it, but wasn't that what a good man would do, contribute his fair share? He had a college degree. A heaviness landed on her heart. She hadn't known what to expect, but she never thought she'd be the one supporting them both. And she wasn't bourgeois. Whatever that really meant. She just wanted certain things, and right now it was freedom from living with a tribe of people.

"I just want to get our own place and make our own life."

His eyes moved from hers to something of interest over her shoulder. He waved and smiled and instantly three students, two females and a male, slid into the booth. Will introduced them as members of the movement. Will talked on about Karl Marx and Mao Tse Tung. The two women hung on every word, enamored with Will's eloquence.

So this was what he did all day while she waitressed. Recruiting a revolutionary movement and talking to beautiful young women. She loved him so much and didn't want to feel resentful. Reading *The Wisdom of Buddha*, she had learned right mindfulness. To acknowledge the feeling and free yourself from it. She slowly breathed in and out in a wakeful meditation, but disappointment weighed heavy on her chest. She wouldn't give up on getting their own place.

12

The Letter

Jolie took a shortcut to the bus after work one afternoon. On a quiet, tree-lined street a For Rent sign in the window of a blue cottage with white trim, caught her eye. The monthly rent amount was posted and her weekly paycheck alone would cover the rent. The front door stood wide open despite the drizzle. Country music floated out to the sidewalk. She walked up the stone path and saw a man in coveralls singing along to the radio as he painted the living room. She knocked on the open door.

He turned. "What can I do you for?" he said.

"I'm interested in the house. Are you the owner?"

"Yep, and it's times like this I wish I weren't," he said. "Are you a student?"

She hesitated. "No. I'm a waitress."

"Good. That's good. Students just tear this place up, and all I do is fix it back up. I'm in a constant state of déjà vu. Do you know about déjà vu?"

She smiled. "Yes, I do."

"Do you have wild parties?"

Jolie laughed. "No, no wild parties."

"Then it's yours. It'll be move-in ready in two days."

He reached out his paint-splattered hand. She shook it. It was callused and warm. She smiled at him. She had just rented a house. They would be free of the commune.

Elated, she walked to the bus stop. Will was warming to the idea of moving after his last political disagreement with Bill and Peter. The tension between them made her uncomfortable.

That night in their room, she worked up the nerve to tell Will. Her hands gripped both knees. "I rented us a house today," she blurted out.

"You what?"

"I rented a house today. It's the cutest cottage. Wait till you see it."

"What's wrong with this house?"

"I want our own house, free from all these people and the drama."

"So you don't want to be part of this utopian social experiment? This isn't free enough for you?"

She glanced at him. Was he being sarcastic or was he serious? She shook her head. There was a long silence. "I can walk to work. You won't have to get up at five in the morning to drive me."

"Always thinking of others. I guess I'm fine with it. There are too many big egos around here, plus I need a place to hold meetings."

Her stomach flipped. Meetings? All she wanted was a quiet house.

At dinner the next night, Will broke the news of their move.

Michael groaned. "No more donuts?"

"Tom will want to interview you on why you're leaving," Bill said. "He's been tracking what works and what doesn't."

Jolie stiffened. Interview them? "It's none of his business why we're leaving," Jolie said.

Everyone looked at her in surprise.

"Right on," Deidre said.

∽◯

All winter rain fell in a steady drizzle. Jolie trudged to work in the dark, rain pattering on her umbrella. She reversed her route in the afternoon, walking home through the gray mist. Often she stopped at the library. She read book after book, curled up in the cozy cottage waiting for Will to come home. He was usually at C.J.'s Coffeehouse or the student union until early evening.

One day he surprised her with a puppy. He brought home a cream-colored fluffy ball of fur with big brown eyes. When he walked, he swaggered from his wagging tail. She named him Bilbo Baggins, a character in *The Hobbit*. She couldn't wait to get home from work and take him for walks in Hendricks Park. On weekends, Will joined them.

Deidre stopped by one afternoon. Jolie made rose hip tea and served it to her on the couch.

"Here is your dose of vitamin C."

Deidre took the cup. "Your house is so warm and inviting." She stroked Bilbo who lay at their feet.

Bright blue madras print curtains hung in the windows; an antique bookcase was filled with used books she'd bought one by one. A small antique Persian rug sat under the window for meditation. That splurge had cost her two weeks of tips.

Jolie nodded. "It is peaceful."

"I like your Buddha. Where did you get it? It looks ancient!"

Jolie picked up the small bronze Buddha. He sat cross legged with the index finger and thumb of both hands touching at their tips. The circle they formed represented the wheel of dharma or fate. "I found him at the antique store where I bought the rug. I think he's quite old." She set the Buddha back on the bookcase.

"Where's Will?"

"He's out drumming up recruits for the movement. How's everything at the House?"

"Pretty much the same. We have a new couple in your old room. They know Will. They're into the socialist movement big time and are trying to get all of us involved. It's ruffling Bill's feathers."

"How's Michael?" Jolie asked.

"We're closer since the encounter session. He's coming to meet my family in Portland this weekend. Wish me luck...they don't understand the whole commune thing." Deidre got up. "I've got to get back. We're in charge of dinner."

After she left, Jolie sat cross-legged on the rug to meditate. Instead of the usual peace it gave her, she was overcome with homesickness. She did feel sick. So this was why they called it a sickness. Tears flowed from her closed eyes. She wished she could tell Deidre the truth, tell her everything. Bilbo rested his head in her lap, and she stroked his fluffy fur. Meditation would be futile today.

She got up, made another cup of tea, and sat at the kitchen table. From her leather wallet, she pulled out the small folded note her mother had written on the day she'd left home. The yellow smiley face grinned back at her from the Have a Nice Day stationary. Her lower lip trembled as she smiled back. If she couldn't phone them, she'd write to them. She reached for the notepad and pen. Words began to flow on the page. She addressed an envelope, slipped the letter inside, and put it in her leather-fringed purse. She'd buy a stamp tomorrow after work.

13

Castles Made of Sand

Jolie arrived home from work one day in early March. Bilbo wagged his tail and nuzzled her as she shut the door. A pile of their belongings was stacked in the middle of the small living room.

"Will?" He was never there when she got home from work.

He emerged from the bedroom.

"What are you doing?" Jolie said, puzzled by the pile.

"It's time to leave town," he said.

"What do you mean?"

"C.J. caught up with me. There was a guy with intense blue eyes at the coffeehouse who might have been a private detective. He had our photos and was asking around if anyone knew us or had seen us."

Her stomach flipped. A private detective?

"Michael also found me at the student union. The same guy had been to the commune asking about us."

A detective went to the commune? She panicked. "What did they tell him?"

"C.J. said he didn't recognize us, but the Big Yellow House members told him that we had stayed with them briefly but didn't know where we were now."

She stood frozen, her heart thudded. Her dad must have hired a private detective.

"Pack some of your things. We're leaving tonight."

"Tonight? Where will we go?"

"We're on a Greyhound bus to New York at six forty."

New York? She'd never been to the East Coast. "Why New York?"

"They'll never find us there."

"What about the puppy and our things in the house?"

"Michael said he'd come and get Bilbo later tonight. I gave him my guitar and told him they could take anything we leave. It's good karma for the help they gave us when we first got here." Will hugged her close. "Don't worry, we'll start over again."

She stepped back and looked around the house.

"The bus tickets just about wiped out our money. It takes three days to get to New York. Pack some food," Will instructed her.

She didn't move. Her thoughts swirled.

"Come on, Little Wing. Have you lost your sense of adventure?"

"Do you know anyone in New York?"

"No, but there's a big Revolutionary Youth Movement there. We'll figure it out, don't worry."

They had to go. If they were caught, Will would go to jail for corruption of a minor. She resigned herself to leave. She'd never imagined going to New York to live.

Tears fell as she packed. She had to leave her sweet puppy, her warm, furry little love. At least Michael and Deidre would take him. He'd be happy with all the attention at the commune. From the bookcase she selected her three favorite books: a volume of short stories by Hemingway, *The Prophet* by Kahil Gibran, and the small, worn copy of *The Wisdom of Buddha* that Jasmine had given her. She packed the small Buddha statue, her best clothes, and rolled up the small Persian rug, lacing it to the bottom of the pack.

Will handed her a bus ticket. "We're going to the bus station separately. Act like we don't know each other. You go first and get on the bus. I'll get on after you."

Jolie took the ticket and looked into Will's eyes for a long moment. He broke her gaze and looked down at Bilbo tangled at their feet. Was this really happening? A detective was looking for them? She looked around their house again. Everything seemed surreal. Will wouldn't lie to her, would he? Through tears she bent down and hugged Bilbo.

"Jolie, you have to get going."

She rose and hoisted her pack on her shoulder, grabbed her purse, and started off on the ten minute walk to the bus station. Her mind raced as she walked through the night. What if Will didn't get on the bus? No, he wouldn't put her on a bus to New York City all alone. What if he missed it? Then what? He had all of their money, except for her tips from today.

At the bus station, she looked around nervously. She didn't see their pictures posted anywhere or any men that looked like detectives. The terminal wasn't crowded, but the few people that sat and waited were not the type she wanted to be around. Scruffy drifters, all of them. She found an empty bench and waited, wary of everyone.

A loudspeaker boomed: "Portland, Denver, New York City; line number eight, now boarding."

She hurried outside and was the first in line to board. The bus driver studied her ticket and looked at her. "So...you're going to New York City?"

Jolie nodded, unable to speak, her throat shut down in fear.

"I'm the driver until Portland. You need to transfer buses there. There's a two-hour layover then get on the bus headed for Denver," he said.

She forced a smile and moved toward the back of the bus. Thrusting her pack into the overhead rack, she slid into a window seat. Outside, passengers stood in line to board. She watched and waited for Will. Her heart began to pound.

14

Ticket to Ride

~~

At the last minute, Will stepped onto the bus, tall and handsome. A wave of relief flooded her. How could he look so relaxed? He sauntered halfway down the aisle and made eye contact but did not smile as he slid into an empty seat a few rows in front of her. She stared out the window, her heart still pounding as the bus lurched out of the station.

The bus driver drove through town in the light rain and turned onto the highway. In the dimly lit seat, she replayed the events of the day. A detective had been close on their tail. How did he know to look for them in Eugene? She had never mailed the letter she had written to her parents. It had been in her purse to mail, but when she bought a stamp at the post office, it was no longer there. Had she dropped it, and someone mailed it? Had Will destroyed it? She would never ask Will about it. He would be furious.

Jolie stared into the rain-streaked darkness. She'd hurt her parents, but they still wanted her back. She lied to the people who had befriended them. What did the Big Yellow House friends think about them now? She hadn't called the Mill Race Café to tell them she wouldn't be back. Tomorrow, Georgina would be worried. She hated lying to everyone. She leaned her head against the window, exhaled, and closed her eyes. A vision of New York swarming with millions of people sprang to life in her mind. What would they do there? How would she cope with all of those people?

The bus pulled into the Salem depot. The interior lights brightened. A few people got off, and three army soldiers in uniform got on with their duffle bags and found seats ahead of Will. When the bus was back on the highway headed to Portland, Will walked back and sat down in the vacant seat next to her.

"We're going to New York!" He smiled and took her hand.

She sat silent. How could he be so upbeat?

"There's an even bigger RYM operation there. We'll meet new people from the movement."

"Do I have to get a job there?"

"Yeah, we'll have to start over."

She closed her eyes and pushed the thoughts out of her head.

In Portland, they waited separately for the bus to Denver. Jolie had to move seats twice to avoid conversations with men asking her where she was going. If Portland was that creepy, what was it going to be like in New York?

Finally it was time to board the bus. Jolie handed the driver her ticket.

"New York City! You transfer buses in Denver. That's in a day and a half."

"Thanks."

"You take care of yourself there, missy."

Jolie walked toward the back. Will was already on board. At least she wouldn't wonder if he was getting on. Why did she think that? He was caring and protective. She was just jumpy. It had been a long day. She slid into a window seat a few rows in front of him and put her purse on the seat next to her. She did not want the company of a stranger. She leaned back and shivered. She hugged herself to warm up. That morning had been a normal work day, and tonight they were on a bus to New York City. Will's comment made her anxious: "They'll never find us there." Was that because of all the people?

Once the bus was on the road, Will came and sat next to her. He reached for her hand, and they settled in for the long ride through the night, east to Idaho, Utah, and beyond. Exhausted, she leaned against his shoulder and fell quickly asleep and into a dream. A large smiling Buddha loomed on the edge of a clear blue lake. A candle burned on the altar below the Buddha and pink lotus flowers poked their delicate heads up through lotus pads. Temple bells chimed softly and a gentle breeze sang in the tree tops. Her father stood on the far shore, arms outstretched chanting: "Come home. Come home, Jolie, please come home."

She woke in the dark. Will was asleep. The bus hummed along a lonely rural highway somewhere in eastern Oregon. The dream had been so vivid; she had seen her father so clearly. She reached for the moonstone around her neck.

They arrived in Denver in the early morning and waited separately for the bus to New York. She sat in a corner reading *The Wisdom of Buddha*, occasionally glancing at Will.

After an hour they boarded the bus for the final leg of the trip. Staring out the window, she tried to envision herself in New York, but no images comforted her. She preferred nature over concrete. Where would they work? Where would they live? She forced herself to think positive—right mindfulness, right thinking, that's what the Buddha taught. There had to be something good in New York. Why else would millions of people live there?

They drove through the middle of America. The flat landscape stretched wide with wheat fields, unidentifiable crops, and cows, lots of cows. Somewhere in Kansas, a siren blared and lights flashed behind them. The driver slowed the bus and pulled over. Two Kansas Highway Patrol officers parked their blinking patrol car behind the bus and walked around to the door.

The officers boarded the bus with their guns drawn. Will drummed his fingers on his knees. After a brief conversation with the driver, one officer strode down the aisle with a paper in his hand, scanning each passenger, his sunglasses hiding his gaze. Jolie tried to look nonchalant, but her chest was tight with fear. Will put a hand on her wildly jiggling leg to stop it. Out the window a herd of cows stared at them with gentle brown eyes from behind a barbed wire fence.

After looking at each passenger, he made his way to the front of the bus. He handed the paper to the driver, and the two officers got back into their patrol car. The driver announced they were looking for an escaped convict last seen in the Denver bus station. The passengers laughed. Jolie inhaled and exhaled deeply, releasing a torrent of fear. This was not how she wanted to live. She half-smiled at Will. Their freedom was so fragile.

15

2000 Light Years from Home

Before dawn on Saturday, three and a half days after leaving Eugene, the bus rumbled into the New York terminal. Will and Jolie stowed their packs in day lockers at the bus station and started off to explore the city. In the early morning darkness, New York buzzed with people. Long-haired youths begged for spare change. Homeless people slept in doorways despite the cold. The streets were littered with paper and empty bottles. Newspapers blew past. They stopped in a small café for warmth and ordered tea to kill time until it was light.

"I need a shower and a bed," Jolie said.

"First we'll find a room for rent by the week and get a shower, then tomorrow we'll look for work."

"On Sunday?" He did say 'we'll look for work'. That was promising.

"We're almost out of money," Will said.

"It's so big and noisy and grimy."

"Wait till you see it in the daylight. There's music in the parks. The streets are teaming with life. You can get anything in the world in New York. You'll see. You'll love it."

She didn't want anything in the world. She just wanted…what did she want? She didn't know anymore except for a shower and sleep. Everyone in the café looked sleazy. She hunched over her cup. So this was New York.

They hung out in the café as long as possible, ignoring the waitress's glare. Once it turned light, they took the subway to Greenwich Village. They went from hotel to hotel, but there were no rooms they could afford. Frustrated after the tenth hotel, they headed to the East Village, hoping for better luck. On the way, Will paused at a newsstand. Jolie leaned in next to him and read the headline: GREENWICH VILLAGE TOWNHOUSE RAZED BY BLAST AND FIRE; MAN'S BODY FOUND.

The explosion is thought to be from the premature detonation of a bomb as it was being assembled by members of the Weatherman, a radical leftist group. A search for other victims is underway. The four story townhouse at 18 West 11th St. was reduced to flames and rubble.

"Jesus," Will said. "They're making bombs."

"I thought they were non-violent."

"They're changing. They're bringing the war home."

"Do you want to go see the townhouse?" Jolie asked.

"No. We don't want to be anywhere near it. The FBI will be crawling all over the place. This rules out any help from RYM for a place to stay."

Jolie stood transfixed by the article. "Why?"

"They'll all be laying low. Come on, let's try the East Village and find a place to crash."

Will took her hand. Exhausted from little sleep over the past three days, they trudged along the endless city blocks. The sun was up, but it was bitter cold. Jolie looked up at the buildings towering over them. Car horns blared. Did the drivers really think that blasting their horns would unclog the jammed streets? A whirlwind tornado of trash swirled nearby. Lines of laundry strung out of apartment windows whipped in the early morning wind. On a street corner, a black man in a rumpled suit soulfully played a Miles Davis song on his tarnished trumpet, his hat on the ground before him.

They stopped at every hotel and inquired about a room. The hotel buildings were run-down. In seedy, dimly-lit lobbies, shady men sat on frayed couches with women whose faces gleamed with make-up. Most of the hotels' costs were out of their reach. The rooms they could afford were either full or rented by the hour.

Will led her into a packed deli to get out of the cold. They stood inside the door and waited for a booth. Finally someone left, and they slipped into the seat, groaning at the simple pleasure of being warm and sitting. Conversations in harsh New York accents reverberated off the greasy walls. The smell of food cooking made her mouth water. Will ordered the cheapest thing on the menu, grilled cheese sandwiches. They ate slowly, killing time, trying to figure out what to do next. Jolie sank low into the booth. Sleep was all she wanted. Will picked up a newspaper from a stack by the door and read. She put her head back and nodded off, only to jerk awake when the waitress slapped the plastic tray with their bill on the table. Disoriented, Jolie looked up. The waitress towered over her with a scowl.

"Let's go to Tompkins Square Park and check out the scene," Will said.

"Aren't you tired?"

He shrugged. "We have to find a place to stay."

Will paid the bill, and they were back on the street, headed to Tompkins Square Park. They passed through the Bowery. The streets were lined with homeless men and women begging. Drunks and addicts were passed out on the cold ground, their faces pasted to the sidewalk. How could anyone survive even one night outside? She'd read about the Bowery but never imagined she'd be walking through New York's skid row, almost homeless herself. She shivered in the cold sun. Jolie stole a glance at Will. Even if they had money New York would be a rough place. What was he thinking?

They reached the park and walked to the center. Jolie found an empty bench and collapsed onto it. Hippies milled about. A guitar and mandolin duo played an instrumental piece. The tall trees were bare, but small green buds bulged toward the coming spring.

A group of Hare Krishna's in bright saffron robes gathered around an elm tree in the center of the park. They danced, chanted, and clanged small cymbals. Their mantra was soothing. *Hare Krishna,*

Hare Krishna, Krishna Krishna, Hare Hare, Hare Rama, Hare Rama, Rama Rama, Hare Hare.

A ragged group of war protesters filed past with signs: End the War in Vietnam NOW; Peace Now; Get the Hell out of Vietnam. They chanted: "Hell no, we won't go!"

"Let's join them and see if anyone knows where we can crash," Will said.

Will and Jolie wove their way into the crowd and fell into the march next to a lanky long-haired man in his twenties.

"We just got here today from Eugene," Will said.

"Where's that?"

"Oregon. There's a large anti-war movement there," Will said.

"A lot of good any of this is doing us," the protester said.

"Can any of your group help us out? We need a place to stay tonight," Will said.

He shot Will a look. "You're in New York, man, we're all crashing with people who are crashing. We're ten to a room. Sorry, can't help you. There are some shelters in the Bowery, though."

A homeless shelter in the Bowery? No way. She was not going near the Bowery again, for anything.

They moved away from the marching protesters and sat down on a nearby bench. They watched the revolving scene unfold before them, acutely aware of their predicament and alone in their thoughts. Jolie rubbed the moonstone in the soft leather pouch against her chest. She wanted to lie down right there and sleep in the cold sun for an hour, for just an hour. But that's what homeless people and bums did. They couldn't let their guard down. She sat straighter and watched the stream of humanity go by.

Restless, Will rose. "Let's keep moving."

They walked the streets of the East Village hunting for a hotel. Gradually, it became dark. They still had no place to stay. The brownstone houses, lit from inside, looked warm and inviting. The streets were still crowded at night. Up ahead a crowd gathered under a marquee that lit up the sidewalk: "Bill Graham's Fillmore East: Tonight Neil Young and Crazy Horse, The Steve Miller Band, Miles Davis".

Jolie was struck by their attire. The crowd was dressed in silk frock coats and top hats, fringed leather jackets, leather pants, fishnet stockings and mini-skirts, candy striped pants, and paisley print shirts. Jolie watched, mesmerized. If only they could get in. What an incredible line up. The Fillmore was the Church of Rock and Roll.

Will and Jolie milled around with the crowd. Will asked a few people about finding a place to crash for the night. All were sympathetic but offered no help. The crowd thinned as the concert goers entered the Fillmore. The small group that lingered outside looked to be in their same situation. No place to go. Some had backpacks and bed rolls. They wouldn't be of any help. Reluctantly, they walked on. Jolie's mood sunk. If she could just get warm, she wouldn't feel so miserable.

"Now what?" Jolie said.

"Back to the bus station. Our locker rentals expire soon."

And then what? He didn't have a plan. She followed him down a subway entrance. Underground, musicians played for coins among the trash.

"You should have brought your guitar. We could have made a lot of money," Jolie said. "Enough to stay in a nice hotel I bet."

He stopped and took her by the shoulders. "Do I look like a beggar?"

Tears welled in her eyes and she shook her head.

They trudged into the bus station and retrieved their packs. They stood and waited for a bench to become vacant. Finally when a couple got up to board their bus, Will claimed the bench and they sat down. Jolie groaned, tired and disheartened. The station was noisy with departure announcements. The automatic door brought a cold gust each time it opened. Police officers patrolled the area. The station was jammed with travelers and homeless people. It stank of urine. No one would notice them there.

All that could go wrong was happening. She put her hand on the moonstone. Didn't Mark say the moonstone would protect travelers from danger? How were they doing at the ranch? It would be spring there soon. She wished they were back amid the tall firs and stately pines, the intoxicating smell of the forest and the welcoming camaraderie of the group. Right now the ranch seemed like nirvana. She had sunk low to want to go back to that isolated place.

A police duo roused a sleeping bum and escorted him to the door. She thought of her family. They had come so close to finding her. Would that have been so bad? She pulled her knees up to her chest and held them tight. She could call them collect. Will could stay on the run, but she could go home. This was not the life she envisioned. No, she was just tired. She and Will loved each other.

She felt Will's eyes on her but didn't want to meet them. Tears were coming, but she couldn't cry, not here. He reached for her hand. She looked at the sordid scene all around them. She couldn't deny the reality of their situation any longer. They had little money left, no place to stay, and no plan. Where were all of Will's friends now? Where was his master plan for their life?

"Don't look so down, Little Wing," Will said.

Jolie didn't respond but continued to stare at the passing scene, wary of everyone.

"New York isn't what I expected. Let's try another city while we still have enough money to leave," Will said.

"What would be different?" She stared straight ahead, no emotion in her voice.

"The bomb explosion blew any chance of connecting with the RYM. Nobody's talking to strangers now."

"Where would we go?"

"We could go up to Boston. It's not too far. There are lots of colleges and the RYM has a collective there."

She'd read about Boston. Anywhere but here sounded good. "Okay."

"You stay here with the packs, and I'll check the schedule and buy tickets."

"No, I'm coming with you." She was not going to sit there alone in the middle of all the shady characters.

"No, you stay. If we leave the bench, we'll lose our spot and end up sitting on the floor all night," Will said. "I won't be long."

He was right, there were no empty seats in the crowded station. The floor was filthy. Jolie nodded, adjusting the packs on the bench, leaving no room for anyone to sit down. She needed to be strong and remain centered and balanced. Closing her eyes, she silently chanted her mantra, reaching for inner strength. Om. Om. Om.

Sensing a presence, she opened her eyes. Before her stood two policemen. She blinked. A wave of panic rushed over her. The saliva left her mouth. Was this it?

"Do you have a bus ticket?" the taller one asked.

She found her voice. "We're buying them now."

"You can't stay in the station unless you have a ticket," the stocky one said, eyeing the two packs.

"How old are you?" asked the tall one.

"Eighteen," Jolie said.

"Birth date?"

She responded.

"Be careful in here," the stocky one said. They walked off and began questioning a man sitting cross-legged on the floor. The man got up and walked out into the night; a blast of cold air replaced him.

A man in jeans, white T-shirt, black leather jacket, and slicked-back hair approached her. "Horse?"

"Horse?" she asked.

"Dope. Do you want to buy some dope?"

"No, thanks."

He walked off and approached two long-haired guys sitting on the ground. They both got up and followed the man into the men's room. This was going to be a long night. Where was Will?

Two young women walked by with glazed eyes. They wore tight-knit mini dresses and high heels. Their hair was teased into rats' nests, their faces were painted with a pound of makeup, and their lips glistened bright red. A whiff of cheap perfume trailed behind them when they passed. An older, balding man approached them. After a short discussion, he went off with the girl in the black and red dress. Her friend continued to walk through the station. Did they have tickets? She continued to watch the girl.

Where was Will? He had been gone over thirty minutes. How long did it take to buy tickets? What if he had gotten arrested? How would she know? He had all the money. They should split it up in case they were separated. She needed to center herself and not panic. She couldn't meditate in the terminal. She was afraid to close her eyes now. The packs might be stolen. She hugged her knees and cautiously watched everyone around her.

16

Back to Zero

Will appeared around the corner. He waved the tickets in greeting and smiled his irresistible smile. The girl in the tight-knit dress approached him.

He shook his head and continued toward Jolie. She moved a pack from the bench to make room for him. He handed her a Snickers bar. A fleeting smile crossed her face, too tired for much more.

"You were gone an eternity. What did that girl ask you?"

"If I wanted to have a good time," he said.

"Like a party?"

Will looked at her. "You're so naive. That's why I love you. She's a hooker. A hooker on heroin."

"How can you tell she's on heroin?"

"They mostly all are."

"She's a hooker on horse," Jolie said. "Some guy tried to sell me some horse, that's heroin right?"

Will put his arm around her. "We'll be out of here soon. We're on a four thirty a.m. bus to Boston. I'm feeling good about Boston."

They sat together on the bench all night and watched New York's underside. It had been a long four days. Will kept his arm around her. She relaxed a little now that they had a plan. And yet what if it was the same in Boston, and they couldn't find a place to stay?

101

At four twenty in the morning, they boarded the bus to Boston and sat next to each other. There was no need to be paranoid about the private detective. They were invisible in New York. The bus was only half full as it rolled out of the terminal through upper Manhattan. They would be in Boston at ten thirty that morning.

She stared intently out the window, taking in the sights. The route took them through Harlem. They drove past a burned out stone church that sat charred in the darkness. How could anyone burn such a beautiful building? Windows were boarded up on storefronts, plaster peeled off of tenement buildings, abandoned buildings stood next to fire-blackened shells. Men lay on the sidewalks, passed out. Others sat on steps and watched the bus roll by.

She'd never seen such a grim sight. Can this be America? New York? How can these people live here? It was desolate, decrepit, and rundown. They passed a vacant lot with flames leaping out of a pile of trash. Were people camping in the city? What happened to civilized society? What would happen if the bus broke down there? She unconsciously gripped Will's hand, and he rubbed it to relax her grip.

"Doesn't anyone care?" Jolie asked. "This isn't right."

"This is what we're organizing and fighting against," Will said. "Poverty and the lack of equality. If our government spent the same amount here that they spend on one week in Vietnam, these folks would have a chance."

The bus left Harlem behind but she'd never forget the scene. A shiver passed through her.

Soon they were out of the city, heading toward Connecticut. They leaned into one another and dozed, the bus engine vibrated a soothing hum.

They awoke as the bus pulled into Worcester, Massachusetts, the Heart of the Commonwealth, a sign proclaimed. The sun shone on old brick buildings. An hour later they disembarked in Boston.

Jolie asked a woman at an information counter about inexpensive weekly hotels. The woman opened a map and circled an area on Berkeley Street about twenty blocks away.

"It's in the South End. It's an okay area. There's no hanky-panky going on," she said, looking into Jolie's eyes. Jolie strained to understand the strong accent. The woman then circled a bus stop on the map two blocks away and wrote the bus number. "This bus will take you near there."

On Berkeley Street, under a canopy of trees, they walked past rows of old brick townhouses with colonial shutters. A few of the townhouses had been converted into resident hotels. In the first hotel that had a weekly rental sign in the window, they rang the bell at the reception desk. A wizened man with curly white hair shuffled out. He eyed them and their packs.

"How much for a room per week?" Will asked.

"We have no vacancy," the old man said.

"But there's a sign in the window," Will said.

"No vacancy."

They walked back onto the street.

"That's bullshit," Will said.

"We do look a little scruffy." She stroked his five-day beard. They looked like gypsies with Will's hand-woven headband, her small rolled-up Persian rug tied to her pack, and her leather fringe purse.

Three townhouses down, they walked into another hotel that advertised weekly rooms. A plump woman sat at the desk, reading. The lobby was dimly lit, and a stale odor permeated the air. Will inquired about a room. The woman indicated they had a room on the third floor with a shared bathroom. It was cheap.

"We'll take it." Will paid for a week and the woman handed him the key and pointed toward the wooden staircase.

On the third floor, a threadbare oriental carpet runner led them down the hall to the room. The stale odor was stronger. What was it? Will unlocked the door and she followed him in. Sunlight streamed in the tall windows of a large corner room. The paint on the windowsills was chipped. A small wood table and two chairs were set against a wall. On top of an old wooden dresser on the opposite wall was a stack of threadbare towels. In the corner, a hot plate, a can opener, and a small pot sat on the floor. A hot plate? That was part of the smell.

People cooked in their rooms. There was an overhead light bulb with no shade. Jolie pulled back the moss-green chintz bedspread. The bed sagged in the middle.

It was shabby and rundown, but there was a bed with clean sheets, the door locked, and a bathroom was right down the hall.

"This is heaven, pure heaven," she said, smiling.

"That's the first smile I've seen in a week."

Showered and changed, they flopped on the bed and fell into a deep sleep. Two hours later, a siren woke Jolie. She looked around the unfamiliar room. Will sat in the chair, looking out the window. The map the woman in the bus station had given them was spread on the table next to their money. Groggy, Jolie joined him at the table.

"Ready to explore?" Will asked.

"I'm famished. How much money do we have left?"

"We have enough for another week's rent or food, but not both," Will said.

Outside, Will led her through the Back Bay along quiet, tree-lined streets. They paused while she buttoned up her coat. The sun was out but it was cold and her cheeks were numb. She felt refreshed and almost herself again.

A sign hung outside a diner on a sandwich board: Cheap Breakfasts Served All Day.

"Let's splurge." He took her hand and led her inside. They slid into a booth. The mood here was different than New York. Not as rushed. They ordered tea and pancakes and eggs. Jolie held her warm tea mug to her cheeks. When their order came, they smothered the pancakes in butter and warm maple syrup and devoured the feast.

Will picked out the *Boston Globe* Help Wanted section from a stack of newspapers in a nearby vacant booth. "We'll read this tonight and plan out where to apply for jobs tomorrow," he said.

Jolie nodded, but an uneasy feeling crept over her as she glanced at the thick help wanted section. The big city was intimidating.

Outside they turned onto Boylston Street. In the distance, four pyramids and a huge tower trimmed in red sandstone stood out in the skyline: a glorious church. They stopped in front of another building. Jolie stared up at it.

"This is the library? It's beautiful. I can't wait to come back here," she said.

People walked by and didn't seem to notice the grand building. "Everything is so old and dignified. I'm going to learn all about the history and architecture," Jolie said.

"Focus on the future, not the past."

They walked up Newbury Street past vintage row houses, boutiques, and restaurants.

"Look for Help Wanted signs," Will said.

They passed men in long wool coats and women in skirts, leather boots and cashmere scarves. She eyed a handbag in a shop window. The price tag was equivalent to a small fortune. She didn't have anything to wear to an interview, much less to work in these shops. Her vintage clothing would be considered too bohemian.

They turned onto Commonwealth Avenue and walked along the Mall, a wide street lined with grass. Benches and monuments decorated the promenade. At the end of the avenue they stood and gazed at the Public Garden before heading to the Charles River. After three blocks it lay before them. Mystic blue, with rowing teams racing along the banks. They walked along the riverfront and sat on a bench.

"I love Boston," Jolie said. "It's much more laid back than New York."

"Don't let your guard down. All cities have crime," he said, and took her hand and kissed it. They sat on the bench, gazing across the river at Cambridge.

To warm up, they walked back along Arlington Street and wandered into the Public Garden. A path lined with elms, horse chestnuts, redwoods, and ginkgo trees meandered alongside a lagoon. Weeping willows spilled over the banks. Couples strolled hand in hand and children fed the ducks. Jolie was drawn to a large bronze statue of George Washington. She gazed up at him astride his lifelike, prancing horse and stroked the horse's leg.

They walked across Charles Street from the Public Garden into the Boston Common. People were everywhere. Some bicycling, others picnicked on benches; it didn't seem to matter that there was a chill in the air. Everyone seemed happy for the sun and to be outside after the long winter. Jolie and Will walked through the Common, pausing at the monuments and fountains, taking in the history.

"They used to hang people in gallows here," Jolie said, reading a plaque.

Ahead, a small group of about fifty or so anti-war protesters had congregated around a stone-columned bandstand. The protesters, finished with their march, hung around in small groups talking. Two policemen on horseback watched nearby.

Will and Jolie approached the group. Will sought out a clean-shaven, short-haired blond man who appeared to be the leader. He was finalizing instructions for the next protest to be held at the Cambridge Common the following Saturday. When he finished, Will introduced himself. The man's name was Adam. Will talked to him at length about the West Coast anti-war activities and the Revolutionary Youth Movement. Jolie stood next to Will, silently observing.

"I've written a revolutionary socialist manifesto that I plan to publish," Will said.

"Like The Communist Manifesto?" Adam asked, his face lit up at the prospect.

"Along those lines. But I've made it relevant for our government, our corporations and our social inequities."

"Bring it by our meeting place. We hang out at Liberation Books in Cambridge. I'll introduce you to the owner. We need new ideas to organize," Adam said.

Jolie glanced at Will. Their first day in Boston, and he'd already met up with a movement. That was good, if it didn't distract him from looking for work.

The protesters disbanded as the light faded. Jolie and Will walked back toward the hotel. They stopped at a neighborhood Italian grocery and bought food for dinner. In their room, they ate cheese and olives and Italian bread on the small table. It was basic, but they were off the street.

Jolie took the crumpled Help Wanted section Will had been carrying around all day and started reading down the column out loud. "Bus Driver, Cook, Dishwasher, Engineer, Machinist, Medical Assistant, Nurse, Preschool Teacher, Sales, Shipping Lead, Waitress." She looked up. "I'd like to be a preschool teacher."

"Focus on restaurants. People give you good tips, they like you. Plus you get food."

She went back to the Waitress section. "Here are some waitress jobs in Harvard Square. Is that by Harvard University?"

"They're both in Cambridge."

"This one says 'Apply in person Monday–Thursday. Ask for Manager. No phone calls.' There are a bunch in Harvard Square."

"Let's go there in the morning. I want to check out Liberation Books. Cambridge seems to be the heart of the movement."

She glanced at him. Shouldn't work be his priority?

Exhausted by the past five days, they fell into bed. The radiator sputtered intermittently. The bed creaked, and the mattress sagged, but it was safe and warm and one hundred times better than last night's bus bench in New York. Will held her tight. They talked of all the places they would explore and the things they would do.

"I want to live in a historic brick house in one of the quaint neighborhoods," Jolie said.

"Someday. But first you have to score a job."

"What about you?"

"I'll be looking. I don't fit into an eight-to-five job. I need my own gig."

Her heart sank. "But you're the one with the college degree."

He laughed. "All the more reason to be my own boss. It'll be easier for you. You'll find a job in a day or two. You have to. Our money is almost gone."

Her body froze. What if she didn't? What if their money ran out and they were back on the street? "Can your parents lend you some money?" Her voice small in the dark.

"I disowned my father years ago. He was a control freak."

"Like what did he try and control?"

"Me. My mind, my ideals, my politics. Nothing I did was good enough. End of story."

"Don't you miss them?"

"I said end of story. Don't ever mention them again."

Jolie shrank away from his brusque words and lay with her eyes open in the dark.

17

Brother, Can You Spare a Dime?

Monday morning, Jolie stood by the dinged-up dresser where she had unpacked their clothes. A queasy feeling swirled in her stomach. What would she wear to look for a job in this sophisticated city? She picked out a pair of navy-blue wool bell bottoms and a vintage cashmere sweater. It was too cold for a skirt.

Jolie showered and dressed. Her pants fell loose around her waist. She found a safety pin and cinched two inches from the waist band. Around her neck and under her sweater was the moonstone in the soft leather pouch, her amulet of protection. She'd need it today. She sat at the table and made a list of all of the Cambridge restaurants hiring and their addresses. All were located on three streets. Her right leg jiggled rapidly. What if they saw through her lie and knew she wasn't eighteen? She needed to meditate to calm and center herself while Will showered.

Sitting cross-legged on her small rug, she closed her eyes and grounded herself into the earth. She channeled her breath into her core, trying to find peace within. Worrisome thoughts intruded no matter how hard she concentrated on clearing her mind. What if she couldn't find a job? If a job called her back at the hotel, would they hire her if they knew she was staying there? What if she got hired and couldn't keep up with the work? She had to be strong and not held back by fear. She'd gotten along so far. Her mind reeled with the sounds of the city outside the window. She silently chanted om.

They took the Red Line Transit, the T, to Harvard Square and emerged from the underground subway onto JFK Avenue. The Square teamed with pedestrians. People swarmed around Out Of Town, the newsstand in the heart of the Square. The sidewalks were brick, the buildings were brick, and the avenue was lined with bookstores and restaurants. In front of the Harvard Co-op bookstore, they stopped by an ornate iron clock set on a tall iron post.

"This will always be our spot to meet," Will said.

A jazz musician on the corner coaxed notes from a trumpet. The ethereal sound of Miles Davis's "Sketches in Spain" wafted down the street. At a coffee shop, they sat by the window and watched the throng of people stream by. They drank tea and shared an English muffin smothered in blackberry jam.

Jolie looked at the bookstore across the street. That's where she'd rather work instead of a restaurant. Her mom had wanted her to become a librarian because she spent so much time reading at the library. A librarian? Just because she loved to read about travel and adventure didn't mean she wanted to be in charge of the Dewey decimal system. Thinking about her mom made her homesick.

"What if I got a job in one of the bookstores?" she asked.

"It's minimum wage with no tips or food. We need your tips."

He was right. She could buy books with tip money. She took out her list of waitress jobs and oriented herself to the streets.

Will stood. "I'm off to check out the scene." He left some money on top of the check. "I'll meet you at the clock post at noon." He leaned down and kissed her. "Good luck."

Sipping her tea she watched him walk down the street and disappear into the crowd. She ordered more hot water and lingered, trying to work up the nerve to go out. Finally, exhausting her tea bag, she left the warmth of the cafe.

Jolie walked by the restaurants on her list and read the menus. There was a crepe café, a German joint, a restaurant with an ice cream counter, and an Italian place.

She circled back through the streets, gathered her courage, and paused before Brigham's. The sign in the window read, "I Scream, You Scream, We All Scream for Ice Cream." She walked in, passed the ice cream counter in front of the restaurant, and stood before a busy breakfast counter where a middle-aged waitress talked with her customers.

"May I please see the manager?" Jolie asked.

"Frank," the waitress called in a harsh accent.

Jolie stepped back and waited. There was no way she would be waiting tables when she was that old. A man in a starched white shirt and black pants walked over to the waitress. She nodded her head in Jolie's direction. He looked at her expectantly.

She swallowed. "I'm here to apply for the job."

"Come on back."

She followed him to the far counter.

"Fill out this application," the manager said. "I'll be back in a few."

She completed the paperwork and waited for him to return, nervously pulling up her waistband and smoothing her sweater down. The restaurant was packed. The waitresses hustled as the cook in a white uniform and chef's hat flung orders onto a counter and yelled out names. The manager returned, picked up her application, and scrutinized it.

He reached out his hand. "Jolie, I'm Frank."

"Nice to meet you," Jolie said. She shook his hand and winced from his powerful grip.

"You can start tomorrow at the ice cream counter. Your shift is from eleven to seven. If that works out, we'll use you waitressing."

"Really?" Jolie said.

"Really." He smiled. "At least one of my problems is solved. Be here at eleven a.m. sharp. We'll have a uniform and apron for you."

"Thank you," Jolie said. "I'll see you tomorrow." She floated outside into the hum of buses, cars, and throngs of pedestrians. Wow, within fifteen minutes she had a job.

A panhandler stood in front of the restaurant. "Spare change?"

She shook her head. She had nothing to spare now, but she would soon. She glanced down the street at the tall iron clock.

There was another two hours to go before she met Will. Wandering up Massachusetts Avenue past boutiques, restaurants, and more bookstores, she found herself on the edge of Cambridge Common. She drifted along the center path, reading the historic plaques and monuments. The Common had been a staging ground for American Revolutionaries. In 1775, right where she stood, George Washington had taken command of the untrained, starving American army. She wanted to know more.

A constant stream of students passed through the Common. Small groups of young people sat in circles and talked or played Frisbee. Refrains from a steel drum band drifted from the far corner of the Common. Drawn to the Jamaican beat she sat down on a nearby bench. The band moved with the music; their long, braided hair streamed out of brightly colored knit hats.

Sitting back, she relaxed for the first time in a while. She had a new job twenty-four hours after arriving in Boston. A week ago she had been in Eugene and now she was sitting on a park bench in Cambridge, three thousand miles away. Once they got settled she would somehow get a message to her parents, letting them know she was okay. She closed her eyes. They had been so close to finding her.

When the song ended, she opened her eyes. A young man with brown hair falling past his ears shared the bench with her. His backpack was so stuffed with books the zipper didn't close. They eyed each other. On his head was a beanie with a red symbol of a lion and the word *Veritas*.

"Do you go to Radcliffe?" he asked.

Radcliffe? She wished, maybe one day. "No, I just got here yesterday."

"I'm Nick, I'm a student at Harvard." He offered his hand.

"Nice to meet you. I'm Jolie. You really go to Harvard?"

"I'm a first year law student."

"Why law?"

"There are so many inequities in the world. I want to help the underprivileged."

She nodded. They sat there for a minute not saying anything. The reggae beat started up again.

"Hey, since you just got here, can I show you around Harvard? I've got about an hour before my next class."

She looked across the avenue at Harvard. It lay before them in its stoic and intimidating beauty. Turning back to Nick, their eyes locked. Neither looked away. "Okay, that sounds good."

Nick walked her through Harvard Yard and pointed out the hallowed brick buildings from the 1600s. She was awed by the history and architecture. She was at Harvard. They stood in front of the library.

"Can we go in?" she said.

"Students only. But Cambridge has a library. It's on Broadway, about four blocks away."

A sudden gust of wind bit through her coat and a shiver ran through her.

"You're cold." He took off his beanie, placed it on her head, and pulled it down around her ears.

The cap was still warm from his body heat. She pressed her hands over her ears and smiled up at him. "Thanks."

"Come on. There's more to see."

Harvard Yard buzzed with students bundled in pea coats, scarves, and hats. They sat in groups or walked hurriedly to class. Shouts and laughter spiked the air. Nick pointed out the architectural details of columns, arched windows, and leaded glass. When it was time for his class, he pointed her in the direction of the Square. She didn't want to leave the cocoon of Harvard Yard.

"Thanks for the tour." She tugged off his beanie.

"Keep it. It looks good on you." He hesitated. "There's lots more history and architecture in Cambridge to see. How can I get in touch with you?"

"I just got a job at Brigham's, the day shift."

He smiled. "Okay, see you sometime."

She slipped the beanie back on and watched him walk off. He turned and called out, "Ciao."

"Ciao," she called, smiling back at him, trying out the word. She didn't know anyone who really used it. It sounded so worldly.

Jolie walked toward the clock post in the Square. She liked Nick and his altruistic goal. She was no longer intimidated by Harvard after walking around with him. They were all just kids with dreams. A revelation swelled within her. College. She wanted to go to college and study. And she would study hard. She needed to think of her future.

She leaned on the clock post and watched and waited for Will. Streams of students passed by in either direction. The Co-op bookshop window was plastered with posters of events. Inside, the display was filled with textbooks, glossy hardback best sellers, travel books, and T-shirts and hats with the red lion emblem and the word *Veritas*. She fingered the emblem on Nick's beanie and saw her reflection. It was the Harvard logo. She smiled. What did *Veritas* mean? How would she explain the hat to Will? She pulled off the beanie and tucked it in her purse.

In the crowd of pedestrians, Will strode toward her, tall and self-assured. Their eyes met, and he smiled his beautiful, wide smile that he saved just for her. When he reached her, she too was smiling with her good news.

"How'd it go?" he said.

"I got a job. I start tomorrow."

"I knew you would." He hugged her tight.

"No tips though. I have to get promoted to a waitress for tips."

"No tips? We need your tips. It's expensive here, if you haven't already figured that out."

A flash of heat rose and swelled in her head. Her chest seized up. Of course she knew that. Tears welled. Do not cry, do not cry, do not cry.

They zigzagged through the streets. Food aromas wafted in the air. Hungry for lunch, they found a diner on a side street. The cheapest items on the menu were grilled cheese or fried egg sandwiches. They ordered one of each and shared. They debated which was better.

"We can't eat out again until we have money coming in," Will said.

She nodded, still hungry.

"I found Liberation Books and talked to the owner, Martin. The Weatherman bomb blast in New York freaked everyone out. The movement's so fractured now. There's no common platform. It needs leadership." His eyes flashed with an intensity she had not seen before.

"We won't see any change until we overthrow the capitalists and abolish the classes of society." He drummed his fingers on the counter.

She pondered the enormous task. How would it ever work? It would take a revolution, that's for sure. Distracted by the dessert case, her mouth watered at the glistening Boston cream pie on display next to a strawberry cheesecake and lemon meringue pie. When she got paid, she would treat them to dessert.

Outside, they gravitated toward the Charles River footbridge. The bridge's graceful arches spanned the river, skillfully built out of brick and stone. They walked halfway out, staying clear of bicycles whirring past, and looked across at Boston and back to Cambridge.

"I think we should live in Cambridge when we save enough money to rent a place," Will said.

"We could rent an old brick house," Jolie said.

"There are rentals listed on the bulletin board at the bookstore. We could start by renting a room in a house with others," Will said.

Please, not a commune. She would not live in another commune. "Not another commune."

"No, just roommates. But if we found one that was listed at the bookstore, at least we'd have similar politics."

Politics, he lived and breathed politics.

"I met a Harvard law student today, and he gave me a tour of Harvard Yard. It is so beautiful and historic. I want to go to college someday."

"You what?"

"I want to go to college someday."

"You went off with some guy you don't know?"

"Well...I know him now."

"Jesus, Jolie. You just don't go off with guys you meet. Not everyone has good intentions."

"He's a first-year law student."

115

"He could be a psychopath. I'm not kidding. This is a big city, and there are weirdos out there looking for prey. You'd fall right into their trap. You're so naïve."

Her eyes filled with tears. He'd never raised his voice with her before. He tugged her to him.

"Let's go home," he said.

Home? Berkeley Street would never be home. They walked on across the bridge. His words still stung. She remained silent, only half listening to his plans to expand the socialist movement.

In their room, Will counted their remaining money and calculated how much Jolie would make her first four days. When she got paid on Friday, they could afford another week's rent and a meager food allowance.

Lying in bed that night, Will's remark still hurt. If she was so naïve, why was she the one who had landed a job on their first day there? He hadn't even responded to her comment about college.

Jolie was up early the next morning, nervous about her first day at work. While she waited for her turn in the shared bathroom, she meditated. She tried to center herself and breathe. Brigham's restaurant was three times the size of the restaurant in Eugene, and the pace far more frenetic. Would she be able to do it? She focused her thoughts on the green moonstone around her neck, a bright jewel, pulsating with pure vibrations from the universe. She channeled the light into her core. Opening her eyes, the chipped paint on the window sills and water stains on the floor jarred her into reality.

Will walked her to the T station. They could only afford one fare. She hopped on the subway train and found a seat next to students babbling about a professor's unreasonable assignment.

At Brigham's, Frank asked Millie, the older waitress from the day before, to show Jolie the locker room and get her a uniform. Millie muttered something, and Jolie followed her down a greasy stairwell into the basement. In the women's locker room, Millie sized her up and handed her a pink dress and white apron.

"Come upstairs when you're changed," Millie said in her hard Boston accent.

She'd be gruff too, if she still worked there at Millie's age.

She held the uniform, waiting for Millie to leave. Pink was not a color she wore. Out of the corner of her eye she saw something run along the floor. A rat, a big rat. It reached the door just as Millie did. Millie screamed and fled the locker room in a blur of pink. Jolie wasn't sure if she should laugh or be afraid. She quickly brushed her hair and braided it into a single, thick braid that fell down her back. She locked up her clothes and purse and put the key in her pink dress pocket, all the time on the lookout for rats.

Frank trained her on the ice cream counter. There was a cash register, metal milkshake machines, and an infinite number of ice cream tubs in the glass-topped freezer case. He demonstrated how to make a milkshake.

"There's no ice cream in milkshakes here?" Jolie asked, surprised.

Frank looked at her and shook his head. "No, ice cream goes in frappes. Do you know how to make a lime rickey?"

"What's a lime rickey?"

Frank studied her. "Where are you from again?"

"California."

"That figures," he said, shaking his head.

He mixed lime syrup and seltzer water and added a lime twist. It looked so inviting. Her mouth began to water.

"That's it," Frank said. "That's all there is to the counter. The crowds start about noon." He put a straw in the glass and took a sip.

"Am I here by myself?"

"Yes, I'll check on you now and again. Your lunch break is at two thirty. You get one meal a day free."

Jolie oriented herself to the counter. Would she be able to remember everything? Her first customer ordered a coffee milkshake. That was easy. Two squirts of coffee syrup, milk to the line, blend, and pour.

Around noon a line began to form and it never let up. She worked as fast as she could. The customer's eyes were on her every move. She was self-conscience and clumsy, and she was starving. She'd eaten a piece of bread for breakfast. Before she knew it, Millie was there to relieve her for a lunch break. Millie muttered under her breath about what a dirty mess the counter was. Small bits of ice cream had melted on the counter. Jolie had tried to keep it clean but the customers were never-ending.

Jolie clocked out for lunch and ordered from one of the waitresses. She took her food into the back room to eat. There wasn't much of a lunch room. One of the cooks was on his break, too. She sat down across from him at a small table in the corner. "Hi," she said.

He muttered something she couldn't understand and returned to reading a foreign newspaper written in a strangely beautiful alphabet.

Jolie focused on her food. She only had fifteen minutes left on her break. When the cook was done eating, he lit an unfiltered cigarette and offered her one. She shook her head.

"Where are you from originally?" she asked.

"Greece."

"Will you teach me some Greek words?"

He grunted something and buried himself behind the paper.

She returned to the ice cream counter. The line was just as long. It was three o'clock, and her shift was over at seven. Millie had left the counter just as messy. She couldn't keep up with the non-stop customers either.

The afternoon turned to evening as Jolie served lime rickeys, hot fudge sundaes on mint chocolate chip, and an endless combination of flavors. She scooped cone after cone until her wrist hurt. Coffee, chocolate, chocolate chip, mocha almond, Irish cream, rum raisin, peppermint stick, vanilla…she began to analyze the customers by the flavors they ordered. Why would anyone order vanilla when there were countless flavors before them?

At seven p.m., a young college girl arrived to start her shift. Jolie went to change in the locker room, keeping an eye out for rats. Exhausted and hungry, she had survived her first shift.

Outside, she breathed in the fresh night air in the brightly lit Square. On the T, she closed her eyes and nodded off. Her eyes flew open when the train jerked to a stop.

At her stop, she ascended the stairs to the street. She should have asked Will to meet her there. It wasn't the best part of town. Although there were families in the row houses, there were other characters hanging around doorways. At the top of the stairs, she walked toward Berkeley Street. A tall figure leaned against an elm tree. Should she cross the street to avoid him? He moved toward her. Her muscles contracted, and she bolted across the street.

"Jolie."

It was Will. He'd come to meet her.

In their room Will laid out cheese, bread, and canned fish for their dinner. "I went to Boston College and met the RYM representative."

She took a bite of bread and cheese. She had been so busy at work she hadn't even thought about what he had done that day.

"All of the organizations have splintered. I'm going to combine them into a cohesive movement. Separate we have no power, no mass. They're thinking small." His words were weighted with his fervor.

"But didn't you create a splinter group in Eugene?"

"Eugene was for amateurs."

She lay on the bed reading *The Prophet*. She must have read it ten times before, but she craved calm after her hectic day. Her eyes fluttered shut, and she saw ice cream cones.

That week Jolie took the subway every day. On her return in the darkness Will met her outside the T entrance. She ate lunch with the Greek cook while Millie covered for her break. Millie seemed to be melting around the edges and didn't seem as gruff. She didn't interact with Frank much, but she caught him observing her as she worked the counter alone.

Thursday morning she spent their last twenty cents on a one-way subway fare. They were flat out broke, but she still needed to get home that night and get to work the next morning. She didn't get paid until Friday afternoon. When she mentioned the dilemma to Will he nonchalantly told her to borrow it.

She went through the first half of her shift distracted by her problem. Should she ask Millie or Frank to lend her subway fare? What would they think? That she didn't have fifty cents to her name? But it was true. She could take it out of the cash register during a sale and pay it back double when she got paid. No, she couldn't steal, she could lose her job and then where would they be? She could ask the girl student who took over her shift at seven. But what if she didn't have any change on her? Then it would be too late to ask Millie or Frank or get it from the till. She wished she got tips, but only the waitresses did. If she worked hard at the ice cream counter, Frank might transfer her to waiting tables. But that wouldn't help her today. Millie's shift ended at four, Frank left at six, and the cook only muttered in Greek. She'd had no contact with the other staff since she was at the front counter by herself.

When Millie relieved her for her break, Jolie tried to ask, but Millie was already taking orders and tisking under her breath about how messy everything was.

Jolie ordered her lunch and took it into the lunch room. The Greek was eating and reading his paper. She sat down, sighed, and stared at her food, too distressed to eat.

"What, what?" he said. He peered over the paper at her.

She looked up, surprised. He never spoke except for the grunt he uttered when she said "hi." Should she tell him? She was too embarrassed. Her eyes met his. His lower face was obscured by the paper, and the creases around his eyes and forehead aged him beyond his years, but his brown eyes shone warm.

"I don't have subway fare to get home tonight or to work tomorrow," she said.

"You don't have any money? Not even twenty cents?"

She shook her head and her eyes welled with tears. He set the newspaper down and pulled out a worn, brown leather wallet. He took out a dollar and handed it to Jolie.

"Is this enough?"

"Plenty, thank you. I'll pay you back Monday," she said, trying to smile.

He muttered something in Greek and shook his head.

"We were never introduced. I'm Jolie."

"Dimitrius. You call me Dimitri. Now you know a Greek word." He went back to reading his paper.

Despite her humiliation, all the worry fell away. Not only did she have subway fare but enough to buy a can of tomato soup and bread at the Italian grocery for dinner.

What was Will doing right then? Had he even looked for work?

Friday during Jolie's lunch break, the manager, Frank, handed out paychecks. "The banks are closed when you get off work. If you need to cash this today you'd better scoot now. There's a bank two doors down."

"Thank you." She held the precious check in her hand.

Dimitri winked at her over his paper.

Jolie practically skipped down the street. In the bank she approached a young teller in a suit and tie. She signed the check and handed it to him feeling self conscious in her pink uniform with ice cream smudges on the white apron.

"Would you like to open a bank account?"

She hesitated. With this check she could pay another week's rent and have money for groceries and her subway fare.

"The minimum deposit is five dollars," he explained.

She smiled faintly. "Yes, I would." It would be a tight week. Will didn't believe in banks but he didn't need to know. Every week she would save a portion of her check. She would never be penniless again.

18

You Say You Want a Revolution

On Saturday, Will and Jolie headed to Cambridge for the anti-war protest. They were meeting Adam at Liberation Books. Jolie buttoned her wool pea coat and tugged her beanie down to keep out the spring chill while hurrying to keep up with Will's long stride. She'd told Will a customer had left the hat. What was wrong with her? Now she was lying to Will. But he would never let her wear it if he knew the truth and she loved the Harvard emblem.

In Harvard Square, students and shoppers flooded the sidewalks. Will and Jolie crossed the street and a car horn blared. Jolie jumped, startled by the angry blast. The drivers were so rude. They didn't care if pedestrians had the right of way. In California, no one honked.

They walked past Brigham's. She stopped and looked through the window. The long line at the ice cream counter snaked to the door.

"That's me during the week," she said, looking at the girl behind the counter.

Will hadn't stopped and was already halfway down the street. She ran to catch up with him. Wasn't he interested in what she did all day?

Musicians serenaded passers-by, hopeful for some coins. The jazz trumpeter commanded his usual corner with sweet Miles Davis tunes. Panhandlers were out in force with a chorus of "Spare change?" A white-faced mime imitated people, exaggerating their walk.

She followed Will six blocks down the Avenue to Liberation Books. They entered the bookshop to an aroma of fresh coffee. Shelves of books lined the walls. In the middle of the room a plaid couch and a few chairs welcomed readers. So this was Liberation Books. Posters of Lenin, Mao Tse Tung, and Ché Guevara hung on the walls. Underground newspapers were piled high on the table. It was more like a private library. Will led her into the back room where she recognized Adam from the week before.

"Where've you been, man?" Adam said. "We missed you at the meeting Wednesday night."

"Hanging out in Boston," Will said.

A twinge of humble pride spread through Jolie. She looked away, embarrassed. He was too proud to say he didn't have subway fare.

"Did you bring it?" Martin, the bookshop owner, asked.

Will nodded and handed him a hand written copy of his socialist manifesto.

"I'll read it this weekend," Martin said. "Let's get together Monday morning."

Martin introduced them to a group of men and women. Pamphlets and signs for the protest were stacked on the table. In the back of the room, stacks of folding chairs lined the wall. Jolie envisioned the lively meetings held there.

Carrying signs and pamphlets, Will and Jolie set out with the group to the Common. A crowd had gathered near the three historic cannons. The earthy scent of patchouli oil wafted in the air. Musical refrains from the steel band and a string quartet tangled together overhead. Adam quickly took charge, handing out signs and giving instructions for an orderly protest.

"No violence, even if the pigs want to clash. Absolutely no violence," Adam said. "Stay out of the street. Do not disrupt traffic."

After more instructions on the protest route, Adam assigned a handful of people to pass out pamphlets at the entrances to the Common. Jolie was directed to the familiar corner with the steel band. She glanced at Will and their eyes met. She didn't want to separate from him. It was her day off and she wanted to be near him. But he nodded and she headed off with an armload of pamphlets, reading one as she walked: BRING OUR TROOPS HOME.

Over 500,000 US troops are on the ground in Vietnam. Over 45,000 of our sons and brothers have died. 14,501 were killed in 1969 alone. What are we fighting for? Who are we fighting?

The two hundred or so protesters fell into place and began their slow march around and through the Common. Cambridge police stood at attention, their nightsticks ready at their sides. Policemen on horseback were strategically stationed at each entrance. Every twenty minutes, the protesters marched by Jolie. On the first pass, the group had doubled in size. With each pass, the crowd swelled and doubled again. Soon the gap closed from the front to the back, its width spreading outward. The energy level soared. The steel band, drowned out by the chanting of slogans, played on with more passion. Jolie joined the chant that went by at that moment, "Stop the war, feed the poor."

Jolie thought she glimpsed Nick in the crowd, but the swell of bodies merged together, and she lost sight of him. She hadn't seen Will for over an hour. The protesters spilled out onto Massachusetts Avenue. Police on horseback tried to move the mob back onto the sidewalk and into the Common, but the crowd was too large and getting bigger. No one was in control.

Jolie, out of pamphlets, stood firmly-rooted and watched. Someone should be taking photos. She'd never seen such a large protest. She stayed in her spot. She couldn't see Will in the sea of people but he knew where she was. He would find her. Horns blared as one lane of traffic was blocked and drivers tried to maneuver around the protesters. Drivers shouted out of car windows.

"Jolie?"

She turned to find Nick standing next to her in the sea of bodies marching with their signs. "I thought I saw you," she said. Her hand instinctively touched his beanie she was wearing.

"This is a big protest," Nick said.

"I wish I had a camera to capture it. The strength of it," she said.

"You like photography?" he asked.

She smiled and thought of the small Kodak Instamatic she'd left at home. She had taken it everywhere. But she wanted a real camera, a 35 millimeter. "I don't have a camera anymore but I plan to get one. I want to photograph all of this."

"There is a camera store in the Square that sells used cameras," Nick said.

Jolie strained to hear. The crowd was getting louder, chanting "Stop the War." A new line of police stood in riot gear in front of the officers on horseback. The police squawked into their bull horns: "Move out of the street."

"This is getting crazy," Nick shouted over the din.

The mood had changed. The protesters marched on, now chanting: "Hell no, we won't go." A moment later tear gas rained down on the marchers in the street. Nick grabbed her arm and pulled her toward the Square. They had to push their way through the solid wall of protesters advancing toward them. Nick held her wrist and pulled her along. Once they reached the edge of the crowd they ran a block, slowed, and looked back at the melee.

"It won't do any good to get clubbed and gassed," Nick said.

Her eyes stung from the tear gas drifting in the air. They stopped and watched the peaceful protest turn into an all out police assault. The Cambridge Common was too small for the crowd. They couldn't help but spill out into Mass Avenue. She strained to see Will. What if he got clubbed? Or arrested?

The police continued to spray tear gas on the crumpled bodies in the street as the protesters kept up their march around the Common. Those that had been gassed were helped by others onto the grass on the Common. The marchers cut a swath around them. Drivers honked their horns, in support or anger, Jolie couldn't tell.

Jolie and Nick watched in disbelief.

"The police look like gladiators with their shields and armor," she said.

"I was in Chicago the summer of sixty eight. This is nothing."

Jolie couldn't take her eyes from the scene.

"I'm sorry but I've got to go. I lead a study group and they're not going to pass an exam Monday without my help. Can I walk you somewhere?" Nick asked.

He was leaving? She'd never seen anything like it. "No, I'll wait here. I'm with some people back there." With some people? Why didn't she say she was waiting for Will, her boyfriend?

He gave her a brief hug. "Okay, promise me you won't go back."

Jolie nodded.

"Ciao," he said.

"Ciao," she replied, her eyes transfixed on the scene. Police had overrun the corner that Adam had assigned her. A television crew started setting up their cameras. She didn't need her picture on national TV or to end up in jail. Will knew to find her at the clock post in front of the Co-op.

Jolie walked up the block, and began her wait at the clock post. Students streamed in and out of the Co-op bookstore. She went inside. It was quiet and calming, a world apart from the protest a few blocks away. She browsed through the books and stopped before the photography section. Massive shelves were lined with photography guides, darkroom guides, and books of photographs. Turning the pages of a book of black and white photographs, she studied them. Everything looked stark and haunting. When they got on their feet she would buy a used 35 millimeter camera and then she'd buy Will a guitar. He was restless without his music. But first they had to move out of Berkeley Street.

The din of the protest still pounded in her head. Concerned about Will, she went outside and leaned against the clock post. Her eyes searched up and down the street for him.

Finally he appeared beside her. "Why did you leave?" he asked.

"The corner was overrun with police and tear gas." She gave him a hug. "I thought you got hurt or arrested."

"It mushroomed," he said. "The news crews are out in force. It should get some good coverage."

"I wish I had a camera," she said. "To capture it. The real version of the news."

His smile radiated through her. "The Revolution needs a photographer. We'll get you a camera."

She smiled up at him. She would set up a darkroom in their quaint brick house and learn how to develop her own photos.

The subway was crowded on the way back to Berkeley Street. At the hotel, they stopped by the TV in the lobby. Two men sat watching the news on a threadbare couch. Will and Jolie sank into unmatched, overstuffed chairs. Sure enough, there it was on TV, Jolie's corner with the crowd of protesters, snarled traffic, the police on horseback and in riot gear. The news crew interviewed protesters who claimed the tear gas was unwarranted. They were peaceful and unarmed. The crowd size was enormous and the police looked intimidating in their riot gear.

"Look at all of those people coming together," Will said. "All with their own agenda. If only I could harness that energy."

"They should lock them all up," said one of the men on the couch.

Jolie looked at the man. "Who should be locked up? The police?"

"No, the damn communist hippies," he said.

Oh, so now she was a communist hippie? She smiled. He sounded like her dad. But the smile faded instantly when she thought of him. He'd only wanted to love and protect her the best way he knew how.

19

Central Underground

Monday morning, Will accompanied Jolie to Cambridge. They walked into the warm glow of Liberation Books. Adam and Martin sat talking in the overstuffed chairs.

"Hey, guys, coffee?" Adam said.

"Sure," Will said. "That was quite a protest." Will and Jolie made themselves comfortable on the couch.

"The pigs ruined it." Adam handed them cups of black coffee. He smiled at Jolie. "But we got great press coverage."

Jolie took a sip and clenched her jaw, not wanting to swallow the bitter brew. She'd buy some tea for the bookshop with her next paycheck.

"I read your manifesto," Martin said. "It's good. It's really good."

Will regarded him. "Thanks man."

Jolie studied Martin. He was solemn and pensive. His blue plaid shirt was tucked neatly into his jeans, and his black military boots were laced with precision. His short brown hair fluffed out from the sides of his glasses.

"I want to publish it," Martin said.

Jolie smiled at Will with pride. Liberation Books wanted to publish his work.

"We've been talking about starting a new underground press." Adam said.

"The old press crashed and burned last year under its own messed-up internal politics," Martin said.

"What do you think, Will? Do you want to be part of it?" Adam asked.

Will nodded slowly and a wide smile spread across his face. "We can use the paper as a catalyst for the movement. We'll merge all of the separate movements into a single socialist revolution. The paper will be a vital mouthpiece for the movement."

"We're thinking along the same lines," Adam said.

"You can use my printing press after hours," Martin offered.

Jolie looked at the three of them. An underground newspaper? She'd read them all the time in Eugene.

"I was thinking about starting an underground news agency," Will said.

Jolie spun to look at Will. This was the first she'd heard of the plan and what was an agency?

"We'll collect news articles from reliable sources all over the world and send them out to other presses all over the country. We'll start a subscription service for news articles." Will's arms waved in the air as he spoke. "We'll link the nation and the world, not just one city. The socialist manifesto will reach every street corner. We'll build a cohesive national movement."

He always thought big. This was the Will she loved. His dark brown eyes shone with energy. He had never looked handsomer.

Jolie rose, holding her still full coffee mug. "I've got to get to work."

"Bye, Jolie girl," Adam said, smiling. "Have a nice day."

She smiled back at him. She liked Adam. He didn't seem as serious as Will and Martin. He was committed to the cause, but he lightened the mood. Martin and Will talked enthusiastically as she slipped out the door.

Have a nice day. She stood on the corner and pulled her mom's frayed note from her wallet and reread it. She carefully refolded it and tucked it away. "Have a nice day, Mom," she whispered and hurried off to work.

All week Will, Adam, and Martin met daily in the back room of the bookshop, hatching their plans. They decided that Adam would run the Boston/Cambridge underground press, and Will would be in charge of the central news agency. Martin would help find resources. They needed an office, supplies, phones, and a staff.

When her shifts were over, Will met her outside Brigham's. He was always late. The first two nights she worried. But on that night, she was miffed, her body stiff in the cold night air. She had been standing all day and wanted to go home to Berkeley Street, such as it was. He was oblivious about her day. Her work was inconsequential, scooping ice cream was insignificant. Heat spread across her cheeks as she stood and waited. What was she doing with her life? She needed to get involved with something important.

Will appeared, smiling. "I'm meeting a political science professor at Boston University tomorrow. Martin said he has one floor of a triplex we may be able to use as an office."

"What about looking for a job?"

He looked at her. "I just created my job."

"I mean a paying job."

"Money is trivial compared to what I'm doing for the movement."

A heavy feeling weighed on her chest. Money was trivial? Her working hard all day was trivial? He had promised to take care of her and now the burden was on her. She sat silent in the subway train. Maybe what he was doing was more important than money, but how were they going to get out of Berkeley Street?

The next night Will described his meeting with Professor Barnes to Jolie. "He was sitting in his office behind a massive desk piled with books, wearing a brown herringbone jacket. He's this classic aging professor until he opens his mouth."

"What do you mean?"

"He unleashed his theories on misguided U.S. imperialist policies. He even agreed to write an article."

"He's willing to do that?"

"Yes, but under a pseudonym. Some of his theories about U.S. government actions in Latin America seem so bizarre they must be true. Anyway, he offered the use of a ground floor apartment in Central Square, utilities included."

"Wow, really?" Will already had an office, and they didn't even have a house yet.

"He's planning to renovate the triplex in the future, but as long as we keep a low profile and don't bother the student renters on the two floors above, we can use it."

"He's a generous man."

"He gave me the keys, and I checked it out. It's perfect. I'll take you there before work in the morning. We can start the cleanup."

"What cleanup?"

"You'll see soon enough."

Will was up at six the next morning, ready to go to Central Square. He unlocked the first floor of the triplex. Jolie followed him in and surveyed the scene. It must have been quite a party. Furniture was scattered all around, some damaged beyond repair. They could put the rooms in order. The lights worked. The bathrooms needed cleaning. A sturdy wood dining room table survived the mayhem. An old couch could be salvaged if a bedspread was thrown over it. The kitchen plumbing worked. The stove and refrigerator were trashed but usable. It had potential, but a massive cleanup was in order.

"You got this for free?" Jolie asked, looking at the tall ceilings and windows.

"Until he's ready to remodel."

Unearthing cleaning supplies in the crusty pantry, they began the clean-up. Bag after bag of garbage and debris was hauled outside to the curb. After hours of labor Jolie left Will cleaning and walked to the T to catch the subway to work.

Late at night at the end of day two, the underground agency and free press office was ready for business. Jolie, Adam, and Will sat at the big wooden table in the dining room.

"We need a name for the agency," Will said.

"Central Square location, Central Agency, how about Central Underground?" Jolie suggested.

"Central Underground," Will tried out the name. "That works."

"I like it," Adam said.

Jolie's face lit up. She liked the name, too. "Central Underground."

"I have an idea." Will got up and walked to one of the bedroom doors. They hadn't touched the bedrooms yet. She followed him.

"Let's move in here."

She looked around at the austere surroundings. A mattress on the floor was covered with a ragged bedspread. She shot him a glance. Was he serious? She looked back at Adam who peered in behind them, his eyebrows arched.

"I want our own house, not a bedroom in an underground news press."

"You're going bourgeois on me again."

"I'm not going to live in a circus."

"Oh, and it will be a circus," Adam said. "The crowd at Liberation Books will make themselves right at home here."

Jolie stepped back into the dining room. She had to make a stand. "I'm not living here."

20

New Digs

A new Help Wanted sign hung in the window when Jolie entered Brigham's for her shift. She had been working for three weeks and had the job down. Dimitri winked at her as she walked into the back room. She smiled back. After he'd loaned her the money for the subway his demeanor had changed. Instead of ignoring her, he was protective. When she paid him back after she had cashed her first check, he told her to give him her lunch order before two thirty every day. He would have it ready. She would have more time to eat and rest instead of standing around, waiting for her order from the other cook. Besides, he told her, he was the better cook.

Frank caught up with her in the back room before she went down to the lockers. He didn't usually talk to her before her shift. He was friendly enough but didn't have time for small talk. Was something wrong? Was he going to replace her? Is that why the Help Wanted sign was in the window? She had caught on quickly, and her cash register always added up at the end of every shift. She clasped her hands together, her knuckles white as she waited for him to speak.

"How would you like to change jobs?" he said.

Did he mean work nights? She didn't want to be away from Will but she couldn't say no, desperate for the job. "Okay," she said.

"I need you waitressing weekdays from 10:00 a.m. to 6:00 p.m. One of the old birds is going out for surgery. I don't expect her to return. They never do."

A smile brightened her face. That meant tips. "Okay, thank you."

"I'm going to need you to train the new person at the ice cream counter once I hire someone, hopefully today. Millie will train you on Monday. You're a good worker, Jolie. I've been watching you."

She floated down to the basement to change into her uniform. She didn't know how much Millie and the others made in tips, but anything would be better than her minimum wage paycheck. She would save her tips, and Will would get a paying job. They would rent a small brick house. Today, she didn't mind the pink uniform.

Later, on her way to her lunch break, a girl sat at the back counter filling out an application. She looked about eighteen with shoulder-length dark curly hair and a sweet face. She hoped Frank hired her. Jolie sat down at the break table next to Dimitri. He was studying the paper. The Greek print was unintelligible.

"I start waitressing Monday," she said.

"Good. Then you'll be working for me."

"For you?"

His eyes smiled at her over his paper. "I control the orders."

The next day when Jolie arrived at work, Frank and the dark-haired girl stood waiting for her by the time clock.

"Show her the ropes, Jolie," Frank said before he dashed off.

Jolie took her down to the locker room and got her a uniform. Her name was Leah. She had just moved to Boston from New York and planned to go to Boston University in the fall. This was her first job. They changed into their uniforms, and Leah followed her up to the ice cream counter.

Jolie started by teaching Leah how to make change before she moved on to the ice cream creations. It was Friday, and they were slammed. The line grew. Slowed by training Leah, Jolie found it impossible to keep up. But the customers were patient as they waited for their concoctions, watching all types of treats being served before them.

Jolie reluctantly took her lunch break, worrying how Leah would do in her absence.

"Keep an eye on her, she may need some help," Jolie said, passing Frank in the back room. She was glad for the break. Training someone was tiring.

"How's the Jewish girl doing," Dimitri said.

"Jewish? How do you know she's Jewish?"

"She looks like a typical Jewish princess from New York," he said.

"Well she is from New York, but I don't know about the Jewish or princess part."

Dimitri laughed, shook his head and went back to reading his paper. She'd ask Will what it meant. She didn't think you could tell someone's religion from their features, or could you?

Jolie went back to the ice cream counter after her break. Frank was helping Leah. The line was endless, and it was time for Leah's break. She wouldn't miss the ice cream counter, but could she keep up as a waitress? Her heart sank. She'd find out Monday.

Jolie quickly learned the menu and, since she already knew how to make the drinks and ice cream concoctions, the orders flowed. Some of her customers were even interesting. If they were college students she always asked them what they were studying. Jolie and the new girl, Leah, had the same lunch break and quickly became friends. Dimitri still read his Greek paper but he joined in on their conversation when he smoked one of his non-filtered Pall Mall's.

Now that they had her tip money coming in, Jolie was anxious to move. Will wanted to live in Cambridge, closer to the action and the Central Underground office. He found an advertisement posted on the bulletin board at Liberation Books. There was a house to share in Cambridge between Central Square and Kendall Square. He called and set up a time to see it on Saturday. The address led them to the second floor of an old brick triplex.

A young man greeted them at the door and invited them in. Another man joined them in the kitchen. They introduced themselves as Daniel and Sam. The apartment had high ceilings and hardwood floors. Soft light poured through the tall windows.

"I teach high school in Roxbury," Daniel said. He had dark curly hair and behind his rimless granny glasses, his large brown eyes looked kind.

"Roxbury?" Jolie said.

"Boston's black ghetto," Daniel said.

Sam was studying engineering at M.I.T., the Massachusetts Institute of Technology. His sandy-blond hair and long side burns melded into soft facial hair that was overdue for a shave.

Daniel led them on a tour. The apartment had three bedrooms, two bathrooms, a large kitchen, dining room, and living room. Off the back hall was a covered porch that overlooked a green space.

The back bedroom was vacant. Jolie glanced around. It was furnished with a bed and dresser and some odds and ends of furniture. It was clean and it wasn't a commune. They walked back into the kitchen.

"So you're starting a new underground press?" Sam asked Will. Sam had posted the ad in the bookstore and was a member of the Students For a Democratic Society (SDS). An explosion of political diatribe ensued between the two.

Daniel and Jolie eyed each other cautiously. "We don't cook much," Daniel said.

"I can tell." The kitchen looked like it was used to make coffee, open a beer, and maybe make a sandwich. "I love to cook."

"You do?" A big smile spread across his face. "I'll chip in for groceries if you cook once in a while. Sam is hardly ever here."

"Sure." Her eyes darted about the house. It was large and clean and sparsely furnished. There was a TV on in the living room. The news announcer's voice droned in the background and then a Shake and Bake commercial blared. "Is Roxbury like Harlem?" she asked.

"It's smaller but just as scary. The schools close when there are riots."

136

"Riots?"

"Last year after Martin Luther King was assassinated they tore the school apart. It looked like a war-torn battlefield. But it's fairly safe here. They'll rob you, but not rape you. In some neighborhoods you need to watch out for everything, but not here."

Robbery and rape? She'd have to be more careful.

Will and Jolie rented the room and planned to move in the next day. On the walk back to the subway, she talked nonstop. "I can get a library card now. And I can invite Leah over for dinner. It's an easy walk to Central Square and Central Underground. It's only two T stops from Harvard Square, or I can walk. I can't wait to move."

Will emerged from his thoughts and squeezed her hand. She didn't care that she had to pay all the rent. She wanted out of the Berkeley dive.

The next day in the new house, she cleaned their room and the bathroom. She unpacked their meager belongings into the antique walnut dresser. Over the previous weeks, she'd bought new sheets, a blanket, and a turquoise madras-print bedspread. After making up the bed, she looked around the room. This was good. She could see the green field in the back from the bedroom window. The other two bedrooms were at the front of the house and shared a bathroom, which made the back bedroom and bathroom more private.

She went out and shopped for groceries at a nearby market. She had a kitchen to cook in. No more hot plate dinners. Daniel hovered in the kitchen, talking to her while she made spaghetti and chocolate chip cookies.

After dinner, Will sat in the living room with Daniel and Sam, talking. Jolie went into the back bathroom. At Berkeley Street she wouldn't have even considered taking a bath, but now she filled the claw foot cast iron tub with hot water and lavender oil and took a long soak while she read Hemingway.

That night in bed, Jolie lay her head on Will's shoulder.

"Did you hear Daniel say that in this neighborhood they might rob you but not rape you?" she said.

"Hmmm."

"Would they rob us at nighttime, or when we're gone in the day?"

"I don't know, baby. Don't think about it. We don't have anything to steal anyway."

He was right. They didn't have anything now, but she wanted things. A camera for her and a guitar for Will to start with.

21

Save the Planet

Jolie and Will walked along the musty banks of the Charles River most mornings on the way to the Central Underground office. She breathed in the earthy smell. The trees were thick with pink and white blossoms that floated in the spring air.

Central Underground was officially in business. With an address and two phone lines, news stories poured in by phone and mail from sources all over the country, Latin America, and Vietnam. Will needed to recruit more student volunteers to keep up with the flow of information. Jolie worked a few hours every morning, sorting mail and organizing the chaos before going to work. When she stopped by after work to meet Will, it was always in worse disarray.

One evening after work, Jolie dropped by the office, as Central Underground became known. Will was on the phone as usual. He raised his index finger, the one minute sign.

"Jolie girl, you look happy," Adam said. He worked at the long wooden table on the layout for the next weekly edition. He was always clean shaven and kept his blond hair trimmed.

"I just saw a poster for a National Earth Day demonstration this Wednesday, April 22. Jolie said. "People are finally realizing we're all connected to the earth and the universe."

"Yeah, we've had some calls. There are events all over the nation, all ignited by last year's Santa Barbara oil spill."

She smiled to think the oil spill may have had a positive outcome. And then her smile faded. The spill had been a catalyst for a lot of events; her being enrolled in an all girls Catholic school, leaving home with Will, living in communes, fleeing Oregon, the Berkeley Street dive. It had been a year of living on the edge. Her life had changed so much. "Good, maybe something positive can come from it. Corporations need to be held accountable. They shouldn't be able to pollute and then raise prices to clean it up," Jolie said.

Will stood next to her. "Earth Day?" He shook his head. "Sounds like a one-time event for tree huggers."

"You used to care about it. It's our planet. If we don't save it, nothing you do here will be of any use," she said.

"I have a single focus now. You need to align your passion with the movement. We could use some serious help around here," Will said.

Jolie inhaled deeply. She did do a lot of work. Both before and after her crappy job. But she also had other interests. "We can only survive with the survival of other species and the earth. It's even spelled out in the *Diamond Sutra.*"

"The *Diamond Sutra?*" Adam said.

"An ancient Buddhist text."

"Get your head out of that Buddhist mumbo jumbo," Will said.

Adam grinned and shook his head. "Maybe you should write an article, connecting the dots for our readers."

"Don't encourage her," Will said.

Why didn't Will ever take her seriously? She would write an article. She'd include Ralph Waldo Emerson's philosophy on the over-soul and man's connection to the universe.

On Wednesday morning, before Jolie's shift, she and Will went to the Earth Day event at Boston Common. Will had agreed only because he didn't want her to go alone. The Common was packed with a diverse crowd of workers, businessmen, labor leaders, students, and long-haired youth.

A man on the bandstand spoke. "For the first time, groups are united here today to fight against polluting factories and power plants, toxic dumps, contaminated streams and rivers, the loss of wilderness and the extinction of wildlife. We need to work together to create a sustainable environment."

Will and Jolie eased up toward the stage. The speaker lamented: "The Cuyahoga River outside Cleveland caught fire last June. The Connecticut River, the Hudson River, the Mississippi River, and rivers in New Hampshire, and Maine and here in Massachusetts are so polluted if a person fell in they would dissolve."

After two other speakers took the stage, Jolie leaned into Will. "I have to get to work or I'll be late."

He nodded and brushed her lips with a kiss. Reluctantly, she left him standing near the stage. She wanted to stay, listen to the speakers, and get involved. She glanced back at Will as she walked through the crowd. He was talking to an attractive young woman with dark hair and long bangs that partly covered her eyes. Her high cheekbones and full pink lips were striking. Jolie's heart thudded. Did he know her?

All day at work she flashed to the woman and Will. Were they still hanging out together?

The next day, reports came in to Central Underground from around the nation. Earth Day had been a success. Will's headline read: Twenty Million Gather to Save the Planet. Adam included Jolie's article urging respect for all forms of life on earth, but limited it to four paragraphs. At least she got to make the final edits. Adam told her it was a thoughtful piece of writing. Despite Will's objection, he placed it on the back page, prime space in the paper.

On Thursday, April 30, President Nixon addressed the nation. Sam called them into the living room to watch the broadcast. Nixon announced the invasion of Cambodia. He was attacking the headquarters of the Viet Cong.

"Our involvement is supposed to be winding down," Will said.

"Lies, all lies," Sam said, absently stroking his long sideburns.

Will called Adam, and they met at the office. They worked all night on a special edition of *Central Underground Press*, writing articles calling for protests and immediate student strikes. The paper was on street corners by early morning. Volunteers distributed the paper around the city and to all the colleges.

The nation responded to Nixon's invasion of Cambodia with outrage. Students went on strike at over four hundred fifty campuses. The protests continued over the weekend. On May 5, the National Guard fired on unarmed protesters at Kent State University, killing four and injuring nine others.

Will's headline screamed: INVASION HITS NERVE—FOUR MILLION STUDENTS STRIKE. Students and protestors clashed at twenty-six universities and colleges. The National Guard had been called in to twenty-one campuses.

"Nixon was escorted to Camp David for his safety," Adam said. "He's calling the protests a civil war."

"How can it be a war if only one side has weapons?" Jolie asked.

"We're at war against the war," one of the students said.

At Central Underground the phones rang constantly with news pouring in. Will, Adam, Sam, Jolie, and a cadre of student volunteers worked tirelessly getting the articles coordinated. They typed the stories and cut and pasted pages for the press. Will was in his element. While he hadn't slept more than a few hours in days he was energized by the events unfolding. He organized the volunteers and the news was flowing out of Central Underground. But more volunteers were needed. It was hit and miss who would arrive to work the next day.

"One hundred thousand peaceful protesters showed up in D.C. and one hundred fifty thousand in San Francisco," Will said to Jolie and the small group working on the next issue. "They showed up spontaneously. Just think what we can do if we organize the movement."

More and more student volunteers showed up at the office. Boston University and seventy-four other colleges across the nation announced they would stay closed for the remainder of the school year.

Everyone shared in the camaraderie of the office. Jolie worked with them before and after work and on weekends. Strangers became sisters or brothers or lovers. The office teemed with enthusiasm and sexual energy. The male students outnumbered the women, but the women didn't mind. Jolie thought they liked the attention. Relationships flared and eventually burned out. Adam liked the flow of women through the office and had flings with all that succumbed to his charms—and charming he was.

Central Underground had taken off in a short period of time. Will supplied other free presses with a subscription service for fifteen dollars a month. Not everyone paid on time but Central Underground News Agency continued to supply them with the news. The *Central Underground Press* consistently sold fifty thousand copies a week. Both were starting to make money.

One evening after work, Jolie found Will and Adam sitting with a group of students drinking beer. The mood was festive.

"What's the occasion?" Jolie asked.

"We cut our first paycheck." Will held up his bottle in a toast.

She hadn't doubted the success of the agency, she just hadn't envisioned Will earning money from it.

"I'm proud of you guys. You had a vision," she said.

"Come work fulltime with us," Will said.

"That's a great idea. We need you around here," Adam said.

Flattered, she smiled. She didn't like waitressing, but she wasn't planning to give it up. The tips were good—so good that she'd begun depositing most of them in her bank account. She still kept the account a secret from Will, not because she didn't trust him, but because she planned to surprise him someday if they needed money fast. Plus, she liked her independence.

The front door opened, and two striking young women, a blonde and brunette, walked in with a pizza and a twelve-pack of beer. They set them down in the kitchen and hugged Will and Adam. Will kissed them both, lingering an extra moment with the brunette. Jolie's stomach flipped and heat rose to her face when she recognized her as the dark haired girl from Earth Day.

"This is Marlena," Will said.

"Hi," Jolie replied.

"Hey," Marlena said, tilting her head toward Jolie, giving her the once over.

Will moved away to take a phone call. Jolie took a deep breath to squash the jealous pang. In *The Wisdom of Buddha*, she had learned that misery originates from within. Let it go. They were just volunteers in the movement. She exhaled slowly.

22

The Weight

~~~⌒~~~

Jolie's station at Brigham's, a long U-shaped bay, was always flanked by customers. Her regulars waited for a spot at her counter, much to Millie's ire. They called her the California girl. She was the one with the accent. An older professor who loved classical music always wanted to talk about California's Governor Reagan. They joked with each other and disagreed about politics. The constant stream of college students who ordered coffee or frappes became familiar faces. A Cambridge cop with the thick Boston accent took a liking to her. It was hard to imagine that she was friendly with a cop. And there was Nick.

Shortly after she started waitressing, he slid onto a stool at her bay. "Black coffee, please."

She smiled. When she worked the ice cream counter, she had told him about Will and the underground news press and agency. She was surprised he had come back to see her.

"I wondered where you went," he said. "You weren't at the ice cream counter. I didn't recognize you with your hair up. It's beautiful."

Her checks warmed. She felt her hair. Today she had coiled two braids around her head Norwegian style. "Coffee?" Nick said again.

"Oh, sorry," she said, laughing nervously. She poured him a cup and went off to take another order. She came back and poured more coffee. "How are your classes?" Was her hand trembling?

"Hard and competitive, but interesting. I still want to take you on a historic walking tour some weekend."

"I'd love that, but *Central Underground* has taken off. It consumes my weekends."

"I know, everyone's reading it. It's far better than the other rag that went under. People trust the content."

She smiled at him and moved away to take an order. She tore off the order sheet and put it on the counter for Dimitri.

"Who's your boyfriend?"

"Pardon me?"

Dimitri nodded his head to Nick.

"Oh, he's just a friend."

Dimitri's eyes twinkled and he wore an amused smile but said nothing more. Her cheeks warmed again. She returned to offer Nick more coffee.

Nick came in two or three times a week and waited for a seat if her bay was full. They talked about civil rights, women's rights, the war, Nixon, environmental degradation, and the books they were reading. Jolie kept putting off Nick's offer for the historical tour. She said she was too busy at Central Underground. She was confused by her nervousness. Was she being untrue to Will when she talked with Nick? She liked to talk to him. Their conversation was effortless and he listened to her. Will seemed far off when she talked to him, like he was in another world. It made her feel her ideas had no importance.

Every week for the past month Jolie had gone into the camera store in the Square to look at cameras. When she picked out the one she wanted, Niles, the sales clerk, amused with her earnestness, put it aside, slightly hidden from view in the display case until she could afford it.

One evening after Will went back to the office, she poured over the books on photography she'd gotten from the library. Daniel came in the living room and peered over her shoulder.

"I have darkroom equipment at my parents' house. I can dig it out of storage this weekend when I go home."

"Really?" she said. "I'm getting my camera this weekend."

"I'll teach you how to develop photos. You'll have to buy new processing chemicals and paper."

"Okay. Where can we set up the darkroom?"

They looked around. Daniel walked into the small windowless utility room off the kitchen. The room contained an old laundry sink and cleaning supplies.

"In here. This is perfect," Daniel said. "I've been wanting to take black-and-white portraits of my students. To give them something."

"I can help you develop them if you show me what to do."

"It's a deal."

She went back to the books and studied the darkroom process. She glanced at the clock, eleven p.m. When was Will coming home? He was so consumed with the office. Was Marlena there? It was too late to walk there by herself.

⌒⌒

Today was the day. It was Saturday in late May. The weather was warm and the sky a deep blue. Jolie walked to the office with Will. She'd baked cookies the night before, some for the house and some for the office. She felt guilty for not spending the day working with him, but today she was going to buy her camera. The cookies were her peace offering.

The streets flowed with pedestrians in the summer-like weather. Jolie wore a skirt, a pale blue T-shirt, and leather sandals, happy to feel warm weather. On the front steps of the office, several volunteers waited for Will. They had retrieved the mail from the mailbox and picked up more stacks wrapped in rubber bands that the mailman had left on the porch. They followed Will inside. Adam and more volunteers streamed in behind them.

Jolie placed the cookies on the kitchen counter and turned to leave.

"Where do you think you're going, Jolie girl?" Adam stood with his arms crossed, a mischievous grin spread across his face as he pretended to block her departure.

She smiled. "I'll be back later." She ruffled his neatly trimmed blond hair.

Will waved to her, a phone to his ear. Back in the bright May morning she ducked into the nearest T station. At Harvard Square, street musicians belted out tunes on every corner.

In the camera store she walked over to the used equipment case. Niles, the clerk appeared. She pulled out her wallet and set it on the polished glass counter. "Today's the day."

He took the camera out of the case and handed it to her. "It's all yours."

"It's beautiful." She turned the camera over in her hands, feeling the sleek body and weight of the lens.

Niles walked to the back of the store and returned with a well-worn black leather case and a colorful webbed strap. "These go with it."

She looked up at him. She knew they were sold separately.

"Thanks."

"You'll need film. Black and white or color?"

"Black and white, please."

He set four rolls of Kodak film on the counter. "Your first film is on the store if you promise to bring in some of your photographs."

"Really? I will."

He showed her how to load the film so as not to expose it. She paid and walked out of the store. The camera hung from the strap around her neck. Overjoyed, she stood buoyant on the sidewalk with a new eye for seeing the world. Tomorrow she and Will were going to another anti-war protest in the Common, but this time, she'd be there as the photographer for Central Underground. She had a new purpose.

She wandered into the Cambridge Common, past a string of panhandlers dressed in faded denim jeans, ragged plaid shirts, love beads, and leather headbands. They looked so young, like boys. Were they runaways, too? At the entrance to the Common, a trio of musicians played a Grateful Dead song. She snapped a photo of the motley group in their army jackets and cowboy boots. She continued on, looking for more subjects.

A small group of Vietnam Veterans Against the War, dressed in their camouflage army fatigues, had gathered in a peaceful protest. She took a few photos. These guys had been there and had seen the war firsthand. They were lucky to have survived.

One held a sign: Q: And babies? A: And babies. She shuddered. The sign referred to the My Lai massacre and the Army's Criminal Investigation hearings into the Vietnam tragedy. U.S. soldiers had killed five hundred unarmed men, women, and children. She met the eyes of the young man holding the sign. Lifting her camera she gave him a hopeful look, her way of asking permission to take his picture. He nodded. She carefully composed the shot and took his photo. Their eyes locked when she lowered her camera. He smiled at her. His shaggy dark hair fell just below his ears and his dimples disarmed her. It was hard to imagine that this young man was even old enough to be in the army, much less to have already served in Vietnam. He flashed a peace sign, and she smiled back at him. His blue eyes were haunting. What had he seen over there?

She walked on, glancing back at the protesters. She met the eyes of the young soldier again, and she felt his pain sweep through her. She wanted to give him a hug. A lot of good that would do after what he'd been through.

She found a park bench and sat next to two girls wearing Radcliffe T-shirts. In the warm sun, she watched a stream of students pass. When she went to college, what would she study? How could she get in? She hadn't even finished high school. The two girls on the bench talked and laughed. She felt so lonely. If only she had a good friend like Zoe to talk to. She had come close with Jasmine and Deidre but Will told her never to trust anyone with the secret of her age so she always kept her guard up.

She thought of the Vietnam Veteran she had photographed. He looked to be her older brother's age. She hoped her brothers didn't get drafted. The elation of her new camera quickly crashed to an ache for her family. She'd been gone from home for ten months. How were her parents doing? They had been good parents. She was the defiant one, following her own path. How did they explain to family and friends that their daughter just disappeared? Tears filled her eyes. They must be ashamed. Daughters didn't just wander off. She hoped they weren't being judged for her act of independence. She wanted to call and hear their voices and let them know she was safe, but Will thought her parents' phone was tapped and they could trace incoming calls. She couldn't mail a letter. The postmark would give them away. She needed to find a way.

23

All Good Things Are Wild and Free

Nick ambled into Brigham's after the lunch mob was gone and slipped into Jolie's bay. He ordered coffee.

"What's happening?" she asked.

"I've got finals this week, and then I'm going home for the summer."

"You're going to Chicago for the whole summer?"

"I have an internship at a law firm. Doing grunt work, but I'll be back home with my folks and younger brother. I actually kind of miss them."

Jolie didn't reply. She missed her family too. She scanned her bay. Everyone was content with their orders. It would be a long summer serving customers while he was helping the poor, doing something worthwhile with his life.

"Why so sad? Are you going to miss me?"

Heat spread to her face, and she dropped her order pad. He always had that effect on her. "Yes, I think I will."

"A bunch of us are going out to Walden Pond this Saturday to celebrate the end of finals. Come with us."

She hesitated. Will wanted her with him at Central Underground on the weekends. He didn't like her doing her own thing, alone or with others. But there were plenty of volunteers there, and she'd read Thoreau's *Walden* in school and now she'd get to go there. She'd bring her camera.

"Well...okay. One of my favorite quotes is from Thoreau."

"Which one?"

"'All good things are wild and free'."

Nick smiled and rose to leave. "See you at ten Saturday morning. Meet us at the entrance to Harvard Yard across from the Common."

A wave of anticipation swept through her.

"Ciao," Nick said.

"Ciao."

❧

That night Jolie talked to Will about buying a VW Bus. She had saved more now that Will had some money coming in, although most of his money was spent on improvements at the office. She opened a small tin and pulled out a stack of cash, separate from her bank account. It was only a portion of her tips. "I've saved enough money to buy a bus. We can go camping on weekends and explore Maine, Vermont, Connecticut, and New Hampshire. They're all only an hour or two away."

"I'd rather visit D.C. and check in with the national scene."

"But it's summer. Let's explore the lakes and streams and the ocean at Cape Cod, the calmness and the energy, the yin and yang of nature. We can do both."

"The yin and yang of nature? I've got an agency to run. I don't have time to contemplate my navel in the woods."

She sat silent. He was obsessed with the agency. They were like yin and yang. She longed for peace and harmony, and he was organizing for a revolution. Why did he always put down her spirituality? It was part of her and it kept her grounded.

Will picked up the stack of bills. "It would be good to have wheels, though. How much is here?"

"Five hundred dollars."

"You saved five hundred dollars?"

❧

In the evenings after work, Daniel and Jolie set up the darkroom. Jolie had purchased the photo developing supplies from the camera store. They cleaned out the utility room and created a lightproof space. He constructed narrow work tables on either side of the cast iron laundry sink. They laid out the film and print processing trays, hung hooks for the tray tongs, and strung an overhead line with clothespins to hang the developed film and prints. Daniel positioned the enlarger, safelight, and lightproof paper holder. In his organized teacher style, he wrote out notes on the development technique and tacked them to the wall above the work table.

"We're ready to develop," Daniel exclaimed. In a practice run with the lights on, he walked her through the film-loading process and developing sequence.

She excitedly held the two rolls of film from the weekend before. With the lights out in the pitch-black room, they proceeded to develop her first negatives. What if she screwed up? All of her pictures would be ruined. She loaded the first film roll into the spool and put them into the development tank, checking the gasket to make sure it was sealed. She walked through the steps out loud in case she forgot anything. At the end of the process, Daniel flipped on the light, and she unfurled the roll of film and hung it up to dry.

The following night, Daniel taught her the process of creating a contact sheet, a thumbprint-sized preview of all the negative images. From this she selected one photograph from the anti-war demonstration. It was an image of a young woman in jeans and a tie-dyed T-shirt holding a sign with her left hand that read Give Peace a Chance. The woman looked right at Jolie and gave her the peace sign with her right hand. They processed a test strip, playing with the exposure until they settled on the best contrast. Daniel showed her how to create an eight-by-ten print of the negative. The first print was botched when she overexposed it. She tried again, following the steps exactly. The resulting photograph was stunning in its simplicity. The woman's eyes stared back at the observer.

"It's magical. I can't wait to show Will."

"Nice," Daniel said. "Well, I'll leave you to it."

She was high on the whole process, experimenting with the tones of light and dark. She was anxious to show Will and Adam the contact sheet for any photos they wanted to use in the weekly press.

She picked out another of the Vietnam veterans' protest and developed a print. The veteran with the My Lai sign stared straight back at her. He was smiling, and his dimples added a sweetness, an innocence, but his haunted eyes brimmed with an inner turmoil. His gaze unnerved her. She clipped the print on the line to dry.

On the back porch, she inhaled the fresh air. Darkroom chemicals lingered when she breathed. When would Will be home? He stayed late every night, preoccupied with managing Central Underground. He liked the far-reaching network, all connected to the common aim of revolution. He was part of the inner circle now, part of a band of brothers. The cadre, linked across the nation, had powerful personal bonds and he was at the heart of it.

Restless, Jolie left the house and walked to the office. Will, Adam, and some students were sitting around the work table. Pizza boxes lay open on the kitchen counter. Marlena was there, a constant fixture at the office. A bad vibe inched up Jolie's spine. Her intuition told her she was not to be trusted. What was it about her? The group discussion continued.

"The national media is only covering ten percent of the demonstrations. They're purposely blacking them out," Will said. "It's a crime of silence and inaction."

"Meanwhile, two hundred U.S. soldiers are killed each week in combat," Adam said.

"We'll keep them on the front page," Will said.

Jolie looked around at the group. There were at least ten people she didn't recognize. She was proud of Will but worried by his visibility in the movement. The FBI read every free press article and was infiltrating protests and meetings with undercover agents. A message was taped to each of the Central Underground phone lines: *This phone is tapped.* A constant reminder to the volunteers.

Will had told her about one guy who hung around Liberation Books. Will and Adam were sure he was an informant. They purposefully led him on with false information for the fun of it. She glanced around. Marlena now sat next to Will. Did she have to sit so close? Marlena repeatedly flicked her bangs out of her eyes, glancing at Will as he talked with the others.

Jolie went into the kitchen to make tea and was surprised to find it fairly clean. Two young women were putting away dishes and organizing the chaos amid a discussion. She put on the tea kettle and sat and read the latest issue of *Central Underground.*

Jolie observed the two women while she read. They were pretty college students, dressed in shorts and T-shirts. They sounded smart as they debated whether communism was a good thing for the people or a single-party dictatorship. It bothered her that women were assigned the more menial chores, typing and mimeographing. At the office, a woman's point of view was talked over. The Movement was male-dominated, the same as in broader society. Nothing had changed there. Where was the equality they expounded on?

Adam jarred her out of her thoughts. "Hey Jolie girl, can you mock up this layout for me? It's Will's masterpiece."

The headline read: CONSTITUTION ATTACKED!

"Amendment 1: Congress shall make no law...abridging the freedom of speech, or of the press."

The article listed the most recent FBI raids on underground newspapers and reported on the ensuing court trials challenging free speech. All the cases had been thrown out of the courts.

"Anything for you." She glanced over at Will and Marlena. Anything to get Will home sooner.

24

Walden Pond

Saturday morning dawned muggy under a faint blue sky. Will came in the kitchen. "What are you doing?"

"Making trail mix and brownies." Jolie slid a pan of brownies out of the oven.

"We have to get to the office. I have people coming in from New York."

"Remember? I'm going to Walden Pond today."

"No, I don't remember. I want you to meet them."

She stopped stirring the nut mixture. "We talked about it twice. I'm meeting work friends and we're driving to Walden Pond."

Will shook his head. "I don't want you out with people I don't know."

She took a deep breath. She spent all day at work with people he didn't know. "I want to see where Thoreau wrote *Walden*." She placed the nuts on a cookie sheet and slid them into the oven to toast.

"If you'd rather spend your time at some pond, go ahead."

She looked up at him. He stood resolute, waiting for her to give in. Her head pounded. She didn't like disagreeing with him, but she wanted to go to Walden Pond. She wanted to meet new friends other than those at the office.

156

"Don't forget there is a meeting here tonight and I promised every-one dinner." He turned and walked out the door.

She stared at the closed door. He hadn't even hugged her good-bye. Her stomach flipped. Why did he always get into a bad mood when she had her own plans? She didn't mean to make him upset. It put her in a low mood too. He just wanted her with him. She could call Nick and cancel. But she really wanted to go to Walden Pond, and that was what she was going to do. She'd cook a good dinner tonight to make up for it.

A burning smell rose through the kitchen. She bolted to the oven and took out the blackened nuts. The morning was going downhill fast. She wanted to bring trail mix and brownies, and now all she had were the brownies.

Jolie stood at the entrance of Harvard Yard, anxious about meet-ing Nick's friends. She looked down at her outfit and smoothed her skirt. Would they be dressed like preppy college students? A white VW bus pulled up, and the German horn bleated a greeting. The back door opened, and Nick jumped out and waved her in. He crawled in behind her and pulled the door shut. They sat on bench seats covered with Mexican serapes. Nick introduced her to Chase, Allison, Preston, and Stella, all students at Harvard and Radcliffe.

Chase adjusted his ball cap and drove the sputtering bus down the avenue. Jolie scanned their clothes, relieved to see cut-off jeans and T-shirts. Chase eased the bus onto the highway and headed north to Concord. Preston sang along to the Rolling Stones' "Street Fighting Man" on the radio.

"Something smells good." Nick said. "What's in the bag?"

"I baked brownies," Jolie said.

"Yum, we never get anything homemade on campus," Stella said.

The group was in high spirits. They'd finished finals and had the whole summer ahead of them. Chase drove into downtown Concord. Blinding white churches with tall steeples stood stoic next to brick houses with rooster and horse weather vanes. Nestled alongside were stately colonial-style houses with wrap around porches shading wooden rocking chairs and porch swings.

"It's so quaint," Jolie said.

"More like Puritan," Allison said, and everyone laughed.

Jolie laughed too, although she wasn't sure what was funny. Chase stopped in front of a grocery store in an old brick building. They piled out of the bus. Jolie snapped a few photos of the historic buildings and tree-lined streets. Inside the store, they bought picnic food and two bottles of wine.

"We have one more stop before Walden Pond: Author's Ridge," Chase said. Allison smiled at him and turned his cap askew.

Chase drove out Bedford Road and turned onto a narrow lane. He killed the engine in a small parking lot at the foot of a hill. A sign declared: Sleepy Hollow Cemetery.

Jolie warily scanned the landscape. Paths led to headstones and small monuments that were rooted under towering evergreens. Sleepy Hollow Cemetery? She glanced at Nick and his friends. They didn't seem like morbid people. Still, maybe Will was right. She shouldn't have gone off with people she didn't really know.

"Allison, you're the English major, you lead the way," Preston said.

They hopped out of the bus. Jolie hesitated.

"Come on," Nick said, holding out his hand to her.

She reluctantly took his hand, and they trailed after Allison along a broken stone path to the top of a rocky ridge. They came upon a granite marker resembling a headstone with an arrow pointing ahead to Author's Ridge. Allison led them along the path and abruptly stopped.

"Wow," Jolie said.

Before them, in close proximity, lay the graves of Henry David Thoreau, Ralph Waldo Emerson, Nathaniel Hawthorne, and Louisa May Alcott. Emerson's nameplate was attached to a huge uncut slab of pink granite. This was his gravesite? Jolie glanced around. The cemetery was oddly beautiful among the rocks and trees.

"Hawthorne's *Scarlet Letter* was the first great American novel," Allison declared.

Thoreau, they confirmed, was the father of naturalists and conservation. Emerson, the father of Transcendentalism, the mystical unity of nature and humankind. At least Jolie had read some of their work before, thanks in part to the bookshelves and long days at the ranch and the Big Yellow House.

"What about Louis May Alcott's *Little Women?*" Chase said.

"Never read it," Stella said.

"Me neither," Jolie and Allison said in unison. The three smiled at each other.

"The coolest thing," Preston said, "is they all lived at the same time here in Concord and were friends."

"Let me get your photo," Jolie said to the group. "Friends on Author's Ridge." They posed by Thoreau's marker. Nick's smile embraced her through the lens. What a beautiful group of friends.

"Take mine by Emerson." Jolie handed Nick her camera. She sat cross-legged in front of the pink granite boulder, her hands in a prayer position against her chest. She smiled up at the cameraman.

They walked back down the uneven stone path, crammed into the bus, and drove off to the "Pond," as Nick called it. Chase eased into the parking lot. They gathered their picnic and walked along a trail. Small boats dotted the water. It was noon, and the main swimming beach was crowded.

"This is a lake, not a pond," Jolie commented. She was glad she'd brought her bathing suit.

Around the lake, past Thoreau's Cove, they took a side trail and stopped at the site of Thoreau's cabin. Jolie took a photo and stood before the marker in awe. This is where he wrote *Walden*.

A quarter of a mile down the trail, Chase lead them onto a small path that ended at a secluded cove with a sandy shore and grassy bank. Stella and Allison spread out sheets for picnic blankets. Preston opened a bottle of wine and passed around paper cups. They sat in a circle and toasted the beginning of summer, final exams, Henry David Thoreau, and anything else that came to mind. Jolie sat quietly, with a smile, observing the group of light-hearted friends and their celebration, raising her glass to toast but not really drinking. Stella sliced the bread, apples, smoky gouda, and brie.

"To the feast," Chase toasted, and they dove in to eat. A boat motored by, leaving a small wake on the glassy blue water. After most of the food had been eaten, Jolie unwrapped the brownies, and Nick passed them around. The conversation hushed as they bit into the rich, chewy chocolate.

"These are the best," Stella said.

They lay back contentedly in the sun.

Sometime later, Chase sat up and looked out over the lake. "The coast is clear. It's time for a swim."

Stella dropped towels at the shoreline. "We have to be careful. We don't want to get a ticket from the park ranger."

"My father would cut me off," Allison said.

Jolie stood with them at the shoreline holding her suit. She was never comfortable showing her body. The others quickly undressed and dove into the water.

Oh, what the heck, she thought. She left her suit by her clothes and dove in after them. She caught up with Nick and they swam together far out away from the shore. The water was clean and cool, the sun warm on their faces.

"I'm glad you came," Nick said. "You're not afraid this far out?"

"I love the water. I could stay out here all day."

They stopped swimming and floated on their backs. She made sure her breasts were underwater.

"Do you have a girlfriend back home?" She had surprised herself by asking.

"Not anymore. Angela and I split when we went off to different colleges."

"Oh." Angela. What was she like?

"It's going to be a long summer, not seeing you," he said.

"Can I get your address in Chicago? I'll send you a photo from today."

He smiled and nodded. "I'd like that."

They floated for a long time, talking. The others were back on shore.

He came up close to her. "Do you know how beautiful you are?"

"No." Embarrassed, she dipped underwater and resurfaced.

"Well you are." He touched her cheek with his fingers. A row boat approached lazily from the other shore. "Race you back." He took off swimming toward the shore.

They grabbed towels from the rumpled heap and quickly dressed. The others, already dressed, lay in the sun. Allison announced it was time for the poetry contest. They each had to recite at least two lines of a poem or an essay and the theme was nature.

Jolie glanced at Nick. He hadn't told her about this. She shrank inward. These were Harvard and Radcliffe students. She'd look like a fool. It was a mistake to have come.

Allison, having the advantage of being the English major, had to go first. Stella said she was at a disadvantage, being a psychology major. Preston moaned that his head had been in pre-med books all year. Nick and Chase were law students and were assigned to go second and third. Jolie, relieved, would go last. They were so competitive. Nick winked at her. Did she look as terrified as she felt?

Allison recited a beautiful sonnet, a lot longer than two lines.

It was Nick's turn. He stood and faced them with a big smile, ready and confident for his performance. Jolie snapped his picture.

"The sea hath its pearls,
The heaven hath its stars;
But my heart, my heart,
My heart hath its love.

Thou little, youthful maiden,
Come unto my great heart;
My heart, and the sea, and the heaven
Are melting away with love!"

"Ohhh!" The group swooned and turned to look at Jolie. Her cheeks flushed warm.

Chase recited a few lines of something, but Jolie wasn't paying attention. Her mind raced to think of a nature poem.

Preston stood and beamed. "My turn." He cleared his throat dramatically.

"There sat one day in quiet,
By an alehouse on the Rhine,
Four hale and hearty fellows,
And drank the precious wine."

He took a bow.

"What does that have to do with nature?" Allison asked.

"The Rhine River."

A few boos erupted from the group.

Stella stood and recited a Carson McCullers verse and then it was Jolie's turn. She wasn't about to stand up. She cleared her throat, looked at Nick and in a soft voice recited: "'The only prophet of that which must be, is the great nature in which we rest, as the earth lies in the soft arms of the atmosphere; the Unity, the Over-soul, within which every man's particular being is contained and made one with all other; the common heart.'"

They stared at her. Unnerved by the silence, she said, "Emerson, from one of his 'Nature' essays."

"That was beautiful," Stella said. They all clapped.

"I think it's a tie between Allison and Jolie," Chase said.

"What about the wine on the Rhine?" Preston asked, and they responded with laughter.

The guys got up to play Frisbee.

Allison turned to Jolie. "How do you know that essay?"

"I've read about transcendentalism. I don't understand all of the philosophy, but I believe in the over-soul and the connection with man and nature and the universe."

Allison and Stella nodded.

"There are a lot of religions with a similar philosophy. Buddhism for one," Jolie said.

"It would be a good topic for a paper next quarter," Allison said.

"You can study that in college?"

"Sure. You can study philosophy or theology," Stella said.

Jolie imagined herself studying philosophy and talking in depth with others. When she tried to talk to Will about transcendental concepts, he turned the conversation to Marxism and the revolutionary movement. He dismissed her interests and mocked her spirituality. He always made her feel small. But these were intelligent people who welcomed her interests.

They sat back and watched the guys playing Frisbee, leaping for the disc and showing off tricks. The sun warmed her. She was at Walden Pond with people she was becoming comfortable with and enjoying the day. She didn't want it to end. The poetry contest had been terrifying, but she had held her own.

At the end of the afternoon, they hiked back around the pond to the parking lot, completing the loop trail. Nick and Jolie trailed behind the others. "You should look into enrolling in college," Nick said.

Jolie hesitated, her stomach tightening. "I will. When I've been here long enough to pay in-state tuition." She hated lying to him. She liked him, and his friends.

"I can help you look at all of the colleges. There are grants and loans and I bet you could even get a scholarship."

"Okay, when you get back from Chicago."

On the way back to Cambridge, Jolie and Nick sat next to each other on the bench seat and exchanged addresses. In front of her apartment, Chase idled the engine.

"We'll all get together in September," Nick said. He hugged her good-bye, brief but tight.

"Ciao," they all called.

"Ciao." She stood and watched them drive off.

Nick rolled down the window and shouted, "Send me a photo…of you." The horn bleated twice.

She couldn't remember a better day. Smiling, she climbed the flight of stairs to the apartment. The house was empty. Good, everyone was out. She lay on the bed, and a dark mood descended upon her. It had been a great day, why was she down now? The group promised another trip to the pond in September before school started. She'd taken some good photos. She should be happy, but she couldn't shake the deep loneliness in her core.

Tomorrow she was going to see Leah's new apartment. At work, she and Leah had quickly become friends. They often talked in the locker room while on the lookout for rats. Leah would cheer her up.

Sam's booming voice in the kitchen jarred her from her thoughts. She remembered the meeting that night and her mood shrank even more. She was on the hook to cook dinner. That was the last thing she felt like doing, but Will expected it. Lately, instead of holding meetings at the office or the bookstore's back room, Will, Adam, and Martin had been holding them at their houses. She knew they were paranoid about the FBI. Still, she wondered why they were being so mysterious, like they were plotting something.

In the kitchen, Sam introduced Jolie to Ginger, his new girlfriend. Her face was framed with beautiful auburn hair and her brown eyes sparkled. Jolie warmed to her instantly.

"I'm going out to buy groceries for dinner," Jolie announced. She grabbed her purse and walked down to the corner store. She'd make oatmeal raisin cookies for Leah as a housewarming gift. Leah hadn't been to her house yet. She wanted to invite her over for dinner sometime when Daniel was around. They might hit it off. She smiled at the idea. She'd work on that.

When Jolie got back, Will, Adam, Martin, and a man she didn't know were sitting in the living room talking with Sam and Ginger. Steve Miller's "Quicksilver Girl" floated from the stereo. Someone had brought a twelve-pack of beer. Will came into the kitchen and put the beer into the refrigerator. The man followed him. Will introduced her to Leon, a friend in the Movement from New York.

"How was Walden Pond? All poetic and polluted?" Will asked.

"Beautiful. I can't wait to get a VW bus and explore the entire countryside. There's so much history here."

"History? We don't need to go back in time and revisit history. We need to focus on the future," Will said.

A knock on the door interrupted their conversation. She was relieved. She didn't want to talk about the day. Her mood was still blue. Will answered the door. A tall man with short black hair stood with Marlena. He looked at Jolie. His beady eyes traveled all over her. Jolie shot Will a glance but he was oblivious, his attention fully on Marlena who was smiling at him with full plum lips, flicking her shiny dark hair. A jealous pang shot through her.

Will introduced her to Coulter. She said "hi" in a welcoming way, but an uneasy feeling flooded her. Something was not right about them. Maybe if she got to know them better she'd feel differently. Will invited them into the living room and put on the new Miles Davis album, *Bitches Brew*. They sat back and listened.

Jolie could partially see them from the kitchen where she made dinner. She didn't mind being alone in the kitchen cooking. She liked to cook for others but not tonight, and not for Marlena and Coulter. Her mind wandered off to the day at the pond. The sweet sound of Miles Davis floated in from the living room.

When dinner was in the oven, she joined the others in the living room.

"The FBI is busting papers for swear words. We don't need four letter words to make a point," Adam said.

"We write the real story, not hyped jargon. That's why *Central Underground* is so successful," Will said.

"The beacon of truth," Leon said.

"We don't need harassment from the man. They can't win in the high court but they sure can make our lives miserable with false arrests, bail, and legal battles. I don't want anything to do with the law," Adam said.

"What's the word on Eldridge Cleaver?" Coulter asked.

Will looked at Adam and back to Coulter. "It's no secret he's in Algeria."

"We're working on a story with him," Adam said.

"Isn't he incognito?" Coulter asked.

Will smiled. "We have contacts."

Jolie sat up straighter. "You're not going to promote Cleaver are you? He's a rapist and promotes violence. I thought we are trying to include women in the Movement. This will only alienate us more."

"She's a feisty little one," Coulter said.

Will laughed and didn't see the fire Jolie's eyes shot to Coulter.

"What do you think?" Will asked the others.

Sam jumped in. "We should support Huey Newton's nonviolent reform ideals over Cleaver's."

"But it would be good to hear from Cleaver, in exile and all," Coulter said.

Jolie glanced at Will and then to Coulter and Marlena. She rose, marched into the kitchen, and got out the cookie ingredients. Ginger joined her.

"Tea?" Jolie asked. She poured her a cup and slid a spoon and the honey jar toward her. "I don't like violence, and I don't like rapists, and I'm not going to idolize Eldridge Cleaver because he's an exiled Black Panther."

"You are a feisty one!"

Jolie shot her a glance, but Ginger was smiling, her wavy auburn hair falling softly around her face. Jolie relaxed and laughed.

"We need you in the Women's Liberation Movement. Come with me to a meeting Saturday. We meet at Boston University," Ginger said.

Women's Liberation. Jolie liked the sound of it. "Sure."

"Good, I'll pick you up Saturday at one thirty. I'm supposed to be getting beers," Ginger said. She grabbed two bottles from the refrigerator and her cup of tea and went back into the living room.

Jolie's mind swirled with the prospect of the Women's Liberation Movement. She'd get to go on campus. She'd ask Leah to join them. Sisters working together. The Socialist Movement wouldn't change women's rights anytime soon. Coulter's comment bothered her. If a woman expressed an opinion, men think she's feisty. Will had even laughed. There was no equality in the socialist movement, only hollow words. Women weren't taken seriously even though they put in their time and had valid ideas.

~⁓◯

Later, Jolie and Will lay in bed, talking with the lights out. Jolie turned to him. "What about Marlena and Coulter?"

"What about them?"

"I get a weird vibe from them. Did they meet at Central Underground or did they show up together?"

"Hmm, not sure. She's in college, I forget where. I think she showed up first and then Coulter came around."

"Well, don't invite them to our house again. I get an uneasy feeling about them. Maybe they're part of the FBI, you know, like informants."

He burst out laughing and hugged her. "You're crazy!"

"I don't feel good about them."

He couldn't stop laughing. "I love you."

"Don't laugh. I'm not kidding." Would he ever take her seriously?

A car engine roared and stopped in the field behind the house. Doors slammed and voices floated through the night air. The car began a high speed circle around the field. Jolie and Will got up, dressed in the dark, and sat on the back porch and watched. Occasionally the car stopped, and teenagers switched drivers. After about fifteen minutes of joyriding in circles with the headlights off, they stopped the car in the middle of the field and began stripping anything of value. Soon flames glowed inside the car. The car doors were closed and the windows were up. The teens crept to the edge of the field to watch.

"Should we call the cops?" Jolie whispered.

"Let the neighbors call. We don't want anything to do with the law."

One by one the windows exploded from the heat, flames leapt from inside the car. A siren wailed a few blocks away.

25

There is No Free Country
Without a Free Press

Sunday morning Jolie woke before Will, excited about going to see Leah and her new place. She eased out of bed and looked out the window. In the middle of the field sat the charred remains of the car.

Will joined Jolie at the kitchen table where she sat with Sam and Ginger. They drank black tea and ate English muffins smothered with thick strawberry jam.

"I'm going to Beacon Hill to hang out with Leah today," Jolie said.

"I thought you were coming to the anti-war protest with me," Will said.

"Don't you remember? I'm going to see her new apartment. Come with me."

"I'm not interested in bourgeois Beacon Hill."

"I love Beacon Hill with its gas street lamps and quaint old houses," Ginger said. "I wish I could live there."

"We're going to the Public Garden," Jolie said, trying to lure him to the park. Couldn't he take a break from politics for an afternoon?

He shook his head. "Yesterday a pond, today a garden. Is that what you'd rather do? Where is your duty to the cause?"

The room was quiet and she sensed his mood. Why didn't he ever remember her plans? He was probably overwhelmed at the agency. When they first arrived in Boston he used to like walking through the Public Garden. Those days seem so distant now in more ways than one. "Leah's expecting me."

Will held her gaze. She had disappointed him again.

She left the house with her camera slung over her shoulder and the cookies for Leah. Will's mood cast a pall on her day. She walked to the nearest T station and headed for Beacon Hill.

On Chestnut Street, she walked along old brick sidewalks and looked for Leah's address. The row houses had tall white columns and black shutters. The small yards were fenced in black wrought iron. Pink and white flowers spilled from flower boxes that hung from wrought iron balconies. It was enchanting.

She found the address and walked up a flight of stairs. She tapped the brass lion door knocker. Leah opened the massive door, hugged Jolie, and pulled her inside. Jolie stood dwarfed by the tall windows dressed with curtains that flowed onto hardwood floors. Ornate layered crown moldings adorned the ceilings.

"It's beautiful," Jolie said. She handed Leah the package of cookies.

Jolie followed Leah into the kitchen. It was elegant with tall wood cabinets and built in storage. How could she afford this place?

Leah unwrapped the cookies and set them on the counter. "I love oatmeal cookies. I can't cook a thing."

"This place is amazing," Jolie said.

A girl walked into the kitchen. Jolie looked from one to the other. Were they twins?

"This is my roommate, Sarah."

"Are you sisters?"

They both laughed. "No," they said in unison. "We know each other from New York. We live in the same neighborhood in Brooklyn and go to the same synagogue," Leah said.

"And now we're roommates going to the same university," Sarah said as she took a bite of a cookie.

At one time that had been her dream. She and her best friend Zoe were going to be roommates in college. A wave of remorse swept through her. She shook it off. She had chosen Will and love and a different path.

"These are delicious," Sarah said. "I wish I could learn to bake."

"It's easy, you just follow a recipe," Jolie said, "or improvise."

Leah and Sarah looked at each other and laughed. "We tried a recipe the other night. It didn't quite turn out like the picture," Leah said.

"We ended up eating Chinese take-out," Sarah said.

Leah gave Jolie a tour of the rest of the apartment. Jolie marveled at the elegance of the interior architecture.

"In California, there isn't anything this old."

"We need some art on the walls," Leah said.

"I can print you some black and white photos as a housewarming gift if you want."

"Perfect," Leah exclaimed. "Photos would look good on these bare walls. Can you make them before my parents visit next month? I want the house to look good."

Jolie nodded, taking in the rooms. It already looked good.

Leah and Jolie said goodbye to Sarah and walked out into the May sunshine. Jolie snapped a dozen pictures as they walked through the neighborhood, experimenting with close ups of architectural details. They strolled down Beacon Street through the Common. It was already crowded with families and couples and a motley group of anti-war protesters. Jolie scanned the group and recognized some of the regulars. She'd forgotten to ask Will where his protest was today. A tinge of guilt flickered through her. She'd look for him on the way back. They crossed Charles Street and entered the Public Garden.

"Wow," they exclaimed in unison. Flowers, laid out in patterns, bloomed in a riot of colors: blue, rose, apricot, pink, and white. The trees that had been bare in March were now in full leaf.

They meandered along the paths, looking at the flower displays and reading the names on the tree plaques. Burr oak, English oak, Norway maple, red maple, silver maple, American elm, Belgian elm,

Scotch elm, and a Kentucky coffee tree. They passed a silk tree, a tulip tree, a weeping pagoda, and a tupelo tree.

"I love the tree names," Jolie said.

They came to the lagoon. A tour boat with an oversized white metal swan paddled by. The passengers sat on wooden benches as the swan boat glided across the water.

"Do you want to go on a boat ride?" Leah asked. "I'll treat."

Jolie smiled at her and looked out at the swan boats. "Too corny, but they're fun to watch."

"You're right," Leah agreed, and they walked on. They stopped before a large wooden sign engraved with a map of the Emerald Necklace.

"The Emerald Necklace?" Leah said.

Jolie read: "'A continuous chain of nine parks linked by parkways and waterways.'"

"Let's do all nine parks this summer," Leah said.

Jolie studied the map. "We could do it all in a day. It's only seven miles."

Leah glanced at her. "Seven miles?"

"I've hiked over ten miles a day backpacking with my brothers."

"Backpacking?"

"Hiking and then you camp."

"You mean you camped outside?"

"In a tent. You've never been camping?"

Leah shook her head.

"This is only seven miles, in a city. We'll bring a picnic. We'll get Will and maybe our roommate Daniel and some others to join us."

They found a spot on the grass near a huge dawn redwood. Leah spread out a blanket, and they lay back in the warm sun and tried to guess the age of the tree.

Jolie propped up on her elbows and watched the swan boats glide by in a steady parade. "I went to Walden Pond yesterday with Nick and his friends."

"Without Will?"

"He was busy."

"He's not jealous?"

"I said I was with friends from work." She didn't mention the skinny-dipping.

Leah raised her eyebrows and looked at Jolie. "Do you like Nick?"

"Yes, and his friends. He and Will are very different." Laughter drifted across the water. She returned her gaze to the boats, her face somber.

"Are you okay?" Leah asked. "You look sad."

"I am sort of sad. Maybe I dread going through the summer in my dead-end job."

"I'm quitting when school starts," Leah said.

Jolie looked over, surprised. "You are? How can you afford your apartment?"

"My parents are paying for it. I only took the job to show them I can work and be independent. I didn't want to stay in New York all summer, waiting for school to start." She twirled a yellow dandelion. "They don't let me go anywhere without twenty questions and fifty warnings."

"Sounds like my parents," Jolie said. She had wondered how Leah could afford the expensive apartment but now it made sense. She lay back and closed her eyes pushing away a tinge of envy. She had chosen her path. But what about the future? She needed a plan or she'd end up waitressing forever like Millie.

They soaked up the sun and talked about why there weren't more women doctors and politicians.

"I'm going to a Women's Liberation Movement meeting at Boston University next Saturday with Ginger, my roommate's girlfriend." Jolie said. "You should join us."

"It can't be too radical if it's held at my school, right?"

"I don't know. We'll see Saturday."

"Hey, let's drive to Cape Cod some weekend in my car. We can rent a cottage, swim all day, lie in the sand dunes, and eat saltwater taffy. At night we can dress up and go out for seafood."

Jolie laughed. "That sounds idyllic."

When the sun got too hot, they rolled up the blanket and walked back to Leah's. Jolie stopped along the way to photograph flowers and people in the park. How would the flower displays look in black and white?

They passed a few anti-war protesters who lingered on the grass. The rest must be at the other end of the Common. She should walk over and see if Will was there. But she didn't feel like a protest today. All she wanted to do was go home to the darkroom and develop the negatives from Walden Pond. They strolled back to Leah's house and stood out front.

"Do you want to come over for dinner some night? I want you to meet our roommate, Daniel," Jolie said.

"Is he Jewish?"

"I don't know. Does it matter?"

"I can only date Jewish guys," Leah said, "but Daniel sounds Jewish."

Jolie looked at her friend. She was serious. "I'll ask him tonight. I'm going to head back to Cambridge," Jolie said.

"Do you want a ride home?" Leah asked.

"No, thanks, it's so nice out. I'll take more photos on the way and then take the subway. See you at work tomorrow."

They both groaned at the thought and hugged good-bye.

Jolie walked along, taking an occasional photo. A warm breeze lifted her feather earrings against her checks. Leah had cheered her up somewhat. They were going go to Cape Cod some weekend and rent a cottage on the beach. She hadn't seen the ocean forever, it seemed, and she'd never seen the Atlantic.

When Jolie arrived home she escaped to the darkroom with the roll of film from the pond. Re-reading the instructions Daniel had tacked to the wall, she turned out the light and worked slowly through the developing sequence. The darkroom was calming. After processing the film, she unfurled the roll and clipped it up to dry.

While the negatives dried, Jolie looked at the contact sheet from the previous roll she and Daniel had developed. There were a few good photos of protesters to print for *Central Underground.* One caught her eye. Staring back at her from the contact sheet was a young woman with long black hair parted in the middle. She wore bell bottoms and a tank top. The sign she held read: Sisters for Liberation. She set up to print and dipped the paper into the developer and watched the image slowly appear. She had learned to control the contrast of black and white. The print had emotion and mystery. Every time she stepped into the darkroom her senses heightened with expectation. The excitement of the unknown. The magic of the print.

She printed a few others and hung them up to dry. They were good. She couldn't wait to show them to Will.

She scanned the negative strip from Walden Pond. The majority were of Nick and the others fooling around in the cemetery and at the pond. She quickly developed a contact sheet. Her favorite was the photo of Nick smiling at the camera, his hair tousled, reciting his poem. In the photo Nick took of her next to Emerson's grave marker, she looked relaxed and happy smiling up at him. She'd print it and send it to him along with the shot of the five of them by the gravestone on Author's Ridge.

She breathed in the quiet of the house. In the bedroom she lit myrrh incense and sat cross-legged on the Persian rug to meditate. Jasmine had taught her to meditate on the ocean to heal sad emotions. She envisioned small waves lapping on a white sand beach. When she couldn't sleep she used the same image. Her mind wandered to Nick. He would have already landed in Chicago by now and was probably at his parents' house, eating a welcome home dinner. Her family would be having their traditional Sunday barbeque. She had to get a message home soon. She would send a photo without any landmarks. Her thoughts slowed as she breathed. A blue hole like a tunnel emerged. The blue light was calming and drew her in. She tried to fall into the hole but remained on the edge. Tears flowed down her cheeks.

The bedroom door creaked and her eyes flew open. Will stood in the doorway.

"What's the matter, Little Wing?"

"Nothing, I'm fine."

He leaned over and put his hands on her shoulders. "You're crying."

She rose and hugged him.

"I feel sad."

He hugged her tighter and kissed her on the forehead. "It's probably just hormones."

"I want to contact my folks and let them know I'm safe."

His body stiffened. "It's too risky for us to do that. I can't let you contact them. I still wonder how they found us in Eugene."

"You have acquaintances all over the country. Can't one of them mail a letter for me?"

"I wouldn't trust anyone with that letter."

She closed her eyes. Another wave of tears spilled. Will wouldn't help her but she would find a way without giving away their location. Somehow, she would find a way.

Monday morning, Will was in the kitchen reading the paper. "Do you want to see some photos?" Jolie asked.

He followed her into the small darkroom. "Not bad," he said. "We'll run all of them this week with your name, J. Cassady, in the byline."

She attempted a smile. "I like this one." She pointed to the Sisters for Liberation photo.

He moved toward her and gave her a tender hug. "Are you still sad?"

She shrugged and tried to swallow the lump welling in her throat.

"I'll walk you to the T." Will stroked her cheek. "And after work, stop by the office. We'll walk home together."

She smiled. This was the Will she loved more than anything.

After work, Jolie stopped by the office. In the dining room-turned-workspace, a lively debate was underway. Will smiled at her and nodded to an empty chair. The usual group was there, Adam, Miles, and some student volunteers. Marlena and Coulter sat at the end of the table. They were discussing advertising in the *Central Underground Press*.

"The advertisements keep us in the black," Will explained.

"It's a sellout to corporate America," Coulter said.

Will drummed his fingers on the table. "Oh, come on, man, all the big advertisers like the record companies pulled out of the free presses last year. That's where the big money came from, full page ads. Now they won't touch us."

"Why'd they pull out?" a student asked.

"The FBI scared them off. Accused them of giving active aid to U.S. enemies," Adam said.

Will smiled. "We are the force of evil."

Jolie watched Coulter and Marlena. Did she see a subtle glance between them when the FBI was mentioned?

"We only accept ads from supporters of the movement," Adam said. "Most advertisers sell the papers at their businesses. They boost our readership."

"Vintage clothing stores, astrology readers, head shops, and rock concert promoters are hardly corporate America," Miles said.

"We're not giving up the ads," Will said.

But Coulter wouldn't let it go. "What about the personal ads? You're not selling a revolution, you're selling sex." He grabbed a recent paper and turned to the last few pages.

"'Groovy-looking guy with tight round buttocks will do erotic posing.' And what about this one: 'Jim's rubs for men are sensational and groovy. Day and night service.' Or 'Tall, dark, handsome, 33-year-old white executive wishes to meet attractive female swinger—'"

Adam interrupted. "What are you, a prude or something?"

"Some buy the paper just to read the ads," a student piped up. "You have to admit, they are amusing."

"Sex? Is that what you're promoting?" Coulter asked.

"It's free speech, purely free speech. There's no free country without a free press," Will said. He stood up indicating the discussion was over. "Time to close her up."

Everyone rose to leave. Jolie stayed seated, waiting for Will to put away any material left out. He only opened the office now if he or Adam were there. Strange people had turned up. He wasn't as trusting as he had been two months earlier. Jolie's stomach tightened as Marlena gave Will a prolonged hug before leaving with Coulter. Will and Jolie walked home hand in hand.

"Is Coulter trying to undermine the paper?" she asked.

"That's a little radical. I think he's a little uncomfortable with the love revolution."

"He gives me the creeps." Marlena, too, or was she jealous of her sophistication? Will was obviously attracted to her.

26

Sisters for Liberation

One morning, after Will left for the office, Jolie sat down at the kitchen table to write Nick a note to send with the two photos.

"Hey." Daniel bounded in. "I have a whole week off before summer school starts. What have you been up to?"

She nodded toward the darkroom.

"Let me see."

In the darkroom he turned on the light. "Wow, you've been busy."

Jolie pointed to a small stack of eight-by-ten photos. "Those are my disasters."

"That's how you learn."

"Expensive mistakes. The photo paper costs a fortune."

She laid out a set of photos from Walden Pond. "I printed these with multiple exposures, but I can't decide which are the best."

They examined the prints.

"Light has form and meaning because of darkness, and darkness because of light," he said.

"I think of the light as hope and innocence, and darkness as despair," she said.

They agreed upon the best exposures. Jolie made notes and they walked back into the kitchen.

"Thanks. Do you want some tea?"

Daniel smiled and nodded.

"Are you Jewish?" Jolie asked.

"With a name like Daniel Shapiro?"

She looked at him, helpless. "No, seriously."

"I'm Jewish, all right. Isn't it obvious?"

"No. How do you learn those things?"

"You just grow up knowing or your parents teach you."

She did have a lot to learn. "I want to invite my friend, Leah, over for dinner. Will you join us? She's starting at Boston University this fall."

"Let me guess…she can only date Jewish guys?"

They set a date for the upcoming Saturday night. Maybe Sam and Ginger could join them.

Glancing at the clock she realized she'd have to write the note to Nick later. It was time for work. She didn't know what to say to him anyway. Carefully she tucked the photos away in the darkroom.

Friday morning before work, Jolie pulled together her favorite photos of protesters, the Public Garden and historic buildings. She placed them in a large envelope, and headed to the camera store. Niles, the clerk, was there as usual. She gave him the list of supplies she needed.

"I brought some photos for you to see," she said.

"Hand them over."

She hesitated and then laid the large envelope on the long glass counter. He removed the prints and spread them out. Standing back, he viewed the photos. He took his time. Jolie stood still in the long silence. She gulped. She'd get better. There was so much to learn.

Niles looked up from the photos. "You've got a good eye. The detail is incredible. It's intimate."

"Really? Wow, thanks."

"Will you leave some with me to display in the store?"

Jolie looked around and didn't see any other photos except Kodak advertisements.

"I want to add some life in here," Niles explained. "I need some art. Something interesting to look at."

"Okay." She still had the negatives although no two prints were exposed exactly alike.

He picked out the ones he wanted to hang. "I can't display politics here but people and architecture will work just fine."

He assembled the items on her list and set them on the counter. "The same deal: the film's on the store if you bring me more photos. I need something to look forward to in my week. Everyone takes the same old pictures. Yours are different."

Jolie floated out of the store on a cloud. Her photos were going to be shown in Harvard Square. She couldn't wait to tell Will and Daniel. And Nick. She needed to write to Nick.

1970, The Year of the Revolution was the headline for *Central Underground Press* that first week in June. Will's article expounded on the duties of a revolutionary: One must advance the revolution, not just talk about it. Ideological debate was out and the Socialist Revolution was in. His Socialist Manifesto had been reprinted as an insert. The article and manifesto were distributed nationally with one of Jolie's photos. It was well received and the independent presses clamored for more.

Saturday morning, Will went into the office early. The agency was swamped. Jolie's happiness about the whole day before her was tinged with guilt. Will wanted her to work at the office, but she'd begged off. She wanted to go to the library. The Women's Liberation Movement meeting was that afternoon and that night Leah was coming for dinner. She hoped Will remembered about the dinner but she doubted he would. The Socialist Revolution had swallowed him up.

That afternoon Ginger pulled up in front of the apartment and honked. Jolie ran down the stairs and hopped into the sky blue VW Bug. "Leah is meeting us there," Jolie said. As they drove off, Jolie raised her arm in the air. "Sisters unite."

Ginger laughed and turned up Carole King on the radio. Jolie was happy for the ride. She wanted to get to know Ginger better. The past week Ginger had occasionally hung around the house with Sam. She always sat quietly in the living room sketching cartoons in her notebook. Going to Boston University would be less intimidating with Ginger. Crossing the bridge, the Charles River glistened below. Boats zigzagged through the water.

Ginger pulled into a large parking lot next to beautiful old buildings set along the river.

"This campus is huge," Jolie said.

"There's almost twenty thousand students."

Twenty thousand? That was a small city. They walked ten minutes across campus, climbed the stairs of an old brick building, and found the meeting room. The room was half full. Some women looked like students and others were older. Leah stood across the room, and Jolie waved for her to join them. More women streamed into the room.

A petite woman in her thirties stood at the professors' podium and welcomed everyone. She introduced herself as Elaine Wood. She had chin-length auburn hair parted off to the side and wore a white blouse and a black skirt.

"I want to start our meeting today with a proposal. A plea, really. Women have made some gains in the past few years but we're losing ground. Our forums don't have any structure. We've lost when we should have gained. Gaining and seizing power is critical to our situation. Women are the majority, fifty-one percent of the population—" she waited for applause to die down, "—but we have no power in any of the movements. Yes, there are women's rights organizations in most cities but they are fractured and not connected. We need to build one organization to empower women with a united vision. We must take the offensive again and begin a united fight in what will be a long but worthwhile battle." She paused again to wait out the applause.

Jolie looked around at the women. Marlena sat across the room, taking notes. She looked up and their eyes met. Marlena? Here? Maybe she had misread her or was she infiltrating the women's movement too?

"What about the women's subgroups in the other organizations?" someone asked.

"It's just lip service. Name one thing that has been gained," Elaine said.

"She's right," a woman said. "The men dominate the discussions. Our needs are diluted. Women are assigned to backstage and the kitchen."

Jolie nodded. That hit a nerve. It sounded like the office.

"Should we remain splintered across the other organizations without a common strategy, or join the Women's Liberation Movement?" Elaine asked.

"Join," everyone cried. Applause thundered through the room.

They discussed the platform based on women's needs. They would use the platform to recruit the support of all women. A platform with specific actions.

A current reverberated through the room. Jolie's body pulsed with an adrenaline high. This is how Will must feel. She had supported some of his ideas but most seemed lofty and unattainable. Here, they talked of specific rights and needs of women. Their platform was tangible, and all women would benefit from equal rights, equal work, equal pay, equal education, funded childcare, maternity leave, accessible birth control, the right to abortion, and the right for women to control their own bodies. These specifics were never discussed in the caucuses of the Socialist Revolution or New Left. It was always vague ideology and not day-to-day reality.

Elaine talked about the need for leadership to gain the support from the other women's groups. Jolie's mind raced. *Central Underground* could help get their platform out to other free presses. She glanced at Marlena. She was still scribbling away in her notebook.

When the meeting ended, Ginger, Jolie, and Leah walked across campus to the parking lot, elated with the united power of sisterhood.

After they dropped off Leah, Ginger and Jolie continued to talk, invigorated by the meeting. They strategized on how to recruit sisters from the other movements. They would use their own power, their own style, to focus on their own issues. They'd get the word out nationally through the Central News Agency.

"Brace yourself," Ginger said, "the split from the other movements will be hostile."

"But it's the right thing to do," Jolie said. "We can't wait for some far-fetched revolution to give us equal rights."

"I agree, but women have been the glue in the other movements. Creating one Women's Liberation Movement will piss them off."

"Men will always control us unless we stand up."

Ginger glanced at her and then back to the road. "And Will? How are you going to handle Will?"

Jolie grimaced. She hadn't thought that far ahead.

27

Summertime

⌒◯

The doorbell rang. Daniel looked at Jolie, his eyes wide. Was he nervous? She opened the door. Leah stood radiant in a summer dress and sandals, her black curls shining. She handed Jolie a bouquet of fragrant pink and white Asiatic lilies. Jolie glanced at Daniel, still frozen against the sink.

After Jolie introduced them, Will, Sam, and Ginger drifted into the kitchen. Jolie put the flowers in a makeshift vase, and Daniel poured wine. Janis Joplin's "Summertime" played on the stereo and Will sang along, his voice rich and low. He was mesmerizing. Everyone stopped and listened. He looked at Jolie as he sang, and she lost herself in his dark brown eyes, warmth spreading through her. She never tired of looking at him. This tender side was the Will she loved. She needed to buy him a guitar.

At dinner, Leah asked Daniel about his teaching job. "But why Roxbury High School?"

"I was hoping to make a difference in their lives."

"So are you?" Sam asked.

Daniel frowned. "I can't seem to get them interested in anything."

Jolie breathed deep. The scent of the flowers in the vase was intoxicating. She smiled inwardly. The mood and the music were perfect for the dinner party. "Daniel's going to take a portrait of each student in his summer school classes. I'm going to be his assistant." Jolie said.

"No way. You're not hanging out in Roxbury," said Will. "It's a burned out rat hole."

Jolie stared at Will in shock. These were the very same people he was trying to raise out of poverty. He must be concerned about her safety. "I'm only helping in the dark room."

"Roxbury can be intimidating, especially for a white guy," Daniel said. He told them about the riots and lootings after Martin Luther King was assassinated. "It was a war zone. It's still an urban war zone. Vacant lots are filled with trash. Arsonists burn anything flammable. No one even bothers to board up the burned out buildings anymore."

"Then why do you stay there?" Leah asked.

"I am hoping to get through to one or two kids and help them get into college. They are desperate to get out of there. They just don't know how. I'm going to give it another year."

Jolie heard the compassion in his voice and respected his selfless-ness. He was doing something specific. She looked forward to helping him with the portrait project.

Later, Jolie took Leah aside and showed her the apartment and darkroom. Their apartment wasn't as spacious and didn't have the architectural grandeur or as good a location as Leah's, but it was clean and comfortable and she was saving money for their own place.

They stood in the dark room. "So, how do you like Daniel?"

Leah smiled. "He's cute. And smart. I admire his dedication to those kids."

They looked at some photos.

"Look at his eyes." Leah said.

The print of the Vietnam vet with the My Lai sign hung by a clip. Despite his smile, there was obvious pain in his eyes.

"What did Will say about these?" Leah pointed to the prints from Walden Pond.

"He hasn't seen them yet. He's so busy at the office. Check out these contact sheets. If you like any, I'll print them for your apartment."

"Wow, okay."

Jolie stacked the Walden Pond photos and tucked them away. If Will saw them, it would only put him in a bad mood.

Leah picked out two photos from their day in the Public Garden. "I like these. I'll buy the frames. Hey, can I ask you a favor?"

"Of course."

"My folks are coming to visit from New York next weekend to see the apartment. Sarah and I are all freaked out because we want to cook them dinner, but it would be a disaster if we did. Can you join us and help cook?"

"Sure, but why not just go to a restaurant? Your neighborhood is full of them."

Leah's brown eyes widened. "We can't. We want to show them we're independent and doing fine on our own, but we need your help. I have to warn you, they're very kosher."

"What's kosher?"

"You've never heard of kosher? There are Jewish laws on what can be eaten and how it's prepared."

"Laws?"

"They're more like customs. Don't worry, I'll fill you in. I have the kosher part down. I just don't know how to cook."

"Oh, okay," Jolie said.

They went to join the others. She'd be happy to help cook for Leah's parents. But what in the world were the kosher laws? Now she was freaked out. She'd have to get some tips from Daniel.

Sunday morning after Will went into the office, Jolie went out to the back porch to read. Daniel wandered out with a cup of coffee. He sat next to her and surveyed the stack of open books on the table. "What are you studying so intently?" He flipped through a book on Boston's history.

"I'm mapping out my route of historic places to visit and photograph. A walk through the American Revolution." She glanced at him. His curly hair was uncombed and his wire-rimmed granny glasses were smudged. "Geez, give me your glasses. How can you even see?"

He handed over his glasses. "Hey, we could do that with my class instead of the portraits."

"It would get them out of Roxbury," she said. "They can take the photos."

"They don't have cameras, but they all need extra credit to pass summer school. This would be a good assignment."

"I could ask the camera store if they could loan me a few used cameras for the day."

He shook his head. "Loan them to kids from Roxbury High? You're a dreamer."

"It's worth a try." She sipped her tea. "Hey, there's a free concert in the Cambridge Common today. Will and I are going. Do you want to join us?"

"I have to visit my folks today."

She hesitated. "Can you give me a Jewish lesson?"

"A what?"

"I agreed to help Leah cook for her parents next Sunday, and I don't want to blow it. She said they were very kosher whatever that is."

"Oy vey."

"Oy vey?"

"It's a saying in Yiddish. It means 'woe is me'."

Would she have to learn a language too? "I thought I would stick with Italian food, like lasagna. That should be safe."

He shook his head. "You can't mix milk and meat."

"There's no milk in my lasagna."

"Cheese."

"Oy vey," Jolie said.

Daniel laughed. "And no pork. Animal foods must be from mammals with split hooves that chew cud and fish must have fins and scales."

She looked at him incredulously.

"That's just the start. Kosher kitchens are very complicated. You have to use separate cookware and tableware for milk and meat dishes."

Did Leah and Sarah have two sets of cookware? "What about you? I've totally blown it cooking."

"I observe in varying degrees and certainly not the food rules. I love your cooking. I just don't eat pork."

What had she gotten herself into? But she couldn't back out on Leah now.

Daniel rose. "I'll borrow a kosher cookbook from my mom for you."

She smiled up at him appreciatively.

Jolie arrived at the office dressed for the concert in her new fawn-colored short suede skirt, wide leather belt, lavender silk blouse, and sandals. A leather craftsman on the avenue had made the skirt and belt for her and a black leather vest for Will.

Will smiled as she walked through the door with her camera slung over her shoulder. Will, Coulter, Adam, an older man, and some students sat in the living room on an assortment of chairs and couches amid ringing phones and hammering typewriters. All heads turned to see who had caught his attention. The conversation simmered as she leaned on the door frame and listened to Will talk about his article series on the My Lai massacre.

"That's old news," Coulter said.

"Old news? The real truth has yet to be told," Will said.

Jolie silently took her camera out of the case and snapped a photo of the group. Coulter's eyes narrowed at her. She sucked in her breath at the intensity of his dark eyes.

"Lieutenant Calley was already tried and charged," Coulter said, shifting in his chair.

"There are two stories. One is the massacre of five hundred unarmed Vietnamese civilians by U.S. troops, and the other is the cover up. We need the real story about what happened," Will said.

"I agree," said the older man. "There's an army investigation underway. We don't know what really happened over there other than it was horrific."

Will introduced the older man to her, Professor Barnes, the owner of the house. "It's nice to finally meet you," Jolie said. "Can I make you some tea?" She set her camera down.

"I'd love some," the professor said.

Coulter stood up and looked out the window to the street. The professor followed Jolie into the kitchen. Dirty mugs littered the counter and the sink. Jolie put on the kettle and began washing the dishes. "Black tea or jasmine?"

"Jasmine sounds delightful," he said.

She poured the tea and the fragrant scent of jasmine flowers filled the room. Will joined them in the kitchen, and he and the professor talked more about My Lai. Jolie opened and read a stack of mail, sorting it into piles.

"Here's a letter to you, Will," Jolie said. "It says you wouldn't include Black Power groups in the Socialist Movement if you knew what they were really saying about the Socialists. It's signed from 'a friend'."

Will took the letter from her and read it. "This is bogus. What do you make of this?" He handed the letter to the professor.

The professor studied it. "It seems that someone is trying to manufacture a divisive split between different factions of the movement. The Black Power groups most likely received a similar letter slandering the Socialist Movement."

"Who do you think is the 'someone'?" Will asked.

Jolie's eyes rested on Coulter still standing by the window. "The FBI?" She whispered.

"I wouldn't put it past them. Check with your Black Power connections and see if they got a similar letter," the professor said.

Jolie poured more tea. Their conversation turned to the growing strength of the Socialist Movement across the county. She got up and finished cleaning the kitchen and started to pick up the other rooms. She felt Will's eyes follow her as she talked with the students and then Adam.

"Jolie girl, we hardly see you anymore. If it weren't for these constant reminders, I'd think you were a figment of my imagination." Adam nodded toward her photos tacked up on the walls.

She started to smile when she noticed her camera. It was on the table where she'd left it, but it was out of the case with the film door open. "Who was using my camera?" She looked around. Adam and the others shrugged. "We wouldn't touch it."

"The film is ruined now." She advanced the roll and removed the film. All of the photos had been exposed. Who would do that? She glanced around the room again. Coulter was nowhere to be seen. When had he left? She retrieved a new film canister from her purse and reloaded the camera.

When the professor left Will strode through and announced, "We're closing her down this afternoon. The free concert rules."

On Monday after work, Jolie found Will on the back porch, sitting rigid his leather notebook open in his lap.

"You're home? What's the matter?"

"We printed a false story about Nixon's timing to withdraw from Vietnam."

"How could you?"

"Exactly. How could we? Marlena said she verified the facts. I asked her twice as the story seemed odd. She said it was from the *Village Voice* and you know...they're credible."

"What did she say?"

"It was a typo."

"A typo? What do you think?"

"I don't know, but I reassigned her duties to sorting mail. I'm printing a retraction. I've never had to print a retraction. Our credibility is sacred."

"I still get a bad vibe from her. I think she's trying to undermine the agency and the paper. Coulter too."

"Oh, she's all right. There's a lot of information coming through the office. I think she just screwed up, that's all."

Why was he defending her?

Will snapped his notebook shut. "Coulter is getting on my nerves, though."

Jolie flashed back to the dark look Coulter had given her after she snapped the photo. "I think Coulter was the one who exposed my film."

"Nah, it was probably some student checking out the camera and didn't know what they were doing. It's no big deal."

Her eyebrows arched. Two week's worth of carefully composed shots was 'no big deal'?

"I saw your prints from Walden Pond. Who are those people?"

She inhaled quickly. He had gone through her photos. Guilt filled her. The day at Walden Pond had been so idyllic. "Oh, they're... friends."

"What's with the cemetery?"

"We went to Author's Ridge."

"I thought you said you were going with work friends."

"One of them is a customer. They're students at Harvard and Radcliffe."

"That Harvard guy again?"

She nodded. Her chest tightened with guilt. He was jealous. "Let's go out there this summer and swim," she said, anxious to change the subject. "We'll invite Ginger and Sam, Daniel and Leah. We'll pack a picnic and swim all day."

He scanned her face for a long moment. "Sure, but not this week-end. I'm tied up at the office. People from D.C. are coming up and the professor's stopping by with an article."

Ginger stopped by that evening to see Sam. They all sat in the living room, watching the ten o'clock news. America was at war with itself. Police constantly clashed with anti-war protesters or were shooting it out with the Black Panthers. Campus bombings of ROTC buildings were rampant. Conspiracy trials were underway in major cities for various trumped-up charges. Hordes of demonstrators scuffled with police outside courthouses. Reality played out in a surreal theater, the streets.

"Look how plastic that news guy is in his polyester suit. Why aren't there any women news anchors?" Jolie asked.

"We'll fix that, won't we? Jolie and I joined the Women's Liberation Movement," Ginger said.

Will looked at Jolie and then Ginger and back to Jolie. "You what?"

"We joined the Women's Liberation Movement," Ginger repeated.

191

"What about the Socialist Party's Women's Caucus?" Will asked.

Jolie looked to Ginger for strength and then back to Will. "That's not going to get us anywhere anytime soon. There are too many women's groups around the country with no real focus. We're consolidating the effort," Jolie said.

"But we're fighting for equality of all classes," Will said.

"We are not 'classes'," Ginger said. "We are humankind."

"Women can't be free in an un-free society," Sam said. "Your liberation will come from the rest of us."

Jolie inched to the edge of the couch, her back straight. "We have the power behind us. We are the majority. We're not going to wait for your revolution."

"I can't believe this." Will shook his head.

"We need your help to get our message out about our platform and what we're doing around the country," Jolie said.

Will locked eyes with her. "You expect our support when you're undermining the power of the Movement?"

"Yes, we do." She sat tall and watched him. Breathe. Yes, his woman-child was standing up to him. She had joined a movement and hadn't talked to him about it. He thought she was vulnerable and naive. Her inner strength swelled. She saw in his eyes that it scared him.

28

The Three Jewels

The chrysanthemum flowers burst open under the boiling water, un-furling their petals like a kaleidoscope. Jolie took the pot of tea to the back porch along with her dog-eared copy of *The Wisdom of Buddha*. It was finally the weekend.

Will came out later and sat down next to her. "What are you reading?"

She held up her book. Will tilted his head back and rolled his eyes.

"I want to join the Buddhist Temple. It's right around the corner. I want more guidance on the eightfold path."

"I don't think so."

"What do you mean?"

"Don't waste your time on that stuff. You spend too much time in dreamland now with that little Buddha statue."

"Meditation helps me stay calm and centered. It's the heart of Buddhism. I want to get to the next level."

Will laughed. "What's that, enlightenment? There is no enlighten-ment in this life. Buddhism is like a cult. The more you give to them, the more they'll take from you."

Buddhism had expanded her view of life and there was so much more to learn. She gathered her inner strength. This was one thing he wouldn't control. "It's not a cult. It's been around for thousands of years. It teaches us to transform our suffering into mindfulness, compassion, peace, and liberation. It's teaching me how to be responsible for my life." There, she had said it.

"Well, I feel somewhat responsible for your life, and I don't want you getting sucked into some religion. It sounds like you're already half brainwashed."

She looked out over the field and retreated inward. He just didn't understand. She'd get him to read about it. Or maybe the professor had a positive opinion about it.

He rose and held her chin in his hand and kissed her. "I'm only trying to protect you, Little Wing. I'm off to the office. Are you coming by later?"

She nodded. If she had time she would, but her day was planned. Today she was going to buy him a guitar. She wanted to surprise him.

She waited for him to leave before going into their room to meditate. She lit a stick of patchouli incense and set it by the small Buddha. Sitting on her rug she meditated, breathing deeply to try and clear her mind. Will puzzled her. Didn't he feel the stress of leading their double life and feeling like they could never let their guard down? Their lives hung on a fine thread that could break at any time. Meditation kept her anchored and calmed her troubled emotions. Following her breath, her thoughts cleared. Sometime later, a siren from down the street roused her from the peaceful state.

She sat down at the small writing table and wrote a note to Nick. She wanted to mail the two photos.

Nick,

Work is a drag. I hope your internship is going well.

Here are two photos from our trip to the pond. Thanks for inviting me. I have taken lots more photos and some are on display in the Harvard Square camera shop.

I joined the Women's Liberation Movement last weekend. Sisters for Liberation! I'm going to see Gloria Steinem speak next week. Have you heard of her?

Write back.

Miss you,

Jolie

She slipped on a vintage silk top and blue jean bell bottoms, grabbed her camera and the envelope for Nick, and walked out into the glorious day.

In Central Square she mailed the letter. As she walked she unconsciously chanted, *The universe has a song, and the song is you.* It had come into her thoughts when she meditated earlier and now it was silently playing in her head. She smiled. It was a blissful summer morning and she was off to buy Will a guitar.

Up ahead a familiar figure walked toward her. She kept her gaze trained on him. Their gap closed. It was Coulter. A wave of panic spread over her. Even if he wasn't with the FBI he gave her the creeps. They both stopped on the sidewalk.

"Hey Jolie, are you headed to the office?"

"Probably later."

His beady eyes drank her in. "Where are you going?"

It wasn't any of his business. She searched for a polite response. "I'm just out and about."

"Do you want to do it?" Coulter asked.

Jolie looked at him quizzically. "Pardon?"

"Do you want to do it? My place is two blocks away."

"I don't want to do anything with you." She strode off, heat rising to her face.

"Hey, what about free love? Especially from you California girls."

Jolie looked back to make sure he wasn't following her and continued walking. She couldn't believe he'd propositioned her. At the office he had acted like a prude. It was just an act. What a jerk. Will would go crazy if he knew.

Her bliss was now shattered. She wanted to retreat from the world. She gripped her moonstone in the pouch. A torrent of angry responses she wished she'd said to Coulter flowed through her mind. She'd be ready for their next encounter.

She stopped abruptly. Her thoughts surprised her. They didn't reflect a Buddhist's virtuous mind. They were the opposite of right thinking and right speech. She silently chanted *the universe has a song, and the song is you* back into her consciousness.

She walked a few more blocks and stopped before the Central Sales Company. This was the place. Inside, the store was crammed with musical instruments. Several rows of guitars, mandolins, saxophones, and other shiny brass instruments hung from the ceiling.

An older man wearing thick black glasses greeted her. "Welcome. Have a look around. I'm Ed if you have any questions."

She eased slowly through the crowded store, looking at guitars. Strains of a classical guitar came from the back room. Her mood lifted.

Ed came over after she had walked around a few times. "What are you looking for?"

She should have brought Will, but she'd wanted to surprise him. "A used acoustic guitar. A good one."

"You've come to the right place. We price them fairly and we don't haggle. What you see is what you get."

Jolie looked at the rows of guitars gleaming under the lights, not knowing where to start. She'd had a guitar at home and had taken lessons. She could strum a few songs but she didn't know the first thing about picking one out for Will.

Ed looked at her. "How much do you want to spend?"

"I have one hundred and twenty dollars. It's a present for my boyfriend."

"Oh, you're in good shape. If it was me, I'd be looking at that Ibanez over there." He walked down an aisle, reached up, and took down a guitar made from dark wood. He handed it to her. She cradled it against her chest and strummed a few chords. It felt right and sounded good. The price: one hundred dollars.

"I'll take it. I need to buy a case, too."

"A case comes with it. I'll tell you what. If he doesn't like it, he can trade it in within the week."

She smiled at Ed, relieved Will could choose another if he wanted. He was very particular about some things. "Thank you."

She walked out with the guitar. Her bell bottom jeans swished against the black case. She couldn't wait to give it to him that night. He needed to play music and mellow out. At the house, she set the guitar by the stereo.

She had the house to herself. She settled in with *The Wisdom of Buddha,* but her concentration waivered. Her conversation with Will earlier that morning was unsettling. Buddhism was not a cult. It was an individual practice, unique to each person. A path to free oneself from suffering. Didn't he want her to find peace?

She inhaled deeply, and as she exhaled a feeling of boldness welled up inside of her. Nobody would own her. Nobody would control her or her spirituality. She set the book down and left the house.

The sun blazed overhead in the humid afternoon. After five blocks she turned into an open wooden gate and onto a stone path. In that instant she entered another world. Irish moss cushioned the ground between large stepping stones. Street sounds faded into the gentle rush of falling water. Koi darted between lotus pads in a pond and disappeared under a small waterfall. She was drawn to the stone benches on either side of the pond but continued on the path and stopped before a massive wooden door. She pushed the heavy door open and walked inside.

It took a moment for her eyes to adjust to the muted light inside the high-ceilinged entry. Sandalwood incense filled the air.

A man with a shaved head wearing a saffron-colored robe approached her. His light brown skin shone against the silk robe. "Welcome to our temple." Peacefulness radiated from him and something more, an aura of rarified energy. She felt instantly calm and safe in his presence.

He oriented her to the temple and showed her the meditation rooms and library. In the cool wooden sanctuary, life outside disappeared and a peaceful protection descended, a refuge from the city.

"At our temple, it is not so much about teaching but about experiencing," he told her. His lilting voice and accent was mesmerizing. "Through meditation, we naturally progress beyond. We have faith in the Three Jewels—Buddha, Dharma, and Sangha."

Jolie smiled at him, not knowing what to say.

"We invite you to continue your journey with us. Join us in meditation. Learn and practice the eightfold path and you will be liberated."

"Thank you. But how do I start?"

"My child, you have already started. You are here, aren't you?" She held his gray-blue gaze. He seemed to be searching her eyes for something. "You are welcome here any time."

He handed her a schedule of meditation and yoga sessions, and she walked out of the temple infused by a sense of calm. Her body seemed to float. She'd read about the Three Jewels. The name alone created beautiful colors in her mind. She was one step closer to liberation. Will didn't need to know about the temple just yet. An increasing sense of freedom filled her.

⌒◞

"The professor came by the office and brought a Vietnam vet," Will said that night. "I put him to work right away. He's quiet but has been around and wants to help."

"Hmm," she said. Her thoughts were on the temple and when she could go back. She needed to pay attention.

"The professor wrote an article on the My Lai investigation. I don't know where he's getting his information but it's good stuff."

"Maybe from the vet?"

"He was in a different command. He was there around the same time, though."

"Invite him over sometime," Jolie said. She wanted to know more about what it was like in Vietnam.

"Adam's running the article this week under a pseudonym. I'm sending it out to all the other presses for publication."

Jolie could hardly contain herself with the surprise for Will. After dinner, he went in to the living room to put on an album. She followed him. He stood eyeing the guitar case.

"Whose guitar is this?"

"It's yours."

"Mine?"

"I bought it for you today." She sat on the couch, gripping her hands together. What if he didn't like it?

"You what? What about the money for a VW bus?"

"I still have five hundred dollars saved in my tin. Let's start looking for one."

She had more saved in the bank. Most of Will's money went directly back into the agency. He didn't believe in banks, but she worried about getting robbed. She'd vowed to herself months ago that they would always have a cushion. It gave her peace of mind, knowing that they wouldn't be on the street if they had to leave quickly again. His hand rested on the case.

"Go ahead. Open it up."

Will laid the case on the floor and snapped open the lid. The guitar glistened. He took it out of the case, turned it over and over, and then strummed a few chords.

"It's so fine, thank you." He bent to kiss her. "An Ibanez, what a beauty."

He sat down next to her on the couch and played one of the songs he had written. His fingers moved smoothly across the frets and his voice was a mere whisper. Jolie put her head back and closed her eyes. Melancholy fell over her like rain. She should be happy, shouldn't she?

29

The Door Gunner

Sunday, Jolie woke to guitar strains coming from the far end of the house. She wandered into the living room. Will smiled at her, relaxed and happy, his hair tousled from sleep. His hands moved quickly across the strings and a riff burst forth. "I love this guitar."

She smiled back. This was the Will she'd fallen for. Not the moody Will who didn't approve of her friends or anything she did or read. Her guitar man was back.

"Leah is picking me up later. We're shopping for groceries for the dinner with her parents tonight."

Will shook his head and kept playing. He thought Leah was a spoiled rich princess. On the dining room table, Jolie laid out six of the photos she had printed. Will stopped playing and stood beside her.

She adjusted two photos. "These are for the paper." One was a Vietnam veteran in his army uniform holding a sign: End Mass Murder in Vietnam. The other was a student with short hair wearing a Harvard shirt. His sign referred to the ROTC: Get the War Machine Off Campus.

"Yeah, we can use these two," Will said. "The vet photo can run with the My Lai story."

Two of the other photos were from the concert in Cambridge Common. The first was a close-up of Will smiling back at the camera with a bandana around his forehead. His sunglasses reflected Jolie taking his picture. The other was a couple dancing, their arms flung in the air, frozen. The fringe and feathers that adorned them were captured in fine detail.

"I like the one of you." She rose up on her toes and kissed him.

The other photos were taken around Cambridge. One, taken from a bridge over the Charles River, as a sculling boat approached. In unison, eight men dipped long oars into the water; the resulting pattern rippled behind.

Jolie pointed to another print capturing the fine detail of Georgian architecture. "This is Longfellow's House. Before Longfellow, George Washington lived there and used it for his headquarters while he planned the Siege of Boston."

"The Siege of Boston," Will repeated, a faraway look in his eye. "The Siege of America, that's what we're planning."

Leah's white Chevy Nova idled in front of Jolie's apartment. She honked twice. Jolie dashed down with the cookbook Daniel had borrowed from his mother and two photos she'd printed for her. Sarah was at the apartment when they arrived with the ingredients for chicken Creole, purchased from the kosher grocery store. Jolie propped up the cookbook and showed them the recipe. Her hunch had been right. Leah did have two sets of cooking utensils and dishware, compliments of her mom. Before long, the Creole was simmering in the pot. All they needed to do was make the rice. Leah and Sarah had set the dining room table. A vase of white lilies adorned the center. White linen napkins floated like swans on the plates.

Jolie brought out the two photos from the Public Garden she'd printed for Leah.

"Oh, these are perfect. Let's go buy frames and hang them up."

"We can't leave the Creole cooking," Jolie said.

"I'll stay," Sarah said.

"You have to stir it every five minutes or it'll burn," Jolie said.

Jolie and Leah walked three blocks to the neighborhood variety store and picked out two black frames. Walking back to the apartment, they passed a vintage clothing store.

"Let's go in," Jolie said.

"Used clothing?"

"It's vintage. Every item is unique."

Leah followed her inside reluctantly. The scent of rose buds engulfed them. Racks overflowed with one-of-a-kind clothing in silk, velvet, and lace. Jolie held out a sheer silk blouse.

"You'd look good in this. Try it on."

"You can see right through it," Leah said.

Jolie moved to another rack and picked out a camisole. "Wear this under it."

Leah tried it on. The butterfly-thin layers of silk clung to her body. "I love it," she said.

Jolie picked up a black beret and tried it on. "That's you," Leah said.

Leah bought the silk blouse and camisole, and Jolie the beret and a black velvet jacket.

Jolie wore the beret as they walked down the street to the apartment. They smiled at each other. "My first score in a vintage clothing shop," Leah said. Jolie did a ballet leap high in the air, euphoric with their finds.

From the first floor hallway they could smell the Creole. "That smells incredible," Leah said.

Sarah was in the kitchen, standing up reading a book at her stirring post. Leah and Jolie unwrapped their purchases.

"I've never been in a vintage clothing store before," Sarah said, "but that stuff is cool."

When Leah's parents arrived, Leah wore her new silk blouse and Jolie her black velvet jacket.

"Where in the world did you get that blouse?" her mother asked. "It looks like something my mother would have worn in the roaring twenties."

Leah and Jolie exchanged smiles. Jolie stayed in the kitchen while Leah and Sarah gave the parents the tour of the apartment. When they returned to the kitchen, Leah's mother marched to the stove. "What are you girls cooking?" She inspected the simmering pot and cookbook, all the time muttering something.

When they sat down to eat, Leah's mother raved about the flavors of the Creole.

"Jolie picked out the recipe," Leah said.

Leah's mother looked at Jolie. "You'll have to share it."

"I'll copy it for you after dinner," Jolie said.

Leah's mother's eyes still rested on her. Was something wrong? She sat up straighter.

"Jolie," Leah's mother said, "how old are you?"

Jolie swallowed. "Eighteen."

"You look so young, much younger than eighteen."

Jolie froze and squeezed her legs together under the table to keep them from jiggling. She didn't know how to respond.

"Where are you from?" Leah's father asked.

"California."

"California! That's where all the flower children are," Leah's mother said.

"You're a long way from home," Leah's father said. "Why are you in Boston? Are you going to school?"

"Not this year. I'm saving money for school, though." She squirmed in her chair.

"What about your parents?" he said.

"Oh, they still live there."

"No, I mean, can't they help you with college?" he said.

"Not right now," Jolie said. She glanced at Leah. Why hadn't she helped cook and gone home before they arrived?

"You're so young to be in this big city, so far from home," Leah's mother said.

"Mom, let her eat. Tell me what my big brother is up to."

203

Relieved to be out of the line of questioning, she listened to their conversation about people she didn't know, hoping they wouldn't ask any more questions.

Leah's mother turned to Jolie. "Leah and Sarah are coming home for the Fourth of July. Why don't you drive down with them?"

"That's a great idea," Leah said. "I bet there are tons of vintage stores in SoHo."

"We'd love to have you as our guest. You're a very nice young lady," her father said.

"Yes, you have to come," Sarah said.

New York. She could call her parents. She could mail a letter from there. "Well, okay. I'd like that."

"Then it's settled," Leah's mother said.

After Leah's parents went back to their hotel, Leah drove Jolie back to the office. "Thanks for everything. I think they'll be more comfortable with me on my own now."

"They're both really nice," Jolie said, thinking about her own parents.

"We'll have fun in New York and you'll get to meet my brother."

"Let me run it by Will."

"You have to come. You can't change your mind with my mother or I'll never hear the end of it. She loves guests. She's probably already planning it right now. My poor dad."

Jolie hopped out of the car and lithely sprang up the steps to the office. The evening had been a success. She'd helped her friends and best of all she had a plan to contact her parents.

Inside the office, it was dark except for a candle flickering in the living room. She walked toward it. Will and Marlena sat on the couch.

"Jolie." Will said, rising.

Jolie froze. A jealous demon pulsed from the pit of her stomach to the top of her head. She couldn't speak.

Marlena got up. "I have to go."

"Wait, we'll walk you to the T," Will said.

"No, that's not necessary." She walked out of the house without so much as a glance at Jolie.

"How was the dinner?"

"Fine." That was all she could manage to whisper. She turned and walked toward the door.

"Wait." Will blew out the candle and followed her out, locking the door. "What's the matter?"

Jolie was silent and kept walking.

"We were just talking. She was lonely and wanted to talk."

She was too emotional to respond. She was lonely too but whenever she talked about her feelings he half listened or changed the subject. Could she trust him when she went to New York?

Monday morning, after Will left for the office, Jolie headed to the temple. She entered the temple gate and the sound of the waterfall enveloped her in an aura of calm. Inside the massive carved door, she left her sandals next to a half dozen other pairs. Sandalwood incense hung in the air. She walked through the long corridor and entered a meditation room. A monk sat cross-legged with other students. She sat on a mat and he began to speak.

"You must become aware of the first four noble truths on your journey to nirvana. The first noble truth is that man's existence is full of misery."

She listened intently. No one's life was perfect, but was everyone as miserable as she was?

"Misery originates from within. That is the second noble truth. Your cravings or your choices lead to your suffering."

Was she responsible for her misery? How could that be? She wanted happiness. She sought out happiness.

"The third noble truth is that misery can be eliminated."

Jolie glanced around at the other students, serene in their cross-legged posture. She shifted her pose and relaxed. She had created her own misery, and it could be eliminated. But how?

"The fourth noble truth leads us to recognize there is a noble path from misery to well-being. When we practice mindful living, our right view will blossom and all other elements of the path will flower. The eightfold path is indivisible and all one. Starting with the four noble truths, we practice turning the wheel through each one."

They chanted three oms and breathed into meditation. Jolie's mind reeled with the flowering paths and the wheel.

Will was home when she came in from work. He tried to hug her, but she stiffened.

"Jolie, I'm sorry. I didn't realize how jealous you are of Marlena. I love you and wouldn't hurt you like that."

"I think she's bad news."

"Here, I got you something," Will handed her a package wrapped in the Sunday comics.

Jolie slowly unwrapped the package. It was a hardcover book titled *Alfred Stieglitz Photographer.* "Thank you."

Did he really think a book would make her feel better? She set the book on the table and flipped through the pages. She was instantly drawn to his work. His photographs were art.

On Wednesday, Jolie went straight home from work and didn't bother stopping at the office. She was tired. Tired of waitressing. Some of the people that came in were interesting and her tips were good, but it wasn't meaningful. What she wanted was an education.

She showered and sat cross-legged on the Persian rug in their bedroom. Meditation would brighten her mood. She lit sandalwood incense and set it on the small Buddha altar.

Her thoughts went straight to California and her parents. Were they thinking about her too, right then? She focused on her breathing. Coulter's face flashed before her. Should she tell Will about Coulter? She tried to erase her thoughts. She envisioned the temple, the hushed meditation rooms and the monk who had shown her the library full of translations of Buddha's teachings. She lapsed into peaceful breathing. Voices from the kitchen brought her back to reality.

Will and a young man sat at the kitchen table, drinking a beer. He introduced her to Charlie, the Vietnam vet. Their eyes locked, and she smiled in recognition. It was the guy with the dimples and haunted eyes she had photographed. Up close his face was handsome and his eyes the color of robins' eggs. His body was trim and muscular. He still looked too young to have been in the war.

"You?" Charlie said. His dimples widened in his smile. "You live here?"

She nodded, staring into his blue eyes. What was it about his eyes? Pain? Loneliness? They seemed burdened.

"You've met before?" Will looked from one to the other.

Jolie nodded. "I took his picture a few weeks ago at a demonstration."

Will asked Charlie about his plans.

"Well, I've been back from Nam for two months. I visited my family for a few weeks, and now I'm here applying to colleges." He paused. "I'm not sure what to do, really, but I need a job this summer."

"Where is your family?" Jolie asked. Will shot her a look. She wasn't supposed to talk about family.

"North Carolina."

"I could use you at Central Underground," Will said. "You can be in charge of the war related articles. I can pay you a small salary. The demand from our subscribers for articles has skyrocketed. I can't keep up."

"That would be good. I like what you're doing," Charlie said.

"Coast to coast, there are about 125 weeklies that all need news," Will said. "Combined, they have over a million paid subscribers and that doesn't count the local distributers."

Charlie let out a low whistle.

"Yeah, we are making some noise." Will turned to Jolie, "What's for dinner, Little Wing?"

"Hmm, I hadn't planned much." Her mood was so low when she'd come home she had forgotten about dinner. "How about grilled cheese sandwiches and tomato soup?"

"Okay with you Charlie?" Will said.

"Sounds like comfort food." Charlie's eyes met hers again. She smiled, hearing the faintest hint of a southern drawl.

Jolie got out tomatoes and began combining ingredients in a pot for the soup. Will went into the living room to change the album. Richie Havens' "Motherless Child" poured out of the stereo. Will turned it up and played along with his guitar.

Charlie stayed seated in the kitchen. "I thought about you. I didn't think I'd ever see you again, and now I'm here in your house."

"You thought about me?"

"Yes. Most people give me the cold shoulder when I'm in my uniform but not you. I had a strange feeling as you walked away. Like you hold the key to something. Something I need. Then you were gone, down the street."

She didn't hold the key to anything. She was just a girl. She was searching for her own peace. It was out there somewhere, she just hadn't found it yet.

She stirred the soup. "What was Vietnam like?"

"I don't like to think about it. It's hard to describe. It was atrocious. Yeah, I think that sums it up. Atrocious."

"Were you drafted?"

"Yes. I went through boot camp and was shipped to Hawaii for training and then boom, we were dropped into the jungle of Vietnam. I was scared shitless."

"I hope my brothers don't get drafted."

"I hope they don't either. It's a crappy war."

"What did you do there?" She wasn't sure she should have asked and was relieved when he began to talk. Maybe the comfort of the kitchen, the music coming from the other room, and the fact that she had brothers put him at ease. She sat down across from him and sipped her tea.

"I was a door gunner on a helicopter."

"A door gunner?"

"Yes, a gunner."

Charlie proceeded to tell her about the gunner's job: standing out on the helicopter skid, in a harness with the door open, machine gun in hand, providing reconnaissance for the infantry on the ground. She sat speechless.

"The ship would dip and dive around the tree lines and villages. We were looking for Viet Cong soldiers. Our mission was to draw their fire, and then we'd engage them."

"You mean, you wanted them to shoot at you?" Her eyebrows arched in horror.

"Yes, we had to draw them out, then we'd shoot back and protect our men on the ground. Our guys went door to door in the villages, looking for Viet Cong soldiers. When the battle was over we'd swoop in and pick them up and fly back to the base."

Jolie tried to envision this baby-faced twenty-something-year-old, standing out on the skid with a machine gun, killing men.

"Weren't you afraid, standing out there?"

"Yes, you're so vulnerable in that position. But sometimes, flying high over the jungle with the cool breeze flowing over your face, it was beautiful. Then you'd see a line of Viet Cong soldiers on a trail in the jungle and the adrenaline just takes over." Immediately his expression turned anguished.

Jolie sat there looking at Charlie. "You're so lucky to be back safe."

"They wanted me to sign up for two more years, but no way. It's no place for me. It's no place for anybody."

They sat in silence for a long moment. She had wanted to know about Vietnam and now she felt sick.

"Hey, do you want another beer?" Jolie asked.

"Yes, please."

She liked him. He was polite. The front door opened, and Daniel came in, frazzled, holding a folder of papers in his hand. Jolie introduced him to Charlie.

"Smells good," Daniel said.

"Do you have to grade all those papers tonight?" Jolie asked.

"Yep."

"I'll help you later," Jolie said.

"That would be great."

Will came in and helped Jolie make the grilled cheese sandwiches. That was one thing he could cook. They sat in the dining room, eating and talking.

"Did you take any pictures in Vietnam?" Jolie asked.

"I did...but...I don't want to look at them any time soon."

"Sorry, Jolie is curious about everything. She wants to understand the universe and everything in it," Will said.

She frowned. Why did he treat her like a child? She wanted to learn more about the war. She wanted to see a real soldier's photos not what they broadcast on the news.

"No harm in that," Charlie said, looking at Jolie. "I'll bring them over sometime."

Their eyes met. Those pained eyes didn't match his baby face and soft-spoken demeanor. He did need something, but what?

30

Pussy Power

Ginger's horn honked twice and Jolie sprang down the stairs to the waiting car. They were going to hear Gloria Steinem speak at Boston Common, but first they were stopping at Leah's.

"I can't wait to hear Gloria speak," Jolie said. "Let's write an article about it and I'll get Adam to print it."

Ginger smiled at her enthusiasm. They parked and walked up the steps. Leah and Sarah were in the kitchen, eating bagels and cream cheese and something pink.

"Help yourselves," Sarah said, pointing to the bagels.

"I love lox and bagels," Ginger said.

"What's a lox?" Jolie asked.

"Cured salmon, try it," Leah said.

Jolie followed their instructions and assembled a poppy seed bagel with cream cheese and lox and took a bite.

"Umm," Jolie said, enjoying the smoky salmon flavor entwined with the soft cream cheese and warm bagel. "Why don't they have these at Brigham's?"

"We'll eat these everyday when we go to my parents in New York," Leah said.

"You're going to New York?" Ginger said, looking at Jolie.

"For the Fourth of July."

"Will's okay with you being gone that weekend?" Ginger asked.

"He doesn't know yet. He shouldn't mind though," Jolie said.

"I don't know…he keeps you on a pretty tight leash."

Did he keep a tight leash on her? Weren't guys supposed to protect their woman? "I feel pretty free."

〜♋

A huge crowd had attended the Gloria Steinem event and her speech was eloquent. She warned there could be no simple reform. It would have to be a revolution.

Jolie and Ginger had written an article about the event and it was set to run in the press with two of Jolie's photos. One photo showed the sea of women in the background and was focused on a woman holding a sign: Rise Above Oppression. The other photo was of Elaine Wood and Gloria Steinem on the bandstand. The headline: WOMEN UNITE FOR LIBERATION.

Jolie dropped by the office on her way home from work. She was tired from serving customers all day but their story and her photos would be in the new *Central Underground Press* issue. She smiled inwardly. This was their revolution, for women and by women.

Will, Adam, Coulter, and Charlie were in the living room, discussing how to expand the paper's readership. The teletype machine Will recently installed clattered incessantly with stories coming in from around the world.

"We'll include not only politics in the press but poetry and cartoons," Adam said.

She listened for a while, not wanting to interrupt but dying to see a copy. Where were they?

"It should only include politics," Coulter said.

As usual he continued to clash with the others. Why did Will keep him around? She tried to ignore him but he was a fixture there now.

"With more content, the papers will appeal to a wider audience," Will said. "Our political message will reach far more people."

She glanced around and saw a stack of freshly printed papers by the door. She sailed over and picked one up. Will looked her way and the conversation died. All eyes were on her. The photographs of the event and the article were on the front page. They'd made the front page. The headline jumped out at her. She stared at it and looked at Will and the others. Adam was smiling. She stood rigid, anger exploding in her head.

"We put it on the front page for you, Jolie girl," Adam said. "It's a good article."

She looked back to the headline: PUSSY POWER.

"Who changed the title?"

"Marlena," Adam said.

"Marlena? This wasn't Marlena's story to change."

"It'll sell more papers," Adam said.

"Pussy Power? You guys don't get it, do you?"

"She thought it was catchy," Coulter said.

Jolie's head jerked to look at him. "Fuck you, asshole." She stared at the cover and back to the group.

The men glanced at each other.

"I told you she'd be pissed," Charlie said softly.

"I didn't know she had it in her," Adam said. "She's always so sweet." Coulter was silent.

She stormed out the door, taking the paper with her. Will caught up with her on the sidewalk. "Marlena's got to go," she said.

"We can change it before we send it to the agency subscribers."

"She's undermining the paper and maybe even us."

Will clasped her shoulder with his left hand. "No. No one can undermine us. You've got to believe that. You and I have to stick together. She was just trying to sensationalize the headline. Come back in. I only have another hour of work to finish."

She glanced back at the house. Coulter stood watching them from the window.

"No, I'll see you at home," she said.

She walked back to the house, humiliated. Did they really think that headline was acceptable? She was even more determined to support the Women's Liberation Movement. They'd start their own damn paper. She'd talk to Ginger. And what would Elaine think? The paper had already been distributed in Cambridge and Boston. A sinking feeling overcame her.

At the house she was greeted by Daniel who sat at the dining room table, grading papers. She unfolded the paper on the table in front of him.

He scanned the front page. "That's kind of rude. The photos are good though." He looked up at her.

She was unable to speak, tears welled in her eyes.

"There's a letter for you on the kitchen table."

Jolie left the paper where it lay and went to get the letter. She never got letters. She took it into the bedroom, sat on the bed, and opened it slowly. It was from Nick. Inside was a card with an Andy Warhol painting. It was from his tomato soup can series. She smiled, remembering their lighthearted debate at Brigham's on whether Warhol's paintings were art or a gimmick. She had considered them commercial illustrations but Nick thought they were clever. Inside the card was a letter. She unfolded the yellow legal size paper and read:

Dear Jolie,

Thanks for the photos. I'm happy to hear you're showing your photographs at the camera store.

My internship isn't too exciting. I'm researching court cases and delivering documents all over the city on my bike in the sweltering heat.

I'm looking at the photo of you by Emerson's gravestone. There is something very different about you from the other girls I meet. Maybe it's your innocence and quest for knowledge or the way you stay true to yourself. Anyway, don't ever change.

See you in September!
Nick

Next to his name he had drawn a peace sign and a little cartoon man trucking along. She smiled again. She put the letter in the card and tucked it in her drawer. She lay back on the bed and closed her eyes, thinking of the day at Walden Pond. She felt so tired. In the morning she would go to the temple. It always revived her spirit.

She woke a little while later. The room was dark. She must have dozed off. She heard Will's guitar coming from the living room and went out to join him. Daniel was watching the news.

Will glanced up at her as she came in. "I thought I'd let you sleep."

"Listen to this," Daniel said, looking at the TV.

Will stopped playing and Jolie eased onto the couch next to him. Massachusetts Senator Ted Kennedy was about to be interviewed. The news announcer proclaimed the House of Representatives had approved the Senate's proposed amendment to the U.S. Constitution to extend the right to vote to citizens eighteen years of age or older.

"Those who are old enough to fight are old enough to vote," the Senator said. He stated America's ten million young people between eighteen and twenty-one were fully capable of the privilege. The bill had been sent to President Nixon for his signature.

Will raised his fist. "Right on."

Jolie and Daniel did the same, their mood jubilant.

Daniel turned to Jolie. "You can vote now."

Could she? But that wouldn't be right. She wasn't really of age.

She looked from one to the other. "Just think. Ten million more voters. There's a revolution right there." And half of them were women.

Jolie hadn't yet told Will about the trip to New York in two weeks. It was Friday and she planned to cook a good dinner and bring it up. Jolie walked into the house after work with two sacks of groceries. George Harrison's new album *All Things Must Pass* moaned from the stereo. That meant Daniel was home. She put the groceries down and joined Daniel, Sam, and Ginger in the living room.

Ginger thrust her hands on her hips and tried to hide her smile. "'Pussy Power?'"

"We need our own paper," Jolie said.

"Oh come on, it was cute," Sam said.

"Our movement has been reduced to *cute*? You'll see," Ginger said.

"I got stuff for dinner. Can you stay?"

215

"I'd love to. I haven't had a good dinner since the last time I was here," Ginger said.

"Count me in," Sam said. "I'll do the dishes. How's that for equality?"

Jolie rolled her eyes and went to shower off the restaurant smell. When she came back into the kitchen she found a full house. Will, Daniel, Adam, and Charlie stood in the kitchen, talking with Sam and Ginger about an incident that happened the day before.

"One of the *Central Underground* paper hawkers was arrested for loitering and selling the papers without a permit," Will said, filling her in. "They held him overnight in jail."

"I found out this morning and went down and demanded his release," Adam said. "I told Boston's finest that permits are not required to sell papers."

"That's harassment, plain and simple," Daniel said.

All heads turned to Daniel. He never said much in this group, always overpowered by more dominant personalities.

"It'll backfire on them. We'll put it on the front page," Will said.

Jolie started cooking. Good thing she'd shopped for food. She needed to talk to Will. They shouldn't taunt the police. What if it backfired on Will and he landed in jail? She looked up to find Charlie's gaze on her. They shared a smile. He was a gentle spirit despite his Vietnam stint.

Ginger offered to make the salad. "I'm working on a satirical Pussy Power cartoon to run in the next issue. So far I have a lion as the pussycat."

"How about a lion, a tiger, and a black panther? Sisters for Liberation!" Jolie said.

They laughed. Will came up behind them and put his arm around both of their shoulders. "What are you two conspiring about?"

"Pussy Power, the revenge," Jolie said.

"Remember, I didn't have anything to do with it."

Jolie glanced back at him. But he hadn't stopped Marlena, had he?

The group moved into the living room. Charlie stayed in the kitchen with Jolie.

"I got into Boston University," he said.

"What are you going to study?"

"Psychology."

Jolie told him about the commune in Eugene with all of the psychology graduates, their endless conversations on the psyche and the intimidating two-day encounter session.

"Sounds crazy."

"I sometimes wonder how they're all doing."

She wished she could write to Deidre. She thought of all the people they had deceived and all of the people they continued to deceive. She'd lied about her age, running away and her last name. Her name never sounded right when she said it. The lies hung like a cloud over her.

"Don't you stay in touch with them?"

"I never really felt like I was part of it. The big experiment." She wanted to be honest with Charlie and tell him everything. He made her feel protected and was never judgmental. But she couldn't tell anyone the truth.

He sat silently at the kitchen table, gazing into space. "You okay?" she asked.

"I don't know. I think about my Nam buddies constantly. Each and everyone was a friend. Sometimes when I close my eyes, I'm back there, standing on the skid, high above the jungle, the cool breeze whipping through me and I just want to go back."

"You really think that? That you want to go back?"

"It feels like a part of me is still there. It's hard to get adjusted here."

She walked over to him, leaned down and gave him a hug. "No, you're staying here, Charlie. You're not going back there. We're your friends now."

Over dinner the conversation flowed, first about music and then to the upcoming draft lottery. The lottery would determine which men born in 1951 would be called for military duty. Jolie thought of her older brother. He had been born in 1951.

"In the past six months only half the inductees have shown up at the induction centers," Will said. "And of those that do show up, over ten percent refuse to go."

"What happens if you refuse? Do they arrest you? Isn't it better to just not show up?" Jolie asked.

"There's a lot of confusion and misinformation," Sam said.

"We should start a Question and Answer column in the paper," Adam said.

"You have your first question," Ginger said.

"It would add work," Adam said.

"It might be worth it to set any misinformation straight," Will said.

Jolie raised her glass. "We can call it 'Letters to the Underground'."

"We can get some Harvard law students to do research for us," Charlie said.

Will cocked his head and looked at Jolie. "Jolie has a law student friend at Harvard, don't you?"

She was caught off guard by his tone. The others looked at Will and then to Jolie.

"Yes, I do," she said, meeting Will's gaze and then looking around at the others. "His name is Nick." Why was he uneasy about her friends and her outside interests? How could they possibly threaten him? She caught Charlie's eye and he grimaced.

"So it's agreed," Adam said and raised his glass "'Letters to the Underground' is officially launched."

After the toast, Ginger turned to Jolie. "What do you plan to do in New York?"

Will gazed at Ginger quizzically, "New York? We're not going to New York."

Jolie rushed in. "Leah and Sarah are driving down over the Fourth of July weekend. Leah's Mom invited me to stay with them. They all want me to go."

"This is the first I've heard of it."

"Let's talk about it later," Jolie said, glancing around the room. Ginger mouthed "*sorry*".

Later in their room, Will was somber. "Why didn't you tell me about the trip to New York?"

"You've been so busy. I really want to go."

"I don't know. I don't want you being away from me."

"It's only a weekend."

"What were you planning to do there?"

She frowned. A feeling that she was in trouble and talking to her father swept over her. His tone sounded like her father's when he didn't approve of something. She didn't like hearing it in Will's voice. "Go to art museums and vintage clothing stores and eat lots of home cooked food."

"What if something happens to you?"

"What could happen? We'll be at Leah's parents' house on our best behavior." She wasn't looking forward to going back to New York after their first experience, but the need to call home was overpowering.

"I thought you didn't like New York, or did your little friends change your mind?"

Little friends? "It will be different this time. I'll have a place to stay, good food to eat and money to spend."

"Let me think about it."

Ginger was right. He did have her on a tight leash. But she had to go. She'd been writing the letter home in her head for weeks. And she wanted to call and hear her parents' voices. New York was her opportunity.

31

I Got a Feeling

Jolie emerged from the busy restaurant when her shift ended and headed straight for the T. On the crowded sidewalk, someone tugged her right arm. She drew back violently.

"Hey," Will pulled her toward him. "It's me."

"What are you doing here?"

He let go of his grasp. "Taking you out to dinner."

"What's the occasion?" She rubbed her arm.

"You're always cooking for everyone."

"I like to cook."

"Yes, but not tonight."

They wandered around the Square, savoring the warm evening. Fragrant garlic and herb scents spilled out to the sidewalk. They followed the aroma to an Italian restaurant and were seated by the window. A candle flickered in a red glass holder on a green-and-white checkered table cloth. She smiled. The tablecloth and candle were similar to the ones her mother used when she cooked Italian food and they ate outside on the patio.

She glanced over the menu at Will. Taking her out to dinner? It wasn't like him. Despite the tightening in her stomach, her mouth watered at the profusion of choices. They ordered and ate warm bread from a basket.

"Let's talk about the trip to New York," Will said.

Her body was taut on the chair. She had to contact her family.

He studied her. "You can go...but I have an errand for you."

"An errand?"

"I have a letter for you to deliver to Leon. You met him at the house a while ago. We know our phones are tapped so I can't call and I don't trust the mail."

"Leon? I'm not sure I remember what he looks like."

"He's tall with brown hair."

"That sounds like half of New York."

"Don't worry, he'll remember you." Will smiled.

He reached for her hand and walked her through the instructions. She was to call Leon and set up a meeting place near Leah's house and hand him the envelope. She was to go alone. Leon would be expecting her call.

Relief poured out of her. She was going to New York. Goose bumps spread up her arms as she envisioned the call home. And she'd be helping Will too.

Their salads arrived and Will said nothing more about the trip. He changed the subject and proceeded to tell her that when he went into the office that morning, there was no dial tone on either phone. The phone service had been shut off.

"Did you pay the phone bill?"

"Of course, those are our life lines. I called the phone company from a pay phone and they said service would be restored in a few days." He paused and leaned in closer. "I think someone is messing with us."

She glanced around the restaurant. "Like the FBI?"

Will nodded. "The phone company was very vague about why we were shut off and how soon service would be restored. They seemed confused about the whole thing."

"That's scary."

When they finished dinner, they walked hand in hand down the avenue toward Central Square. It was dark now, and the street lights cast a mellow glow on the sidewalk.

"I don't want to take the subway tonight," Will said. "Too many people underground." He put out his thumb to hitch a ride.

Apprehension filled her. She'd never hitchhiked in Cambridge before and certainly not at night. "The subway isn't crowded this late."

"I can't go down with the moles."

The moles? She did it every day. Twice a day sometimes.

A dark-colored, two-door Mustang pulled over. Will opened the passenger door and bent down. The driver was a stocky white man in his forties.

"Going near Central Square?" Will asked.

"Sure, hop in."

Will flipped the passenger seat forward to let Jolie into the back seat. She slid in. Will sat shotgun and made small talk with the man. They had absolutely nothing in common, but Will could talk with any-one. With only a slit for a window in the back seat, Jolie peered out the front. The driver's silhouette was lit from the dashboard. He wore a suit and his buzz cut looked military.

A few blocks later, the driver stopped at a red light and looked over his right shoulder at Jolie. "You're a buxom young thing. Do you swing?"

Alarmed, she sat up rigid. Swing? Did he say swing? "No."

The driver looked at Will. "How about you?"

"No."

The light turned green, and the man drove on. Jolie leaned for-ward in the dark, reached around Will's right side, and squeezed his shoulder.

"We'll get out here," Will said. "Thanks for the ride."

The man looked straight ahead as if in a trance and kept driving.

"Pull over, we'll get out here," Will said.

"No, I'll get you closer." The man continued to drive.

"Stop the car, we're getting out," Will demanded.

With a sudden turn, the man pulled over and double parked. The engine idled. Will got out and started to depress the latch to flip the seat forward for Jolie. The driver stepped on the gas. Tires screeched and the door closed with the abrupt surge. He drove off into the night.

Will's shouts grew faint as he sprinted behind the car. Frantic, Jolie struggled with the seat latch and screamed for the man to stop and let her out. His right hand flailed at her in the back seat. She cowered in the corner to avoid his blows.

"Shut up."

She continued to scream.

"Shut the fuck up."

Panic set in. She stopped screaming and looked out the front window. Trapped in the back seat, she had to get a grip and come up with a plan. Think, think, how could she get out of there? Where was he taking her? Her heartbeat hammered in her ears. The city no longer looked familiar. The horror of her situation numbed her thoughts.

A few miles later, he turned off the main street into a residential neighborhood. After three blocks he pulled into a driveway of a single family home. The car lights shone on a large two story brick house.

Did he live there? She stared straight ahead, terrified. Now what? He turned off the engine.

"Please let me go, just let me go now."

"Stop talking. If you so much as utter a sound, I swear I'll strangle you. Understand?" His entire persona had changed. His voice was low and deliberate, venomous. In the back seat, she nodded and clutched her purse. He got out, opened the passenger door, and pulled the seat forward. "Get out." He was like a demon in the darkness.

When she didn't move, he reached in, grabbed her arm, and yanked her. His strength propelled her out of the car and she stumbled against him. She cried out wincing at the pain that shot through her arm from his powerful grasp. Her leg scraped against the car frame. He shut the door and dragged her up the dark front porch steps. She frantically searched the neighborhood hoping to see someone who could help her. Not a soul was in sight.

In the dark, the man struggled with his keys in the first of three locks. Dread paralyzed her. Who had three locks? He briefly released his grasp on her arm, needing two hands to open the lock. When it clicked open, he grabbed her arm again and shoved her back against the house, facing him. She had missed her opportunity to escape.

He inserted the key into the second lock and once again released his grip to turn the lock. It was now or never. She swung her knee hard into his groin. It met its mark. He cried out and doubled over in pain as she dashed down the stairs. On the sidewalk, she sprinted in the direction of what she thought was the main street.

Adrenaline surged through her. He shouted something but she didn't dare look back or slow her pace. His shouts grew louder. She ran harder. Keep running, keep running, keep running.

She passed people on the sidewalk but did not slow down. Block after block she ran, faster and faster, her purse rhythmically hitting her hip. She no longer heard his shouts. Had he stopped? She quickly glanced back.

A few people were on the street, but no one was running after her. When she reached the main street she did not slow down. Two blocks later a T station sign beckoned from the corner. With an extra surge, she raced to it and ducked down the stairs into the subway station.

Stopping at the turnstile, she gasped for breath. She never liked it underground in the subway with the hordes of people, but now they would shield her. Her lungs burned from the exertion. She glanced anxiously at the steps, expecting to see the man at any moment. She scrambled for a token in her purse, inserted it and slid through the turnstile. She stood next to the tracks, blending in with the others. On the map, the big circle rested on North Quincy, the Red Line. Her eyes remained glued to the entrance, and her heart thudded in her chest. Time stood still until she finally heard the train approach.

At her stop, she emerged up the steps. She would not feel safe until she was home. Her instinct was to run the last three blocks to the house. Instead, she hurriedly walked home. Would Will be there? As she approached the house, she saw two figures on the steps. She slowed her pace.

One figure stood. "Jolie?" It was Daniel.

The other stood and ran to her. "Oh, thank God," Will said and hugged her to him.

She had never seen him so distraught.

Daniel spoke up. "Will didn't know what to do. He was paralyzed. I don't know why he wouldn't call the police right away. One more minute and I would have."

Her body began to tremble. "What would he have done to me?"

He held her tighter. "I don't want to think about it."

32

Fireworks

⌒◯

On Friday morning, Jolie paced back and forth on the back porch while Will slept. Her bag was packed for New York. The letter to her parents was tucked in the bottom, and the sealed envelope for Leon, along with his phone number, was in the side pocket. Feeling guilty about leaving Will for the weekend, she went into the kitchen and made a double batch of chocolate chip cookies. He could take some into the office for Charlie and Adam and the others.

Will came up behind her and put his arms around her. "I don't want anything to happen to you."

She inhaled and her body stiffened. "Don't worry. I'm not hitch-hiking. I'm never hitchhiking again."

The terror of that night played in her mind like a movie that wouldn't stop. She had wanted to find his house again and call the police. Daniel encouraged her to report it. He kept insisting that they had a description of the car, and she could probably locate the neighborhood again. But the police could unveil her secret, her true identity. It weighed heavily on her that the evil man was still out there and other girls could fall victim. The day before she had finally gotten up the nerve and used a pay phone in Harvard Square to call the police. She described the car, the man and his North Quincy neighborhood and the three locks on the door. The officer on the phone thanked her and encouraged her to come in to the station. In a panic she hung up.

"I don't want you to go." She felt his body shift behind her and he held her tighter.

She stared straight ahead and willed herself to be strong. "I'm going. Leah is picking me up at ten." He turned her around and looked into her eyes.

"Leah said we're going to the watch the fireworks tomorrow from a rooftop." She was looking forward to it. Anything to get her mind off the attempted kidnapping.

"Oh, so you're getting all patriotic now?" From his sly grin, she knew he was kidding.

Around ten, a horn honked out front. "They're here," she said.

Will held her by the shoulders facing him. "I'll miss you. Make sure you call Leon. The letter has to be delivered tomorrow."

She nodded and picked up her pack and camera. "Bye." She grabbed a bag of warm cookies and bounded down the stairs to the waiting car.

Jolie hopped into the back seat of the white Chevy Nova. She looked up at the house. Will's imposing figure stood in the living room window, watching them. She waved to him. Leah and Sarah waved, too. Will smiled and flashed the peace sign as they drove off.

"He's so handsome," Leah said.

"Is he a real revolutionary?" Sarah asked.

"I guess if the FBI thinks you're a revolutionary, maybe you are," Jolie said.

"The FBI?" Leah and Sarah said in unison.

"Just kidding," Jolie said.

Leah drove south on I-93. James Taylor crooned from the radio. Jolie sank back into the seat. They were going to New York.

"I can't wait to go to SoHo and check out the vintage clothing stores. You have me hooked now," Leah said.

"Me too. Look at this cool blouse I got at the vintage store by our house," Sarah said, tugging at the sleeve of her blouse.

Jolie peered over the seat at Sarah's silk blouse. Delicate beading adorned the scooped neckline. "Good find."

"My mother is so excited we're coming. She's making a ton of food. She said she wants to fatten you up."

Jolie sat back and listened to the music while Leah and Sarah talked. She was nervous about going back to New York, but knew she would be safe staying at Leah's parents. It was going to be a good weekend. If she could just get the image of that evil man out of her head.

Sarah passed back a *Vogue* magazine. Jolie flipped through the pages. "I can't believe they are trying to force us into the midi," Jolie said. "They're saying the mini was the sixties and the midi is the seventies."

"Nobody's listening," Leah said.

"They're hideous. Half way below your knees." Sarah said.

"Let's all get hot pants this weekend," Leah said.

"Your mother would never let you wear them," Sarah said.

"I'll wear them in Boston," Leah said.

They laughed and continued their banter about clothes. Four hours later, the New York skyline was visible. Leah drove through the congestion into Brooklyn and the Borough Park neighborhood. Jolie looked out the window, fascinated. Many of the men had long beards and wore small round caps. Others wore black jackets and black pants with white dress shirts and black fedoras. Some wore fur hats. Fur, in the summer? Jolie asked about the clothes.

"They're Orthodox Jews. They live strictly according to the Torah," Sarah said.

"You can tell which movement they follow by their hats. The little round caps are called yarmulkes," Leah said.

They passed a woman wearing a shawl over her head. "If you are an Orthodox married woman, you are not allowed to show your hair," Sarah said.

"What are your parents?" Jolie said.

"Both of our parents are modern, but kosher. You'll get to meet my parents tomorrow at the temple," Sarah said.

"The temple?" Jolie asked.

"The synagogue." Sarah looked at Leah. "You forgot to tell her we go to prayer on Saturday?"

Leah looked at Jolie in the rearview mirror and raised her eyebrows. "Sorry."

"I'm sort of a Buddhist," Jolie said.

"Sort of?" Leah said.

"Well, I adhere to the teachings but I do kill spiders when they come in the house. So technically I violate one of the teachings and probably won't obtain enlightenment."

Leah and Sarah looked at each other and burst out laughing.

"Being a Buddhist should get you off the hook for tomorrow," Leah said, pulling into the driveway of a large three-story house.

Sarah hopped out and grabbed her bags from the trunk and ran up the steps. "See you later."

Leah drove another block and pulled into a driveway with a similar style three-story house. She sounded the horn once. The front door opened, and Leah's mom beamed at them. They slung their packs, purses, and Leah's oversized laundry bag over their shoulders and followed Leah's mom into the house.

Dark antique furniture and thick Oriental rugs welcomed them. Jolie scanned the built-in bookcases laden with books. A massive fireplace with a carved wooden mantel anchored one wall. Black-and-white photographs covered the walls on either side. The people in the photos posed for the cameraman. The clothes, dark and thick, looked like scratchy wool. Were they relatives from Europe? What kind of camera did they have back then? The room was like a museum adorned with hand-painted ceramic vases and oil paintings.

Leah's mom led them into the kitchen. Two platters were piled high with small sandwich squares and bite-sized cakes. It was all for them. They washed up and sat down at the table. They were starving, and Leah's mom watched approvingly as they ate and talked about Boston until they couldn't eat another bite.

"Let's get you settled," Leah's mom said to Jolie. They picked up their bags, and Jolie followed them upstairs to the third floor where Leah and her brother's bedrooms and a guest room were located.

"This will be your room when you come to stay." Leah's mom led them into the guest room.

Her room? She was already being asked back? "Thank you," Jolie said. An antique four-poster bed with a white chenille bedspread awaited her. An armoire and matching dresser were set against a wall. Intricate lace doilies had been placed on the dresser. "It's beautiful." She put her bag down and followed Leah to her room. Leah's mom went back downstairs to start dinner.

A pink canopy bed and light pink walls gave the room a soft glow.

"My room at home is pink," Jolie said.

"I hate it."

"Me too. Why do they assume we like pink?"

A thundering noise approached from the stairs. A second later, a tall young man burst in. He moved toward Leah and without hesitation put his arms around her waist and whirled her around.

"You have no idea how much I've missed you," he said. He noticed Jolie and seemed startled.

"Missed you too. This is my friend, Jolie. Jolie this is my brother, Zack."

They surveyed each other in silence. His tall lean frame hovered above her. His square jaw and smile were framed by a halo of longish black curls, just like Leah's. She resisted the urge to touch them.

"It's good to meet you," he said.

A radiant smile spread across her face. "Nice to meet you too."

Leah and Zack launched into catch-up mode and quickly filled each other in on friends and events. Jolie liked it here, in this big welcoming house. Leah's mom stood at the door, smiling.

"My baby's home," she said. "Dinner is at six and your father will be home soon."

They all went to their rooms to clean up and change. Before Leah and Jolie went downstairs, they dabbed patchouli oil on their wrists and neck. Jolie followed Leah as she dashed down the stairs two at a time to greet her father.

"Welcome home, princess," he said, hugging Leah. He stood back and sniffed. "What is that musty smell?"

Leah's mother lit two candles on the dining room table and carried in the homemade challahs. The warm, yeasty-smelling bread was covered with an embroidered cloth.

They took their places at the dining room table. Leah's father stood over the bread and said a prayer in Hebrew. They toasted with glasses of wine and began to eat the braided challahs.

"This embroidery design is beautiful," Jolie said, admiring the cloth that had covered the bread.

"My grandmother made it," Leah said.

Leah's mom's eyes rested on Jolie. "It's a dying art. Where did you get your blouse?"

Jolie looked down at her handmade peasant blouse. An embroidered garland of intricate colorful flowers entwined the neckline. "I made it," Jolie said.

"It's beautiful work," Leah's mom said. She got up to bring the food to the table. "I'm not used to seeing embroidery on clothes."

Dinner conversation turned to Zack, a second year student at New York University.

"He's not home much," his father said.

Zack smiled. "I study a lot."

Leah's father turned to Jolie. "Are you joining us for prayer service tomorrow afternoon?"

Jolie could see Zack rolling his eyes next to his father as he lifted his glass of wine.

"Actually, I'm a Buddhist," Jolie said.

Zack snorted and choked on his wine. When he recovered, he said, "Did you know about one-third of North American Buddhists are Jews?"

Jolie looked at him, puzzled. You could be a Jew but not Jewish? "I learn something new every day," she said. She would have to talk to Daniel to understand what Zack was talking about.

"Tell us about your family," Leah's father said.

Jolie swallowed. "Well, I have two brothers. One is in college and one is a senior in high school."

"That doesn't make sense," Leah said. "You said they were both older than you."

Jolie's mouth opened but nothing came out. She was on a tight rope. "Ah...well...I meant the one in high school is taller than me."

Leah cocked her head, absorbing the response. "Oh, well brothers usually are."

"They're Dodger fans," Jolie said.

"The Dodgers used to be New York's team," her dad said, and then he proceeded to tell them the history of the Dodgers.

Jolie sat on edge, half listening. Will warned her to never reveal information. She needed to get her story down.

Zack joined them later in Leah's room. Leah and Jolie sat on the bed. He flipped through a stack of records and put on Cream's *Disraeli Gears* and straddled the desk chair. When "Tales of Brave Ulysses" came on they got up and danced around the room. Zack kept changing the music, taking requests like a D.J. Their parents called up good night from the floor below and he turned the music down a notch. Jolie couldn't take her eyes off his beautiful black curls.

"I'm proud of you, Leah. You moved out of the house and to a different city for college. I honestly didn't think you'd survive. And I hear you actually cook now."

Leah looked at Jolie with unspoken gratitude.

When they couldn't stay awake any longer, they went off to bed. Jolie lay in the luxurious guest room feeling very small in the grand four-poster bed. A wave of isolation washed over her. Why was she overcome with sadness and a deep loneliness when she was surrounded by this family who welcomed her? Was it because she missed Will? No, not yet, anyway. She felt for the moonstone in the suede pouch around her neck.

She closed her eyes. It was her family she missed. Tomorrow she would call them. Would they be angry with her? What if they weren't home and she'd come all this way for nothing? She could still mail the letter.

Drifting off to sleep, she began to dream. She was below the surface of emerald-green water, looking up at a faint shaft of sunlight.

She swam up and up but couldn't break through the depths to the sunlight. She was drowning. She could see the surface and fought to reach it. There was a weight on her chest, and her lungs couldn't hold out any longer. Struggling, she finally broke through the green depths and woke, gasping.

Startled, she lay breathless in the dark. Where was she? She sat up and was comforted by the sight of the four-poster bed. Leah's house. The vivid emerald-green color stayed with her. It was the color of the heart chakra, the fourth of seven major energy centers in the body. Jasmine had taught her that each chakra has a color and a function. If one is blocked, the body is unbalanced.

She lay back and inhaled, expanding her heart, the chakra center for acceptance, love, and compassion. She breathed out, sending energy to the base of her spine. She breathed in, moving energy back to the heart center. She breathed this way for a longtime, letting her breath move energy. Her mind was void except for the deep emerald-green color she floated in. At last she fell asleep.

The next morning, Leah, Jolie, Zack, and Sarah sat at the kitchen table planning the vintage clothing shopping spree. Zack knew a route to SoHo with only one train change. Leah's mom hovered, trying to figure out the attraction to old clothing. She looked happy to have Leah back for a few days and the house full of life.

Jolie slipped out of the kitchen and went to the phone in the living room. She dialed the phone number Will had given her and asked to speak with Leon. He came on the line and they arranged a meeting two blocks from Leah's for later that afternoon. She wanted to get it over with. Will had instructed her that she had to deliver it that day, the Fourth of July.

The foursome bade their good-byes and promised to be back for the late afternoon prayer service. When they got off the subway in SoHo, the temperature hovered near eighty-five degrees. The sidewalks swarmed with people.

They found a string of vintage stores and went into each, combing through the racks of clothes and accessories. Leah squealed in delight when she found a 1920s flapper dress. Zack stood inside the door of the shops, making faces at their finds, sometimes approvingly. Jolie held up a delicate sleeveless dress in white cotton and lace for Sarah, who tried it on.

"You look like an angel," Jolie said.

Jolie tried on a silk blouse with intricately layered white lace stitching on diaphanous material; the bodice hugged her breasts. It was pure art. She came out of the dressing room.

"Ooh la la," Leah said.

"Is it too tight?"

Zack shook his head. Her face grew hot.

Jolie bought the blouse, a 1930s black beaded cocktail purse, and a silk peacock print scarf in brilliant blue, green, and turquoise hues. She wore it around her forehead, tied at the side.

In the last store, Jolie held up a navy-blue military jacket, Sergeant Pepper style, to Zack. "Try it on."

"I can't wear that."

"Yes you can, go ahead, try it on," Jolie said.

He slipped it on and they stood side by side, looking in the mirror. The jacket transformed him. Leah and Sarah came over.

"Wow, you look so handsome," Sarah said.

"It's you," said Leah. "You have to get it."

Jolie and Zack smiled at each other.

"You're corrupting me," he said, holding her gaze.

"Me?" She reached up and ran her hand through his curls, smiling back at him in the mirror. She loved those curls.

Zack bought the jacket, and they headed down the street, hot and sweaty in the July heat. They passed a pizza joint and went in and bought large slices of pepperoni pizza and Italian sodas. Sitting in the window on well-worn stools, they ate and watched throngs of people pass before them. Women were dressed in jumpsuits, and hot pants. Couples wore stylish designer fashions, despite the heat. Shirtless men in jeans wearing beads and bandanas walked with their chicks dressed in cut-off jeans or miniskirts, colorful blouses, bangles, chokers, and love beads. Jolie had her camera poised, snapping shots of the circus around her.

"Here comes a midi," Jolie said.

A fashionable couple walked by. The woman wore a white pleated midi, a sleeveless white silk top and a white beaded choker around her neck.

"What's a midi?" Zack asked.

"The opposite of a mini, but shorter than a maxi," Jolie said.

The girls laughed. Zack shook his head, baffled.

On the train back to Brooklyn, they made a pact to wear some of their vintage finds to the dinner after the prayer service.

Back at the house, Leah's mom was finishing cooking, and everyone scattered to bathe and get dressed. Upstairs, Jolie sat on the edge of Leah's bed. "Are you sure you don't want to join us?" Leah asked.

"No thanks. I'll stay here and meditate and maybe take a walk around the neighborhood and take some photos."

When Leah and her family left, Jolie reread the letter to her family, addressed the envelope, and slipped it into her purse along with the envelope for Leon. What was inside Leon's envelope and why did it have to be delivered that day? She wanted to read it, but it was sealed.

Jolie walked to the corner where she had arranged to meet Leon. She stood and waited, looking at all the passers-by. A man in his mid-twenties approached. She noticed his clothes first. He wore a tall black top hat and a long dark coat. He looked like the mad hatter. He was tall and had brown hair but she was sure she had never seen him before.

Her eyes darted around the street, her stomach in knots.

"Are you lost?" he said.

"No, I'm waiting for a friend," she said.

"I could be your friend."

She backed away. Where was Leon? She noticed a man across the street watching them, a newspaper under his arm. The mad hatter shrugged and walked on. She turned and walked down the street. The other man had crossed the street and was walking toward her. He had short brown hair and was smiling. He looked vaguely familiar.

"Jolie?" he asked.

She nodded, too anxious to speak.

"I'm Leon."

She exhaled.

"You have something for me?"

She pulled the envelope from her purse and handed it to him. He put it in his newspaper. "Tell Will thanks for the support."

Still unable to find her voice, she smiled briefly.

"The agency he's created is amazing. Stay cool." He turned and walked off.

She watched him disappear around the corner. Lightheaded from unconsciously holding her breath, she exhaled deeply, the delivery was done. But her relief was short lived. The phone call would be much harder.

She continued on to the phone booth she'd seen by the corner store, a few blocks from Leah's. She slid in, closed the accordion door, and pulled out her coin purse filled with quarters, dimes, and nickels.

She dialed the operator and after depositing the coins according to the operator's instructions, the call was placed. The phone rang once. She envisioned the dining room where the phone sat on a corner table. The French doors would be open overlooking the ocean. It rang twice.

On the third ring she heard, "Hello?"

"James?"

"Yes?"

"It's Jolie."

"Jolie! Where are you?" Her brother's voice sounded so close and wonderful. Her pulse surged.

"I'm out here...somewhere." She wanted to tell him but thought of the private detective in Eugene.

"We're worried sick about you."

"I'm fine. I'm safe. How are you?"

"Where are you?"

"Can I talk to Mom or Dad?"

"They're not here. They're out of town for the weekend. They're so torn up about you. Dad has been searching everywhere. He's been traveling, trying to find you."

He'd been traveling? She thought of him searching for her.

"He thought he found you in Eugene but you vanished."

Had it been her dad in Eugene? "I know."

The operator broke in requesting another coin deposit. Tears blurred her vision as she dumped out the coins onto the shelf and deposited the required amount.

"Jolie, come home."

"Not now. I have a life out here." She looked out the phone booth window to the park across the street.

"We all want you back. You won't be in trouble if you come home. Everything has changed. They just want you back. Nothing is the same here without you."

"I will, someday. I just wanted to let you know I'm safe and I'm doing well. Please don't worry about me."

"Of course we're worried about you. Can you call back soon? When Mom and Dad are here?"

"I can call back tomorrow."

"They're not back until Monday. Can you call then?"

"It's hard. I don't want the calls traced."

"They'll be crushed they weren't here to talk to you. I almost don't want to be the one to tell them you called."

Her heart pounded in her ears and her throat closed up. "I want to talk with them too. Tell them I'm fine and I love them. I'll try and call again soon."

"Jolie, just come home."

"I'm mailing a letter."

"Do you need anything?"

"No, I have everything I need, except for you guys." The operator broke in, asking for more coins. She deposited the last of the coins. James updated her with the goings-on of the family. Tears streamed down her face. She couldn't wipe them away fast enough. She was talking to her brother. It was so good to hear his voice. When she ran out of coins, all she could hear was, "Come home, Sister, please just come home."

Jolie hung up the phone and slumped to the floor in the phone booth. Crushed by a weight, she hugged her knees and sobbed. After a while she became aware of tapping on the glass.

She heard a woman's voice. "Are you okay?"

She looked up to see two women standing next to the booth, waiting their turn. She stood up and walked out. Numb, she crossed the street to Sunset Park. The park was full of families with Fourth of July picnics spread out on blankets on the grass. Footballs, baseballs, and Frisbees flew by. She found a tree away from the action and sat cross-legged on the grass in the shade. Across the park the skyline of Manhattan stood out. Her head hurt from crying and her entire body was in knots. She thought contacting her family would ease the pain but now she felt worse.

Overcome with nausea, she replayed the conversation. Her parents were torn up and she'd hurt them inexcusably, but they still loved her. She couldn't face them now. Or could she?

But what about Will? He loved her, too, and they'd started a life together. She wanted to be with him. She tried to balance her emotions. She must be deeply flawed to have done something that horrendous to her family. Girls didn't just leave home. What was wrong with her? She closed her eyes, fighting back tears, but they flowed through in a river.

They still loved her.

A Frisbee grazed the grass near her and sunk to the ground. She rose, tossed it back, and started to walk back to Leah's. At the edge of the park she paused. The Statue of Liberty loomed far off on the skyline. She snapped a picture of it and walked on. Near the corner store was a mailbox. She took the letter out of her purse, kissed it, and whispered, "Please forgive me." She dropped it into the mail slot.

She'd done what she came to New York to do.

Leah and her family were still out. Upstairs, she washed her face with cold water; her head pounded from crying. In her guest room, she meditated. Her mind was stuck on Anahata, the heart chakra. She focused her energy flow into the heart and inhaled the color of emeralds, envisioning an emerald-green line flowing through her body and through all of her energy centers. Later, when her eyes blinked open, she was calm, but her heart was raw with a dull pain.

She showered and laid out her clothes for the festivities. The last thing she felt was festive. She dressed in a fringed skirt, sandals, and the vintage blouse she'd bought that morning. The undulating lines of lace on the blouse reminded her of waves lapping at a shore. She took the blue-green peacock-colored silk scarf and tied it around her neck. Voices and footsteps came up the stairs. There was a knock on her door. Leah looked in.

"We're back. Are you okay? You look so, so, oh I don't know, serene...but sad."

Jolie nodded.

"Meet me in my room." Leah dashed down the hall.

Jolie and Zack met up in Leah's room. Leah wore her flapper dress. Zack wore the Sergeant Pepper jacket, despite the heat. Leah was hyper and tried out some flapper dance moves. Soon they were trying to outdo each other. The doorbell rang, and they bounded downstairs. Sarah and her parents had arrived for dinner.

Sarah stood in the foyer in her new vintage sleeveless lace shift, looking cool and crisp in white with her dark curls. Leah's mother and father turned to see the three of them standing behind them in the living room.

"What in the world?" Leah's mom said, looking at Zack in his jacket. Zack saluted. Her eyes landed on Jolie's scarf. "Is that a Versace?" She came closer to inspect.

Leah's mom laid out platters of food, and they ate in the formal dining room. As daylight faded, they raised glasses of wine and drank. It was time for the fireworks on top of Leah's father's office building, ten blocks away.

The adults drove, and the foursome walked. On the streets, thousands of people were seated in chairs or stood, waiting for the fireworks. The girls followed Zack, snaking their way through the masses of revelers.

On the rooftop garden Jolie was on top of the world. A spectacular view of the city skyline lay before them. She took out her camera, adjusted the exposure, and snapped photos of the skyline and Leah, Sarah, and Zack. Boom, boom, boom…the sky lit up in bursts of color in endless designs.

She was in New York, on top of a building with a garden with her friends, watching the incredible celebration. It was a very different experience from the first time she'd been in New York only three months earlier. Her thoughts turned to her father. He was still searching for her. A wave of sorrow overcame her.

A bird burst forth in song outside the window. Jolie opened her eyes. The room was dark. The big house was quiet. She rose, peered out the curtain, and saw the bird in the elm tree. The street was still. She dressed and went downstairs.

In the living room, she was drawn to the bookcases. She went from shelf to shelf, reading the titles, running her finger over the spines. There were so many books to read, a sea of knowledge. Startled by a rustling sound, she turned. Leah's father watched her from his deep velvet chair with the Sunday paper in his lap. He smiled at her, and they exchanged good mornings.

"The fireworks were amazing," she said.

"There were more than fireworks last night."

Was their music too loud after they got home?

He held up the front page of the *New York Times*. A smoldering building with blown out windows stared back at her. "Some crazy group tried to blow up the Bank of America. They did a pretty good job of it, too."

"Was anyone hurt?"

He shook his head. "Thankfully, no."

Will despised the Bank of America, the symbol of capitalism.

In the kitchen, Leah's mom poured her a cup of tea, fragrant and sweet. Jolie asked her for her bread recipe, and she sat at the kitchen table, copying it onto a recipe card while Leah's mom fussed about the kitchen.

The bank bombing haunted her. Who was behind it? She'd have to get a copy of the *Village Voice* before they drove back to Boston.

Eventually Leah and Zack came down. Zack wore his jacket.

"Did you sleep in that?" his mom asked.

He ignored her and addressed Jolie. "What do you want to see in New York today? Central Park, the Statue of Liberty, or the Modern Art Museum?"

"The girls have to be on the road by early afternoon," his mom said.

Zack rolled his eyes.

"There's a Sunday flea market," Leah said.

"I'll go wherever you want to take me," Jolie said.

"Then Central Park it is," Zack said.

Leah's father strode into the kitchen. "I'm going out to get bagels."

Zack stood. "I'll go with you."

"Not in that jacket, you won't."

Zack shrugged and slipped it off. Minutes later the doorbell rang, and Sarah came in.

When Zach and his dad returned they placed the assorted bagels, lox, and cream cheese on the dining room table.

Jolie savored a still warm bagel. "This is the best bagel I've ever had."

Leah's dad beamed. "They're cooked in water."

"In water?"

He nodded.

How do you cook a bagel in water?

Zack led the girls to the subway. They emerged in the middle of Central Park amid lush greenery and trees. They walked south along a path. People on bicycles and roller skates, some wearing hot pants blew by them. They had only covered a portion of the park when it was time to head back to Brooklyn.

Later that afternoon, the three girls stood by Leah's car in the driveway.

"Visit us any time, Jolie. You're a lovely girl," Leah's mom said.

Zack gave them all a hug. He looked at Jolie. "I want to see some photos from this weekend."

"I'll send you some," she said, smiling as she thought about some of the crazy people she'd photographed.

Leah's father stepped toward Jolie, holding a large paper bag. "I went and bought another dozen bagels for you to take back. Nobody can make a bagel like we do in New York. They try, but they're just not the same."

Jolie stepped toward him, gave him a hug and a brief kiss on the cheek, and took the bag. The bagels were still warm.

"Take care of these girls for us," he said, nodding toward Leah and Sarah.

"Oh, I will," Jolie said, trying to smile, fighting back tears.

The car ride back to Boston was quieter than the ride down. They were hot and tired but happy. Jolie was glad to have the back seat to herself. She looked out the window and soaked up the passing scenery.

"I liked Zack," Jolie said. "What about you Sarah, are you attracted to him?"

"No. We're like brother and sister. We're close, we hang out together, but that's all. Why?"

"Oh, just wondered."

"Are you attracted to him?" Sarah said.

"Well, he is damned cute with those curls." She smiled. "But I love Will."

The girls laughed.

"He liked you. I could tell," Leah said.

"How could you tell?" Jolie asked.

"He wouldn't have come with us to SoHo or Central Park if you weren't there, that's for sure."

"Well, even if I didn't have Will, and we fell in love it wouldn't work out. I'm not Jewish."

Leah and Sarah laughed. "That's our lot in life," Leah said. "But I guess you could always run away together. They'd have to forgive you both sometime. He is their flesh and blood."

"Bridge Over Troubled Water" came on the radio, and Sarah turned it up. Jolie leaned her head back on the seat and closed her eyes.

33

Magic Bus

$\sim$

They rolled into Cambridge at six that evening. Leah dropped Jolie in front of her apartment. She sprang up the stairs. In the living room she found Will and Charlie. Will played the guitar, and Charlie sat reading the Sunday *Globe*, the headline on the front page stared back at her: BANK OF AMERICA BOMBED DURING FIREWORKS.

Will stood up, put his guitar down and opened his arms. "I missed you." He wrapped his arms around her tightly.

She turned her face up to his, and he gave her a long kiss. "I gave Leon the envelope."

"I know."

How did he know?

Will released her from his embrace. "I have a surprise for you."

"What kind of surprise?"

"Follow me."

He walked toward the front door. Jolie gave Charlie a quick hug, and they followed Will out to the street. A few houses down he stopped and turned toward the curb.

"Here's your bus."

A sapphire-blue VW bus was parked before her. She looked at Will and then back to the bus and then to Charlie.

"Get in," Will said, opening the side door. They climbed in the back and sat on the bench seats.

"It's perfect," Jolie said, running her hands over the seat.

"Charlie found it. We've been looking for a while, and he found this sweet deal."

They got out and inspected the engine and the exterior.

"Let's go for a drive," she said.

Jolie sat in the back to experience the bus feeling, and Charlie sat shotgun. Will drove out to Memorial Drive and along the river. Skullers sliced through the water. The front windows were down, and the breeze blew fresh against her skin. Will and Jolie smiled at each other in the rearview mirror. They had wheels. There was no need to hitchhike now.

"I love it. We can fix it up for camping," she said. "We can go to the White Mountains in New Hampshire or the Green Mountains or Maine. Charlie, you can come with us."

"Wait a minute, who's going to run the office?" Will said.

For the next few days, Jolie worked in the darkroom every morning before work, developing the photos from New York. She studied the different characters and scenes she'd shot. She printed a few of the fireworks and the shot she'd taken of the Statue of Liberty from across the river in Brooklyn. Her favorite was the one she'd asked Leah's father to take of the four of them on the night of the fourth. Leah glowed in her black flapper dress next to Sarah in white. Zack stood tall in his military jacket with Jolie next to him, her scarf tied around her forehead, blonde hair spilled out the sides. It captured their weekend. She printed it to send to Zack. There were so many more photos to play with.

She showed them to Will one evening. She described the fireworks show from the rooftop garden and the view of the New York skyline. "I was on top of the world."

"Baby, don't get sucked into that bourgeois stuff by those people."

She stared numbly at the photos and retreated into silence. Those people? They were her friends. Or as much as she could have good friends while keeping her true identity under wraps. That night had been one of the most thrilling moments of her life but now the memory of it was tarnished by his words.

⌒◌

Will and Jolie planned a camping trip to the White Mountains for the weekend. They shopped at an Army/Navy store for camping supplies and early Saturday, with the bus packed for the trip, they left for New Hampshire. Will wove through thick traffic amid blaring horns to the interstate.

"I can't wait to get back to nature," Jolie said.

"The ranch didn't cure you of that?"

"I wonder about them sometimes." She unconsciously ran her fingers over her moonstone pouch.

"That's the new thing. Getting back to the land. Hippies are moving out to the country. We did that. And now we need to focus on the Revolution, and you can't do that in isolation."

His socialist utopia vision was becoming more urgent, more strident, and possibly more violent. He was obsessed with the Bank of America bombing in New York. He followed all of the news reports, but there were no leads, and no one had claimed responsibility.

They drove north. She flipped through the radio stations and settled on Otis Redding's "Dock of the Bay." The bus purred along in the slow lane, its top speed fifty-five miles per hour. "Old Blue," Jolie said. "Let's name the bus Old Blue."

They arrived at the campground three hours later and pulled into a campsite. They got out and stretched. A stand of fir trees dwarfed them. The afternoon sun was high and glistened off the lake. They changed into bathing suits and walked down to the lakeshore. Jolie waded out and dove in, swimming underwater for some distance. The water was so refreshing and pure. Will dove underwater, and she swam to escape, squealing, but he caught up with her with his broad strokes.

He brought her to him in an embrace, water beaded on their faces and hair. It was so good to get out of the city.

After swimming for some time, Will got out and lay on a towel on the shore. Jolie floated on her back, weightless and one with nature.

"Aren't you ready to get out?"

"No, never." She somersaulted into the depths and resurfaced some distance away.

He lay back, closed his eyes and fell asleep. Jolie got out of the water and lay beside him on a towel. It was quiet except for the wind, high in the trees. The scent of fir and pine floated on the warm breeze.

On Sunday morning, Will was ready to pack up and drive back to Cambridge. He paced around the camp like a caged animal, anxious to get back to the office.

Jolie wasn't as eager to leave. "I'm going down to the lake for one last meditation."

"Why do you waste your time on that?"

"Meditation? It calms my emotions. I feel stronger and more stable yet serene."

"I'm ready to roll now."

"Just give me twenty minutes. Relax...play your guitar."

She sat cross-legged at the lake, her thoughts flowed through her mind in a torrent. They hadn't even been there for twenty-four hours and he was ready to leave. If he didn't want her meditating, what would he do if he found out about the temple? Despite the stillness she couldn't quiet the chatter in her mind, knowing Will was ready to leave. She wanted to spend the day hiking and reading by the lake, communing with nature. The city was harsh and ungracious. She opened her eyes and looked out over the blue-gray water glistening in the morning sun. At least the temple awaited her.

34

Helter Skelter

They returned to the city midday Sunday. Will went into the office, anxious to find out what he had missed. Jolie cleaned the camping gear and repacked it, ready for their next trip. She wanted to be back in the woods by the lake. Or better yet, in the lake. Restless, she left the house for the temple.

Daniel was home when she returned. Jolie poured mint iced tea, and they went out to the back porch. Fragrant mint leaves floated with the ice cubes. They hadn't caught up for a while, and she was eager to talk. Jolie told him about New York.

"I have photos to show you." She hurried into the house and brought out a few. "I have so many to print."

Daniel picked up the photo of Zack, Leah, Sarah and herself. "Look at you Bohemians! Who's the guy?"

"Zack, Leah's brother. Leah asked about you."

"Yeah?"

"I told her about the photo project with your students. She said she'd help if we needed her."

"We need her. We're on for next Saturday. Ten kids have signed up. In addition to Leah, it would be good to get one more adult to come with us."

"I'll ask Will if he can come."

Daniel's eyebrows arched, and he shook his head. "It'll never happen."

"It doesn't hurt to ask. I'll go to the camera store tomorrow and see if they'll lend me a few used cameras for Saturday."

He shook his head again, smiling, and got up. "You're such a dreamer. I'm going for a bike ride along the river."

"You mean girl watching?"

"Well, that too." He smiled sheepishly.

Jolie gathered her notes about Boston's history, grabbed her camera, and walked to the office. She wanted to type up the historic site list for the student field trip.

At the open door of the office she stood in disbelief. "What happened?" she asked.

The place had been ransacked. Mail was strewn on the floor. File cabinets were overturned in the living room. The teletype machine lay on the floor, on its side, silent. *Communists* was scrawled on the wall with dark pink lipstick. Will, Adam, Charlie, and the professor sat in the kitchen.

"We've been raided," Will said.

"You mean robbed?" Jolie said.

"Raided," Adam said.

Sam and Ginger walked in with a half a case of beer, pretzels, and chips and set them down on the kitchen counter. Ginger and Jolie hugged.

"I think we could all use one of these," Sam said, as he opened beers and passed them out.

"Vive la revolution," Will toasted. "They'll never stop us."

Everyone echoed the salute and clinked bottles.

"Who is 'they'?" Jolie asked.

"The FBI, most likely." the professor said.

Jolie looked at Will and froze.

"The FBI?" she mouthed, unable to speak.

Will put his arm around her shoulder. "It's all right, it's going to be all right." He squeezed her tight, and looked into her eyes. "They're raiding free presses all over America."

Her stomach flipped, and she slipped into the bathroom and leaned against the porcelain sink, tears falling. The FBI was in their midst. What if Will got arrested?

"Are you okay?" Charlie said, outside the door.

She splashed water on her face, took a few deep breaths, and went out.

"It's just harassment to stop the paper. All they did was slow us down," Charlie said.

They went into the kitchen, her face still blotchy from tears. Ginger handed her a cup of tea, and they went into the living room. Ginger recounted the events. Charlie had come in that morning and the place had been turned upside down. Names and phone numbers of other underground press contacts had been taken. Eldridge Cleaver's Algerian contact information was gone.

She could hear the men in the kitchen, talking loudly. The incident had invigorated them. Jolie followed Ginger back into the kitchen. Ginger put the chips and pretzels on the table and sat on Sam's lap. Jolie picked up her camera and started taking pictures of the disarray. When she'd finished photographing, she set her camera down and leaned against the kitchen counter, listening. She hadn't hung around the office lately, but the group seemed smaller.

When there was a lull, she asked, "Where are Coulter and Marlena?"

"I haven't seen Coulter for a week or two, but it's summer. Everyone's getting out of the city," Will said.

"I haven't seen Marlena for a while," Adam said.

"The writing on the wall looks familiar, like Marlena's," Jolie said.

"You're being paranoid again," Will said.

"Those two never sat true with me," Jolie said.

"Nah, they're okay," Adam said.

"I don't know," the professor said. "I tried to contact Marlena through the school directory for a teaching assistant role, and she's not listed as a student. I didn't think much of it. Maybe she uses a different name around here. Some people aren't who they say they are."

Jolie and Will's eyes locked.

"Do you think they're informants?" Ginger said.

"I'd say it's a pretty good bet if they don't come around anymore," Sam said. "They're probably already on another assignment."

They debated Coulter and Marlena's involvement in the break-in. Jolie was sticking to her intuition. Charlie started looking for Marlena's handwriting on something, anything.

Jolie looked around at the chaos. "Since we're not calling the police, is it okay if I start to straighten up this mess?"

"Have at it, Jolie girl. We've already done an inventory and know what they took," Adam said.

Jolie began to straighten up the chaos, stacking piles of mail and organizing files. When the professor left, Will put on a Stones album, and everyone sprang into action. Adam righted the file cabinets, and Jolie put files away.

Driving back to the house that night, Jolie asked Will, "Do you think it was the FBI?"

"Well, it sure wasn't the Black Panthers."

She shot Will a look. "I'm scared. What were they looking for?"

"Anything to shut us down."

"What if you get arrested?"

"We're not doing anything illegal. They couldn't find anything, so they trashed the place. It's happening all over. Intimidation and harassment is the name of their game."

The meeting with Leon flashed through her mind. Something about the meeting had not felt right. And then the bank was bombed that night. But she had given him an envelope, not a bomb. "What was in the envelope I gave Leon?"

"Oh, just some contacts he needed."

She had to get a grip. The FBI raid was getting the best of her. She tried to shake off the dark feeling.

At the house, Jolie went into the dark room and developed the negatives from the break-in. Her hand trembled as she hung the negative strip up to dry.

35

History Lesson

~~~

The next morning Jolie went to the office early with Will. She typed up the historic site list and a homework assignment for the field trip. Will was preoccupied with a story he'd started about the break-in.

"I need to stop by after work to mimeograph some stuff." She kissed Will and walked out the door into the morning.

Jolie headed to the camera store in the Square. Niles's face lit up with a smile.

"Haven't seen you for a while. What's up?"

"I need some film and a favor."

"We've got film. What's the favor?"

Jolie told him about the field trip.

"You want me to loan you cameras for Roxbury High School students?"

Niles pondered the unusual request. "I trust you, and I certainly want to give amateur photographers a start, but the cameras aren't mine to lend."

Her expression went flat with disappointment. "I know, it's a lot to ask." They stood facing each other.

He studied her. Silence filled the store. "Can you have them back the same day?"

"Yes! I can, I will. This Saturday. I'll have them back by closing. Thank you. You won't be sorry. I'll show you their work once we get it all developed." She gave him a quick hug. He blushed at her show of enthusiasm. "I'll see you Saturday morning. I'll buy the film then. I have to run or I'll be late for work." She dashed out of the store and down the block.

After work, Jolie stopped at the office to mimeograph the field trip homework. Will, Charlie, and some of the student volunteers were there. Jolie greeted everyone and went to work on the mimeograph. The ink ran on the paper, making an inky black mess after being tipped over in the raid. She dismantled and cleaned the machine, her hands stained with ink. After refilling the fluids, she finally got a clean run.

Will came over. "What are you working on?"

"The field trip with Daniel's students. We're on for Saturday. I'm printing their homework."

"You're really going to waste your time on that?"

Charlie and Adam turned to listen.

"We've been planning it for weeks."

"Well, I didn't think it would ever happen."

"Come with us. We've going to the Boston Common cemetery and Park Street Church."

"I don't have time for that."

"We need one more adult. We're responsible for the kids."

"Those kids are more street-smart than you could ever imagine," Will said.

"I know, that's why we need to keep an eye on them. Come with us. Maybe you'll convert one or two to the cause."

"No, not my thing," Will said.

"I'll go," Charlie said. "I could use a history lesson."

"Good," Will said. "Make sure she comes back in one piece."

Adam looked at Will and then to Jolie. "I'll tell you what. I'll publish their photos, with their names, if they're any good. But they have to create a caption with a revolutionary tie."

Jolie looked at him, stunned. "Really?" She wanted to dance and leap from room to room, but in the presence of the others, she maintained her composure. The students would get their photos printed in *Central Underground Press.*

At home, she set the folder of homework sheets on the kitchen table and changed into darkroom clothes. She developed the contact sheet from the photos of the raid and a few prints from the camping trip. There was one of a reflection of the tall trees shimmering on the lake. She felt she was back at the lake. Her favorite was one of Will playing guitar at the campsite, sitting in the open side door of Old Blue. Will could look at the contact sheet later when he got home. He was working late on the story about the break in, checking facts from other presses that had been raided.

She went into the kitchen to make dinner. Daniel sat at the table, reading the homework assignment.

"You crack me up," he said.

"What do you mean?" A wave of self-doubt flooded her. Was it too basic for high school juniors?

"I mean, you made it fun. This will keep them busy, thanks."

"Charlie is joining us, along with Leah. And guess what? Adam will print their photos in the press if they're any good."

"Wow, wait till the kids hear that."

"We have four cameras. Yours, mine, and two from the camera store."

Daniel's eyebrows arched in amazement. "You're full of surprises."

She grimaced inwardly. If he only knew.

Saturday morning, Jolie picked up the two cameras and bought eight rolls of film with the money Daniel insisted she take. Charlie and Daniel were waiting for her when she got back to the house. They loaded all of the cameras with film and preset the apertures. There wasn't time to teach the students about exposure settings. When they got off the T at Park Street Station, Leah stood near a small group of kids.

"Mr. Shapiro," the kids called to Daniel as soon as he came up the subway steps. The kids were early. The idea of getting published in

Central Underground Press had created a buzz and now twelve students had signed up for the field trip.

Daniel greeted the kids, said hi to Leah, and then he checked off their names while they waited for a few others. When they all had arrived, Daniel introduced everyone and then split them up into groups and gave a quick orientation to the cameras.

"Hold still, focus on your subject, press the shutter down, then advance the film." He gave them the rules for the photo publication and instructed them to stick together with their leader.

While he was talking, Jolie studied the group of boys and girls. All were black except for two Hispanics. In the fall they would be juniors in high school. It suddenly dawned on her that they were the same age. She hadn't interacted with kids her age since she'd left home. They looked so young and carefree. It was hard to relate to their youth. She felt so much older. Jolie took their picture as they stood listening to Daniel.

Jolie gave Charlie, Leah, and Daniel paper to record the students' names by the photo number. It was going to be a challenge keeping them straight. And then they were off. Every group wanted to start at the Granary Burial Ground.

Jolie's group had two boys and two girls. They bantered with each other as they walked.

"Where're you from, Miss Jolie?" the girl named Coretta asked.

Brandy, the other girl jumped in. "Not from around here, I know that."

Jolie laughed. "California."

"California!" one of the boys said. "Dang, I've never been out of Boston."

"I went to New York once," Brandy said.

"I want to go to California," Coretta said.

In the cemetery, they looked for the names on their sheet, clamoring for the camera when they found one. Jolie stood in the shade of a tall elm tree with the two girls while the two boys traded off taking photos.

"What's that thing around your head," Brandy asked.

Jolie touched the sky-blue gossamer silk band with beads sewn in a vine pattern. "A headband. You can also wear it as a choker." She untied it and then retied it around her neck.

"Oh, I saw one of those chokers in a magazine," Coretta said. "It's cool."

"I made it. Can you sew beads?"

"Yeah, we did a bead thing in home economics," Coretta said.

"But it was stupid," Brandy said. "That's cool."

"I have more of this material and I have some beads. I can sew you the bands if you sew on the beads. Every design should be different. I can send it all with Daniel."

The girls looked at her. "For how much?" Brandy asked.

Jolie cocked her head and looked at the girls. "For nothing."

They eyed her cautiously. "Okay," Coretta said.

"What kind of beads do you like? I have glass beads, shell beads, African beads—"

"African," they both blurted out at once.

Jolie felt her headband. "They'll look cool on this silk."

The guys returned and handed Jolie the camera. They were ready to move on.

Three hours and many rolls of film later, they completed the assignment. Daniel bought everyone a cold drink at a concession stand. Throughout the day, she could tell the students liked Daniel by the way they kidded him. Jolie collected the cameras, labeled all of the film, and put everything in her backpack.

"When can we see the photos?" one of the kids asked.

"We'll have the contact sheets ready in a few days, and you can pick your best photos for printing," Daniel said.

They watched the kids walk down the T station steps.

"Do you think we should go with them?" Jolie asked.

Daniel laughed. "They'll be just fine."

Leah invited Daniel, Jolie, and Charlie back to her apartment. They walked the few blocks to Beacon Hill. Inside, Leah offered them iced tea and poured pretzels in a bowl. Exhausted, they sank into the couch and chairs in the living room.

"Jesus, Daniel. How do you do that all day? I'm spent and I only had three kids for a few hours," Charlie said.

"The kids are okay. The worst part for me is walking the three blocks from the subway to the school and back. It's scary," Daniel said.

"They're good kids, though," Leah said.

"Mine were really into it," Jolie said. At her feet was the backpack with the cameras. Her fingers kneaded the straps. When they finished their tea, she stood. "I have to get these cameras back."

Sunday morning, Will went to the office to meet the professor. Daniel and Jolie developed the eight rolls of film. When they finished, she stepped out onto the back porch and took a deep breath of fresh air. She loved the darkroom, but the chemicals were acrid and biting in her nose and throat.

Daniel came out and joined her. "Will sure puts in a lot of time at the office. You're a revolutionary widow."

"I don't mind. It's his passion."

"Don't you think he's kind of obsessed with it?"

"He is dedicated to the cause. Anyway, I have my own plans today. Ginger is picking me up later. We're going to a Women's Liberation meeting."

"You're both obsessed," Daniel said, smiling at her. "Does Leah go to those?"

"Yes, and her roommate Sarah, too. We're planning a women's strike in August."

While Jolie waited for Ginger, she sewed the headbands for Brandy and Coretta. She opened her cigar box that held an assortment of loose beads and she selected the African beads that seemed to represent each girl. She put the headbands, beads, needles, and thread into two bags with their names on the outside.

Jolie handed the bags to Daniel. "Can you give these to my girls?"

He read the names. "Your girls? What is it?"

"A sewing project."

"Sewing?"

"You'll see. I'm sure they'll be wearing them soon." Ginger's horn beeped. "See you later. I'll be back to work on the photos." Jolie grabbed her purse and camera and dashed out the door.

Ginger put the blue VW Bug in gear and they drove through the tranquil Sunday streets to Boston University. It was the first meeting since the Women's Liberation Movement article ran in *Central Underground Press.* Jolie was nervous about seeing Elaine after the headline had gone wrong.

Elaine stood in the front of the room, talking to a group. More women streamed through the door and helped set up. Jolie and Ginger took Elaine aside. "The headline was a mistake," Jolie said. "We were betrayed."

Elaine shook her head. "No, it's okay. Some of us talked about it, and after we got over the initial shock we realized we can use it to our benefit. We'll show them we have a sense of humor and power."

The lecture hall quickly filled up. There were twice as many women as last month. Jolie looked around. Marlena was nowhere to be seen.

Elaine took to the podium with the microphone and opened the meeting. She reviewed the platform that was aligned with the national strategy they'd agreed upon at the last meeting,

"1. Equal rights and equal opportunity in jobs, pay, and education

2. Establish childcare centers

3. Repeal the anti-abortion laws"

Applause rang out. Elaine continued, "This will appeal to women everywhere. The August strike will commemorate the date fifty years ago when the 19th Amendment was ratified to allow women the right to vote. It will also commemorate the resurgence of a major political movement for the liberation of women everywhere."

There was more applause. Elaine, dwarfed by the podium, had a huge effect on this crowd. Part of it was Elaine, and part of it was the future they would create. "Tell your mothers. Tell your sisters. Tell your coworkers. Make your signs. Let's show up in force!" Elaine said.

Ginger and Jolie sought Elaine out after the meeting. Leah and Sarah followed.

"We want to help get the word out about the strike," Jolie said. "We can print posters and bring them to the next meeting."

"With this crowd, we can post them all over town," Ginger said.

They sat down and created a draft poster with the date, time, location, and message. They would use Jolie's photo of the sea of women at the last rally and Ginger would try her hand with the art work.

❦

Jolie and Daniel took down the eight contact sheets Daniel had developed while she was out. At the dining room table, Daniel looked at the thumbprint-sized photos on the sheets with a magnifying lens while Jolie cut the negatives, fit them into plastic sleeves, and labeled them.

"There are some interesting shots here," Daniel said.

"Interesting good or interesting bad?"

"They're good. Some are so serious. I like the ones you took of them taking pictures."

"You wanted their portraits so I got one of each of them in action. You know, for when they're famous."

Daniel laughed. "Here, your turn."

She eagerly scanned the contact sheets. "Wow, they really dug that cemetery."

Jolie labeled the negatives while Daniel labeled the contact sheet photos with the student names. When they were done, Daniel placed the contact sheets and negatives in his portfolio case.

Jolie was restless. There was a meditation session at the Buddhist temple in a half an hour, and Will was never home until later. She told Daniel she was going out for a walk and would stop at the grocery store to get something for dinner.

The temple was cool, the hushed atmosphere tranquil. Jolie went into a meditation room and joined a group. On the altar, candles glowed, and white flowers smothered the bottom of the Buddha statue. Blue smoke from sandalwood incense wafted through the room. They sat cross-legged on mats on the hardwood floor, facing the altar, eyes closed, hands in prayer position resting on the chest bone. The monk led three oms to the Three Jewels: Buddha, Dharma, and Sangha.

The monk spoke in a hushed voice. "Peace starts within each of us. We cannot bring to the outside world what we do not have inside of us. Peace starts within our own hearts and minds. Once we have found it, and it is entrenched within us, we share it. Let your breath take you deep into your inner stillness. Find the deeper water of peacefulness within. Start by chanting silently: May I be at peace."

Sometime later a bell rang softly, and Jolie became aware of her surroundings. She opened her eyes and slowly focused on the room. Sublimely serene, her body felt weightless.

She arrived home with an armload of groceries. Will stopped playing the guitar and came out to the kitchen.

"I've hardly seen you all weekend." He hugged her. "I thought you were going to stop by the office. We could have used your help."

"Daniel and I had a developing marathon for the student photos."

"The story and photos we printed Wednesday of the raid are causing quite a buzz. All of the papers are carrying it this week." He gave her another embrace, more tender this time. "You look very sweet. And you smell good, too. What's that scent?"

"Sandalwood."

Incense from the temple clung to her hair and skin, but he didn't need to know about the temple.

36

Dazed and Confused

Jolie took the stairs to the house two at a time Wednesday after work. She was happy to be home. She paused at the door. It stood open a few inches. She cautiously approached and stopped at the threshold.

"Will? Daniel?" No response. "Sam?" She inched the door open a little wider. "Anybody here?"

She eased through the door and paused. The apartment was silent. Someone probably didn't close the door all the way, and the latch didn't catch.

"Anyone home?"

The kitchen and dining room looked normal. She walked into the living room. Nothing was amiss. She walked back through the house and shut the front door. Gingerly, she walked through the kitchen to the darkroom. She stopped short and sucked her breath in.

Photos and negatives lay strewn on the darkroom floor. The developing equipment was knocked over. The instructions Daniel had written out and tacked to the wall lay torn into pieces on the counter.

Heart pounding in her chest and ears, straining for any unusual sound, she moved through the hall to their bedroom. Dresser drawers were open, and the contents dumped on the floor. In the corner, her cigar box of beads was up turned. Silver beads, glass beads, shell beads, and turquoise beads littered the hardwood floor. Her small collection of books lay scattered about.

What did they want? It was so destructive. The only thing of any value was her camera. The bottom dresser drawer where she kept it was open. Her camera was gone. Tears welled in her eyes as she searched the room, but it was nowhere to be found.

They'd stolen her camera, her sole defining possession. It had become a part of her. She felt violated. She sat down on the bed, stunned at the deliberate chaos of the robbery. After a moment, she went into the kitchen and dialed the office. The line was busy. She dialed the other phone line and a volunteer answered. She asked to speak with Will.

"He's on the other phone."

"Please tell him it's Jolie, and it's urgent." What if someone was still in the house? Unsettled, fear washed over her.

Will came on the line. "What is it?"

"Can you come home? We've been robbed," she said, her voice shaky. She hung up the phone and stood rooted by the kitchen table. She heard footsteps coming up the stairs. Daniel came in the door and stopped when he saw her.

"What's wrong?"

"We've been robbed."

She heard Old Blue come up the street and soon the sound of footsteps on the stairs. Will and Charlie came through the door.

"I came home and the door was open slightly," Jolie said. They followed her as she walked through the path of chaos in the darkroom and their bedroom.

"My camera's gone," Jolie said.

"No, not your camera!" Charlie said.

Will grimaced and methodically went room to room through the rest of the house. They followed. In the living room, the stereo, television, and Will's guitar were there. Will walked into Sam and Daniel's bedrooms. Everything appeared to be untouched, unlike the upheaval in their bedroom and the darkroom. Daniel's camera sat on his bookshelf.

In the corner of the dining room sat Daniel's portfolio. Daniel opened it. The student negatives that Daniel and Jolie had carefully catalogued the Sunday before were safe inside.

Daniel looked at Jolie. "That's a relief."

"Those are worth more than any camera," she said, tearing up.

Will put his arms around her. "Don't worry, I'll get you another one. I'm just glad you're safe."

They moved into the living room and sat down. Charlie brewed tea and brought her a cup.

"Thanks," she said, taking the cup. She looked at Will. "Who did this? What do they want?"

"What do you mean?" Will said. "We got robbed, that's all."

"This wasn't random. I feel like they targeted you and me. They destroyed our bedroom and the darkroom. They stole my camera. They didn't touch your guitar or the stereo or Daniel's camera. I don't think they even went into the other bedrooms. I don't know if they took any photos or negatives."

Charlie shot Will a look.

"What?" she said, looking at Charlie.

"Charlie found some of Marlena's handwriting. We compared it to the writing on the wall. It does look like Marlena's," Will said.

"I have no idea what you're talking about," Daniel said.

"We think Marlena is an informant for the FBI," Charlie said.

"Which chick is Marlena?" Daniel asked. "The voluptuous one with the gorgeous brown hair parted down the middle?"

"Yeah, that chick," Charlie said.

"The FBI?" Daniel said. "I just passed her this evening with some older guy hurrying down the street to the T a few blocks from here. She recognized me but didn't say anything. They were in a hurry."

"Marlena? You saw her this evening?" Jolie said.

"I didn't remember her name, but I definitely remember her."

"Go look through your photos and negatives and see if anything was taken besides your camera," Will said.

Dazed and in shock, she walked into the darkroom and flipped on the light. She sat on the floor, picking up the negatives and printed photos that lay in disarray around her. Someone had been in their house, their bedroom. An uneasiness spread through her. Daniel came in and started straightening the photo equipment.

"Oy vey. Did they have to make such a mess? Why would the FBI come and steal your camera?"

"Maybe they're harassing us for publishing photos of the raid at the office," Jolie said.

"Well, there are more cameras where that one came from," Daniel said.

"Right on," Jolie said, cheering up a bit.

She sifted through the prints and negatives, putting them back in order. The only photo missing was the one of Will on the camping trip, sitting in the door of Old Blue playing the guitar. That was strange. A tinge of jealousy burned through her. Had Marlena fallen for Will? Her jealousy turned to panic. Or maybe they weren't done with him yet. Now they had a photograph of him. Could they trace him back to California?

Later that night, Will and Jolie picked up the tangle of clothes strewn on their bedroom floor. Jolie carefully folded everything and put them back in the drawers. She scooped the beads into the cigar box and arranged her books on the shelf. She held out the small tin she kept their savings in. The only savings Will knew about.

"They didn't touch the money."

"Let's get out of the city this weekend. We'll go camping in Maine," Will said.

That was a surprise. The last trip, he couldn't wait to get back. She hesitated. She and Daniel had plans to start printing the student photos and there was a workshop at the temple Saturday with a Buddhist monk from Tibet. She'd bought a book on Tibetan Buddhism. But he didn't care about the student project and she couldn't mention the temple. If she didn't go he may never want to go again.

"Okay."

"Charlie wants to come too. He's never been to Maine."

"Well, that makes three of us."

He wrapped his arms around her. "Don't be so glum. I'll get you another camera."

"It's not that. I'm scared. The FBI might have been here, in our house, our bedroom. What if they find out who we really are?"

"They won't. We have new identities now."

"They took your photo with them."

37

As Tears Go By

On Saturday, Will and Jolie packed Old Blue with food and camping gear and drove north. Jolie sat cross-legged behind Will and Charlie on the bench seat, overjoyed they were leaving the city. She quietly hummed "Here Comes the Sun" as she took in the new scenery. Two hours later, they were on a rocky coast in Maine. Will drove through the campground. The lone pay phone by the showers looked out of place among the towering trees. Her head tingled at the sight of it. Could she risk a call home?

Will pulled into a campsite. They walked to a massive granite outcrop and watched the waves crash far below. Jolie stood between Will and Charlie and linked arms. They breathed in the clean air, tinged with the sea, spruce, and fir.

"We need to get out of the city at least every other weekend for the rest of the summer," Will said.

She smiled. That would never happen.

"Let's walk down to the beach," Will said.

Maybe he did like nature, or maybe he liked it when Charlie was around to talk to.

Later, they sat at the picnic table. Will strummed his guitar, working though a new song he was writing. Jolie stood and stretched. "I'm going to go meditate."

"How did you learn to meditate?" Charlie asked.

"My friend Jasmine taught me. It's part of my life now. Do you want me to teach you?"

"Yeah, I'd like to try it. You seem to be at peace with the world. Maybe it would help me."

At peace? He had no idea how conflicted she was. Nobody did.

Will rolled his eyes. His fingers deftly worked out a melody.

Jolie and Charlie walked down to the rocky outcrop. The ocean stretched for miles below. They sat on a flat granite slab in the afternoon sun.

"Start by making yourself comfortable. You'll need a mantra."

"A mantra?"

"It's a word or a saying that you chant silently to calm the thoughts that fill your mind. I'll share mine with you. It's 'om'."

"Om? That's it?"

"Yes, om. Chant it silently."

"What does it mean?" He looked at her quizzically.

"In one translation it means 'to become'."

"To become what?"

She smiled, remembering her own questions to Jasmine the year before at the ranch. She knew so much more now. "To become free from suffering. To become liberated and happy. To become anything you want to become, I guess."

"Oh, okay. I'm ready."

"Close your eyes and let the sun warm your eyelids. Breathe through your nose and relax. Breathe in, expand your diaphragm. Breathe out and release. When you exhale, your belly wants to touch the front of your spine. It's the way babies breathe."

Gulls cried overhead.

"Breathe in and out slowly. Quiet your mind. Focus your thoughts on love and kindness. If your thoughts stray, focus on your breath and chant om. Release your troubles and give in to the tender embrace of solitude."

They sat in meditation. The sound of the surf breaking on the rocks below faded into the atmosphere. The phone booth popped into her thoughts. It would be too risky to make a call with Will so near. She pushed it aside and chanted om.

After some time, she emerged from the depths of calm. Charlie still had his eyes closed. His shaggy brown hair ruffled in the breeze. She unlocked her stiff legs and stretched on the rock.

Charlie opened his eyes. "My butt is asleep." He straightened his legs.

She laughed. "We're sitting on granite. How was it?"

"It was calming," Charlie said. "I can't turn off all of my thoughts and images, but it does take them down a notch. I think I fell asleep."

"It takes practice. What kind of images go through your mind?"

His brow furrowed as he traced a mineral vein in the granite with his finger. "Stuff from Nam."

She slid over and gave him a fleeting hug.

Will was writing in his leather notebook when they returned to the campsite. "Well?" He looked expectantly at Charlie.

"I learned how to breathe like a baby and chant."

Will shook his head. "You're both wasting your time."

"No," said Charlie. "I liked it. I'm going to try it again. It takes practice."

Jolie smiled and suppressed a laugh.

Charlie pitched his tent while Jolie got out their picnic dinner. Will started a campfire. After dinner they talked by the roaring fire, mesmerized by the flames and cricket song.

The phone booth by the showers called to Jolie. It hovered in her thoughts. She was still haunted by the phone conversation she'd had in New York with her brother. She could call home from Maine. She had enough coins. She always had a purse full of change from tips.

"Jolie?" Will startled her. "I was talking to you. Why are you always a million miles away?"

"Pardon?"

"Pardon? You're so polite," Will said.

Why did he criticize her for being polite? "It's ingrained. My dad wouldn't allow us to say *what* or *yeah*. It had to be *pardon me* or *yes*."

"Same here," Charlie said.

⌒◯

Sunday morning, Jolie and Charlie went down by the cliff to meditate. They sat cross-legged on towels.

"Breathe. Let your energy flow through the channels of your body. Bring your mind home. When you exhale, release your body into tender gravity. Be held how you want to be held. Find your now."

"My now?"

"The present moment is all that exists. Our minds worry about the past and the future, but the now is the true self. Be in the moment and experience peace. Be here now."

"Be here now. Okay, I'll try and find my nowness."

Jolie peeked at him. His eyes were closed, and his dimples were exaggerated by his grin. She smiled to herself and closed her eyes. "Rest in your mind's pure awareness. Chant your mantra to calm the mind." An amber glow from the sun spread through her.

On the way back to their campsite, Jolie stopped at the showers and told Charlie she'd see him back at camp. The phone booth pulled her like a magnet. When Charlie disappeared on the path through the trees, she walked into the booth and shut the glass folding door. She lay out coins in stacks, took a deep breath, exhaled, and dialed 0. When the operator came on, Jolie fumbled for the correct change and the call was placed. The phone rang twice.

"Hello?"

"Hi, Mom." Her voice squeaked like a little girl.

"Jolie?"

"Yes, it's me."

"Oh my god. Jolie honey, are you okay?"

"I'm safe. I wanted to let you know I'm fine."

"Oh Jolie, where are you?"

"Somewhere out here." She struggled to get the words out. Her mom's voice soothed her.

"Honey, are you in New York?"

New York? The postmark from the letter, or did they trace the call? Jolie choked up. "I love you. I love all of you."

"We love you, too. We're sorry we pushed you away." Anguish poured out of her mother's voice. "The Catholic school idea was just wrong. Your dad can't forgive himself. We just want you home."

Had her mom finally stood up to her dad? "How is Dad?" Her voice choked.

The line was silent.

"Mom? Are you there?"

"I'm here."

"How is Dad?"

Another long pause ensued. "I find him outside on the deck at night, sitting in the dark. Have you ever seen a grown man cry?"

She could not imagine her father crying. The pressure in Jolie's chest rose to her head. Her throat closed up. It was like she was drowning. "I have to go," she whispered.

"No, please…don't go. Talk to me, honey. Where are you? We just want you home with us. I'll come and get you."

She had to get off the phone. Will said they could trace the calls from their phone.

"I can't come home right now. I'll call again. I love you. Give Dad a hug for me. Tell everyone I love them." She hung up the receiver. The image of her father in tears was etched in her mind. Why had she hurt the people that meant the most to her? They still loved her and wanted her to come home. A wave of guilt and remorse washed over her as she leaned against the glass. She could never undo what she had done to them.

38

Come Together

After they returned from camping, Jolie devoted her spare time to the student photos. She developed prints before she went to work and again in the evenings with Daniel. The darkroom was small and they were limited to how many they could print in one session. Daniel added another drying line. Prints hung everywhere in the small space. The finished photos were spread out on the dining room table and chairs. Summer school was out in two weeks and they had to finish the project.

"Why are you doing this?" Will asked, one night in their room.

Her mind raced. What was it now? He didn't like her interest in meditation and Buddhism, the Women's Liberation Movement, the Roxbury High photo project, and her so-called bourgeois friends.

"Doing what?" Her stomach tightened and she held her breath.

"Why are you spending so much time on the photo project? You're preoccupied with it."

"I'm doing it for the students."

"You'll never see them again."

"That doesn't matter. You should have met them. And their photos are good."

"You've spent so much time and energy on this. I could have used you at the office."

"We'll be finished soon. His students are so excited. Is Adam still going to print them in *Central Underground?*"

"Yes, but he'll need some kind of a story to go with the photos. You know, the lead-in article. The who, what, why, where, and when. We'll run them next Wednesday. I just want you to be done with it."

Didn't he see that she enjoyed the project? But it wasn't worth arguing about. She had to learn to shake off his slings and arrows and not be so sensitive. His criticism would make her stronger, and besides, was it so bad that he wanted her all to himself, all of her energy focused on him?

⟳

By the end of the week, all of the photos had been printed, including the ones Jolie had taken of the students taking pictures. She spent the weekend with Will at the office. She laid out the special photo insert, six photos per page.

"You're going to use up a lot of ink, Jolie girl," Adam said, looking over her shoulder. "It will cost you."

Her head snapped around, and she saw the twinkle in his eye.

"Sorry to hear about the robbery," Adam said.

"What do you think about the Marlena theory?"

"It does piece together. As revenge for her betraying us, we're writing an article: 'I Slept with an FBI Informant'."

Jolie looked at him, her throat tightening, "Who slept with her?"

Adam looked around the office. "Well, me for one."

Her stomach and chest tightened. She ran though the interactions she'd seen between Will and Marlena. Was Will writing the 'I Slept with an Informant' story? She willed herself to stop thinking any negative thoughts. In the Buddhist practice of right mindfulness, love is spoiled by insecurity and possessiveness. Focus on love, compassion and wisdom. Marlena meant nothing to Will.

She regained her composure. "Would you do me a favor?"

"Anything for you, Jolie girl."

"Can you print posters for the Women's Strike for Equality? I'll have the layout ready in a week."

"Women are striking?"

Jolie smiled. "All over the country."

"Sure, just clear it with Will."

Why did she have to clear it with Will? Weren't they equals? Jolie finished up the photo spread, proofed it once more, and walked over to where Will stood with Adam and Charlie. She set the layout before them. "It's print ready."

"It's about time," Will said.

"I'm going to get groceries on the way home and cook a big dinner," she said. "I haven't cooked all week."

"We know, Will's been complaining," Charlie said.

Jolie looked at Charlie and Adam. "You're both invited, of course."

She walked out into the warm Sunday afternoon. The photo project had been all-consuming. Her mind was full of the images. When she closed her eyes at night or in meditation, the photos were there, burned into her retinas. At least they weren't images of Vietnam like Charlie had.

Jolie turned the corner and automatically walked through the open gate and up the stone path to the temple. Soft pink lotus flowers with yellow centers were open to the sky, stretching tall from the lotus pads floating in the pond. If only she had her camera to capture the beauty, the peacefulness. Giant koi swam serenely below the lotus pads. She'd bring Charlie here sometime.

She removed her leather sandals inside the temple door. The floor was cool on her feet. In the meditation room, golden-colored candles and frankincense incense burned on the altar. Delicate pink and white flower petals lay beneath the Buddha statue. A handful of students sat cross-legged, waiting. The monk instructed them to place their hands in prayer position against their chests with a pound of pressure. A harmonic tenor filled the room as they chanted three oms.

"Bring your scattered mind home," the monk said. "All the fragments of ourselves will become friends. Follow your breath."

"To fly you need two wings. Compassion and wisdom," the monk said. "Compassion comes from the heart. Breathe light into the heart. In time, wisdom will come to you and liberate you from suffering."

The image of her father crying rose in her mind. Fighting tears, she breathed deeply. She had to heal the pain in her heart. Jolie imagined a ball of emerald light hovering above her head. She breathed in, drawing the energy through the crown of her head until it flowed down, filling her heart center with warm, positive energy. She breathed out, creating a protective aura around her.

When meditation was over, Jolie was in no hurry to leave. She stretched her legs, stiff from sitting cross-legged. She got up and walked out with three other women she had gotten to know. The women stopped at the counter in the lobby and looked at the class schedule.

Cheyenne looked at Jolie. "Do you want to come to yoga with us?"

"It enhances the practice," Molly said.

She wanted to learn yoga, but she hadn't wanted to go alone. "Sure, I'll join you," Jolie said.

"See you Thursday morning then," Willow said.

They walked out into the late afternoon sun and went their various ways. Yoga at the temple, one more thing she'd have to keep from Will.

Monday night, Will and Jolie watched the news. The reporter was broadcasting from the Statue of Liberty: "Today brought the first hint of actions to come. Over a hundred women went to liberate the Statue of Liberty, unfurling a banner on her pedestal reading *Women of the World Unite*, sending a message to the world of the upcoming strike and march."

Jolie jumped up from the couch. "Did you see that? I wish I'd been there."

"What are one hundred women going to change?" Will asked.

Ignoring his question, she rushed into the kitchen and called Ginger. "We're going to change the poster design. We'll use a photo of the Statue of Liberty I took from Sunset Park and create a banner with Women of the World Unite on it."

On Jolie's way home from work on Wednesday, she stopped at the office to drop off the final design of the strike poster. She handed it to Adam for printing.

He held it out at arm's length and whistled softly. "Roll over, Beethoven." He looked at Jolie and then to Will with a question in his raised eyebrows.

"Go ahead, print them. She even talked me into publishing the damn thing," Will said.

Jolie gave Will a hug. "The strike is going to be big."

"Yeah, right. Probably fifty women will show up," Will said.

It was press day. She was anxious to see the student pictures published. A stack of papers sat next to the door, hot off the press. She picked one up and carefully opened it to the photo spread. There was Daniel, talking with his students while they looked on with rapt attention. It was followed by her short article on the class field trip. She focused on their photos, slowly turning the pages. Tears blurred her vision.

She looked up. Will and Adam stood watching her. "Thank you, it's beautiful."

Will walked over and stroked her hair. "Not as beautiful as you."

Jolie and Will left the office together, driving home with a stack of newspapers for Daniel and his class.

The next morning Jolie went to the temple for yoga before work. She grabbed a mat and stretched with the other students. A male yogi led them through yoga poses. "It is through the breath that we can truly link the mind to the body," the yogi said. "Let your breath guide your movement and let your movement follow your breath."

They followed his breathing techniques and poses. Some poses were easy stretches. Others were awkward and hard to maintain. "Let your body encompass the relationship with your mind. Let your mind encompass the relationship with the earth and then the universe," the yogi said.

Jolie practically floated to the T station, her body buoyant and graceful. In the Square, she stopped in the camera shop. Niles smiled at her from behind the counter. She handed him a copy of *Central Underground Press.* He laid it out on the glass counter, and they looked through the photos together.

"How did you get them to print this big spread?"

"My boyfriend runs the agency."

"Ah, well no one else would give those kids the time of day."

Jolie walked over to the used camera case. "My camera was stolen."

"Your camera? Sorry to hear that."

"I'm saving for another one. Be on the lookout for a good used one."

They talked cameras for a while before Jolie dashed off for work.

Adam stopped by the house that night with a large stack of the strike posters. He set them down and handed one to Jolie. She scanned it quickly. The artwork was well done. The vibrant colors leapt off the page. Adam had gone all out on the detail of the printing.

Her eyes fixed on the banner across the photograph of the Statue of Liberty. She turned to Adam and Will who stood watching her. This couldn't be happening again.

She looked back to the poster and turned to Adam. "You're kidding right?"

"No, we took a vote and this won, hands down," Adam said.

Jolie turned her gaze back to the poster. The banner read: Pussy Power. She looked at the tall stack of posters and stood speechless. Her thoughts exploded and her heart throbbed in anguish. Why weren't they taken seriously?

Adam picked up another poster from the stack and handed it to her. The original slogan, Women of the World Unite, was printed on the banner.

"We're just messing with you, Jolie girl," Adam said, laughing. "I only printed ten of those to get a rise out of you."

Jolie let out a long sigh and shook her head. "You're a cruel man, Adam."

⌒◯

Saturday was Jolie's birthday. She hadn't told anyone and didn't want to a make a big deal of it. Ginger stopped by to pick her up to go to the Women's Liberation meeting. Jolie and Ginger carried stacks of posters down to Ginger's VW Bug. As they drove through Central Square the colorful strike posters were plastered everywhere.

"You've been busy," Ginger said.

Jolie nodded and smiled.

Sarah and Leah met them at the meeting room on the BU campus. They set the posters on the front table and by the door. Elaine's face lit up when she saw the colorful design. Jolie showed her the Pussy Power version, and she howled with laughter. At the end of the meeting, the posters disappeared with the women. Soon they would be on telephone poles and storefront windows all over Boston and Cambridge.

After the meeting Leah, Sarah, Ginger, and Jolie walked to the parking lot. "What's up Jolie? You're quiet today," Leah said.

Should she tell them or just let it go by? "Nothing."

"Ah, come on. Something's on your mind," Ginger said.

"Well, okay. It's my birthday," Jolie said.

They encircled her in a happy birthday hug.

"What's Will doing for you?" Ginger asked.

"I think he forgot."

"No, he wouldn't do that," Leah said. "Would he?"

"We have to take you shopping," Sarah said. "There is a cool district near here called Allston with vintage stores galore. I read the advertisements in *Central Underground Press.*"

Jolie smiled, Sarah was reading the free press.

"I'll drive," Ginger said.

They piled into Ginger's VW Bug and rolled down the street. In Allston, they walked past funky art galleries and cafes, and discreetly taped and tacked up posters. On the corner, two black guys with frothy afros sang. Their vocals burst forth like rolling thunder as they clapped the percussion.

In a vintage store, they looked through the racks of clothes and accessories, caressing the soft fabric and rich detailing. Leah sauntered over to Jolie, holding a black silk-and-satin cocktail dress with sequins and beads dripping from the bodice.

"This is you. I'll buy it for you for your birthday."

"It's beautiful, but where would I wear it?"

"Have Will take you out."

Sarah and Ginger joined them, admiring the exquisite detail of the beadwork.

"Oh, he'll think it's bourgeois," Jolie said.

"He thinks everything and everybody is bourgeois," Ginger said, laughing.

"Try it on," Leah said.

Jolie stood looking at the dress.

"Please?" Leah said.

Jolie reluctantly took it into the dressing room. She slipped the soft silky dress over her head and pulled it down around her body. It fit perfectly. She opened the dressing room curtain. Her friends cooed at the sight of her.

"It was meant for you," Leah said.

"You're positively smashing," Ginger said, in a put-on British accent.

They shopped in more stores and everyone found something unique. Jolie found a black velvet choker with crystal beads that she bought to go with the dress.

It was mid-afternoon when Ginger dropped Jolie off at the house. "I'm coming by later to see Sam. Wear your dress tonight," Ginger called as she drove off.

In the house she found a note from Will on the kitchen table. *Tied up at the office until about 6. 7 p.m. meeting tonight at the house.*

She groaned; not another meeting at the house. He did forget her birthday. Well, she was not cooking for them tonight. She had three hours before he got back. Locking the house, she walked down the street and turned onto the stone path to the temple. In the lobby she taped a poster for the strike in the window and went into a meditation room where a small group had assembled. She sat on a mat and closed her eyes.

"Breath in the light and bring your mind home," the monk said. "The core of your being is the only safe place to call home."

She breathed in. It was her birthday. The day she was born. Unsettling thoughts and feelings rose and fell with her breath like the swell of the ocean.

When Jolie got back to the house, no one was home. She ran a bath and added ylang ylang flower oil to arouse the senses. She slid into the foaming water, breathing the scent from faraway lands. A sense of inner peace filled her. When the water grew cool she got out and slipped on her new beaded dress and knee-high soft suede moccasins. She combed out her hair and tied the black velvet beaded choker around her forehead. Looking in the mirror she debated whether to change. Would Will like it?

She could hear voices down the hall. In the kitchen, Will and Charlie stood by the counter, opening bottles of beer. On the kitchen table was a wrapped present. He had remembered. They hadn't heard her come into the room and when they turned, they both stopped and stared at her. She scanned Will's face. Did he not like the dress? She held her breath.

Charlie gave a soft wolf whistle.

"Watch it buddy," Will said. "She's mine, all mine." Will went to her and gave her a kiss. "Happy Birthday, Little Wing. You look stunning." He nodded to the present on the table. "Open it."

Jolie carefully unwrapped the paper, revealing a plain brown box. She opened it slowly to find three wrapped objects inside. She opened the large one first. Her eyes grew wide. Elated, she held up a 35 mm Nikon camera. And she thought he'd forgotten her birthday.

"Wow, thank you."

Enthused, she opened the other packages. One was a wide angle lens and the other a telephoto lens. She smiled joyfully.

"You're back in business," Will said.

"With a Nikon no less," Jolie said.

"Your new camera for the cause. But no more off-the-wall projects," Will said.

279

Ignoring the comment, she attached the telephoto lens. At the window, she focused on a woman walking down the street. She seemed so close in the lens.

"You could spy on somebody with this lens."

Ginger and Sam arrived with a birthday cake. Adam showed up later with pizzas and red wine. Daniel, Leah, and Sarah walked in sometime later. The party moved into the dining room and living room. Will played guitar. At some point, Charlie followed Jolie into the kitchen.

"I've been meditating, but my mind wanders or I fall asleep," Charlie said.

"Well, that's a start. At least you're not thinking about Vietnam."

He grinned. "You're always so positive. By the way, you look unbelievable tonight."

"Thank you." Jolie put on water for tea. "I've been going to the Buddhist temple around the corner. Promise you won't tell Will, though."

"Why don't you want him to know?" He leaned against the counter next to her.

"He thinks it's a cult, and I'll get sucked in."

"Is it?"

"No. It is spiritual, though."

"I could use some of that."

"Come with me sometime and check it out."

He glanced into the living room at Will. "Maybe."

Jolie followed his gaze. Will had captivated all the girls with the song he played.

"Has Marlena been around?" Jolie said.

"No, I haven't seen her for weeks."

"Can I ask you something?" Jolie said.

"Anything," Charlie said.

"Did Will sleep with her?"

He shifted his weight. "I don't know. I honestly don't know." He paused. "I sure didn't. She's sort of fake or something."

She poured boiling water into a pot of bergamot tea, and they carried the teapot and cups into the living room where the others sat listening to music.

She sat back and sipped the fragrant tea, alone in her thoughts. She was sixteen today. What was her family doing? At least they knew she was safe. She had tried to give them some peace of mind. The vision of her father sitting in the dark flashed through her thoughts. She set down her tea and slipped out of the room, not wanting anyone to see her tears.

39

A Band of Braless Bubbleheads

~~~O

On August 26, women around the country united for marches, protests, and strikes. The Boston Women's Strike was scheduled for five
p.m. Jolie and Leah left work early. They told Frank they weren't feeling well, and it must be highly contagious because they were both sick.
They hopped in Leah's car and drove to her apartment. Leah parked,
and they walked toward the bandstand on the Common.

"Wow, look at the crowd," Jolie said. She had never seen so many
women in one place before. If only Will were here to see, maybe he'd
take them seriously. Hundreds of women had descended upon the
Common. Cameramen and reporters cowered on the sidelines, intimidated by the swell of women.

Elaine introduced the speakers as they took the stage. Curious
bystanders watched from the edge of the crowd. The throng of women
responded to the speeches with cheers and chants. After the last speech,
women and girls linked arms and marched around the Common. Jolie,
Leah, Sarah, and Ginger marched in silent solidarity. Women carried
signs and banners: Women Demand Equality; Don't Iron while the
Strike is Hot; End Human Sacrifice—Don't Get Married. A group of
women marched in academic gowns with a banner reading VERITAS,
Harvard University's motto, the Goddess of Truth. Jolie photographed
everything.

At the house that night, Ginger and Jolie watched the news with Sam and Will. The news man uttered condescending remarks describing the events around the country. He likened it to an infectious disease and claimed the women of the movement were nothing more than a "band of braless bubbleheads".

"We'll show him what a band of women can do," Jolie said.

"We'll boycott their TV stations and not buy the products they advertise," Ginger said.

"Right on," Sam said.

Will shook his head, and got up and left the room with his guitar. Jolie and Ginger exchanged a look. Jolie shrugged and turned back to the TV. The convergence of women in Boston and New York and around the country was overwhelming. Women in Paris and Amsterdam had also taken to the streets.

Jolie spent the weekend printing photos from the Women's Strike. On Sunday, Ginger stopped by with two draft articles. One highlighted the strike; the second article's headline read: WOMEN UNITE: BOYCOTT THESE PRODUCTS. WE WILL NOT BE DEGRADED. Underneath was a long list of household products that were advertised on the major networks. Together, Jolie and Ginger edited the articles and picked out the photos, focusing on the banners, signs, and massive crowd.

"I'll bring both articles to the office and get them sent to all of the other underground presses to run," Jolie said. "We'll show them what an infectious disease can do."

When Ginger left, Jolie packed up the photos and articles and walked to the office. The day was warm, and the breeze carried the faint scent of honeysuckle. She felt so alive. As she approached the office, refrains from Crosby, Stills and Nash's "Ohio" spilled out of the open windows. Adam, Charlie, and a black guy with a huge afro worked in the living room, laying out the next issue. Will talked on the phone in the dining room area and never looked up. She strode over to the guys and set down the packet with the photos and articles.

"Jolie girl," Adam said.

Jolie put her hands together in a prayer position on her heart, bowed her head once, and smiled.

The black guy held out his hand. "I'm T.J."

She shook his hand. "I'm Jolie."

"Don't I know. Your name comes up a lot around here."

"Did you call the *Globe?*" Charlie asked.

"The *Globe?*" she said.

"*The Boston Globe.* They called Will and wanted to run some of the student photos."

"They did? They do?" Why hadn't Will told her? "I haven't heard about it." She looked at Will who was still on the phone.

"I'll find the message for you." Charlie walked over to the desk where Will sat with his feet up and rifled through a stack of messages. He returned and handed her a paper with a name and phone number.

"Thanks. I'll have Daniel call them." She glanced at the paper and slipped it into her back pocket. She looked at Adam. "I've got two articles for you to run and lots of photos."

"I don't know if we have room this week," Adam said.

Her mouth opened slightly to speak but nothing came out. Didn't have room? He could make more room. He could add as many pages as he wanted. She searched his face and saw the sparkle in his eye. She grinned. He always knew how to get a rise out of her. Proudly, she unveiled the photos and the two articles and set them on the long table. Adam, Charlie, and T.J. scanned them.

"A boycott? A lot of good that will do," T.J. said.

"Fifty-one percent of the population are women and we do eighty-five percent of the shopping," Jolie said.

"The chicks that read this paper hardly buy anything," Adam said.

"We've got to start somewhere. Women talk to women, daughters talk to mothers. It's a sacred sisterhood."

Charlie smiled at her. "Sounds like a cult."

Adam flipped through the photos of the strike. Will came over to see what they were looking at. He picked up the two articles and scanned them. She knew they were good.

"Jesus, Jolie. First you spent all that time on the student photos, and then on that strike, and now a boycott?" He flipped the articles back onto the table.

Pain flashed through her. She was aware that all eyes were on her. Charlie shot her a glance and their eyes met.

"You're just wasting your time," Will said. "The Socialist Movement is far more important."

Her throat constricted and she could hardly find her voice. She straightened the articles on the table. "I'm not wasting my time. We have momentum. Look at this crowd." More women had turned out for the strike than any of the Socialist Movement protests. She handed the articles and photos to Adam.

Adam held them up.

"Man, look at all of those women," T.J. said, whistling softly.

"These are good photos," Charlie said.

At least Charlie and Adam were on her side. The phone rang, and someone called out for Will. He went to take the call. She looked at Adam. "Can you run these this week?"

"Of course I'll run them."

Charlie moved toward Jolie and gave her a quick hug. "We're with you."

"Can you send these articles and photos out to all the subscribers?" Jolie said.

"Consider it done," Charlie said.

Jolie glanced over her shoulder at Will as she slipped out the door. His back was toward her, and he was in an intense discussion with someone on the other end of the line. She didn't like conflict between them. Her chest and stomach felt crushed by a weight. Her earlier enthusiasm was squashed. He always made her causes seem trivial. The strike had been a success. They'd drawn a huge crowd, and she had helped make it happen. Will should be proud of her.

Without thinking, she changed her route and walked up the stone path to the temple. Alone in a meditation room she sat on a mat. The room was cool, sheltered from the outside heat. With closed eyes she considered Will's hurtful comment. She was not wasting her time. The monk's words from a previous meditation session came to her: Nothing is permanent, actions have consequences, change is possible. Change was possible. She focused on

285

her breathing and tried to slow the torrent of mental noise. Why hadn't Will told her about the message from the *Globe*? Did it get buried in the pile of other messages? She exhaled and let go of the tension. The sapphire-blue hole slowly appeared through the tunnel of darkness.

40

She's a Rainbow

⌒◯

"This is my last week," Leah said to Jolie in the restaurant locker room. "I'm so sick of ice cream. I can't wait to be done with this place and this rat-infested basement."

"We'll still be friends, though," Jolie said.

"We'll always be friends. Can you come to the Cape this weekend?"

Leah had invited Jolie to Cape Cod for Labor Day weekend. Her parents and Sarah's parents had rented two cottages. Zack was coming, too.

"I'm not sure. I haven't asked Will yet."

"Don't you want to come?"

"Yes, it sounds amazing."

"Then just come. Why do you have to ask permission?"

Jolie didn't respond. Leah didn't really know Will. But she was right. Isn't that what they were fighting for? To make their own decisions?

Leah tied her apron around her waist. "Well, I hope you can come. Zack and my parents keep asking me if you're joining us. They're driving me crazy."

After work, Jolie went straight home. She sat on the back porch with a book in her lap. She too was sick of waitressing. Leah, Sarah, and Charlie were all starting college next month. They were moving on and she was getting left behind. She should study and take the

GED test. If she passed she would earn a High School Equivalency Certificate and then she could apply to colleges. Tomorrow before work she'd go to the Cambridge Library and find out how to sign up for the test.

The front door closed with a shudder. Will found her out on the porch. He kissed her on the top of her head and sat down next to her. He talked excitedly about the Socialist Party march he was organizing for the upcoming weekend.

"We are growing a bigger and more radical Socialist Labor Party."

"The march is this weekend?"

"It's on Labor Day. You're going to take photos, remember?"

"Leah invited me to spend the weekend with her family on Cape Cod. They have cottages on the beach."

"You want to spend the weekend with some bourgeois people, barbequing and drinking cocktails when you could be making history?"

Her heart sank. She needed to be strong. "The cottages sound like fun, and they're not bourgeois. Leah and Sarah's mothers are both supporting the product boycott."

"I need you to come and take photos. This is important to me."

"Charlie can take the photos. I'll lend him my camera. I can develop them when I get back."

He reached for her hand and squeezed it. "No, you need to stick with me."

She knew he wouldn't take no for an answer. Why was she disappointed? He only wanted her with him, by his side. Jolie listened as Will explained the Socialist Labor Party developments.

"Ché Guevara taught us that revolutionaries move like the fish in the sea. The mistrust that so many people have for this country's capitalist and imperialist politics has created an ocean of revolutionaries," Will said. "And there is an ocean of returning students to recruit."

Like fish in the sea. Her mind wandered. Nick would be back next week. She'd plan the hike through the Emerald Necklace Parks for whoever wanted to come.

"We're going to abolish capitalism and reorganize the U.S. into a socialist state. We're preparing the party for war."

This caught her attention. "War?"

"We're becoming a cohesive and disciplined organization." Will paused. "Remember what Fidel Castro said? 'A revolution is not a bed of roses. It is a struggle to the death between the past and the future'."

"But it won't be a real war," Jolie said.

"It depends how it plays out."

The week seemed to drag on forever. Jolie told Leah that Will was organizing a protest on Labor Day and she had to be there. Leah tried her best to change Jolie's mind, but to no avail. Friday came. It was Leah's last day. Dimitri cooked them both a special lunch, and they ate together in the break room. Over the summer, Dimitri had warmed up to Leah.

Leah drummed her fingers on the table. She had four hours left on her shift. She looked over at Jolie who had hardly touched her food. "Why so quiet?"

"Just thinking about the weekend." Jolie looked at Dimitri. "What are you doing this weekend?"

"Working."

"Working? Here?" asked Leah.

"No, on weekends I cook at my cousin's restaurant."

"You never told me that," Jolie said.

"You never asked."

"What kind of restaurant?" Jolie asked.

"Greek, of course, in the Back Bay. Stop in sometime."

Jolie wrote down the name and address on her waitress pad. The closest thing she'd ever had to Greek food was a gyro sandwich from a street vendor.

"You seem sad. I'll call you this weekend," Leah said, getting up from the table. "We'll be bored without you."

Warmed by their friendship, Jolie cheered up as they went back to their stations. After work, she stopped at the camera store. Niles was standing behind the glass counter reading the latest issue of *Central Underground*.

"Nice photos of the strike," he said with a nod to the paper. "You got another camera?"

"It was my boyfriend who bought the used Nikon and two lenses from you."

"Will is your boyfriend?"

Jolie nodded.

"I've heard a lot about him. It was an honor to actually meet him."

She smiled. Will had that effect on everyone.

"I saw the kids' photos in the *Globe*," he said. "They did a nice spread. How come you weren't mentioned?"

The *Globe* had run an article with a picture of Daniel and his class, along with a few student photos. Daniel had insisted she be included, but the last thing she wanted was her photo or name in the paper. "It's all about the students. Thanks again for loaning us the cameras." She walked to the film counter. "I want to try color film. What does it cost to develop a roll?"

"Most photographers use color slide film. You develop the slides and then select which ones to have printed. It saves a whole lot of money." He handed her a roll of color slide film. "The film is on me."

"No. I can afford it. I need to pay."

She thanked him and hurried to the T. She was anxious to start the weekend with her new book, *The Teachings of Don Juan* by Carlos Castaneda, a mystical journey with an Indian shaman.

Saturday morning at the temple, Jolie first meditated and then read in the sandalwood haze of the library. Each book, infused with layers of incense, emitted an intoxicating scent as she turned the pages. A monk sat at the far end of the long wooden table, absorbed in his own book.

She read the Buddha's sermon about the Four Noble Truths. He believed that through individual practice and experimentation one could unlock the cause of one's suffering and be liberated. He stressed the importance of finding out for oneself, thinking for oneself and using one's own senses. The cause of suffering was unique to the individual and so was the path to liberation. She looked at the monk. It seemed so vague. How would she find the key to her emptiness? With each meditation she struggled with the empty space, the blue hole. She had to get through the hole.

She put the book back on the shelf and picked up a small worn volume on chakras, the seven energy centers in the body. She turned to the chakra depicted by sky-blue petals, the color of the blue hole she saw in meditation. It was the Vishuddha energy center, the throat Chakra. She read on. The fifth chakra governed communication, independence, fluid thought, and a sense of security. Knowledge speaks. Wisdom listens. Speak the truth. Live authentically. She put the book back on the shelf, overwhelmed with the multitude of meanings.

On her way out, she read a poster for a meeting that afternoon. "Save the Earth. Open Forum. Turn your concerns into actions." The Forum was at a Harvard lecture hall. Why not? Will was busy preparing for the march on Monday. A few months ago she would have been too intimidated to go on campus by herself, but not now. She would walk to Harvard Square and take color photos along the way.

The house was empty when she returned from the temple. She mixed up a batch of chocolate chip cookies to take to the office on her way to the meeting. Making cookies was always relaxing. While the cookies baked, she played Jimi Hendrix's new album, *A Band of Gypsy's*, and hummed along as she cleaned the house.

Ginger and Sam came in the door as the cookies cooled. "Yum, these are my favorite." Sam reached for a cookie. "We just stopped by to get some of my clothes. We're heading to Nantucket Island for the weekend."

"What's in Nantucket?" Jolie asked.

"My folks have a second home and a sailboat there," Sam said.

"It's full of quaint houses and big mansions, little shops, and restaurants," Ginger said.

"We're going to go sailing, eat fish and chips and drink Bloody Marys," Sam said.

Ginger laughed. "I'm going to lay on the boat, read, and swim."

"Wow that sounds idyllic."

"I thought you were going to the Cape," Ginger said.

"Plans changed. Will has the big march on Monday."

"I think you're blindly in love with a dictator," Ginger said, only half joking. "You should have gone to the Cape. You need to have some fun."

Jolie shrugged and handed Sam and Ginger a bag of cookies as they dashed out the door. Will a dictator? Was that how others viewed him?

She dressed in a pale blue gauzy shirt, cut-off jeans, and sandals. With the color film loaded in her camera, she picked up the large plate of cookies for the office and headed out. A wave of isolation rolled over her, and the familiar ache welled in her chest. She had a whole weekend of adventure ahead, yet she felt so alone. Maybe the gang at the office would cheer her up. She crossed to the sunny side of the street and let the sun warm her face and arms.

She heard the music halfway up the block. Country Joe and the Fish blasted out the open windows of the office, louder than normal. Charlie was there with three other students. They were busy opening and sorting a pile of mail and answering the constant ring of the phones.

"You're looking lovely today," Charlie said.

"Brought you something," she said to Charlie. She placed the cookies on the kitchen counter and looked around. "Where's Will?"

"Don't know. He took off a while ago. Hey, I sent your articles to all the presses. And I sent the boycott article and list to my mom."

"Your mom?" A smile spread across her glum face. She flashed him the peace sign.

"What are you up to?"

"I'm going to try out some color film and then go to a Save the Earth meeting."

One of the students looked up. "I heard about that."

"Nuke the gray whales," Charlie said.

Jolie pushed his shoulder affectionately and left the office.

She walked along the side streets of Harvard Square, her eye focused on color, absorbed in finding photo subjects. Capturing the essence of the composition seemed harder in color than black and white. With black and white, she captured the soul. With color, the beauty of nature became art. She stopped and took a close up of an Icelandic poppy with its brilliant coral flower and bright green leaves set off by delicate tendrils. Harvard Square hummed with humanity. She snapped a photo of a Hare Krishna wearing a shimmering saffron-colored robe.

In the Common, she sat down on an empty park bench and observed the flow of people. She was seeing in color now. She conceptualized a photo series of chakra colors: red, orange, yellow, green, blue, indigo, and violet. Her mood warmed to the color images.

Across the street at Harvard, she found the lecture hall and stood in the doorway, surveying the room. It was packed. A few people in the front of the room by the podium looked vaguely familiar. From Earth Day? She found a seat in the back next to a young woman and took out a small journal and pen from her purse. Her shirt stuck to her back, sticky in the heat. Here she was, sitting in a classroom at Harvard. She smiled to herself. Okay, it was a Save the Earth meeting, but she was in a classroom at Harvard and it was good to dream.

A tall, lanky man with shoulder-length black hair and glasses stood at the podium and thanked everyone for coming. "This is an open forum. Everyone will get a chance to come forward and promote their cause. If we have common causes, we can join forces around the world and save the earth!"

There was a sprinkling of applause. A line had formed on the side of the podium. The first speaker, a middle-aged white man, adjusted the microphone and began speaking.

"There are now 3.7 billion people in the world. We are at risk of global starvation. The U.S. must set an example and produce more food. We need to reduce our population growth to zero or negative zero."

Jolie looked at the woman sitting next to her and caught her eye. They both raised their eyebrows quizzically. Negative zero? What did that mean?

"The U.S. needs to add a tax for babies," the man continued.

How many kids did he have?

The next speaker promoted an anti-nuclear platform. "The spread of nuclear weapons around the world is apocalyptic in the hands of unstable leaders. Nuclear testing and the resulting radioactive fallout is harming the lives of humans and our ecosystems. Nuclear power plants are in our backyards. Nuclear waste is contaminating our deserts and water supplies. The waste lasts thousands of years. We must eliminate nuclear weapons and nuclear power."

Applause started with a ripple and then thundered in the hall. Score one for the anti-nuclear movement. Jolie jotted a note in her journal.

An older woman stepped up to the microphone, cleared her throat, and began. "DDT is in women's breast milk. Mercury is in fish. Dioxin in our food. Lead is poisoning our children. Our rain is acid. The air we breathe is polluted. Our lakes, rivers, and oceans are contaminated with toxic dumping from manufacturing, acid mining, urban runoff, and ships dumping at sea. We even haul our garbage out to sea and dump it! This all must stop. We must regulate chemicals and toxins and require corporations to clean up the mess they have created."

Applause thundered. Another winner.

Another middle-aged white man got up and talked about whales being run over in the shipping lanes in the Atlantic and Pacific Oceans. Someone else spoke of global warming, greenhouse gases, clear-cutting forests, sea levels rising. Another man spoke of invasive species, endangered species, and extinct species.

The leader of the meeting narrowed the concerns into three groups: anti-nuclear, chemical pollution, and land preservation/conservation. Why hadn't anyone spoken of offshore oil drilling and catastrophic oil spills? She should have gotten up and talked about the devastation she'd seen firsthand, but she was too shy to speak in front of all these people. Someday she would.

When the meeting ended, Jolie walked to the front of the room where the leaders of each group stood by sign-up sheets. At the chemical pollution sheet, she wrote her name and phone number. The leader was a Harvard biology Ph.D. candidate, and he'd already set the first meeting date for the same room.

She bounced down Massachusetts Avenue toward the T station, happy with a new cause to embrace for the future of the earth. The streets were jammed on the holiday weekend. A half a block from the T, she heard Old Blue. The low rumble from the hole in the muffler was unmistakable. The bus drove past her on the street and she leapt and waved. A young woman was in the passenger seat. Her long blonde hair, parted in the middle, framed a doll-like face. She looked right at Jolie, and they locked eyes for a brief moment. Will looked straight ahead, his eyes on the road. He hadn't seen her on the crowded street. A sinking feeling filled her.

Jolie stood still and watched Old Blue disappear in the distance. Heat rose through her. Her head hummed and her heart pounded. Who was that woman in their bus? Her bus.

She walked to the T and down the steps. On the packed subway, she sat back and clutched her purse and camera. Her brain was paralyzed. It was like she was being held under water. The woman was probably just a volunteer. There were lots of them. They came and went. She glanced up at the station map. Should she get off at the office or go home? She had only a moment to decide. The subway car slowed for the next stop. People rushed for the door.

She stayed seated, feeling too emotional to interact with the group at the office right now, much less Will. She walked into the empty house, poured a glass of mint iced tea, and went out to read in the cool shade of the back porch.

She was lost in *The Teachings of Don Juan* when the front door opened, and Will called to her.

"Out here," she said.

Will came out on the porch followed by his entourage, Charlie, Adam, and the girl passenger in Old Blue. Adam plunked down a six-pack of beer. Will introduced the girl as Lily.

"You drove by me today in Harvard Square," Jolie said.

"I didn't see you," Will said. Lily and Jolie stared at each other. Jolie perceived a challenge from a rival in her eyes.

They pulled up chairs and sat down. Will sat closest to Jolie and looked at her book. "*Don Juan?* If you're searching for spirituality, you won't find it there."

"It's interesting. I think I was an Indian maiden in another life," Jolie said. "I feel like I have a genetic memory of it or something."

"A genetic memory?" Charlie asked.

Adam and Lily burst out laughing. "I heard he made half that shit up," Adam said.

Charlie silently reached his hand toward Jolie, and she handed him the book.

The heat of humiliation rose to her face. "It's his metaphysical journey and view of the world," she said.

Adam smiled at her as he opened a beer. "Well, when lizards can talk and people can fly, you let me know, Jolie girl."

41

If You Could Read My Mind

On Labor Day, Will, Charlie, Adam, and Jolie piled into Old Blue and drove to Commonwealth Avenue for the march. It was overcast and muggy. The small but growing crowd consisted of students and blue-collar workers. Union members gathered under signs with their affiliated union numbers.

A few men put the finishing touches on a hastily erected plywood stage. A group near the stage waved to Will, and he strode over to them. Jolie stood with Adam and Charlie, snapping photographs. She used her telephoto lens to snap a photograph of the men by the stage. Lily came into view, standing close to Will, hanging on his every word. Her long blonde hair shone despite the sunless day.

"What's the story with Lily?" Jolie asked Charlie.

"She just showed up one day to volunteer," Charlie said.

"She follows Will around like a puppy," Adam said. "I wish she'd follow me around."

Jolie stiffened and watched as Will and Lily walked to where they stood.

Charlie whispered into Jolie's ear. "She's an airhead."

"Well, well, look who's here," Adam said to Lily.

"Hi guys," Lily said.

Charlie looked around at the crowd. "You girls are sure outnumbered here."

"That's the way we like it," Lily said.

"I don't know. I love being around all of my sisters. There's power there," Jolie said.

She looked at Will who returned her gaze. "Yeah, and you spend too much time with them. Let's move to the front of the crowd. You can get better photos of the speakers."

Jolie stood between Will and Charlie. Adam and Lily were squeezed off to the side next to a group of Union members. The speaker tried to get the crowd's attention, but even with the microphone he was drowned out. Adam whistled loudly, and the crowd grew quiet. The speaker introduced himself as the president of the Socialist Labor Party for greater Boston.

"We must wage an anti-capitalist political offensive." He paused while the applause and whistling died down. "Billions of dollars of our taxes are poured into the Vietnam war machine while vital social needs in this country remain criminally neglected by the imperialist government." Whoops and applause erupted from the small crowd. "We must control and use the wealth, created by the workers, in the interest of the oppressed workers."

Jolie took a photo of the crowd cheering and waving their signs in the air.

Will took to the stage and was handed the microphone. "We must unite and revolt. In our struggle for power, the party requires enormous sacrifice from our members. We demand unconditional loyalty and revolutionary firmness of character." More applause and whistling erupted. "We demand you give the party one hundred percent. All party units and individual members must comply with the directives of the National Political Committee."

Jolie leaned in to Charlie and whispered, "Sounds like a cult to me."

He suppressed a laugh.

She glanced around at the crowd. The Women's Strike had attracted ten times more participants than this. Her mind wandered to Leah and Sarah on Cape Cod, and Sam and Ginger in Nantucket. She imagined swimming in the ocean.

"We must attract all students and workers to create a dominant Socialist Labor Party in the U.S.," Will continued.

After the speech, about five hundred participants straggled down Commonwealth Avenue marching to Charlesgate. Jolie photographed a marcher and his sign, Working Class: Mightiest Force in the Land. Lily positioned herself next to Will as they marched. Her arm looped through his. The familiar jealous pang spread from Jolie's stomach to her head. She recalled the monk's words: "Happiness is in your control. Where you focus your thoughts is in your control." She needed to focus her thoughts on the positive. The solidarity of the marchers, their intensity, and their socialist vision. Her mind drifted to her new Save the Earth forum, but the pang remained. Why could she control her thoughts but not her feelings? She needed to grow up, that's all.

42

The Emerald Necklace

"We missed you," Leah said, swooping in to sit on a stool at Jolie's bay. She handed Jolie a bag of saltwater taffy from Cape Cod. Between customers, Leah filled her in on the trip to the Cape. It was hard to talk, but Leah wasn't in any hurry. She nibbled on a grilled cheese sandwich and sipped a raspberry lime rickey.

"Let's hike through the Emerald Necklace parks next Sunday," Jolie said.

"Ask Daniel if he wants to join us," Leah said.

"Are you love struck?"

Leah smiled. "Safety in numbers, that's all. Is Will coming?"

"I'll check tonight. Probably not. I'm going to invite Nick, too." First she had to get up her nerve to call him. "What about Sarah?"

"She's going to New York. It's the last weekend before school starts. Her mom is taking her shopping."

"Like she needs more clothes," Jolie said.

"Don't you like shopping with your mom?"

Jolie nodded. She did, especially in the fall. There was something about new clothes, textbooks and the start of school that was exhilarating.

That night, Jolie cooked dinner for Will and Daniel, and they ate in the dining room.

"What did you do? All of the girls in my classes are wearing those crazy headbands," Daniel said.

Jolie smiled at the thought.

"I got a telex message this afternoon," Will said. "Timothy Leary escaped from prison in California."

"How do you escape from prison?" Jolie asked.

"I think the Weather Underground had something to do with it. I'm trying to verify the rumor."

"Nixon said he's the most dangerous man in America," Daniel said.

"Nixon is the dangerous one. He's got our soldiers blood on his hands. Leary was in prison for possession of the remains of two joints," Will said, shaking his head.

They talked more about Timothy Leary and moved on to other subjects.

"Leah and I are going to hike the Emerald Necklace this Sunday. It's seven miles," Jolie said. "Do you guys want to come?"

"You know I have a standing meeting with the professor on Sundays," Will said.

"Invite him too. You can talk along the way. I'm bringing a picnic."

"We're working on the party platform."

The party platform. She was disappointed, but she knew there was no way she'd change his mind if that was his agenda for the day.

"I'm in," Daniel said.

"Good," Will said. "Now you girls will have a bodyguard."

The next morning after Will went to the office, Jolie rushed to the temple for yoga before work. The class was small with four women and two men and the yogi. They sat cross-legged on their mats with eyes closed, hands resting on their knees, palms up.

"Breathe in the light. Open up your heart. Draw your shoulders down away from your ears and bring your shoulder blades toward your back," the yogi said. "Breathe out and soften your body. Imagine you are holding all of the world's sorrow in your left palm, and all of the world's joy in your right palm. Breathe in the light and open your heart. Breathe out and soften. Let go of the sorrow."

Could the yogi feel her sorrow? Let it go, let it go, let it go. She relaxed and a bright light filled her heart. The yogi led them through yoga sequences. "In yoga, there are two opposing lines of energy. Always engage them. It's like yin and yang."

When the class was over, she floated to her feet. Jolie and her three yoga friends walked out together. At the entrance, Jolie took a flyer with the schedule of classes and put it in her purse. They stood talking outside for a while in the peaceful outer sanctuary of the temple before hugging goodbye and heading their separate ways for another week.

Jolie started her shift, invigorated after yoga. She smoothed her crisp white apron and collected the tips into a separate cup for the waitress who had just finished her shift. The woman who came in to relive her from her shift was not as honest and never left her anything, but that would be her karma.

She looked up as a new customer sat down at the end of the bay. She walked over with a coffee pot and order pad, her long braid swished across her back. "Coffee?" Her mind was on the color photography chakra project she wanted to start.

"I've been gone all summer and that's the greeting I get? Coffee?" the young man said, smiling up at her.

"Nick!" Heat rose to her face. He was back. "Sorry, my mind was somewhere else. You look different somehow."

His brown eyes held her gaze. "I had to cut my hair for the internship and yes, I'll have coffee, please."

Nick sat drinking coffee, conversing sporadically between Jolie's customers' demands. The bay was full now with the lunch crowd, and it was impossible to talk. He got up to leave and confirmed he'd see her at noon on Sunday for the Emerald Necklace hike. He was off to buy his books for the next semester. By his coffee cup he'd left her a tip and a black-and-white postcard from the Museum of Fine Arts for the upcoming *Ansel Adams* photography exhibit. She smiled and tucked it away under the counter next to her tip jar.

Sunday morning, Jolie packed bagel sandwiches and baked two batches of brownies, some for the hike and some for the office. She kissed Will goodbye as he left and handed him the plate of warm brownies. A moment later she heard Old Blue thunder down the street. She waited to meditate until after he left the house, tired of his negative comments about wasting her time.

She emerged later dressed in bell bottom jeans, beaded moccasins, and a vintage, blue silk blouse. She adjusted her black beret and tied the tails of her blouse in a knot at her waist.

Daniel was in the kitchen, finishing a brownie, ready to go.

Jolie grabbed her camera, and Daniel took the backpack. They got off the subway at the Public Garden and waited for Nick and Leah at the entrance. Daniel set the backpack on the grass.

"Guard that with your life. There's something special in it," Jolie said.

"Oh, I will," he said, with a giggle.

Jolie glanced at him. He was in a good mood, as always.

Leah arrived, looking like an angel in a white blouse and Indian love beads. Her curly dark hair fell softly to her shoulders. She and Jolie hugged. Daniel moved in for a hug with Leah that seemed to last more than a greeting. Leah faced Jolie, and she raised her eyebrows and smiled.

Nick arrived, and Jolie introduced them. Daniel grasped his hand and shook it heartily. She hadn't seen Daniel this friendly and relaxed before. It must be Leah.

Nick gave Jolie a hug. "Going French today?" he said.

She smiled and touched her beret. He noticed the smallest things.

Jolie pulled out a map from her pocket and unfolded it. "Here's our route." They hovered around her as she traced the green parkway of the Emerald Necklace through nine parks, ending at Franklin Park. "We'll stop and eat lunch at Jamaica Pond."

"If we make it that far," Daniel said.

They glanced at Daniel. "No man, it's do or die. We're following Olmstead's vision," Nick said.

"Who's Olmstead?" Leah asked, as they started walking twelve blocks down a grand avenue away from the Public Garden.

"Frederick Olmstead is the creative genius who designed this park system a hundred years ago," Nick said. "He was a visionary."

"Connecting man and nature," Daniel said absently.

They walked to the Boylston Bridge and looked out over the Fens. Jolie took a picture of the panorama.

They veered off onto a path and into the public vegetable garden. The stench of manure filled the air. Gardeners weeded and harvested vegetables in communal plots.

"Look at all of that food. I'm getting hungry," Daniel said. "Let's have a brownie."

Leah walked near Jolie and whispered, "He sure is enjoying himself."

"Let's go sit by the Japanese bell," Jolie said.

They walked past the rose garden, a mass of blooms. A heavy rose scent filled the air. Near the bell they sat down on a bench.

"Now, can I have a brownie?" Daniel asked.

Jolie brought out the brownies. "I made these from the Alice B. Toklas recipe. They're not for the faint of heart." She pulled out the wrapped bag. It had already been opened.

"Alice who?" Leah asked.

"Really? I'll have one," Nick said.

Jolie looked at Daniel. She remembered him eating a brownie in the kitchen before they left, but assumed it was from the other batch. She started laughing.

"Ahh, no wonder I feel so fine," Daniel said, with a wide-eyed look.

"What's so funny?" Leah said.

"Daniel's way ahead of us." She took one and passed them around. "There's pot in these. Have one. The Emerald Necklace will take on a whole new feeling."

Leah took one and looked at Daniel who seemed to be enjoying himself. She bit into it. They sat munching brownies, savoring the chewy chocolate bites, looking at the three hundred year old Japanese temple bell. It was a gift from Japan, a gesture of world peace.

With arms linked four across, they continued on the trail through the Fens to the Riverway. At the bridge Jolie and Leah broke away and skipped over, hand in hand, laughing. Daniel and Nick caught up with them and they walked the Riverway path into Olmstead Park.

They walked through the wildflower meadow to Ward's Pond and stood by the banks in their own small wilderness. Jolie spread a faded Madras bedspread on the ground. They sat down one by one and lay on their backs, looking up at the swaying trees.

"You can hear them," Jolie said.

"Hear who?" Leah said.

"We need another brownie," Nick said.

"Yes, we do," Leah said.

Jolie looked at Daniel and fell into a fit of giggles pointing to the backpack.

Daniel passed out more brownies, and they sat up, chewing slowly, staring out at the pond.

"What are you photographing?" Nick asked.

"Green algae, pure green."

"Wow," Leah said.

Along the trail to Jamaica Pond, they stopped at a picnic table. Jolie and Leah spread out the bedspread as a table cloth. Leah took out the cut-up fruit she'd brought, and Jolie got out the bagel, cream cheese, and avocado sandwiches and laid them on napkins.

"What is that green stuff?" Leah asked, looking at the wiggly green things spilling out of the bagels.

"Bean sprouts," Jolie said.

"Bean sprouts? I've never heard of them. I've never had an avocado either," Leah said.

Leah didn't move, still staring at the sprouts.

"I've never had sprouts either," Nick said, "but here goes." He took a bite of the sandwich. They could hear the sprouts crunch with each chew. Jolie and Daniel took a bite. Eventually Leah picked one up and took a tiny bite. "Yum, these are divine," she said, closing her eyes. "It tastes like California."

After lunch they continued along the path through the Arnold Arboretum. They passed through meadows, ponds, and a small forest. Daniel and Leah walked hand in hand in front of Jolie and Nick. Nick put his arm around Jolie. He squeezed her close to his body. A small tremble ran through her, and her knees weakened in a rush of warmth. What she had been trying to push away from her thoughts all summer became clear now. She did feel for Nick. She leaned into him to steady herself. This wouldn't have happened if Will had come along.

Will. Guilt descended, but she shook it off. She and Nick were only friends. He released his arm.

They stopped at the medicinal herb garden used for research. Jolie crushed some leaves between her fingers and a spicy aroma wafted in the air. "Don Juan's shaman would love it here."

"Who?" asked Leah.

"An Indian healer," Jolie said.

Leah looked puzzled.

"I'll lend you the book."

They walked on through Franklin Park to the end of the Emerald Necklace at the edge of Roxbury. They all lingered, reluctant to end the day.

"Is anybody hungry?" Daniel asked.

"Famished," Nick said.

Leah laughed. "I could eat a whale."

"Let's go find Dimitri and his restaurant," Jolie said.

They emerged from the subway in the Back Bay neighborhood and walked along Newbury Street until they stood before a towering blue-and-white sign above a blue awning: The Greek.

Daniel held the door open, and they entered. It was cool, dark, and noisy. They adjusted their eyes to the dim light. The tables were full of families talking loudly. Glasses and silverware clinked. Through the food service window, Jolie glimpsed Dimitri and waved. He squinted at them and then with enormous hand gestures and speaking in Greek, he called out something to the hostess. She nodded and escorted them back into a private room. Photographs of Greece covered the dark, wood-paneled walls. The table was set with a white linen tablecloth. Blue cloth napkins swaddled the silverware. Dimitri came in and greeted them.

"You brought your friend," Dimitri gestured to Nick. His eyes smiled at Jolie.

"All of my friends." Jolie introduced him to Nick and Daniel.

Dimitri smiled brightly at Jolie and Leah. "You look hungry."

"We're starving," Leah said.

"You'll be my guests today."

"No, no," Jolie said. "We want to pay."

Dimitri shook his head, offended, and said something in Greek. Nick responded in Greek, and a rapid-fire dialogue ensued. The hostess brought in a bread basket and tray with three types of olives. Dimitri hurried back to the kitchen. "Well, that's settled," Nick said.

"What?" Leah asked.

"He'll only serve us if we're his guests," Nick said.

"I didn't know you spoke Greek," Jolie said.

"I'm Greek, through and through."

The waitress came in with stuffed grape leaves. Nick took one and held it near Jolie's lips. She opened her mouth and took a small bite. She closed her eyes as she savored the taste of the rice, pine nuts, and fresh herbs. Nick ate the remainder.

Tiropitas—cheese-filled phyllo triangles, and a plate of thick, sliced feta cheese arrived next.

"I think I'm in heaven," Jolie said as Dimitri appeared with a tray of four dips: eggplant, garlic, cucumber, and taramosalata, a caviar made from carp roe.

He and Nick had another brief exchange, and Dimitri winked at Jolie and hurried off again. "What did he say?" Jolie said.

"He always knew you were an angel."

"Little does he know," Jolie said.

They passed the bread basket filled with slices of olive bread, feta cheese bread, and pitas. The tray of dips went around.

Leah groaned. "This is a feast."

Nick laughed. "It hasn't even started. Save some room."

Two waitresses appeared with a layered eggplant dish filled with spicy lamb and a spinach pie made with delicate phyllo dough.

"Moussaka and spanakopita," one said, pointing to the dishes.

"Oh my god," Jolie said, looking at the steaming platters.

One waitress returned with stuffed tomatoes and leafy greens. Daniel's eyes grew big, and he and Leah broke into laughter. Dimitri arrived with a platter of lamb and potatoes and announced, "Arni me patates."

Jolie jumped up and gave him a hug. "This is the most fantastic feast I've ever eaten."

Nick started a slow clap which the others echoed. Dimitri gave a quick bow and hurried back to his busy kitchen. Jolie took a photo of the table and all of the beautiful food.

A while later, they sat back with satiated smiles. One waitress cleared the dishes and brought coffee. The other waitress brought in a creamy custard pie and baklava.

Nick took a fork of baklava and held it out to Jolie. "Try this."

She leaned toward him and opened her mouth for a bite. The flaky phyllo dough, filled with cinnamon and spiced nuts soaked in honey, melted in her mouth. He smiled and wiped pastry flakes from her lips with his napkin. Their eyes locked and a wave fluttered through her. He leaned in and kissed her ever so gently.

43

Falling Stars

The air was crisp and thin and smelled clean. The sunlight was translucent. Jolie walked to work, not wanting to take the subway on the cool fall morning. College students filled the streets. Across the street from a high school, she paused at a newsstand and watched the students through the fenced school yard, streaming to their classes. They were her age, but they seemed so young and carefree. She felt like an old soul, peering in on them. She should be in school. School for her had been easy and boring, but now she wanted to go to college. Dreading going to work, she idled at the newsstand, looking at the magazines. The headline on the *Globe* leapt off the front page: JIMI HENDRIX, 28, FOUND DEAD IN LONDON FLAT. Stunned, she bought the paper and stood on the corner, reading the brief article. Jimi Hendrix was dead. What a tragic blow. She walked to work, numb.

On Thursday morning, Jolie and her three yoga friends emerged from the temple into the bright October sunlight. The women talked and laughed as they walked along the stone path. They lingered near the water fall among the brilliant green bamboo stalks. Jolie hugged them good-bye and walked toward the street. A tall figure leaned against the dark wooden temple gate. It was Will. Jolie slowed her pace.

"So, this is where you go before work?" Will asked. In his hand was the schedule of yoga and meditation sessions she kept at home inside her drawer.

The women stood watching. "Most days," Jolie said. She wouldn't lie to him. She may have secrets, but she wouldn't lie.

"I knew they'd suck you in," Will said.

"Hey brother, yoga is not a crime," Cheyenne said.

"Yoga? Now it's yoga? Buddhism is a damn cult."

"It's not a cult," Jolie said. "Buddhism and yoga have been around for thousands of years."

"Join us sometime," Molly said.

"Come on. I'll drive you to work." He turned and walked toward Old Blue parked down the street. She followed him, glancing back at her friends.

"See you next week?" Willow asked.

Jolie nodded and followed Will.

Will drove toward Harvard Square, silent, his eyes on the road. After a long while he looked at her. "I told you, I don't want you getting involved with cult religions."

"It is not a cult. I love the temple. It's a positive influence in my life."

He shot her a glance. "You don't know who is involved there. They could be wacko fanatics."

"How can you judge something you have no experience or knowledge of? Why don't you come with me?"

Will pulled into a loading zone near Brigham's. The engine idled. "I don't have time for men in orange robes."

Their eyes locked. A fierceness spread through her as she grasped door handle. "The temple is my refuge." She opened the door and slid out. With the door still open she looked into his eyes. "I'm sorry you won't join me but I won't give it up."

His eyes held hers. "I'll pick you up here tonight at seven."

Jolie looked back, eyebrows raised in a question.

"It's getting dark earlier. I don't want you going home alone."

She walked into the restaurant, relieved that Will now knew about the forbidden temple. There were enough secrets to maintain. She didn't want to hide anything from him. She was at last liberated from that secret.

Will picked up Jolie that night and announced he had to go back to the office to finish an article. She followed him into the office. Lily was sorting mail at the kitchen table. She flashed Will a bright smile. It instantly faded when Jolie appeared behind him. Will headed for the typewriter in the dining room.

In the living room, Adam, Charlie, T.J., and a few other men she didn't recognize debated something she couldn't quite hear. Jolie joined them. She could smell incense and maybe hashish? The discussion stopped.

"Jolie girl," Adam said. "You haven't graced us with your presence in days. Where in the world have you been?"

"Will told me she's been hanging out with men in orange robes," Charlie said. His boyish smile and dimples brightened her mood.

Jolie placed her palms together pressing them lightly on her chest and bowed her head.

"Right on," T.J. said.

"What are you guys plotting?" Jolie said, glancing around the room.

"The usual," Adam said. "A united front against capitalism."

"Anyone want tea?" Jolie said. A resounding yes came from the group. Adam introduced her to the guys she didn't know. Jolie went into the kitchen and put on the kettle. Charlie followed her.

"So tell me about this secret cult you've joined," Charlie said. "Will asked me today if I'd go with you and check it out."

She glanced at him. His eyes were smiling. She didn't need Charlie to check it out, but she did want to take him there. "I think you'll like it. Meditation is better there, deeper. I release the outside world as soon as I enter the gate."

Lily paused sorting mail and looked at Jolie. "How's *Don Juan?*"

Jolie ignored her sarcasm. "It's an interesting book."

The kettle whistled, and Jolie brewed two pots of hibiscus tea. She poured a cup for Lily without asking and set it down on the table. "Oh, thanks," Lily said, looking up surprised.

Jolie and Charlie carried the tea into the living room, pouring a cup of the fragrant crimson tea for Will on the way. He hardly acknowledged it, the typewriter keys flying over the page. Jolie sat down with the group.

"So, Jolie girl, I'm dying for some of your home cooking. When are we going to get an invite or are you fasting, too?" Adam said.

She looked at Adam and then to Charlie and laughed. "I guess it's time to plan a dinner."

On the coffee table, the headline of *Central Underground Press* stared back at her: OCTOBER 5, 1970. JANIS JOPLIN, 27, FOUND DEAD IN HOLLYWOOD. Jolie sucked in her breath. "Janis died?"

Three weeks ago Jimi had died and now Janis? A hollowness filled her. Why hadn't Will told her? She moved to the stereo, put on "Summertime" and slumped on the couch. Had everyone lost their way? She glanced in at Will. Lily leaned over him with some mail, her breast brushed his shoulder. Jealousy stabbed her. She leaned her head back and closed her eyes. Nothing seemed right anymore.

44

Freedom's Just Another Word

The next morning, Jolie emerged from the T station into a burst of red and white flashing police lights. Fire trucks and police cars blocked the Harvard campus entrance. Her pace slowed as she walked through small groups of students milling around, talking. The entrance was cordoned off with yellow crime tape. In Brigham's she started her shift, uneasy with the scene outside.

A woman student ordered coffee and told Jolie a bomb had exploded in the Center for International Affairs at one in the morning. No one was injured.

A bomb at Harvard? That was getting close. An eerie blanket of doom draped her. Bombs wouldn't solve anything. At least no one had been hurt.

Throughout the day, all of her customers speculated about who was responsible for the bombing. Was it the Weathermen, the Black Panthers, the students? Will picked her up when her shift was over. He sat impassive as she slid into Old Blue.

"Do you know who did it?" she asked.

"What did you hear?"

"Oh, just speculation. No one has claimed responsibility."

"The FBI will be all over town. We have to be careful."

They didn't talk the rest of the way home, both lost in their thoughts. Though they were innocent, the possibility of another FBI raid frightened her. Even with fake IDs, they could be discovered, couldn't they?

⌒〇

Jolie and her yoga friends walked out of the temple into a light drizzle. She felt light and harmonious.

"Was that your boyfriend last week?" Molly asked.

Jolie nodded.

"He seemed pretty uptight," Willow said. "We were worried about you."

"He's just protective," Jolie said.

"Too much protection can squash your soul," Cheyenne said, "and stifle your freedom."

They stopped and huddled under Molly's oversized yellow-and-red umbrella.

"Freedom is the most important thing that any of us has," Cheyenne said. "You should never let it go, not even for love."

Jolie didn't respond. She hugged them goodbye and set off in the light rain for work. When she glanced back, they stood watching her as they talked under the colorful umbrella. Was Will squashing her soul? He was a strong man. Dominant yet charismatic. That was one of reasons she loved him. That's why everyone loved him. He was a pillar of strength, but she too was strong.

⌒〇

The weather had turned cold and darkness descended by early evening. Jolie missed sitting on the back porch, reading. Like the temple, the porch was her sanctuary from the roommates at times. She wanted to get their own place and have Will to herself. With winter coming, the house seemed closed in.

314

Jolie poured over the For Rent advertisements in the paper until she found it: a quaint two-bedroom brick townhouse close to the office. She could turn the other bedroom into a photography studio and meditation room. In the backyard, she would plant masses of flowers and grow herbs for cooking and tea.

Jolie broached the subject with Will. "I found us an apartment."

"You what?"

"I saw a For Rent ad in the paper. I've walked by it on my way to work a few times. It's a cute brick first-floor apartment near here. It has two bedrooms with a small backyard and porch. It's perfect."

"What's the matter with this pad?"

"I want our own place. We could use the second bedroom for a darkroom."

"You have a darkroom."

"We can afford the rent. I'm tired of roommates, even if they're good people."

"I like it here. We have the run of the place. I know you're safe when I'm not around, plus they love your cooking."

From the finality of his tone she knew the conversation was over. The vision of the brick townhouse crumbled. At least they weren't in a commune. Her bank account was swelling and in the new year she'd try again. She sat back, silent. She couldn't plant a garden in the winter anyway.

In the meantime, she would focus on studying for the GED test. She would surprise Will by getting her diploma. But would she be able to pass? Every morning after he left for the office, she meditated and methodically read through the stack of textbooks Daniel kept in the dining room.

Charlie met Jolie at the house Saturday morning, and they walked to the temple to meditate. "What can I expect at this Buddhist temple?" Charlie asked. "Do I need to know anything?"

"No, I don't want to influence you. Just experience it. It's different for everyone, depending on your demons."

He looked at her. "You have demons?"

Her face flushed warm. "Sure, everyone has something that troubles them. It may seem small to others but huge to them." Her mom and dad flashed before her. Her demon would be giant to everyone.

They passed through the open gate along the stone path and a peaceful feeling engulfed her. The Japanese maples glowed deep red and gold. The waterfall splashed rhythmically on the rocks in the pond. Jolie pushed open the thick door. They took off their shoes and coats in the tall entry and retreated silently across the wood floor to a meditation room. Five men and women sat on mats. Sandalwood incense burned on the altar and the Buddha statue seemed to float on white flower petals. The monk acknowledged their presence. They closed their eyes, and he led them through three oms to Buddha, Dharma, and Sangha.

Jolie snuck a peak at Charlie. His eyes were open slightly, watching the monk. It would take him a while to get settled.

She focused on the monk's words. "Look inward and bring the mind home. Accept whatever thoughts arise. Acceptance reveals the good heart which dissolves unkindness, torment, suffering, and the pain within you. Draw your breath into your heart center. As your chest expands with your breath, your heart opens and expands. The hearts greatest lessons are patience, compassion, and unconditional love. Be kind to yourself."

Her mind drifted to her parents and the pain she had caused them. Would they have unconditional love for her? Remorse gripped her. How could she ever be free from that? She didn't deserve to be free from it. Be kind. Be kind. Be kind. She had Will now. He was what she wanted. She drifted into her breathing.

The monk tapped a clear note on a chime, and it rang long and pure throughout the room. Slowly she opened her eyes. Charlie smiled at her. They sat for a moment, soaking up the inner glow before rising. Silently they padded through the temple, put on their shoes and coats, and walked out into the autumn morning.

Charlie walked to the bench by the pond and sat down. Jolie sat beside him. "I see what you mean," he said. "It is better here. I really got lost in my mind."

Jolie stared at the waterfall. "I was floating, and my heart was beating green," she said.

"Well, don't tell anyone else that. They'll think you're crazy."

They sat quiet for a moment, nodding to others walking by on the path leading to the street. "So there are no initiations or payments required?" Charlie asked.

"No brain washings either. They do accept donations."

"I'm so relaxed. Can I come with you on Saturdays?"

"Only if you wear a copper-colored robe."

He shot her a look. "Yeah, right."

They got up and walked back to the house. Charlie left Jolie by her steps and walked on to the office. "I'll give Will a full report," he called back to her. She flashed him a peace sign and smiled widely.

In November they had their first snow. Jolie stood out on the back porch, watching it fall. She tugged Nick's beanie over her ears and fingered the Harvard logo. The snow had accumulated quickly on the bare field behind the house. The porch light lit up the delicate flakes as they floated to the ground. Daniel, Sam, and Ginger joined her. Will was still at the office.

"I've never lived where it snowed before," Jolie said, her voice small on the dark porch.

They looked her way in amazement.

"It's not winter without snow," Daniel said.

Nick stopped in to see Jolie every week. He usually brought her something: a used book, an aged black-and-white photo postcard of somewhere in the city, a book of poetry, a list of colleges in the area. She looked forward to his visits but never knew when he would appear. He was busy with his classes.

"I'll take you to the *Ansel Adams* exhibit this weekend before I go home for Thanksgiving," he said.

"You're going home next week?"

"Yep, I'm ready for some home cooking too. Are you going home?"

"No."

"What about Christmas?"

She shook her head.

"When was the last time you were home?"

"About a year and a half ago."

"Geez, they must really miss you. You should plan a trip."

She nodded, unable to speak, her throat tightened. It seemed like she'd been gone for years.

"I have to run to class. I'll meet you at the museum at one o'clock Saturday. Ciao." He left her a generous tip, waved to Dimitri and disappeared out the door.

"Ciao," she half whispered.

She went to Millie. "Can you keep an eye on my station? I'll be right back."

Millie nodded. Jolie went into the back room, tears filling her eyes. Everyone was going home for the holidays. Other staff whizzed by in a blur. Not wanting anyone to see her crying, she opened the large walk-in refrigerator door and entered the cold room. She sat down on a cardboard box of produce and put her head in her hands. Tears flowed. The smallest things set her off now. But home for the holidays wasn't really a little thing, was it?

The door opened. She stood up quickly. She was cold now and moved toward the door. Dimitri walked in.

"I thought I saw you come in here, but you never came out," he said. He saw her tears. "Are you okay?"

"I'm fine."

"Did Nick upset you?" His tone was protective.

"No. I'm just a little homesick."

"Ah, I know something about that. Most of my family is still in Greece."

In the bathroom she washed her face in cold water and returned to her customers.

"Are you okay, honey?" Millie said, looking into her red eyes.

Jolie shrugged.

After her shift, she waited out front for Will. He was late again. She finally heard the rumble of Old Blue coming down the street. She slid into the bus, shivering, and sank into the seat. He shifted into gear and started down the street. A few blocks later he turned to her. "Why so quiet?"

She shrugged in the dark. She wanted to tell him how homesick she was but he always brushed it aside.

"No customer reports for me tonight?"

"No."

"Oh, come on. Usually you have something that happened, or you met somebody that was interesting."

"Not today."

Will glanced over at her again. She sat crumpled in the seat. "Tired?" He flipped on the radio and Ray Charles filled the air. She closed her eyes in the dark.

45

You Can't Always Get What You Want

⌒⌒

Saturday afternoon, Jolie sat on the steps of the Museum of Fine Arts, waiting for Nick. She was early, anxious to see the exhibit. And she was excited to see Nick outside of the restaurant. Will would never take the time to see a photography exhibit at an art museum. Nick walked up the street with purposeful strides. His shaggy brown hair swayed with each step. A radiant smile spread across her face and a wave of euphoria filled her. If only she could hold onto that feeling forever.

Nick paid their admission, and they moved slowly through the *Ansel Adams* exhibit, pausing at each photograph and discussing it in hushed voices.

"I've seen some of these in books. I can't believe I'm standing in front of them," Jolie said. "Look at the depth, the layers of light. He captures the natural beauty."

He smiled at her. "He's a master."

After wandering through the exhibit rooms for a few hours they looked around the museum shop and headed to the museum cafe.

They ordered tea and sat at a corner table. Jolie turned the pages of the Ansel Adams book Nick had bought her in the shop.

"What's Will up to?"

"He's at the office, as usual."

"Are you happy?"

Jolie looked into his eyes, surprised by the question. "Happy? What do you mean?"

"Are you happy with him? Does he treat you well?"

Was she happy? Most of the time she felt more wounded than happy. She couldn't honestly say she was happy. "I'm not sure."

"You can leave him, you know. We could be together. We would be happy."

Leave Will for Nick? Her mind whirled. Her feelings for Nick overwhelmed her. It would be a very different life with Nick. But she would have to tell him the truth about her age and that would lead to too many complications. She wasn't who he thought she was. Her life was a lie. She shouldn't even be there with him.

"I can't," she whispered.

"Jolie, I want to be with you. I know in my heart you're the one for me."

She would never start a relationship with a lie. And now the lie was coming between something that could make her happy, really happy. Tears fell down her cheeks. "I can't leave him."

"Don't let him control your life. He's not good enough for you." He reached out and took her hand. "I can help support you in college. You don't have to be a waitress."

"Will and I have been through too much together."

"He doesn't deserve you. I see so much potential in you, so much love and strength, and it kills me that it's being wasted on him."

She held his hand as his words cascaded down around her.

Thanksgiving was upon them. Nick was in Chicago, Leah and Sarah were off to New York, and Ginger and Sam were headed to Nantucket to Sam's parents' second home. Jolie planned Thanksgiving dinner at their house for anyone not going home. Adam, Charlie, and six stray student volunteers arrived mid-afternoon. Jolie greeted them at the door in a black velvet jacket and pants. Layers of bangles jangled on her wrists and a silk-beaded headband adorned her head. The arrivals had even dressed up a bit. Charlie wore a button-down vest over a long sleeve dress shirt. Adam sported a Nehru jacket. Two of the women wore dresses, and the guys wore tweed or cashmere sport jackets that were discarded immediately.

Jolie had thrown herself wholeheartedly into cooking the pilgrim feast. The aroma of turkey, herbs and spices wafted throughout the house. She joined the group in the living room and sat on the couch between Will and Adam. Will played "Can't Find My Way Home" on the guitar, a rippling torrent emanated from the strings.

As small talk ensued, Jolie's mind wandered back to Nick and their conversation at the museum. From the periphery of her mind, she heard Adam talking to her. "Jolie girl, where are you? You're a million miles away."

Jolie looked at him and then glanced around the room. All eyes were on her, including Will's who continued to strum his guitar. "Oh, just thinking," she said. There was a knock on the door, and she got up to answer it. Lily stood with a bottle of wine.

Surprised, Jolie stood unmoving.

"Will invited me," Lily said.

"Oh."

Lily offered her the bottle of wine. They both glanced into the living room. Will smiled broadly at Lily. Jolie took the wine into the kitchen and checked on the turkey. When she joined the group again, Lily was sitting between Will and Adam. Charlie offered her his seat, but she shook her head and sat cross-legged on the floor with her back against the side of his chair.

Later, Jolie laid the feast on the table, and they sat down. Will toasted. "To the cook."

"To the cook." They all raised and clinked their glasses.

"To the turkey," Adam said.

"To the turkey," the group chanted and clinked glasses again.

Dishes of food were passed around. It was quiet for a moment as the first bites were taken. Hums of appreciation ensued.

Will started a lively political discussion. "There are three centers of revolution in the world: Moscow, Peking, and Havana."

"Don't forget Cambridge," Adam said.

Detached, Jolie looked around the table at the group and the food. These were the same recipes her mom used. She had the sudden urge to call her, to hear her voice. She could see her so clearly.

Her thoughts were interrupted by Charlie's voice. "Jolie? What's the matter? You look so sad."

"I was just thinking about my mom."

Will quickly turned to her and held her gaze with a fierce intensity. He didn't want her talking about home. There were too many ways to get tripped up in lies. She looked away and caught Charlie's eye, his eyebrows raised in concern.

46

The Blue Hole

❦

December was bitter cold and brought more snow. Jolie traipsed around the parks in the piercing cold, taking photographs. She had switched back to black and white film. The winter landscapes were too stark for color. The most beautiful place was the temple. Blanketed in snow, the Buddha statue near the pond encircled with tall bamboo brought her peace.

In the dark room she developed the contact sheet and thought about Nick. She hadn't seen him since before Thanksgiving when they'd said goodbye at the museum. Each day at work she looked for him, but he hadn't come. She missed him. His words still echoed in her mind. All of them. He'd surprised her by opening up and putting his heart on the line. That was brave. She'd come close to telling him the truth. It was an impossible situation. He had told her to think about it and to call him if she changed her mind, but he wouldn't wait forever. There was no future for them, yet he tugged at her heart.

She shouldn't think about Nick. Will was her man. She had changed her life for him, and she would stand by him. She clipped the contact sheet up to dry. The temple shots stood out in their intimacy.

In her spare time, she studied for her GED test and attended the chemical pollution meetings. Her passion for the forum was fueled by the gloomy winter. She continually brought their position articles into the office for printing and distribution. Will grumbled, but Adam printed the articles in the *Central Underground Press*, and Charlie sent them to agency subscribers. The subscribers clamored for more. The campaign to ban DDT was in full force.

On a sodden, blustery Saturday, Jolie stopped by the office. She had just come from an anti-pollution forum at Harvard and was delivering an article supporting the ban of DDT and other synthetic pesticides and herbicides. Will was there with Adam, Lily, and some shaggy looking students. The phone was ringing, and the telex chirped continuously. Jolie handed Adam an article to print in the next issue.

"DDT, it even sounds nasty," Adam said.

"I don't get the whole DDT issue," Lily said. "It's like such a small thing in the world to worry about."

"It's actually a big thing. We're all connected to the earth. It's affecting everyone," Jolie said.

"It's not affecting me," Lily said.

"It's hidden," Jolie said.

Lily tilted her head and smiled dismissively. "Hidden? Like Don Juan magic?"

Jolie bristled. "DDT accumulates in soil and water and gets into the food chain. Animals eat the crops, we eat the crops and the animals. The pests become resistant, the farmers spray more powerful chemicals that flow into the rivers and into the sea, the fish die, humans get cancer...."

She stopped. Will had joined them and stood listening. "Anyway, we eat and drink pesticides, and now they're in our bones. It's basic biology. We're polluting the earth and its inhabitants through human carelessness."

"I wish you'd put that passion into things that need to be done around here," Will said.

She glanced out the window. Rain came down in sheets, sideways in the wind. "I can help today."

There was a price to pay for getting her articles published. Adam put her to work laying out the next issue. She strategically put the

article championing the ban on DDT on the front page: DDT: THE
ELIXIR OF DEATH.

⁓͡◦

Jolie walked into the high school in Dorchester one Saturday in
December at the appointed time. A man led her and about fifteen others into a classroom and handed them each a thick GED test packet. A
wave of uncertainty filled her. The weight of the test alone was intimidating. They took their seats at old wooden desks carved with decades
of initials. The man read the test rules and sat down at the desk in the
front of the classroom. He set the timer, sat back, and observed.

Jolie inhaled deeply. Release the tension, focus on the goal. She
still hadn't told Will she was taking the test. She exhaled and tried to
relax. She either knew it, or she didn't. She could always take it again
if she failed.

She bowed her head over the desk, her fingers taut around the
pencil as she read the first question. Calmness settled in as she worked
through each section of the comprehensive exam.

At 4:00 p.m. the timer dinged. "Set down your pencils…now," the
man said. He walked through the aisles and collected the tests. "The
results will be mailed out in January. Good luck, everyone. If you don't
pass, you'll know from the score results what subject to work on."

January seemed like an eternity.

⁓͡◦

Holiday lights brightened the winter gloom. Oversized ornaments
sparkled in storefront displays, and large bows adorned doorways.
Shoppers crowded the sidewalks along with street musicians heralding
holiday music.

Jolie put up blue lights in the front windows of the house. She
relished the holiday mood in the evenings. Daniel was drawn into
the magic, never having had Christmas lights at home when he was

growing up. She put up multicolored lights in the front windows at the office.

She printed and framed photographs as gifts. For Charlie, she selected the temple scene in the snow with the Buddha and pond. Leah would get a photograph of Central Park from their trip to New York.

For Nick, a photo from the Emerald Necklace hike, a landscape shot of Jamaica Pond in stark Ansel Adams style. She wrapped it and brought it into the restaurant. She stored it in her locker, hoping he'd stop in. His last words were to call him if she changed her mind. His phone number was tucked safely into her wallet. But he stayed away. Would she ever see him again?

She stopped by the leather store and bought Will a soft brown leather notebook that he admired every time they went there. He unfailingly picked it up and held it, turning it over in his hands before setting it back down. It was the perfect gift. His old notebook had been missing for some time.

One Sunday afternoon, Will met with the professor at the office. When he came home later he said, "The professor invited us to his house for Christmas dinner."

"Really?" Her face lit up. She envisioned a formal dining room set with china and crystal, drinking eggnog by a roaring fire—

"I declined."

Her vision collapsed. "Why? That would be fun."

"Where are Adam and Charlie and the gang going to go? They all expect to come here."

She didn't mind cooking, and Charlie and Adam always pitched in to help with the dishes, but he should have asked her. Maybe she wanted a change.

"Does Lily expect to come here too?"

"No, she's going home."

Everyone was going home. He moved to her side and stroked her hair as he always did. She stiffened. The gesture maddened her somehow.

As the holidays approached, the colleges went on winter break, and the mass exodus home started. Jolie tried to control her thoughts and not think about home. She had a new life now, and they knew she was safe. She had to let them go.

Things slowed down at the office. Will and Adam worked on the year-end issue. It was shaping up with a memorial to all the soldiers who had died that year. Music icons Jimi Hendrix and Janis Joplin would have separate remembrances. Charlie worked on a satire of the country's failings. Adam selected Jolie's photo of the temple in the snow as the full page cover with a Peace on Earth caption.

On Christmas day, Jolie withdrew to the temple. In the quietness of the vast wood-beamed library, she breathed in remnants of incense and read Buddha's teachings. A different monk sat reading at the far end of the wood table. He acknowledged her with his kind eyes and faint hint of a smile.

She understood the three Noble Dharma Seals and Four Holy Truths, and now worked her way through the Noble Eightfold Path. She read a page and sat back to contemplate the meaning and con-nectedness of what she had learned. It all fit together so perfectly: transforming suffering into peace, joy, and liberation.

The new year rang in with an ice storm. Old Blue wouldn't start in the arctic cold. Jolie rode the subway home every night after work. Her pea coat was too thin for the cutting cold, and she constantly tugged the beanie over her ears. The three-block walk from the T station to the warm house was bone chilling.

One night after work, an official-looking letter addressed to her was propped on the kitchen table. Her GED test results had arrived. Engulfed in trepidation, she glanced into the living room at Daniel and waved. With the letter in hand, she slipped into her bedroom. Her mind buzzed with anticipation. Breathe. She opened the envelope and read. In a daze she reread the short paragraph. She had passed all of the sections. Her High School Equivalency Certificate would be sent to her within the month. With letter in hand, she leapt into the air. "Yes," she whispered.

Will came in and startled her.

"Why the big smile?"

She handed him the letter and waited in anticipation while he read. He'd be so proud of her. She was proud of herself.

He handed the letter back. "A lot of good this will do you."

She turned his words around in her mind. It would do her a lot of good.

"It's a step in my future."

"Your future is the revolution. I have to make a phone call." He turned and left the room.

She reread the letter once more, folded it and placed it in her bottom drawer next to the list of colleges Nick had given her. Nick. Her elation faded even more when she thought of him. He would be proud, but she couldn't tell him. He assumed she was already a high school graduate.

⚬⚬⚬

Jolie had invited Leah to the Georgia O'Keefe art exhibit that Saturday. She had discovered O'Keefe's art when reading the Alfred Stieglitz photo book that Will had given her. His photos of his wife Georgia intrigued Jolie and then she fell in love with her art.

Jolie sat in the grandeur of the hushed lobby of the art museum. She jumped up when Leah walked in. "You're going to love Georgia O'Keeffe's paintings," Jolie said, hugging her. "They are colorful and organic."

"Organic?" Leah said.

"Like primal and indigenous."

"I don't know what you're talking about, but I can't wait to see them."

Inside the exhibit they moved slowly through the large-scale paintings. One depicted a ram skull with a blue morning glory, others were large scale flowers that filled the canvas. In another, the expansive sky and brown cliffs reverberated the stillness, the remoteness, and the beauty of the desert.

They stood in front of a large white flower. A hint of pink seeped from the edges, flowing around and into itself. "It's erotic," Jolie said.

"It's surreal," Leah said.

Jolie stood gazing at the painting, transfixed by the beauty. Leah tapped her arm. Jolie followed Leah's gaze. Her heart thudded. Nick and a girl with shoulder-length dark hair stood in front of a large landscape, holding hands. Jolie stood rigid and watched as Nick and the girl moved closer to them. They looked at ease with each other. She couldn't take her eyes off Nick. Her stomach flipped, and her face warmed. As Nick led the girl to the painting next to where they stood, he saw her.

"Jolie! How are you?"

"Fine. I'm fine." She smiled at him.

"Angela, this is Jolie and Leah."

His old girlfriend? "Angela? From Chicago?" Jolie asked.

Angela nodded and looked confused.

"She transferred to Radcliffe for the winter quarter," Nick said.

"Nice to meet you," Jolie said.

He had moved on. He wasn't waiting for her to change her mind. Standing next to him, her emotions caught up with her. Would she regret not telling him the truth about the tangled web of her false identity? Would he still love her if he knew? She swallowed and regained her composure.

"I have a photograph for you. Stop by the restaurant."

"I will," he said.

"Bye," Leah said, pushing Jolie along. "Good to meet you."

As they left the gallery Jolie glanced back and met Nick's gaze. His brown eyes were sad and devoid of the usual sparkle. He smiled wistfully and shook his head.

On a slushy Saturday, Jolie and Charlie walked to the office after meditation at the temple.

"Do you see a hole when you meditate?" Jolie asked.

"No holes, other stuff, but no holes," he said.

"I see a blue hole when I meditate. It started a while ago and now it is always there. I'm drawn in to it, but I can't seem to let go and get though."

"Keep trying. Maybe it's the window to enlightenment."

They laughed. She glanced at Charlie and warmed with affection. She suddenly realized something. Charlie was more than a friend, he was her liaison. He stood up for her and now they shared a spiritual connection.

"Tell me what the monk meant when he said a wave does not need to die to become water," Charlie said.

"Oh, well, a wave is already water. The ground of a wave is water. As he's said before, we need to look deeply and touch the ground of our being: nirvana."

Charlie stopped on the corner and turned toward her. She stopped walking and continued. "We don't have to attain nirvana, because we are already dwelling in it. It is within us. We only need to touch it through understanding and insight."

"Have you touched it?" Charlie asked.

"Not yet." She smiled.

At the office, they warmed their hands over the rusting radiator. Bob Dylan moaned from the stereo. Lily was sorting mail at a table nearby.

"How's school?" Charlie asked her.

"I dropped out," Lily said, twirling a strand of long blonde hair around her finger.

Dropped out? "Why?" Jolie asked.

"Will wants me here full-time." She beamed an angelic smile.

"You dropped out of college to work here?" Jolie asked.

She nodded, still smiling. "He thinks I'll learn far more here."

Jolie looked at Will, who was talking intently with T.J., and then turned back to Lily, stunned. Her dream was to go to college and Lily had just let it go, for Will. Her throat closed up, and she couldn't breathe. Why couldn't Lily fall in love with Adam or Charlie? Why did they all fall for Will? Without being conscious of moving she found herself on the sidewalk walking in the direction of the house.

"Jolie," Charlie called after her.

His footsteps fell close behind, and she willed herself not to cry.

47

Whisper Words of Wisdom

Spring was just around the corner. Jolie walked to the temple almost daily before work. She continued to see a blue hole when she meditated. In the temple library, she studied Buddha's teachings of the eightfold path. One morning when she entered the library, a familiar monk sat reading. She sat nearer to him than usual. He glanced up as her chair screeched against the floor.

"Can I ask you something?" she said.

"Of course, my child."

"When I meditate, I see a blue hole. It seems to invite me through, but I stop at the edge."

"You are suffering," he said, "but you've come far. The initial stage is earnestness. The desire to understand your suffering." He sat back and looked at her. "The hole may reveal your obstruction, the cause of suffering. Your spirit is asking you to search deeper for what you want."

"I am searching but at the edge of the blue hole I seem to hold back."

"One has to let go to be free. Being free is the only condition of happiness."

She sat silent, thinking through what he had said. *Let go to be free.*

"Cultivate your heart to remove obstructions," he continued. "Your subconscious mind is ready for a new way of life before you are consciously ready. Meditate on it, it will come to you."

"In meditation it will come to me?" she asked.

"The path will reveal itself in your unconscious thoughts. Meditation, dreams, or just walking down the street."

She looked into his shining brown eyes. He paused and then continued. "And when it reveals itself, my child, you must trust and embrace the wisdom that lies within you. It may not be what you expected, but you must listen and trust your own voice, your own inner knowing. The universe does not want you to suffer."

⁓◦

Leah stopped in Brigham's one afternoon and invited Jolie to join her in New York for the weekend. "Daniel's coming with me to meet my parents."

"Daniel's meeting your parents?"

"Yes." Radiance danced from her eyes and smile. "We're going to all the art museums."

"Bagels, art museums, your mother's cooking…I'd love to come," Jolie said.

"Zack's taking us to a huge flea market. There is a whole section with nothing but vintage clothing," Leah said.

That night she stopped in the office on her way home. Some student volunteers still worked while others sat around shooting the breeze. An attractive new girl stood at the table in the kitchen, sorting the mail. Another new recruit. She had a tall frame with jet black hair that fell down her back like silk. Her short skirt, tall platform shoes, and matching apricot lipstick and rouge seemed out of place at the office. Her oversized, silver hoop earrings bobbed as she talked with Adam. Charlie and Will studied a map on the work table. Lily hovered near Will.

"Going somewhere?" Jolie asked.

"I'm driving to California," Charlie said.

Jolie looked at the map. They had plotted the route from Boston to Los Angeles. "You're going to L.A.?"

"Yes, my Nam buddies are having a reunion," Charlie said.

"That's a long drive," Jolie said.

"They're like brothers to me," Charlie said. "Plus, I've always wanted to go to California."

"Are you coming back?" she asked in a small voice.

"Of course."

"I can picture you in the Wild West."

Jolie studied the map, thinking about the long Greyhound bus trip she and Will had taken a year ago.

"I'm going to New York," Jolie said.

Will snapped his head around. "With who?"

"Leah, Daniel, and Sarah, the weekend after next," she said.

"No baby, that's the weekend of the anti-war march in D.C. You're coming with me. We're going to be a million strong there."

Jolie looked at him, her excitement dashed. "But Leah needs me there. You know, for support, when Daniel meets her parents."

"Leah's a big girl," Will said. "Besides, where would you rather be, in D.C. with me at the largest protest ever or in New York?"

The room fell quiet. All eyes were on them, including the new girl. Will looked at Jolie intently. Charlie looked down at the map, tapping it with the pencil eraser.

Not this question again. Where would she rather be? Honestly, if she could be anywhere in the world where would she want to be? The temple? The blue hole popped into her mind. Was it that hard to answer?

The ring of a phone broke the silence. A student held up the receiver. "Will, it's for you."

Will was busy setting up meetings with other presses for the weekend in D.C. and had been working late. One night she stopped at the office after work, not wanting to go home to an empty house. Adam was in the kitchen on the telephone. The melodic voice of Sam Cooke singing "A Change is Gonna Come" floated from the living room. Adam quickly glanced into the work room. Jolie's eyes followed his gaze. Will sat typing. The new girl stood behind him massaging his neck. She stopped when she saw Jolie and pursed her apricot lips.

"Ah, don't stop now baby," Will said, looking at the paper in the typewriter. He pressed his head and shoulders into her.

Jolie turned and slipped out the door. Two blocks later she ducked into a diner. She slumped into an empty red plastic booth. Fireworks went off in her head. Release your feelings, calm the mind and think. The waitress appeared.

"Herbal tea, please."

"We only have black tea, honey," the waitress said.

"Black tea is fine." She forced a smile at the older waitress.

The waitress walked off and Jolie closed her eyes. A wave of emotions churned in her head and her heart. She could hear the monk: "Calm your mind. Reflection brings wisdom. All you need is within yourself. Become your own."

The blue hole appeared, but seemed different. It was sky blue with a warm light at the end. She was falling and falling. She let herself go and fell through.

When she opened her eyes, a white mug sat before her on a chipped saucer. A Lipton tea bag dangled by a string from a small, steaming teapot. She poured a cup and sat in the big booth, drinking tea. It was dark outside now. She was calm, at peace and happy, truly happy. She had let herself go and had emerged with the answer. The answer to the blue hole. The answer to the physical and emotional emptiness that constantly tugged at her.

Three pots of tea and two hours later, Jolie paid the waitress. She left her a large tip and walked home slowly, staying under the street lamps. Near their house, she could see someone sitting on the top of the front steps. As she approached, she could make out Will's profile.

"Jolie." He jumped to his feet. "I've looked everywhere for you. I called Leah. I even went to the temple. Where were you?"

"I lost my way."

"What do you mean, 'lost'? Lost where?"

"It doesn't matter. I'm here now."

48

Fly On, Little Wing

Charlie stopped by the house Saturday morning, and he and Jolie walked to the temple. The monk led them in meditation. "Bring the mind home. Relax, ground to the earth, reflect and breathe," he said in a quiet voice. "Find your ever-present source of inner peace and wisdom to draw strength, courage, clarity, and compassion."

After meditation, Jolie and Charlie sat in the spring sunlight on the bench beside the pond. Pink and white cherry blossoms hung in the trees overhead. Petals floated like snowflakes to the ground and into the pond.

"I'm getting it. I can let go of my thoughts," Charlie said. "I enter a peaceful world."

Large orange koi swam in slow circles under green lotus pads.

"Charlie?"

He turned toward her. His blue eyes were bright and shone with serenity.

"I want to come to California with you."

"What? You do?"

She sat straight and strong, self-assured and at peace. "I want to go home."

"Sure," he said. "I can drop you off for a few days and swing by and get you after my reunion."

They held each other's gaze. "I'm not coming back." She paused and looked into his eyes. Her throat closed, and her heart pounded. "I'm leaving Will."

Charlie stared back at her speechless. His eyes clouded with questions. Finally he asked, "Does he know?"

She shook her head. "He will never let me go."

"This will crush him. You know that don't you?"

"He's strong," she said, staring at a koi circling endlessly around the pond. But she knew that wasn't true.

"I think you're making the right decision but you need to be sure."

"I'm sure."

They sat in silence for a long while.

"I leave on Friday morning after my last final," he said.

"I'll be ready." She smiled at him, a brilliant smile of joy and release. They lingered by the pond, mesmerized by the blossoms floating down around them and swirling in the current.

"Have you ever been to Yellowstone?" she asked.

He smiled at her, dimples creasing his face. "No, but I have a feeling it's going to be one of our stops."

Each day that week felt like a year. Alone with Will, Jolie was quiet. He sensed something after she had returned late from the diner. He was more attentive and left the office when she got home. Thursday night, Will sat at the kitchen table with his guitar, strumming hypnotic grooves while Jolie made cookies. He talked about their upcoming trip on Saturday to D.C.

"Our new world will replace the old world of privilege, imperialism, and capitalism," he said.

"Play me a song," she said.

He paused and played the Beatles' "Blackbird". As he sang, his voice hit her with a force right through the heart. She leaned against the counter and closed her eyes. She would not cry.

Sleep would not come that night. She lay still next to Will and followed his breathing. What if her plan was foiled somehow? He would never let her leave on her own. Morning finally came. Jolie kept to her routine, making tea and straightening the house, her body tight with nerves. She packed cookies for Will to take to the office. He seemed to be dallying, or was she jumpy? She had to relax and not give herself away. She put on a jacket and took a cup of tea out to the back porch. It was chilly, and the air was fresh in the early spring morning.

"Here you are," Will said, coming out to the porch. Startled, her body jerked, and tea spilled onto her leg. He bent down to kiss her. "I'm off to the office."

She rose and gave him a hug. Looking into his eyes, she stroked the outline of his face. "Don't forget the cookies for your comrades."

She waited a moment and went inside. From the living room window, she watched him get into Old Blue and chug down the street. Her heart raced. In the bedroom, she pulled out her duffle bag and packed her camera and a portfolio of negatives and photos. In her drawer was a small stack of clothes that she placed in the bag. Underneath the clothes was her doeskin wallet that bulged with cash from her closed bank account. She slipped it into her purse.

Opening Will's leather journal, she wrote in a shaking hand:

Will,

I will always love you. I have reflected on my life, and you need to let me go. I realize now that without my family, my life will be hopelessly empty. The pain I have caused them is unforgivable. I have to go home and try and make amends.

I won't let anyone know where you are. Think of yourself and the future. Do not come after me.

Peace and love,
Jolie

Closing the journal, she set it on the bed. She looked at his photo on the wall from the day at the concert. She had been in love with him.

Or had she been in love with the idea of him? But now she was disillusioned with the real man.

She picked up her bag and walked out the door, bounding down the steps to the sidewalk. Her heart pounded as she walked to the T. Time seemed to stand still. Was the subway always so slow? Emerging in Harvard Square, she walked to the big clock and waited for Charlie. She was early. Melting with anxiety, she leaned against the clock base. What if Charlie decided not to take her? He was coming back to Cambridge and would have to face Will at some point. But if they pulled it off, Will wouldn't know how she left the city.

She looked at every passing car. If Charlie didn't show up, she could always take a Greyhound. Or a plane, she certainly had enough money.

Relax, relax, relax, she chanted silently.

Then Charlie was there, double-parked in La Bamba, his white station wagon. He waved to her. The car behind him honked. She picked up her bag and floated to the car. He opened the door for her from the inside, and she slid onto the bench seat. He dropped her duffle onto the back seat and drove off.

They didn't speak. Charlie drove out of Cambridge and onto the interstate. Jolie sat cross-legged with her eyes closed, trying to relax and calm her racing heart. Her throat was parched.

After a few miles, Charlie cleared his throat. "You can open your eyes now and breathe." She looked over at him. His eyes were intent on the road, but he was smiling. She let out a long sigh.

"By the way, you're in charge of the radio," he said.

Jolie flipped it on, and music filled the car. She looked out the window at the passing green landscape. She was flooded with joy, and it was no ordinary joy. She was going home. The feeling blossomed as they drove.

Late that night Charlie pulled into a campground in Ohio on the banks of Lake Erie. He folded the back seat down and set up their beds on a foam mattress. They crawled into the sleeping bags he'd brought.

"It's going to get cold here tonight," he said, and pulled a quilt over them.

They lay awake in the darkness.

"You're brave, really brave," Charlie said.

"I don't feel brave."

She lay still under the weight of the quilt.

An owl hooted nearby.

"Owls are good luck," he said. "They're protectors."

"Hmm." She curled up into a ball to stay warm and drifted off to sleep.

The next morning they set off early. Charlie turned the car heater on high to warm their shivering bodies. They stopped for tea and drove on. Jolie studied the map as they inched west. They talked and then fell silent for long periods.

"I bet your folks are excited about seeing you," he said.

She looked over at him. "They don't know yet."

He glanced at her and then back to the road. "Well, don't you think you should call them? Or are you going to just show up and say you were in the neighborhood?"

She laughed. "I'll call. I just need another day." She looked out the window. "It's complicated."

She looked down at the map and traced their progress. She'd call them when they were more than halfway. That felt right. As they drove through the heartland of America, she turned to him. "Charlie, there are some things I need to tell you before we get to California."

"I'm your captive."

Jolie proceeded to tell him her story in a calm and dreamlike voice. He pulled off the highway, turned off the engine and listened with a look of disbelief. When she finished, tears shone in her eyes.

"Jesus, Jolie, I had no idea." He sat there shaking his head. "What Will did is not right. You're just a kid."

"I hope my family will forgive me."

He reached over and took her hand. "They'll forgive you, but nobody should ever forgive him."

They sat in silence and watched a farmer in a green John Deere tractor, plowing his field. He inched toward them in a straight line.

"Let's keep moving," she said.

49

She's Gone

Somewhere in the middle of South Dakota, Charlie pulled into a gas station to fill up La Bamba. It was late afternoon. Jolie got out to stretch. She eyed the dusty red and white phone booth alongside the station. She walked into the gas station store and picked out two orange juices, a pack of Beemans gum, and the Sunday paper. The old man behind the cash register eyed her between looks at Charlie out by the gas pump talking with the younger gas attendant.

The man stared at her outfit, blue jeans with paisley bell bottoms, a tie-dyed T-shirt, moccasins, and a scarf tied around her forehead.

"I need change for the phone, please."

He rang up her items. "Where're you two from?"

"It's not where we're from that's important, it's where we're going." She smiled at him and walked out the door.

Charlie was still talking to the gas attendant. She put her purchases on the front seat, walked over to the phone booth, and shut the folding door behind her. She stacked the coins on the small ledge. What kind of calls had been made from this middle-of-nowhere phone booth? She took a deep breath and dialed the operator. She deposited the first set of coins, and the phone rang twice. On the third ring, a deep male voice answered. He sounded tired.

"Dad?" Her heart beat loudly in her ears.

"*Jolie?*"

"Hi, Dad, it's me."

"Where are you? Are you all right?"

"I'm fine. I'm coming home." She was smiling as she spoke.

"Jolie?" Her mom's voice came on from another line.

"Hi, Mom."

"Where are you now?" he said.

"I'm somewhere in South Dakota. We just crossed the Missouri River."

"I'll come and get you," he said.

"No, Dad, I'm on my way." She looked out the phone booth window. Charlie was leaning against La Bamba, watching her. "I should be there in about two days. I'll call you when we're closer. We're making good time."

"Who are you with?" he said.

"A good friend. He's giving me a ride. I'm safe."

"Please come home," he said.

"I'm on my way. I love you."

She hung up the receiver, leaned back against the glass and closed her eyes. She was going home. She was really going home. A pickup truck blaring country music drove into the station from the frontage road and jarred her from her thoughts.

She opened the glass door and walked over to Charlie who was still leaning against the car watching her. "Everything okay?" he asked.

"Who says you can't go home again?" She smiled a brilliant smile, and they got into the car and drove west.

Charlie drove all night. Jolie talked to him, making sure he stayed awake. At dawn the next morning, they arrived at Yellowstone National Park and pulled into a campsite. The majestic, snow-capped Grand Teton Mountains towered in the distance. A patchwork of snow quilted the landscape. They stood close together and shivered. Exhausted by the drive, they crawled into the back of the car and slept. Jolie woke a few hours later. Charlie sat bundled by a campfire. He had boiled water and made a pot of tea. She poured a cup and sat down next to him on a log stump. She looked up at the mountains.

"I feel so free. Like a weight has been lifted," Jolie said, fingering her moonstone pouch.

"You've been harboring a lot. I admire you."

"You admire me?"

"Yeah, you always stand up for what you feel is right. Don't ever change that."

They stared at the flames.

A pang of sadness shot through her. "What do you think Will is doing right about now?" she said.

"I imagine he's working on the anti-racism, anti-materialism, and anti-capitalism manifesto."

They both laughed.

"He'll survive," he said.

She swirled the tea leaves in the bottom of her cup and sat strong and grounded and clear-headed with her decision.

Charlie got up and put out the fire. "Time to hit the road. But first, I want to see one of the wonders of the world, Old Faithful."

In the middle of the night Charlie pulled into a rest stop near Reno. He fixed up their beds and they slept for a few hours. They woke at dawn with the sound of big rigs starting their engines, vibrating past them. They got up and meditated on the tailgate. Fifteen minutes later, Jolie opened her eyes and went to get her camera.

"I want to remember this," she said. She took a photo of Charlie sitting cross-legged, hair tousled with a three-day beard, smiling back at her on their last leg to California.

Charlie stopped at a roadside café for breakfast. Jolie, bursting with energy, could not stop grinning. She would be home that night. They ordered tea and homemade cinnamon rolls.

"How are you holding up?" Charlie said.

"My mind is wild. I'm joyous and scared and blissful and worried all at the same time."

"Worried about what?"

"I'm worried about Will trying to find me."

"He's not your problem anymore."

"I have a bad feeling. Can you call Adam and just check-in?"

"Sure."

Charlie paid the bill, and they walked outside to the phone booth. The phone book was missing, and the cord that once held it hung limp. She squeezed in next to him. Charlie dialed the operator, inserted coins, and was connected to the office. He asked for Adam. A moment later, Adam was on the line.

"I thought I'd find you there," Charlie said.

"Charlie?"

"Yep. How's it going?"

"How's it going? It is all fucked up here Charlie. That's how it's going. She's gone. Jolie girl is gone. She left Will and no one knows where she is."

Adam's animated voice spilled out of the phone receiver.

"I don't blame her." Charlie fixed his gaze on Jolie.

"Man, the guy had a meltdown. He looked everywhere for her. He even thought she might be with you. He was going to come after you. Then we got him calmed down and assured him you'd never steal his woman. He was frantic. Manic. I tried to give him a sedative to calm him down, but he wouldn't have anything to do with it."

"How is he now?"

"He's in jail, that's how he fucking is. He was all wound up and called in a missing person report last night. The cops came to get more information, and they took one look at this wigged out cat and got suspicious. They took him in to the station. Turns out there was a warrant for his arrest because she's underage."

"Jesus," Charlie said.

"That poor kid. We all cherished her. Where did she go?"

Charlie's eyes were still fixed on Jolie. Tears rolled down her cheeks. "She's with me. I'm giving her a ride home. She'll be home tonight." Charlie deposited more coins and handed the receiver to Jolie.

"Adam?"

"Jolie girl, everyone's been worried about you. Will for one, and Nick and Sarah, and Leah and Daniel, Sam and Ginger. And me...."

She listened, staring into the barren Nevada landscape as he reeled off the chain of events again. A giant tumbleweed rolled by in the distance. "Are you there, Jolie girl?" Adam asked.

"I'm here."

"Will, our pillar of strength, just imploded before our eyes."

She handed the phone back to Charlie and leaned her face into his chest. He reached out his right arm and held her tight as a great wave of sadness filled her. Why hadn't Will taken her note to heart and let her go? Why, why, why had he done this to himself?

50

Far Away Eyes

On the 101 Freeway they passed a road sign. "Santa Barbara, 60 miles," Charlie read. Jolie breathed in and audibly exhaled. A rising anxiety gripped her. She clutched her moonstone. He glanced over at her. "You okay?"

She nodded, pulled down the visor, and peered into the mirror. She'd been gone almost two years. On the inside, she was a completely different person. Had her appearance changed much? The same blue eyes and face stared back at her. Please let them forgive her.

In Santa Barbara, Charlie pulled into a gas station to clean up. They both emerged from the bathrooms looking fresh but road weary. Charlie had shaved and wore a white button-down shirt and jeans. He looked boyish with his shoulder-length hair. Jolie had changed into clean bell bottoms and a silk blouse and had combed her hair. She gave him directions as they drove and soon La Bamba turned up the long driveway to her parents' house.

Nervous energy flowed through her body. Charlie parked, and they got out. He leaned against the car.

"Breathe and stay grounded," he said.

A brief smile met her lips. Her legs wavered, weak with apprehension. How could she come back after being gone for so long?

She walked toward the courtyard entry, and her father appeared. He stood in the doorway with his arms outstretched. It was the same vision of him that she saw in her reoccurring dream, at the pond with the Buddha, except now he was smiling. Charlie stood by the car. Jolie first walked, and then ran. She floated to her father's arms and was enveloped in a bear hug. His blue eyes were wet, but his smile was unwavering. Her mother appeared and then her two brothers. She was engulfed in hugs. Jolie looked over at Charlie who was riveted to the same spot.

"Let me introduce you to Charlie. Oh, and La Bamba."

Charlie moved toward them and shook her father's hand and then her brothers'. He gave her mother a hug. They moved inside. "It looks like you could use a beer," her father said to Charlie.

"And a shower," Jolie said.

The next morning Jolie and Charlie sat out on the deck. The ocean sparkled in the distance and the scent of honeysuckle and jasmine mingled in the air.

"Look at this," Charlie said as he waved his hand at the view. "I can't believe I'm in California."

Jolie smiled and looked at the ocean. The water glinted clean and blue. The oil platforms still loomed on the horizon silently threatening another oil spill.

"And your family. They're so welcoming. Last night after you went to bed I stayed up with your dad and brothers. They wanted to know everything about the war. They really missed you, Jolie. Your dad called me a hero for bringing you home."

She would miss Charlie. His open honesty, his faint accent. She loved everything about him. "You are my hero."

"I have to leave for L.A. soon."

"I'll write you," she said. "I'll let you know what college I get into."

"You better." He paused. "I was wondering something."

"What's that?"

"Can I come out for your birthday when you turn eighteen?"

A laugh spilled from her. It was a deep laugh that had been unconsciously silenced for a while. "I thought you'd never ask." She met his eyes. He had been there for her the whole time.

"I'm sure we can think of something crazy to do for your birthday," he said. "Another road trip?"

"Hmm," she said, with a faint smile and a faraway look in her eyes. "How about a temple in the mountains of Tibet?"

Made in the USA
San Bernardino, CA
05 February 2015